A

Beautiful Biker

Romance

Book Two

by

DD Prince

Thank you very much for reading my work! If you enjoy it, please consider leaving a review, even a short one. It's like tipping your server. Cheers :)

NOTICE:

This book is not intended for those under the age of 18. It contains strong language, violence, and explicit sexual content. If you do not enjoy such books, this might not be the book for you.

Dedication:

To Bertha Prince, my grandmother.

She's still here in body, but Alzheimer's Disease has taken most of her essence away from us.

She always had a stash of romance novels and a half-eaten bag of spearmint leaf candies in her room when I was a little girl.

Thank you for all you've done for me, my siblings, and my cousins, Grandma Prince.

While this is book two in the Beautiful Biker series, it can be read as a stand-alone.

It will, however, be a richer reading experience if you read these books in order.

Book one in this series is called Detour

1

I might be a little bit in love. Okay, lust?

I was definitely leaning in the direction of an *L word.*

I was also leaning against the bar, because I was a little bit tipsy and needed the support.

Who was the object of an L-word? A biker. And this was totally unlike me. I went for the opposite of a biker, usually.

I'd only ever crushed on one biker in my life, but the crush didn't go far, could not go far -—because the guy, my best friend's cousin, is a jerk. He's hot. But he's also a Grade-A certified alpha-hole.

Alpha-hole definition: A hot alpha-male who is also an asshole.

And Jenna (a.k.a. moi)? Jenna don't play dat.

But, this object of my fascination? He was about 6'1" or 6'2", which was a good thing because at 5'7" and liking heels *a lot*, I went for guys at least six feet tall. I rarely wore flats other than at work or around the house and having to lean down to kiss a guy somehow took some of the magic out of the moment for me. Just my personal preference.

So, why a biker? Why *this* biker?

This biker had medium brown hair just past his shoulders. It was wavy, like mine, but not as dark or as long as mine.

It was clean. It shone from across the room. It was the kind of hair that would lighten in the summer sun with the sort of natural highlights that made people who paid me a lot of money for that shit jealous.

I can also spot split ends from across the room and I'd need a closer look, but this guy didn't look like he had any. None.

Many guys his age with long hair refused to trim it, so had split ends. Most of them adapted the grunge look, but no chick wants to see all sorts of hair on a man if she doesn't also want to run her fingers through that hair. I should know; I deal with hair for a living. I can look at a dirty-pretty guy, but do I want to touch him? Not especially. Especially not his dirty hair.

I have a thing about hair.

I've had to sift my fingers through all types of hair. Dirty, clean, long, short, soft, coarse -—you name it, I've probably trimmed it. I dated a guy with dreadlocks once, for about three days. It looked great. It did not feel great. Some girls would still dig it, but with my hair fetish, it just didn't work for me.

Then again, if Jason Momoa, à la Stargate era, wanted to date me, I might just have to deal with coarse dreads.

For a bit.

Then, I'd convince him to let me give him a haircut. I can be pretty persuasive. The guy with the dreads wasn't worth my persuasive skills. He might've been even more high-maintenance than me. And that's saying something.

I don't have a whole lot of choice about the hair I touch at my beauty salon. A customer is a customer and they all deserve to leave my chair feeling great about themselves, so I'm the consummate professional. But outside of business hours, I want to touch hair that feels great.

Anyhoo...

When the biker stepped into the bar, you couldn't help but notice him. He just had that 'it' factor. Tall, fit, piercing eyes, sexy smile. Swagger. Like he owned the joint. But not douche-y, from what I could gather. And believe me, my douche radar is almost always spot-on.

And he had even more going for him than great hair. He had a bit of a sexy Jesus vibe going on. Oh, I know—blasphemous - but this was like a Jared Leto Jesus thing. And we all know there's nothing unholy about the beauty of Jared Leto. Jared was divinely created by a benevolent God. And would our Creator be so benevolent if he didn't want us to appreciate it? I think not.

Those piercing eyes and that long hair? Put sandals on this biker with a flowy white cloak and he could be in an Easter pageant. But, making women swoon and simultaneously repenting because they'd feel bad for how they felt gazing at their Lord and Savior.

This guy was bigger than Jared. Taller. Lean but broad-shouldered. Muscled, but not bulky. And this guy's eyes were piercing. His eyes were green. Blue-green. More green than blue, I think. I decided I had to get closer to tell for sure. And his lips? They were like pillows. His bottom lip had one of those sexy slits in it. Kind of like Angelina Jolie's, but on a man.

I chewed my own lip, practically salivating at the idea of licking that slit. And, of course that got me thinking about him licking *my* slit. Lawd!

Was it hot in here? Definitely. Hot, indeed.

Alas, he was dressed like a biker. And that kind of sucked, because he was hot and there would be even more hotness potential if he'd put on something decent instead of jeans and a leather biker jacket vest thingy with the sleeves cut off. Or never sewn on. I don't know. I know next to nothing about the specifics of biker culture. Though, I probably should. I live in South Dakota and our small city is often crawling with bikers.

But, he had potential because if you likened him to Jared Leto in his Jesus-phase and then Jared Leto with short hair in a suit? You could see that he could work either look. This guy was like *that*. I'd love to cut his hair and take him shopping for a suit.

He wore a navy-blue Henley and jeans that were previously black, now a washed out charcoal grey, and frayed all over the place.

He caught me looking. Damn. I usually preferred that I caught *them* looking.

His eyes traveled from my ankles up to my face. Slowly. Thoroughly. A leg man. For sure. This was a good thing. Not to brag or anything, but I had legs for days. My boobs were smallish, but that was okay, they were perky and as they say, more than a mouthful is a waste. At least that's what I told myself to compensate for my lack of boobage.

I could almost get away without a bra, which I sometimes decided to do, and often to great effect. I had decent hair and big cornflower-blue eyes that looked amazeballs with winged eyeliner. And I knew how to do make-up. Having my own hair salon, I was well-versed in primping. My friend Pippa, also my roommate, rented space there from me to do nails and waxing. She kept me hairless where it counted, and my brow game was strong.

At Jenna's House of Allure, you can come in and get your hair chopped off and /or styled, or get extensions. You can buy all your hair products and tools and top-shelf make-up as well as get all your girlie bits waxed and your ears, eyebrow, or your belly button pierced, too. I'd only had the salon not quite two years, but it was going pretty well, turning a profit.

I'd tried my hand in business. I got a four-year business degree and did time as a teller at Mom's bank, but I absolutely hated it (as can likely be surmised by my referring to it as if it was a jail sentence). I lasted two months. Two excruciatingly long months.

When that went south, Mom was pissed to near-lethal levels, because she'd gotten me "in" there and I'd only worked two months with two weeks' notice when I just couldn't take any more of it and handed in my letter of resignation. Dad did some fancy footwork to calm her down and hired me to work in his real estate office.

I only lasted three months and seventeen days there. And it was longer than I wanted to stay, but I wanted Mom to lose the bet to Dad that "She won't last three months."

It wouldn't have been horrible, but Mom drove me crazy about it. She tried to micro-manage me when she didn't even work there. When I told Dad I couldn't do it any longer, he asked me to give him an extra week before telling Mom I was quitting and going to beauty school, and that was when he came up with the salon idea.

I think I hated working in the same building with either of my parents, because Mom was smothering, and Dad just always seemed like he'd prefer that I weren't me. They were always giving me those looks, the looks that made me know they wished I was more like they were. Especially Mom.

Dad joked almost all my life that my favorite thing to do was do make-up and hair and yak with my friends, and that gave me the idea to go to beauty school. As soon as I told him that I was interested in that, Dad did the legwork and presented his salon plan to me and Mom.

I was shocked. In a good way. Mom was pissed, at first, feeling railroaded, but once she got the chance to think about it and mull over all the ways she could use the shop to pull her puppet strings, she was all over it.

They gave me the keys to the salon, which was established and ready to roll, and it had a vacant remodeled two-bedroom apartment upstairs, getting me out of their house, too. Perfect.

I moved in, moved Pippa in, too. We met at beauty school. We painted and redecorated and made our apartment even more awesome. The salon was already awesome, but I've been slowly making changes to make it more *me*.

The deal was that if I make a success of the salon in five years, it's mine. They'll gift half of it to me and deduct the second half of the original price they paid from my trust fund. If my balance sheets aren't healthy by then, we'll have to talk about whether or not I'd have to pay full value or leave it to them to sell.

Dad is trying to empower me. Mom would hate her friends to think of her daughter as a "lowly hair servant" (Mom's thoughts, not mine). Better that she can say I'm an entrepreneur with a beauty company. But, I'm pretty sure that Mom not only thinks I'll fail, she wants me to fail.

Either way, I was happy to have the option. I don't take for granted the fact that most girls at my age don't have their own businesses where they can do what they want, plus have their own rent-free place to live. And my apartment is fantastic. Big, over the shop, with a back terrace that's connected to the other above-a-store dwellers on the block. All twenty or early thirty somethings, and almost all of us, like-minded.

I am lucky. I can afford to party, have a laugh, and be fairly carefree. I buy expensive clothes, go out as often as I can, and try to extract joy from every situation I can. I'm a good-time girl. My mentality is that I might only get to live once and I ain't Benjamin Button, aging backwards, so might as well live it up while I can look semi-decent doing it. I'm 24 and life is good.

I've been called high-maintenance by guys, it was a sore point with my last two boyfriends, but that's okay. There's nothing wrong with having expectations. I want to have fun. I like nice things. I deserve to be treated well by the person I'm treating well.

I don't date assholes. First sign of assholery and I am outta there. And, I treat the guys in my life well. Really well. Gifts, compliments, attention. I want the same in return. If that's high-maintenance, then it's what I am and what I'll always be.

And, I'm a good friend. My friends are everything to me. I'll give the shirt off my back for them. I have no siblings, but my best friend is my sister-of-the-heart. She lives next door to my childhood home and while she's a lot more conservative in almost everything (except sex. Ella is a total she-perv), she is the best friend I could ever ask for. If I push, she'll usually come along for any ride-or-die *Thelma and Louise* type gig I'm pushing for. She might not like it, it might be kicking and screaming, but rarely will she leave me hanging. Okay, so I usually have to push. But, Ella's awesome.

She's also my Jiminy Cricket -—my conscience.

> *"Jenna,"* Ella will say. *"Shouldn't you save some money? You've gone shopping five times this month already."*

> *"Jenna, why don't we have a quiet night instead of going to the bar? You've gone to the bar three times this week already."*

Growing up, I'd hang at Ella's place as often as I could. It was like the anti-Murdochs. My parents (the Murdochs) used coasters on the table. At Ella's, if you noticed a ring on the coffee table from your can of Pepsi, you'd just sop it up with your sleeve. Or not. Or you'd make a new ring overlapping that ring and create a new design. Nobody would flip their lid.

There was definite contrast between my parents and Ella's folks.

Her parents are cool, almost like hippies. My parents are a banker and a real estate broker.

Her mom wears flowy skirts and sandals with rings on her toes. She dyes her hands with cool henna designs. My mom wears business suits and wouldn't be caught dead wearing white after Labor Day.

My mom followed the rule of having to cut your hair above your shoulders when you hit 40. Ella's mom is late 40s and her hair almost touches her ass. *I don't know who made that rule, but I don't plan to follow it.*

I've never even seen my mom's cleavage. Ella's mom is boobalicious and not afraid to show it.

Ella's dad regularly pinches Ella's mom's ass. I can't count how many times I've seen him grope her by the boob, thinking no one was looking, or having a few drinks and not caring who was looking. I don't think I've ever seen my parents kiss one another on the mouth, except in their wedding pictures. When I was a kid, I'd see him lean over to kiss her mouth and she'd present him with her cheek. Nowadays, I don't think he even bothers to try. When they renewed their vows for their 25th wedding anniversary, he kissed her cheek, for Heaven's sake.

They have side-by-side double beds like 1950s TV parents because my father tosses and turns too much, and it affects Mom's sleep.

My parents believed in diversifying your portfolio from a young age, never missing church on Sundays, and never letting anyone see you sweat.

At Ella's, I could fall on my ass and we'd all laugh together. The Forker clan might go to church, on occasion, but they'd prefer an outdoor revival with people being slain in the spirit surrounded by the glorious music of a huge Southern gospel choir instead of a monotone hymn singalong with no eye contact inside a stuffy church with starched collars.

My family was crust-less sandwiches and tiny china teacups. Ella's family was fried chicken and red Solo cups.

Ella was often embarrassed by her parents and their lifestyle. Her shabby mis-matched mish-mashed house. I loved it over there. I loved that I was free to be me.

Not long after Ella and her family moved in, my parents had a rip-roaring fight. It might've been the only time I ever heard my Dad raise his voice. Mom wanted to move away, not liking Ella's parents or how they kept the property. I was mortified and pleaded with Dad not to let her take my best friend away. I loved having Ella next door. I even snuck over sometimes and slept over, filling my bed with pillows.

Dad assured me that we would not be moving. This was the house he'd grown up in, the house his parents had willed to him. It was a beautiful Victorian style century-home in pristine condition. I never met my grandparents, but Dad talked fondly of them and the house. It was the only thing I'd ever seen my father fight her on. Usually, he let her have her way. He promised me we weren't moving and told me it'd be *my* house someday.

Ella's family went camping. Mine went to stuffy resorts. We had linen napkins. They tore off a square of paper towel. My house wasn't touchy feely. Ella's house *was*.

Of course I loved my folks, even if I couldn't express it and rarely got it back, particularly from my mother. I felt like I had to be on my best behavior with them; I couldn't just be me. And I preferred to be badly behaved. I had champagne tastes and expensive towels in my bathroom that were just for show, but I also had no qualms about getting my Manolos muddy. Like I said, I'm kind of high maintenance. But, I don't think I'm unreasonable. And I don't give birth to kittens when something perfectly washable gets dirty, like my mother does.

Ella didn't want to come out tonight. It was a rare 'leave me hanging' moment, which she was more capable of because she couldn't see my pout through the phone. If I'd Facetimed her, she probably would've caved.

Just before I'd spotted the biker eye-candy, I'd called and tried to coax her out with us. She made an excuse and hung up on me. And then she stopped answering her phone.

I'm not shocked. I'm sort of famous for blowing up her phone when she won't indulge me. She eventually gives in. Unless she turns the phone off, which she's been doing lately.

It was me, Pippa (roommate and the esthetician at my salon), and our friend Andie, who lived next door to us. Her parents owned the bakery next to my salon. Two of our other friends, Stef and Clare, were going to meet us later on. It was early. Way early. And I was already feeling the shooters we'd downed. I forgot to eat that day, the salon was so busy. Clare and Stef had both come in to buy shampoo and chatting with them was what led to tonight. I forgot the fact that I'd skipped food until I'd had two shooters and a vodka and cranberry. I asked the bartender for fifteen to twenty cherries in my drink, so I could say I'd eaten that day, and chased the drink with some peanuts. He was a big burly biker old enough to be my father and he started calling me Cherry after that.

Deke's Roadhouse used to be a country bar, and before that I think it was a titty bar. It had been closed down for months, maybe even a year or longer. The new owners hadn't renovated. They may not have even swept the floor before reopening. There were cobwebs all over the place. But, the drinks were good, and they weren't stupid-expensive, and the music was good-—classic rock. And me, Pippa, and Andie? We were well on our way toward smashed and thinkin' it would be our new hangout.

But, back to the object of my lust...

The object of my lust was leaning against a wall, wearing fawn- colored cowboy boots, one leg cocked and the sole of a boot against the wall behind him. And his eyes were still on me.

I sipped my vodka and cranberry through a straw, catching the tip of my straw with my tongue and then duck-lipping a wee bit to illustrate the fullness of my lips, not that they needed it. I was wearing this lip gloss that was designed to give you fuller lips and it stung like a bitch when you first put it on. The results were slut-tacular. And I made eye contact with him when I did. His gaze darkened in a way that made me quiver in a very personal place.

He was standing beside a tall and wide redheaded biker and a younger, blond, dirty-pretty, scruffy biker. All three of them were probably in their 20s. I'd put him at around 25, 27 max.

A tall, svelte redhead walked by and gave him the side eye. The scruffy blond guy leaned in and elbowed my biker and muttered something and then they laughed.

The blond scruffy guy then approached the redhead. She turned to face him and looked like she was immediately giving him the brush-off, while eyeing *my* biker. I recognized her. She went to our high school, a few years ahead of me and Ella. Paige Simpson.

She was skanktacularly dressed. She batted her eyelashes at the object of my lust. He jerked his chin at her in greeting and then his eyes traveled the length of *her* body, stopping on her boobs.

Great. NOT.

I turned my back to him and scanned the bar, thinking I needed a new fixation. I didn't find one as good as that one.

I spent the next few hours regretting playing it cool with that guy. He hadn't looked my way again. If I'd cranked the charm up one more degree, he wouldn't have even noticed Paige.

I'd clocked him a few times, once at a pool table, then he'd been at a dart board, and he'd disappeared for a while. In fact, it was a long while, leaving me to think that maybe he'd left.

But then, a few drinks later, I was coming out of the bathroom, and I walked right into him. Full body. And phew. He caught me.

By my ass. Both hands on my ass.

"Whoa, run me over, why don't you?" he teased, looking down at me with a sleepy-sexy expression that turned my stomach to jelly and made my toes tingle.

I went to step back but his grip tightened.

"Uh, sorry," I said, a little thrown.

"I'm not," he said and winked.

I swallowed hard.

He squeezed and then let go of my butt.

I didn't know whether to be insulted or flattered. I was beyond tipsy and up close I saw his eyes were a color smack dab between blue and green and it was so unique, so vivid, that I'd felt like a bumbling idiot.

He squeezed by me with sexy smirk on his face and disappeared into the men's room.

I stood, deer-in-the-headlights a moment, and then moved back to my gang. And I was a little bit disgruntled, because I'd been off my game. And I didn't like it.

Several songs and more vodka and cranberries later, Pippa and I were dancing with a couple of other girls. Andie was getting propositioned by a tall, bearded, 50-odd-year-old biker and she was super-cute, but super-introverted and wasn't having much luck fending him off.

"Just dance with me, little lady. It's all I want!" he bellowed at her.

Finally, me, Pip, and a couple of other women all moved in.

I'd said, "Let's all dance!" and the older biker let out a "Yee hah!" and then nearly all the women in the bar all danced in a circle together with him. And that older biker guy could bust some moves!

I saw the hot biker again, watching me, standing off to the side with a couple of other bikers who all had their eyes on the dancing group.

His eyes were on me. And I felt them on me as if there was touching involved.

I swayed a little more, flipped my hair a little more provocatively. I was feeling absolutely no pain at this point, having drunk enough to declare to myself *the* sexy dancing queen. I knew I was working it. He was staring at me with unconcealed lust.

The song ended, and he moved, as if floating, toward me. Yep, I was back on my game.

He dipped me, Hollywood-style, and held me, down, near the floor.

"You a dancer?" he asked, bringing me back up vertically.

I shook my head. And that necessitated me then pulling a lock of my hair out of my mouth. I smiled at him afterwards, as he seemed to be watching me extract that hair from my mouth with avid fascination.

"Hair stylist."

"Gonna need your number," he said.

Mission accomplished. Those stripper exercise classes? They had just paid for themselves.

I smirked. I gave it to him. And I gave him my *real* number, which was something that only happened occasionally. I was picky. I watched him put it into his phone and then we stared at one another, googly-eyed for the last call round, where he bought me a double, not that I needed it. I was sloshed.

"So, what name am I tattooing on my body after you make me fall madly in love with you?" he asked.

Smooth.

"Jenna. Jenna Murdoch."

"Jenna. Nice. Wanna know what name you'll be screamin' later?"

"Oh, that's easy. Papa John's."

He shook his head, looking highly amused.

I shrugged. "All right. Go for it."

"Rider Valentine."

"Ryder like a truck?"

"Rider like a motorcycle rider."

"Ah."

"Good to know you'll never write my name wrong. Most chicks assume it's R-Y-D-E-R."

"You know what they say about people who a-s-s-u-m-e..."

He smiled.

Good name. I didn't know if it was his real name or a biker name, but Rider and I flirted hard the rest of the evening. And the power exchange was definitely not what I was accustomed to. He had swagger. He was definitely interested, but he also knew I was. The dynamic between us was not my norm and I wasn't sure I liked how it was going. Because, it was going so good, I didn't want the night to end.

I don't even know what we talked about; I was so mesmerized by him, I think we mostly talked about me while he took every opportunity to touch me. My hand. My knee. My hair.

I chatted about my salon. I got a little bit out of him; he said his MC was throughout North and South Dakota but with just a few chapters and they were here now because they were growing and had just opened a new chapter, their clubhouse temporarily above the bar.

He said he'd just moved here from Sioux Falls a few weeks back. That's about as far as we'd gotten about him when I think I kind of just launched myself at him in the middle of him talking about his life and mouth-fucked him with my tongue. It was as if I'd been possessed by some lustful beast. And I was. It was the infamous *drunk Jenna beast*. He caught me, again with his hands on my ass.

I managed to stop myself from taking him home with me. But, I did not refrain from putting my tongue in his mouth repeatedly. And touching his hair. And smelling it. It was as soft as it looked, and it smelled great. And there was not even one split end.

"YOU DON'T WANNA TAKE me home with you, I know a nearby place we can go..." he whispered in my ear outside the bar.

I laughed. This wasn't "Can I come home with you?" This was where the convo started, so he was giving me two choices, both of which would end with him having sex with me.

Smooth.

"Naw, I gotta make you work for it." I chose a non-option and winked teasingly, then licked my lips. His mouth was really close to mine, I was leaning against the brick wall outside the bar. We were waiting for a cab.

"And I am worth working for it," I advised.

"Hm. Good play," he winked. "Make me want you."

"Do you?" I asked.

His eyes caressed me as they swept from head to toe to head again. "Oh yeah." His voice was husky.

I pulled a pink lollipop out of my bag and popped the plastic wrapper off with my teeth, then grabbed it and tucked it in my pocket, eyes on him, his eyes on my mouth. I twirled the tip of my tongue around the pink globe and then sucked on it, hollowing my cheeks out.

"Good. Maybe I'll see ya around," I said.

With perfect timing, a taxi pulled up.

I leaned forward, licking the slit on his bottom lip and leaving him with the taste of bubblegum as I passed him the lollipop and hopped in with the girls. He licked his lips and then popped the sucker into his mouth and watched me go, a huge smile on his beautiful face. I headed home, thinking that maybe I was into bikers after all.

His eyes? They were gorgeous, like a tropical ocean in paradise. And when my tongue touched the slit on his bottom lip, it felt really effing fantastic. He was the perfect height for me. I'd have to roll up on my toes to kiss him when I wasn't wearing heels and I liked that idea. In heels, bodies pressed together full frontal, I got to look up at him. I fell asleep that night, still drunk, but smiling at the memory of those lips, those eyes, that hair, and his hands on my ass.

THIS WAS THURSDAY. Friday, he didn't call. It was a busy day at the shop, as Fridays always were, and I went to bed a little bit early, having nursed a hangover most of the day, but despite that, I kept checking my phone. And I brought it to bed with me in case he called or texted. He didn't do either.

SATURDAY, MY BESTIE, Ella, came into my salon.

I'd already decided I was seeking him out and she needed to come with me. Since she was here in person, I could and would charm her into it.

"So, get this!" I pounced on her when she got in.

"Thursday night, I met this guy. Fuck, Elle, he was gorgeous. A biker. Hot biker. Hottest biker I've ever, *ever* seen! You have got to see him. He's new in town and I made out with him at that roadhouse biker bar. Gave him my number. Cannot wait to see him again. Think I'm goin' back to the bar tonight to see if I can catch his eye. I'm a little bit in love, I think." I smiled big. Okay, love was a little bit of a strong word. "Maybe in lust, but love is a definite possibility."

She followed me to one of my salon chairs looking pale, for some reason. "What was his name?"

"Rider. But, maybe that's a biker nickname. I dunno. Met him right at last call. Wish I'd had more time. If I'd met him at the start of the night, I bet I would've brought him home. Fuck, Ella, best kiss I ever had."

If I'd spent the evening talking to him, he'd have gotten into my pants. I knew it. I wasn't a slut, by no means, but it took every ounce of self-control to not go home with him that night. The chemistry I'd felt had been off the charts. I don't think I'd ever felt that much chemistry. Ever.

She asked me what he looked like, so I described him and said he was totally my type.

"Since when is that your type?" Pippa had called me out, coming into the conversation. She was with a client.

"Since I laid eyes on Rider."

I then proceeded to talk Ella into coming out that night. She wasn't easy to convince that day. She was sitting there looking a little bit green around the gills. But, I didn't give up easily.

After some coaxing, I got her talking and she shared a crazy story. She'd been held at knife-point the night before. She'd let me ramble about the hot guy I'd made out with without interrupting me to tell me that she'd been held at knife point during an attempted armed robbery. I was astonished she'd let me blather on before finally spilling about what must have been an absolutely terrifying experience. I would still be hiding under the covers, trembling.

That was Ella, though. She often got stuck in her head. I was regularly pulling her out of it.

She was my bestie, but she had a tendency to over-think things. She was like an old woman trapped in a 23-year old's body. She needed a night out after the night she'd had. And I could use some extra girlie support in my efforts to catch Rider's eye again.

Ella was a real beauty, inside and out. Me and Pip gave her a bit of a makeover, which cheered her up. I used a flat iron to tame her crazy-wild, beautiful blonde curls and she looked movie-star gorgeous instead of her usual movie star girl-next-door cute. The makeover and a money bribe to make sure she had cash for drinks and... mission accomplished. I was seeking out the beautiful biker, Rider Valentine.

MY PHONE WAS RINGING, interrupting my Spotify app, which was playing Uptown Funk, song three on my current 'getting ready' play list, as I was sweeping the blush brush across my cheekbone.

My mother.

Blah.

I hit the button for the speaker.

"Hey Mom," I greeted, feeling that little knot of dread furling in my belly. I always felt that when she called me. She didn't call me up to just say *Hello*. Ever. Her calls had purpose -—usually to express disapproval, or to recommend I do something I wouldn't want to do ... that would result in her temporary approval.

"Jenna? Are you there?"

"I'm here."

"You sound funny."

"You're on speaker. I'm multi-tasking."

"Take me off speaker, please. You know I don't like it."

I put my blush brush down and picked up the phone, hit the speaker button, and put it to my ear. "There. Done."

"I'm off speaker?"

"You are."

"You know I don't like that."

"Sorry, I was busy."

"Doing?"

"Getting ready to go out with the girls."

"Oh. To?"

"Dancing. Cocktails. Just a girls' night out."

"Roy Sotheby's nephew Daniel said you didn't return his call."

I rolled my eyes. "Haven't had a chance, Mom."

"Oh." That 'oh' was so very loaded. And laced with disappointment. In me. I heard that 'Oh' often. Too often.

"But, you have time to go out for *another* girls' night?"

I rolled my eyes again.

"He's new in town and..."

She droned on about him. Blah blah, good job. Blah blah, good family. Blah blah, something, something.

She was always trying to set me up with the sons, nephews, or godsons of people in her social circle. They were sometimes nice guys that weren't really my type, but more often than not, they were far too straight-edged, too serious, too ... chosen by my mother.

The few times they had even a glimmer of promise, they were in the same position as I was -—not looking to be set up by a parent or other relative, so it usually put a cloud over things from the start.

My mother's interference always made it start off with me feeling like I was being dragged along. Daniel Sotheby didn't stand a chance. No matter how great-looking, successful, and charismatic he might be.

She rambled on, laying the guilt on thick, but doing it interspersed with his good points to try to simultaneously guilt me and sell me on marrying the guy immediately.

"Ella got held at knifepoint last night," I cut in. "Ella needs a night out more than Roy WhatsHisFace's son needs to take me out, Mom."

"Oh."

She didn't ask about Ella. Not surprising. Ella's Mom, Bertie, would've dropped everything in life if it had been me that was put in mortal danger like that.

"She's okay," I added.

"Good. Good, good. Nephew. Not son."

"Huh?"

"Daniel is Roy's nephew, not son. Really, Jenna. Are you even paying attention?"

Wow. I was speechless.

"When will you call him back?" she pushed.

Seriously?

"This week. I guess."

"Tomorrow, Jenna. It's rude to not return a phone call."

"I'll try to send him a text."

"Texting is rude. If he called you, call him back."

I rolled my eyes again. There was a beat of silence, then she said, "Your father and I would like to meet with you to go over the books. In detail."

I rolled my eyes.

She did this in punishment whenever I did something to displease her (or wouldn't do something that *would* please her). Then, she could express her displeasure in a way that I couldn't blow off, because she held the strings on my business, my apartment, my lifestyle.

It'd been given, but I'd worked hard for the success I had thus far, and she never allowed me to forget that she had the ability to move the goal-posts and that all they'd done could be un-done.

Dad had said I had five years, then they would transfer it all to my name and wait until my thirtieth birthday for the money, but Mom had added, "Unless there's an unforeseen circumstance."

A very, *very* generalized loophole.

Typical Mom.

2

Rider was dipping me, old Hollywood style again, and he called me *Gorgeous* when he saw me. Seeing him again after thinking about him non-stop for a couple days, he didn't look so bad in these biker clothes after all. He looked damn good, actually.

I'd been in the bar not too long when he'd swooped in and dipped me again.

His jeans tonight were darker. A little frayed in places, but they fit him well. Too well. He had on a motorcycle club vest over a grey Henley. His biceps and shoulders looked particularly defined. He wasn't wearing his fawn-colored cowboy boots. Instead, he had on black motorcycle boots with gunmetal hooks for his laces and buckles at the ankles.

His eyes seemed even more piercing. And his hair again looked and smelled great. And the lips? Just as pillowy-looking as I remembered. He took no time getting me into a clinch. I threaded my fingers into his hair. He did the same into mine, but a bit roughly as he kissed me.

He looked at me with sparkling eyes and walked me to the bar.

And then he took very little time to etch my name into his dance-with-no-pants card that night.

"I've been thinking about you non-stop since the other night," he whispered in my ear. "Thinkin' I got a taste for some more lollipop."

"Hm. Yet, you didn't call?" I challenged, taking a mouthful of my beer but doing it sort of seductively, guiding it to my lips with my tongue.

He smirked. "I lost your number, Starlet. Sad but true. Real happy you turned back up here tonight. Were you lookin' for me?"

"Starlet?"

"Yeah, you're as gorgeous as a movie star. You lookin' for me, babe?"

"No, but it's been a nice side-effect." I didn't bother pointing out that he'd put my number into his phone, so I wasn't sure how he could've lost it.

He smiled, "Yeah? How 'bout I take you home tonight? You got your own place?"

I was pretty sure I'd told him I did. Despite my being hammered, I actually remembered it specifically. Maybe he was as drunk as I was. The alternative, that our conversation and moreover, our kissing, wasn't memorable enough was something I refused to consider. Well, I was trying to stop myself from considering it...

"Mm, maybe."

"Then maybe we should go there." He moved in and bit me where my neck met my shoulder.

"Ouch," I shivered, "Hungry much?" That was sort of sexy but it also sort of stung.

"Starved," he replied huskily and kissed the spot he bit.

"How about we close this joint and see how hungry you are then?" I teased.

"Deal. Only if you can handle feeding an extremely famished man. But fair warning, if I'm starvin' now, I could be hard to handle in a couple hours." He nuzzled his nose behind my ear and then his tongue was in my ear.

Whoa. I felt that right between my legs. That tongue swirl showed some dexterity.

"Oh, I think I can handle it," I said, with confidence. "But starving or not, that doesn't mean you're gonna close the deal tonight, there, handsome."

"We'll see. I can be pretty irresistible," he warned.

That was usually my line. But it wasn't something I usually said aloud.

Ella re-joined us, looking really freaked out. She'd been hauled away by Rider's brother, who was also *smokin'* smoking hot. Turned out, we were swooning over brothers.

Rider's brother Deacon was the one who rescued her from the Circle J armed robbery the night before. Ella and I'd already had a quiet moment in the ladies' room where she confided that she'd stressed about the fact that my biker might've been the same guy who'd rescued her, and she was worried that we were both in lust with the same guy.

I'd joked that if we both married our bikers we'd wind up sisters. She'd been like a sister to me almost all my life anyway.

Deacon had proven himself chivalrous. In addition to saving her the night before, he also chased off Ella's ex, Jay, who was sort of being stalker-weird at that bar that night. Jay had come in after our pow wow that morning and overheard Pippa on the phone with her boyfriend Joe, telling him about our plans, so I was icked-out by him showing up that night at Deke's Roadhouse.

Rider's other brother Spencer was also present, and he was also a hottie. He had a John Mayer vibe goin' on. Pouty mouth. Chin cleft. Short at the sides and floppy on top pompadour hairstyle. But, after less than five minutes in his presence, my alpha-hole radar started going off. He was definitely at little bit of an alpha-hole.

He was drunk when we got here, and he'd been undressing Ella with his eyes ever since. Deacon looked like he was itching to punch Spencer in the mouth.

Ella's dad's band was performing at the bar that night and they started playing Journey's *Open Arms*. Turned out Rider's father was owner of the bar, and the Valentine brothers also owned the adjacent two businesses. And, Rider's father was President of this new chapter of the Dominion Brotherhood MC.

I loved this song. I made a swoony face, I guess, because Rider took the hint, grabbed my hand and took me to the dance floor and he was light and smooth on his feet.

Wow.

I took dance lessons from age 3 until I was 14 and hadn't had a non-professional dance partner as smooth as him...ever. He might have even rivaled some of the professional partners.

I was feeling a little bit tipsy. And more than a little bit lightheaded at being in his arms. Rider was tall and lean, but he had muscle. Broad shoulders, a tight stomach. A super-tight ass. I felt safe. I really liked that feeling.

But then I felt something weird in the pit of my stomach as he spun and twirled me around, singing in my ear. There was a sharp tugging, pulling inside of me. I know we'd only just met so the song he was singing, he was just singing, it's not like he was singing it *to me* as if to say he felt about me the way Steve Perry felt in that song.

But then, he kissed me, and it felt like... like no kiss I'd ever felt. It felt like he was *it* for me. The room was spinning, but we were still. We were the only solid thing in that place. He felt like *the one*. The one me, Ella, and her gran talked about. The man that was perfectly designed for me. The only man that could make me feel like there was a possibility of happiness with one other person for the rest of my life.

It was silly to feel like this so soon after meeting a guy who wasn't even my type and I was a little freaked out, but a whole lot something else...

Ella's grandmother, Gran Izzy, had set the bar high with us since we were little, telling us it was better to be alone than be with a man who didn't deserve us. Could this beautiful biker in front of me deserve me? Or, was he just a charmer? Was I just ready for something real and wanting it so badly that I was trying to make it so?

We made out on the dance floor so hot and heavy that we heard whistles and catcalls afterwards. The music had long stopped and there were a lot of eyes on us.

"I'm taking you home," he said against my mouth.

I nodded. I was a little dizzy. I needed to lay down. With him on top of me.

"I need your hot body naked against me. Can't wait for last call."

I nodded again, enthusiastically. He also had mindreading talents, evidently.

"Pippa, take care of Ella," I said, passing her on our way out. "See you later. Going back to our place. Put Ella on the couch. Get her blankets?" If Ella got smashed, she'd fall asleep anywhere. She'd need someone's help getting to the couch.

Even drunk, Pippa was an expert at taking care of drunk people; almost as much as Sober Ella. I should know; as my roommate, she'd had to take care of my inebriated ass many times.

She saluted me. We got outside, I was nearly jogging behind him to keep up, and then I saw a small crowd gathered, watching something. Was there a fight?

Oh. Nope.

It was a rare Ella Show. Ella kicked her foot high and her shoe sailed across the parking lot and landed on the windshield of her dad's truck.

Damn. I hated missing an Ella Show. She was my sensible bestie, but on the rare occasion she let her hair down, it was always entertaining. Rider was leading me in the other direction, and as much as I loved an Ella Show, I had one purpose. I was all about getting alone and naked underneath this beautiful biker. He flagged someone over. Two bikers followed us. Rider tossed his keys high and a dark haired super-sexy biker caught them.

Where the fudge did all these hot bikers come from?

He opened a car door and hit the thing that made the front seat fold over and waved me in.

One biker got in the front and Rider and I climbed in back. The other biker got into a car beside the muscle car.

"What's happening?" I inquired.

"Jesse's gettin' us home. Mick's followin' in his car to take Jess back, leaving my car for the morning."

"Oh. You're stayin' all night, are you?" I asked, leaning into him.

"Gonna need all night for what I have planned for this beautiful body. These are our D.D's for the night."

"D.D's?"

"We always have members on hand sober at a night like this. Sometimes I'm that sober one. That usually sucks."

"I bet." I leaned in toward him.

He met me half way and caught my lips with his and grabbed a handful of my hair to hold me to his mouth. My breath caught.

"Easy, there," I extracted my hair from his hand. He was being quite passionate, but he'd pulled it a bit roughly.

"No way I'll go easy on you," he said, his mouth at my ear, "That'd be a fuckin' waste of a night. A night where you've spent the whole night making promises to me."

I giggled and started kissing him. His tongue was in my mouth and I was seriously horny. And drunk. And did I mention horny?

"I promised nothing..."

"With your words, no, but with your body language, with those bedroom eyes? Fuck yeah you did." His thumb slid across my nipple.

And something about his seriousness turned my bones to water.

"Where we goin', Ride?" The guy who was driving asked.

I called out my address and in no time at all, we were there. I was half way to climaxing by the time we were, though, because he had his hand in my shirt, he'd been rubbing me between my legs over my jeans, and I'd grabbed his package and gave it a squeeze.

"Ooh," I said against his mouth as I squeezed. "This seems rather promising."

"Fuck, yeah, gorgeous. I promise you won't be disappointed."

That was when I noticed we'd stopped. Home. Where the bed was. *Yessss...*

His hot biker buddy gave him keys and I fumbled to find mine. They exchanged looks and I caught a glimpse of something shiny pass between them. Did Rider just pass the other guy a gun? I did a double-take. Maybe that wasn't a gun.

The two bikers left in the other car and I went to the back staircase. Rider following me.

"That was nice of them," I pointed out, trying to decide whether or not to ask if that was a gun.

My salon, having the upstairs apartment, was in a free-standing building, but from the back there was an alley to the left that could take you to the front entrance and the space between buildings on the right was too small for even a person to fit through. I had a back roof terrace that overlooked the parking lot and there were rigged bridges on both sides from the roofs so that neighbors could easily travel from roof to roof. I had a back staircase from the parking lot up to my apartment. We could've also gone in from the front, as there was a door beside my salon's storefront that had a tall staircase that led upstairs.

Before I could finish pondering about the gun, he started to kiss me. He kissed me all the way up the stairs. He was ridiculously good at kissing. I couldn't stop touching his hair. I wanted him inside me. Badly.

The terrace was big, it had an overhang, and I often used it like a carport. We'd had a party a year or so back to coerce a bunch of friends and neighbors to lay patio stones on my section of it, but it didn't have railings around 1/3 of the perimeter. My ex-boyfriend Ryan had been the one who'd gotten the project started, but hadn't finished. He gave up putting effort into us (I was too high-maintenance. Whatever.) and on my deck, so there was still a stack of lattice and a bunch of lumber to go up.

We had a patio with a chimenea and some Adirondack chairs around it. I had a little barbecue, too, and then a covered door that had trellis surrounding it, which I'd woven fairy lights and a fake (but pretty) zero maintenance ivy plant through. This led to my kick-ass kitchen and then we were in the hallway that led off the kitchen to the two bedrooms, the main bathroom, and then it opened up into my spacious living room, which had a wall of windows that overlooked the main street. My windows were covered with white sheers with jewel-toned polka dots on them. They were currently pulled back with sashes and you could see the traffic lights from the street below. My living room had white walls and white leather furniture with jewel toned throw pillows in turquoise, pink, and yellow. I had glass coffee and end tables. And a disco ball that hung from the ceiling. My salon and apartment were between a bakery and a health food store. It smelled amazing in the mornings, when the baking got going, and every day I woke to the smell of baked goods. It was a good thing that aroma didn't have calories, or I'd be 600 pounds.

I had great neighbors, too, and we often cruised from roof to roof with drinks and appetizers, at night. Andie was generous with the baked goods. My neighbor on the other side, Lara and her husband Andre did amazing things with Triscuits and their toaster oven. I frequently handed out free booze and I had the kick-ass chimenea.

Rider and I were all over one another on the way to my bedroom, which was huge and kick-ass, done in champagne, peach, mauve, and teal with a big ensuite bathroom.

I couldn't wait to feel him all over.

I had a fleeting thought, as we kissed our way into my bedroom, while I was undoing the third button on his shirt and scoring his chest with my nails as I did it hungrily, that I might slip out in the morning for warm croissants for breakfast for us. I had about a dozen jars of various jams in my fridge from a recent bake sale at Ella's grandmother's nursing home. Did I have coffee? Probably. Milk? Hm. Maybe not. But, I had some French vanilla creamer. Or, I could dash to the coffee shop on the next block.

We were in my room. My room had a big bed with a ruffled white duvet that was ridiculously expensive. I didn't sleep with it on, it was just for show, along with the dozen or so pillows that made it look like it was a set in a magazine shoot.

"One sec, I'll get this off."

I pulled away from him and started lifting my pillows up to put them on the trunk at the wall by my bed.

He let out a little growl and had my shirt and was pulling it over my head. "Let's get this off. Then let's get you off. Then me, off." His lips vibrated against the back of my shoulder. "Then you again, huh?"

"One sec," I giggled, glancing over my shoulder while trying to set my pillows nicely on the trunk. I was now in my bra, jeans, and high heels, and he was drinking me in with those gorgeous eyes, his front teeth rooted in his full bottom lip.

He spun me around, picked me up by the waist and tossed me onto the bed. He threw his shirt over his head and it landed behind him somewhere.

As I landed, I bounced, and it made me giggle.

"One sec, I just need to get this duvet off." I tried to sit up.

"What?" He laughed, pinning me on my back, his mouth on my stomach, moving up as he worked my jeans buttons undone.

"My duvet has to come off. It's white. Watch your boots." I had a champagne-colored carpet and hoped his boots weren't full of mud. Most people knew to take their shoes off at the door when they saw all my lush carpet coming in. But, his eyes had been on me, or closed, as we'd made out all the way in. I had a steam cleaner, so it was okay, if there wound up being mud.

He leaned back and looked at me like I was from outer space.

"One sec. Up!" I rolled off to the floor, landing softly on my knees, and then I waved him off the bed.

He stood up, his eyebrows furrowed as he scratched his chin. I pulled the bedspread over and over so that it was folded as I went and then set it down across my hope chest.

Underneath the duvet was a pale peachy-pink comforter that I actually used, and there were still six pillows on my California king-sized bed with the plush mauve headboard. I grabbed him by his belt buckle and pulled him toward me.

"Fuck, babe," he was rolling his eyes.

"Sorry, it's like $1700 for that duvet. It's just for show. We're good. There. See?"

"You sure?" he asked, looking a little annoyed.

"Oh yeah," I said, moving toward him. I pushed him back and climbed up.

He smiled as his head hit the pillows.

"Damn, your hair looks awesome on my pillow," I said, and then I caught my first glimpse of his naked upper body.

Gulp.

I ran my hands up his chest. It was sexy. He had lots of ink on his muscular arms. Full sleeves up to his shoulders. Loads of tattoos. Letters, pictures, logos. His MC logo, his last name, black roses, an eagle. A really cool vintage-looking motorcycle. The tattoos were all black and grey and it was like a beautiful muted canvas. His chest had zero tatts. I ran my hands over his silky muscled hairless chest. His right nipple was pierced. Holy shit, that was hot. A silver ring was there.

I tongued it. He made a sexy man-moan that vibrated between my legs and then I was undoing his pants.

Commando. And wow.

When his dick was out, I just about choked on my tongue. Not only was it extra-thick, but it was also pierced, just below the head.

I ran my thumb over the two side-by-side silver studs. I looked up at his face. His eyes were looking smug. He put his hand behind his head.

"Like what you see, gorgeous?"

I'd never been with a guy who was pierced down there before. I stared at it a minute.

He also had a tattooed black shaded heart on his pelvis, to the right, a raised scar going through it and done up like an arrow, with the name Valentine in white tiny script.

"Appendix scar?" I asked.

"Mm hm," he answered.

"I got one, too." I informed him.

"Show me," he commanded, huskily.

"In a minute," I whispered, and my eyes moved back to his dick. Maybe I stared at it too long, because he flipped me and then I was on my back. I was still in my bra and my jeans and I still had stilettos on. I kicked them off and his hand went to my undone jeans. He pulled them down and off, leaving me in my demi cup red and black silky bra and red Spandex thong.

"Mm," he said, looking at me. Tracing my scar with his index finger. And then his finger slid over to my panties. He kept going, pulling them down. I was glad I'd gotten a Brazilian three days earlier.

He unhooked my bra, which hooked in the front and then his mouth was on a nipple.

"Very fucking nice," he muttered against my boob and I threw my head back and absorbed the feel of his touch.

"Tell me what you want. What do you want?" he asked against my nipple.

"You. Inside me," I whispered, loving the feel of his hair, woven in my fingers, all over my chest.

A growl rumbled up from his belly and his hands moved up and down my body as he tongued my nipple. His fingers went between my legs and then his other hand was reaching into his jeans pocket, producing a condom.

"Put that on me, gorgeous."

He went back to work at my nipples with his mouth and my pussy with his fingers. I'd never put a condom on a guy before. I'd always thought of that as the guy's department.

I fiddled with the wrapper until I got it open, having trouble focusing, because of what he was doing to me. And countless alcoholic beverages probably didn't help.

The condom was sticky. I made a face. I rose on an elbow and he watched as I reached down and fumbled a little, or maybe a lot, because he finally... after what felt like forever... took it from me and finished getting it on.

I sighed in relief. He got poised at my entrance.

"You're nice and wet." He rubbed his dick along the seam of me, making eye contact that was super-duper sexy. "And this rubber is lubed, but I'm big. Gonna go slow for starters. You good?"

I nodded. "Good news. And yeah. I'm real good."

He was working my clit with his fingers, as he moved slowly, advancing inside, and at the sight of his naked body looming over me, I was melting into the pillow.

His eyes traveled up and down my body and the look on his eyes was the most sensual expression I think I'd ever seen.

I was still feeling the effects of the booze and feeling in awe of the beauty hovering over me. God, this biker was a sight to behold. All that hair, those soft lips, the sexy eyes, the muscles and tattoos, and holy... a peen piercing. Could this get any better?

It did get better. Oh God, he was thick.

I winced. He kept advancing slowly, carefully, rubbing my clit, turning me to nothing but a puddle of need as he sank inside and began to move. Slow. Deep. Eye contact.

Whoa...

I got the fastest and best orgasm of my life, the piercing rubbing inside me while his fingers were against my clit. If I wasn't so hammered, I'd be embarrassed at how quick it happened.

"Fuck. Fuck, Rider, Fuck that's... don't stop." I was typically mute during sex. It must be the booze. And the piercing. And the thickness. And the hip action.

"You like that?" he said into my ear, his voice low and husky and *oh so sexy* as his cock and fingers worked some sort of voodoo magic on my girlie bits.

My God. Every man needs a peen piercing because *Oh My God.* I had never asked for a guy to *not* stop. I typically didn't make much noise during sex. Even when I came, it was usually quietly, a little gust of breath, maybe a bit of sound at the very end, but never had I *ever* been this verbal.

He surged forward in me, deep, so fucking deep, and he went faster and faster and harder as I was coming, and then he repositioned, and the sensation revved up. And he knew what he was doing. This was intentional, taking my orgasm from out-of-this-world to out-of-this-universe. I was coming in multiple places, because he also had my nipple between his thumb and index finger, and the way he was moving in and over me in deep strokes was rubbing my clit while also rubbing me inside with that piercing? Heaven.

I wrapped my legs tight around his thighs and let out a long and loud stuttered sound that I didn't even think I was capable of. It almost sounded musical. It was as if I was an opera singer and I'd just hit the highest note of my career.

And then I blanked out and was like a ragdoll. I was never so loose in my life.

"Phew," I said and blew my hair out of my eyes. "Holy shit. Holy shit."

He kept going. And then he flipped us so that he was on his back and I was riding him. But I was drunk, sated and boneless, and ruined, so I just kind of... flopped.

He started to grunt, like he was close. And then he grabbed my hair and was pulling it a little too hard as he ravished my neck with kisses and nibbles, and then bites.

I shivered.

He let go, flipped us so I was on my back, and then he grabbed the headboard and began ramming hard into me. Rutting. Like he was driven by carnal need and nothing else.

Wow, that was sexy.

He reached under me and then my right ass cheek was in his hand as he made me spread wider by using his knee to push my legs further apart.

I felt something foreign back there, right on my... asshole? My asshole? Wait...

I clenched my cheeks, "Nope, not that kinda girl. Not unless there's a four-carat ring in it for me." I giggled, thinking it was funny.

It was one of my ongoing sex jokes that anal required, at minimum, a 4-carat diamond. I swatted at his arm to get his hand away from there.

He grunted and didn't laugh at my joke.

And then he flipped me onto my belly and then was going in from behind. The way he threw me around was crazy-hot. But I was getting dizzy.

Oh shit. That was deep. It was so deep that I wasn't sure I could handle it. And he pulled my ass cheeks apart, so I felt super self-conscious that he could see my winking one-eye. How could *that* be sexy?

He had a handful of my hair. He pulled it a little too hard as he was thrusting into me.

"Ow, my hair." I whined, and tried to clench my butt cheeks against his separation of them. He let go and buried his mouth in the back of my neck. I could feel his whiskers, feel his soft lips.

I moaned. It felt good.

"How 'bout a little ass slapping?" he asked, lips right against my ear. "Float your boat?"

I laughed, "Not unless you want a kick in the nuts."

He laughed against the ridge of my ear and then pinned me by holding my arms above my head. He was thrusting hard, his pelvis hitting my backside, making a slapping noise.

"Fuck, you've got a sexy ass. Love to fuck you up the ass. This ass is sexy enough, I'd maybe consider pullin' a heist to get you that ring."

I giggled, but ew.

I didn't say ew. But, I thought it. I had no desire to get fucked up the ass. Exit only!

Blah. I was starting to get a headache.

"Work you up again," he said, lying me on my back and then his mouth was between my legs.

Holy shit.

That felt good. That felt crazy-good.

"Drape your legs over my shoulders."

I did.

"Up on your elbows. Watch."

"What?" I laughed.

"I want you to watch, okay?" His face was serious. So serious that I couldn't come up with a smartass remark. So, I nodded and got up on my elbows.

The throbbing was increasing between my eyes. I was drunk and to that point where I needed to go to sleep.

But then he sucked my clit hard and I forgot my headache. Instant headache cure. I watched him do it, and it was so sexy. The sight of his tattooed shoulders, the sight of his hair, and the combo of the sight *and* feeling of what he was doing between my legs? I felt it building. I started to tremble.

"Watch how I lick you," he ordered, eyes on mine with so much heat I could feel it scorching my skin. I rolled my neck back and my eyes closed anyway. It was too much. Too much sensation. I was suddenly being moved and he flipped and had me sitting on his face, "Climb on my face reverse cowgirl and suck my cock."

I turned over and followed his order. Man, this was hot. The dirty talk? The bossiness? Surprisingly hot.

"Ridin' the Rider..." I chanted and smiled big but then looked down at his cock, which was patiently waiting for my mouth.

I was never really into sucking guys off. I tried the occasional lick or kiss and maybe a suck and supplemented it with jacking the guy off until he came. I tried this with Rider.

"Suck, gorgeous. Suck it. Been thinkin' bout how all that gorgeous hair of yours would feel on me, on my balls. Take me deep."

His dirty talk? Holy moly. Half of it, I almost wanted to scrunch up my face and tell him off. But for some reason, it was making me tingle instead.

I didn't like the taste of the latex in my mouth, but I didn't know him well enough to go bare, so I tried to get enthusiastic about it. And I could taste me, too, which really was way out of my usual comfort zone. It did *not* "float my boat".

He was enthusiastically licking me between my folds, putting pressure on my clit. And then he did something and before I could process, I was coming again, his cock firmly and deeply in my throat. And then it dawned. He'd had fingers in me, on my clit, and he'd he tongued my asshole.

Fuck, that's dirty.

I came huge. A big...massive...shuddering orgasm, with his big pierced dick in my mouth, that piercing clinking against my back molars. He started thrusting into my face and then he came. I felt the expansion and warmth in the condom he was wearing.

I pulled him out of my mouth and collapsed on his pelvis.

He flipped me and then righted my body effortlessly, so I was at the head of the bed. He yanked up the blanket and tucked me in. He was gone to the bathroom.

I was destroyed. I was completely and utterly ruined for any other man. Ever. I just got fucked, and I also just got my butt tongue-fucked by the father of my future children. For sure. And he tucked me in. I smiled.

"HEY GORGEOUS; GOOD morning," I heard a deep sexy voice say. I felt warmth near my ear and smelled minty mouthwash.

"Hi," I said, as I opened my eyes. "Whoaaaaa. Make the room stop spinning, please and thank you."

"Two Tylenols. Big bottle of water on your bedside table. I gotta ride."

"Hm?" I sat up. Ouch. My head. I put it back on the pillow, my hand over my eye.

"Not Tylenol. My liver's already working too hard."

He chuckled. "Huh?"

"Advil is processed by the stomach, Tylenol by the liver."

"Advil bottle was empty, babe."

Shit.

He was dressed, showered, ready to go.

"Oh. Sorry, Liver." I popped the pills into my mouth and washed them down. "What time is it?"

"Dunno, close to noon, I think. Gotta drop Ella's car off to her with Deacon. Me and Joe are goin' to do that now."

"You and Joe?"

"Yeah, babe. Gotta go. Okay? See ya."

"Wait." I grabbed his wrist, "I was gonna make you breakfast."

He smiled.

"I was gonna... wake you up with breakfast and dessert." I ran my hand up his chest.

"Raincheck? D and Joe are pollutin' your street."

"Huh?"

"Cars are runnin', babe, burnin' fuel," he clarified.

"Oh. Okay." I shrugged. I was feeling a little shy suddenly in the morning light under his intense turquoise gaze. Something was weird with him. I couldn't quite put my finger on what.

He kissed me right on the lips and it was quick, but it was still hot.

"Great night, gorgeous. Later?"

"Yeah," I said, smiling, hoping he saw how great it was for me, hoping he saw that I really would've preferred that he stayed. But then something gripped me like a vise. Fear of rejection. I didn't like the look on his face. It was sort of ... serious. The playful expression I'd been getting from him thus far wasn't there.

I tried to lose the desperate lovesick look I was probably giving off. I shrugged, "Yeah. Sure. Cool."

I wondered if he'd come right back after he helped Deacon get Ella's car to her. I wondered how Ella's night had gone.

"See ya," I waved and then took another swig of my drink, trying to act like I didn't care as much as I did.

He leaned over, and I thought he might kiss me again. But, he chucked me under the chin and left.

Chucked me under the chin?

What?

I was sitting there, trying to process that, when I heard talking outside over the sound of motors running, so I hopped out of bed, peeked out my window, which overlooked the back parking lot, and saw him get on a motorcycle and follow a convoy of Ella's car and Joe's. Rider's orange muscle car was still parked here.

I called Ella. A couple times. And then I texted Ella. And then while I lazed, replaying the night in my mind, Ella finally called me and without as much as a *Hello*, asked about her car.

She hated her car. It was this big snot green 70s muscle car that her father gave her. And he was so proud of it that Ella drove it in misery, barely able to afford the gas because it was such a gas guzzler. It was funny to hear her sound worried about it.

"Duuuude. Where's my car? Haha. Well, hello to you too, bitch."

"Sorry Jen. Feelin' rough. I blame you and Pip. My car?"

"Isn't it always my fault when you have a hangover?" I laughed. But, I laughed too hard and hurt my own ears. I closed my eyes and finished, "Deacon picked it up. Rider and Joe followed him there with Joe's car and Deacon's bike. Rider spent the night, Ella. Oh. My. God. Omigod! I think

I'm a little bit in love. I think I've met the father of my future children." I felt myself slipping toward a daydream, seeing a wedding, babies. I'd never thought I wanted that. It was sort of weird to not only daydream about that but to daydream about it with a biker, a type I'd never even considered might be my happily-ever-after type.

Me and Ella were both dating bikers.

But Ella's biker might not be what she was looking for and I needed to clue her in to what I'd heard. Spencer had said a couple of things snidely at our table about him being a player and king of the one-night-stand, during the time Deacon and Ella had disappeared at the bar, and I hadn't had a chance to get her alone since then yet, to feel things out.

"But listen Ella, I need to talk to you about Dea—-"

"Oh, that's good. Listen, I'll call you back." She cut me off, sounding distracted, and then the bitch hung up on me before I could tell her about my concerns about Deacon.

I closed my eyes and decided to go back to sleep. I'd feel things out with her later, when I could open my eyes without this level of brain pain.

A while later, I woke up and peered out the window, seeing that Rider's car was gone. He must've come back and gotten it. I asked Pippa if he'd come back up. She told me he hadn't. I pushed away the way that made me feel.

I also realized I didn't get his number and he had said he'd lost mine. Which still made no sense, since I'd watched him put it in his phone. Well, he knew where I lived.

3

I was having trouble getting ahold of Ella. And I very much needed to talk to her about her 'beautiful biker'. The things I'd heard the day after the bar were twice as bad as what I'd heard when I was already concerned.

When I finally felt somewhat human on Hangover Sunday, Joe and Pippa were having a quiet night in front of the TV. I hung out with them and while we ate Chinese take-out, they told me all about the Night of Terror on The Terrace.

Rider's brother Deacon was bad news. Bad, *bad* news. Super jealous and abusive, according to Joe who'd heard that from Spencer, the youngest brother.

It was looking like I'd landed myself the right brother. The middle one. But, he hadn't come back up when he got back to get his car. Joe said he hadn't said much that morning.

All we knew about these guys so far was that the oldest one, Deacon, was a possessive stalker psycho. Sure, he'd saved Ella from the armed robbery, but that didn't mean he was boyfriend material. Spencer, the youngest brother? He was a coke-head loudmouth asshole.

I'd heard a few things at the bar the night before that had me concerned as it was, but my concern went from the yellow zone to the burning white-hot zone when Pip filled me in.

While me and *my* beautiful biker were doing the dance with no pants, Pippa, Joe, Spencer, and a few other friends from the bar were over, having a fire, drinking beers, and chillaxing on the rooftop terrace. Lara and Andre had even come by.

All of us 'roof' people, as we were known, were like moths to a flame whenever one of the other rooftop dwellers had a fire. The party went on until nearly dawn. But things didn't stay in the chill zone, though, when Deacon arrived and beat up Spencer and then dangled him from the part of the roof where the railings hadn't yet been put up. I needed to get that shit put up, stat.

I also needed to talk to Ella, faster than stat, about the things that Spencer had reportedly said about Deacon and how possessive and abusive he was in relationships.

I was freaked right out by the idea that my best friend could wind up with a guy like that. Someone who would hurt her or make her afraid. I'd never seen her as excited about a guy as I had with Deacon. She would be heartbroken. But, she needed to know.

I also needed to be careful. If Deacon was what he sounded like and Spencer was a Coke-head, could I trust that Rider was really a good guy?

I CAN'T LIE AND SAY I didn't care that Rider didn't call me Sunday. I cared. I would appear nonchalant on the outside, but as that saying goes, inside, I was 'chalant as fuck'.

Late Monday morning, I demanded Ella come into the salon, which she did, and I told her what I'd heard about Deacon. She didn't wanna hear it and was ready to cover her ears and pull a "La la la", on me, so I had to do some quick blurting. Because, it was important.

I'd heard Rider's brother had put a girl in the hospital. And that he'd done time in jail for beating another girlfriend's brother almost to death. And while they'd been partying on my terrace, not only had Deacon beat the daylights out of Spencer and dangled him from the roof, but Spencer had also said that was because he'd been hitting on Ella. He'd also said that another girl had left the country to get away from Deacon's possessive ways.

My bestie needed to know all this, whether she wanted to or not. And I took no joy whatsoever in telling her, watching her expression drop like someone had kicked a puppy. The vision of us being sisters by bikerly association was fading fast.

Boo.

And then she'd told me that her ex, who was turning out to be like a bad smell that just wouldn't go away, was more than just a stalker-weird problem. He didn't smell bad. He looked like a catch, actually. Good-looking, good job. Tall. Nice hair. But, he wasn't a catch. Good looks were where Jay Smyth's good qualities ended.

Deacon had warned her that Jay had been saying some pretty personal sex stuff about Ella in public and he had a right to be protective after that, but with all the other stuff we'd heard about Deacon, Pippa and I both agreed that Ella needed to protect herself where Deacon was concerned. No way would Ella put up with some guy with a track record of beating up women.

And Ella told us that Deacon had pilfered her keys Saturday night and used them to sneak in Sunday night. She'd woken up with him in bed with her! All of this freaked me out even more. I was worried for her.

When she was on her way out, shoulders slumped, and clearly broken-hearted, I told her I'd try to broach the subject with Rider carefully, to see what he thought of Deacon's history with women. But chances were, she wouldn't care. The info we had was enough to disqualify him as boyfriend material.

I didn't want this thing with them to muddy our waters, so I would try to be Switzerland with Rider about it. But, when it all boiled down to it, Ella was my best friend. She came first.

LATER MONDAY AFTERNOON, I heard the roar of motorcycle pipes and it was so loud I turned my attention to the street. I saw several bikers with Dominion Brotherhood vests on, riding past the salon. But, I didn't see *him*.

That was when I got a text from my mother, reminding me to contact Daniel Sotheby.

I wrote Daniel Sotheby a text immediately afterwards. I needed this over with.

> **"Hey, Daniel? This is Jenna Murdoch. My Mother and your uncle are trying to play matchmaker - they want us to meet. I'm kind of swamped this week but can probably squeeze in a**

> **fast coffee. Unless you're not game, in which case we can pretend we met and just didn't hit it off."**

He answered almost immediately.

> **"Good to hear from you, Jenna. I saw your photo and heard a lot about you and I'd love to meet for a drink. Whenever you have time, let me know. Here's my photo."**

I stared at the screen and I was pleasantly surprised. Glasses. And sexy. And he looked pretty buff. This was *totally* my type. He was in a nice suit. He had a tan that didn't look like a fake 'n' bake tan. He had dark wavy hair and blue eyes. Daniel Sotheby totally had a Henry Cavill-Clark Kent thing going on.

Mom did good; looks-wise, anyway.

But the thing was, I was thinking *Oh, he's kind of movie star gorgeous.* And yet, I couldn't get my mind off the guy who'd dipped me Hollywood style and called *me* Gorgeous.

The guy who'd kissed my neck and did that thing with his tongue...and that thing with his dick. And even that thing with his tongue in my fanny.

I felt my blood get hot at the memory, and weirdly, not in a grossed-out way.

And how he sang in my ear. And danced like we were a couple of pros from *Dancing with the Stars.*

He was in my head. He was under my skin.

I was standing there, holding my phone, my eyes closed and warmth washing over me.

I had it bad. This was not good. It was especially not good that he hadn't called.

I had an idea what my life would look like with a biker like that. My parents would hate him. But life with him might be like life at Ella's house versus life with Daniel Sotheby, who would fit right in at my parent's stuffy country club. A place where I didn't particularly want to fit in.

I didn't want to go for coffee with Daniel. I didn't wanna spend my spare time at the country club rubbing elbows with snobs. I wanted to ride on the back of Rider's motorcycle, arms around his waist. I wanted to live in my parents' house with a husband and kids, but take the stuffiness down a notch so that it looked good but had the feel of Ella's house where there was laughter, family game nights, being real. And kisses and hugs and where you were allowed to screw up sometimes and where things didn't have to be 100% perfect all the time.

I shook myself back to reality and replied to him.

"Super busy today but I'll get in touch in a few days and we'll set a time. Cheers."

"I look forward to it." was his reply.

I put my phone down and all thoughts of Daniel Sotheby left my head. Thoughts of Rider, though? They were in my mind more than I would ever want to admit to him.

IT WAS TUESDAY. I WAS at the biker bar and a little bit drunk, being biker eye-candy, but not for Rider. He wasn't there. Plenty of other bikers were and several of them had been watching me with what looked like avid interest.

The bartender put six cherries into my drink and gave me a wink. He remembered.

I liked Deke's Roadhouse.

I came in wearing a swingy skirt and a tight top, and very high heels.

Pippa kept looking at her watch, wanting us to go. She told me she had plans to meet Joe at our place at 8:00 and it was already 7:45. I was taking my time with this drink, hoping Rider would show up.

Pippa muttered, "Drink up. I wanna go! Goin' pee." She wandered to the bathroom.

I figured, let Joe wait a bit. He had a key to our apartment and he never hesitated to make himself at home when Pip wasn't there. This was all I had going tonight. Trying to catch Rider's eye. Wherever he might be.

Deacon walked in and headed toward the bar. He glanced at me, and he looked more than mildly irritated. He looked like he wanted to crush someone's skull. He turned away from me and ordered a beer. As it was put down in front of him, the door opened, and I saw Deacon do a double-take at something outside.

Spencer was suddenly in front of me, before I had a chance to follow Deacon's eyes. As he sat down, I saw the back of Deacon as he stalked back outside.

"Hey, Blue Eyes. How's it goin'?"

"Hi, Spencer. It's goin'." I smiled and took a sip of my vodka and cranberry through my straw.

Spencer's eye was a bit purply. He looked like he'd definitely been on the wrong end of a fight.

I wondered if Ella had ended things with Deacon yet.

"It's goin' down smooth tonight." Spencer downed the rest of his beer and then put the bottle on the bar with a flourish.

"Where's your brother?" I inquired.

"Ride? Likely workin' or doin' something for the club. Why?"

I shrugged, "Just wonderin'."

"Wonderin' if he wants to come back to your place again?" Spencer leaned in. He reeked of booze. He was tanked.

"Not necessarily," I said and took another sip of my drink.

He gave me a knowing look.

"Hm. Well, trust me, if he wants seconds, he'll sniff around ya."

"Seconds?" I was a little bit, no *a lot* offended.

He waved his hands defensively, "Just teasin', Blue Eyes. My brothers aren't really one-woman men, though. You know? Not like me. Ride's got a whole section in his phone of bitches' phone numbers who want him to come back for seconds."

I snickered to hide the involuntary dive my stomach just took.

"Oh, and where's your *one woman*?" I asked.

"I'm still searchin' for her. Tried a few on for size lately, but nothing special in this town that's available." He was watching Pippa coming toward us. She was texting, her honey and highlighted-with-caramel hair swaying, her face smiling, obviously getting something good from her text conversation. She ignored both of us and sat on the barstool beside me.

"Though gotta say," Spencer continued, eyes back on me. "Wish I'd started lookin' a day earlier. You or your little blonde friend caught my eye before D and Ride and I'd've had either of ya. You're both foxy as fuck." He was staring at my mouth.

"And you're drunk as fuck. Go away." I waved my hand at him as I chased my wayward straw with my tongue and took a big sip. I realized instantly that this was the wrong move. He was still staring at my mouth and now his gaze was darkening.

"Oooh, she's spirited," he remarked with a big grin. "No wonder you caught Ride's eye. He likes 'em spirited." He turned back to the bar and signaled to the bartender.

"I amend my earlier statement. Give me your brother's number and then go away."

"Relax, just mean you're both potential girlfriend material, rather than biker bunnies. It's a compliment."

"Whatever. His number?" I raised my eyebrows.

"He didn't give you his number, babe? Maybe you didn't make that much of an impression."

"Don't be an asshole," Pippa snapped, her eyes off her phone and glaring at Spencer as I simultaneously said, "Fuck you."

He reared back, amused at our aggression.

I took the straw out of my glass and tossed back the rest of my drink and ate the cherries at the bottom. I reached for his phone, which was lying on the bar. He let out a teasing laugh.

I hit his *home* button. Password protected.

Damn it!

"Gimme his number, Spencer," I ordered.

"Have a drink with me. No two drinks. Two shots. Barkeep!" He slammed his palm on the bar and the big, no *huge*, grizzlyish biker with a long beard and a big belly who looked like he belonged on the set of the tv show *Duck Dynasty* looked down his nose at Spencer. He'd been friendly with me, definitely not stingy with the cherries, but looked like he was annoyed with Spencer.

"Spence?"

"Three shots of tequila, Little John."

"Make that two, Little John. None for me. I'm goin'." Pip said and gave me a look. "You not comin'?"

"I'll have a drink with Spence," I shrugged. "Go. I'll catch a cab."

"I still want three. I'll drink hers," Spence said.

Pippa rolled her eyes at me, swung her big slouchy purse over her shoulder, and then she left. Spencer's eyes were on her ass the whole way out. Then again, several other sets of eyes were, too. Pippa taught yoga classes as well as Pilates in addition to doing nails and waxing and she had a great butt.

"GIMME YOUR BROTHER'S number," I whined, kicking my feet like a tantruming toddler. I'd had two shots of tequila and another vodka and cranberry and was feeling no pain.

Spencer laughed at me.

Spencer was really, *really* good-looking with his brown with amber flecked eyes and his muscled arms covered in ink, that sexy flop of dark hair falling in his eyes. He also had dimples when he flirted. He kept flirting, but it was feeling harmless and I didn't return the flirtation. And I had my sights set on Rider.

I slammed my fist on the bar and got angry. And then, I pounced. I tried to wrestle the phone off him. We wound up on the floor of the bar, all tangled up with discarded peanut shells and *who knew what* else.

Yick.

"All right, all right," he relented, laughing his butt off, and helped me to my feet, looking totally amused.

"Passcode!" I demanded.

Shit, I just did that in a skirt. I didn't bother glancing around to see if I could tell whether or not anyone had seen my undies.

"6969," he said.

"Such a pig," I grumbled, and unlocked the phone then found "Ride" in his directory and copied the number onto my phone.

"Gotta tinkle. Be right back," I said, and Spencer was snickering and putting his phone into his front jeans pocket, dusting dive bar debris and peanut shells off his jeans.

Sitting on the toilet, I sent a text to Rider.

"Hey sexy."

My phone buzzed from my handbag while I was washing my hands.

"Who's this?"

"I'll give you a hint. You spent the night with me very recently."

There was a long delay where my phone didn't text back, and it niggled at me. Of course. How many women had he recently spent the night with? I didn't even wanna know. The term 'recently' was subjective, too.

Clearly, I wasn't in his phone.

"...and I've got a really expensive duvet that you did NOT get dirty. LOL."

He replied seconds later.

"Duvet. You crack me up, gorgeous. I'd like to get your duvet real dirty. Too bad you're not that kind of girl."

I smiled.

Clearly, he was waiting for some sort of hint before replying. I pushed away the oily feeling that threatened me. We weren't exclusive. Yet. We were new. But, I wanted him to want that exclusivity. And I was good at making men I had in my sights want me.

"My duvet is pure and unsullied, and practically priceless. But another night with you? I'd consider letting you soil that duvet REAL good."

I wrinkled my nose in delight, pleased with myself.

"How would I be invited to do that? Tell me.

It buzzed again.

"In detail. Maybe I'll bring a 2-carat ring with me."

I giggled.

"4 carat. Minimum. Why don't you meet me at Deke's Roadhouse and we can talk -—maybe explore all the ways there are to dirty my duvet?"

"You there now?"

"I sure am."

"Be there in fifteen."

"Hurry. Or I'll start without you."

I sashayed back out to the bar, feeling like I was walking on air, and ordered another drink. Spencer was chatting up a cute redhead with huge boobs.

My beautiful biker didn't show up. Around an hour later, I took a cab home alone. And I was kind of butt-hurt about it and let Spencer know it, too. It wasn't like me to sit around and wait for a guy.

I made *them* wait. I was more than annoyed. And I let that all hang out rather loudly.

He shrugged it off, telling me he would try not to feel too wounded that I'd spent the night bitching about hanging out with him. As my cab got there, I saw Spencer walking up the stairs outside of Deke's Roadhouse to the upper floor, the Dominion Brotherhood clubhouse, and he was holding the hand of busty cute redheaded girl.

RIDER TURNED UP IN the morning at my salon just before lunchtime. "Sorry, Starlet," he said when I looked up from the magazine I was reading, sitting at the reception desk, between appointments. Pippa was in her back room, with a client.

I raised my eyebrows and gave him a cold glare.

"Emergency last night," he said.

I narrowed my eyes at him and flipped the page. I couldn't decide whether to play it off bitchily or like I didn't care. I guess what came next was a bit of both.

I shrugged with one shoulder, "All right." I flipped the page on my magazine again.

He looked at me a beat and something in his eyes threw me. Was he disappointed with my reaction? Was this the wrong play to make?

A long moment passed where I felt really small under his gaze. I didn't like that feeling. At all.

He looked like he was about to leave.

"So, uh, Ella and Deacon. Can I ask you your opinion objectively?" I asked quickly, hoping to salvage the conversation.

"Objectively?" He folded his arms across his chest, looking at me suspiciously.

"I've heard some things. Ella is like a sister to me. Is it a bad idea for her to get involved with him?"

"No. Not a bit." He did not hesitate.

"I heard some things through the grapevine. He's got a history of violence against women?"

"Not at fucking all," Rider spat, looking annoyed. "Spence. Fuck," he grumbled.

"No?" I asked, hopefully, but also feeling a little bit sick, because if it was all bull-pucky, it might already be too late. Ella may have already given Deacon *the finger*.

"No. It's bullshit. There's a lot of shit that went down between Spence and D and between D and the women he chose to spend his time with. He's been fucked over a coupla times by bitches and had his heart broken, too. He had a girlfriend get murdered, a girl he was ready to propose to fucked off on him when he was ready to get serious, partly because Spence was in her friend zone and didn't wanna be there and he went about sabotaging her thing with D. And there was a psycho chick who pitted D and Spence against one another using her pussy first and then her fists and a fucking crowbar when D decided her pussy wasn't worth the hassle. That cunt's in jail doing 25 to life for murdering some other poor bastard who fell for her shit. My brothers got away not unscathed by her bullshit, though. Your girl Ella would be a lucky bitch to hold D's attention."

"Oh God." I was clutching my throat. 99% of the time around Rider, up until that point, had been flirty and lighthearted. Except that morning after. And this. This was *so far* the opposite of that, it made my blood curdle. He looked ready to rip someone's head off. I chose to ignore his usage of the 'c' word, even though it was like nails down a chalkboard for me. Because, Rider looked pissed. Beyond pissed.

He continued. "Couldn't have a better guy in your corner. Been a long time since I've seen him get serious about a girl. Your girl is a lucky girl to get that from a man like my brother. That he's even interested after the shit he's had to deal with? She's a lucky girl. God's honest truth."

"Really?"

"Truth," Rider vowed. "Spence is jealous, and Spence is dealing with shit right now and he's tryin' to drown his sorrows in booze. Booze makes him an asshole, particularly toward Deacon. He needs to slow down his drinkin'."

"I'm sure the cocaine isn't helping," I muttered.

Rider lifted his brows, "Cocaine?"

I waved my hand, "Never mind."

He growled, "Fuckin' great. You know this for a fact?"

"I know he tried to get Joe to score for him. That's all I know."

"Fuck sakes."

I didn't like the look of him pissed. It was pretty scary, actually.

"I need to call Ella. I told her what I'd heard from Joe and Pip, and I need to tell her I got it wrong." I reached for my phone. I hoped it wasn't too late for Ella. If it was, it'd be my fault. Shit. Shit...

"They've already sorted it. I saw her bright and early this morning with him at his place. The only thing left to be sorted is Spence." A muscle was working in his jaw. He looked annoyed.

"What do you mean?"

"Spence is lucky that Deacon overlooks shit with him. Deacon is no slouch and he doesn't generally overlook bullshit from anyone, but he lets shit roll off with Spence. Anybody else, it'd be bad."

"Oh?"

"Yeah. Deacon can be the scariest motherfucker I've ever seen. And I've seen some scary fuckin' mofos."

"Yikes," I said. Not sure what else *to* say.

"But that scariness won't come at Ella. It'll shield her. She's got nothing to worry about, givin' her heart to my brother."

I felt a little melty at that. I smiled.

"Well, he did dangle Spencer from the roof," I said.

Rider snickered, "Yeah, wish I'd seen it."

"Not me. Didn't sound like fun. I think you and me were havin' a whole lot more fun while that was going on, anyway."

He stared at me a beat, something working in his eyes. His lips tilted into a smile.

I smiled back.

His smile got bigger.

Our eyes locked for a second and my knees went to Jell-O.

He cleared his expression. "Another reason I'm here, beyond apologizing for not turnin' up last night, is to warn you about Fork."

"Fork?"

"Jackal. Ella's cousin. Blond guy. Huge."

"Christian Forker?" He was blond. And huge. He was probably 6'7".

"Fork and the other Jackals from his charter are hanging around Aberdeen extra. They don't like that The Brotherhood are here. They really don't like that Ella's with *my* brother. Figure she'll tell you about it but in case she hasn't, or in case she doesn't drive the point home, I wanted to get in front of this. You gotta keep quiet about anything to do with the Dominion Brotherhood versus the Jackals. Anything."

"Okay..."

"And a coupla their bitches were clocked last night bein' moles and saw *you* with Spence at the Roadhouse. One of those bitches snapped a pic with her phone. If they think you're with him, they might hassle ya."

"With him? I didn't give any indication of anything *with* him."

"Heard you tackled him in the bar," Rider said, sort of emotionless, "Took him to the floor, straddlin' him."

No, not emotionless. Cold. His eyes were cold when he said that.

"I was wrestling his phone off him to get *your* number," I croaked out, feeling my face going red.

I did tackle him, but was it really seen like that? Is that why Rider didn't show? He thought I was flirting with his brother?

"I spent two drinks and two shots trying to bribe him to get your number. I had no desire for his company otherwise, believe me."

I folded my arms across my chest.

His expression didn't change.

I swallowed. "Is that why you didn't show? You thought I was playing games between you and your brother?"

He shook his head, "Nope. Said I had an emergency. I don't bullshit, Jenna."

I rolled my eyes, but my heart sank. That was the first time he'd called me 'Jenna'. Until now I'd been "Gorgeous", "Babe", or "Baby" or some other pet name.

I didn't like the tone in his voice when he said my name. I also didn't believe him. Maybe he had an emergency, but he clearly had an opinion about me "straddlin'" his brother. Why the heck did I do that? In a skirt, no less. And there were pictures of it?

He narrowed his eyes and it made my heart sink even deeper. I looked away from his penetrating gaze.

"Okay, well, uh...thanks for the warning about Chris and the Jackals. And thanks for... setting me straight about Deacon." I snapped the magazine I'd been reading shut and dropped it on the table in my waiting area. I moved to the door, opening it to wave him out. He didn't move. He was working his jaw muscles, looking annoyed with me. More annoyed.

What the heck for?

I glared at him, tight-lipped, not wanting him to be annoyed with me, not sure why he was so annoyed, but not wanting him to have an upper hand. I always avoided giving men the upper hand. In my experience, they'd use it to hurt you.

He rolled his eyes and then his expression cleared and the new look on his face was even worse than the last one because this one was as if he clearly couldn't give two shits that I was now in a dirty-look-showdown with him. He moved toward the door.

Shit.

Shit!

I was screwing this up with my attitude. Deacon and Ella's thing? I might've screwed it up. Was I screwing up me and Rider, too? Before we even got a chance to be a *me and Rider*.

"Rider?" I stopped him with my hand to his arm as he was passing me.

He looked down at me, at my hand on his arm, and then his gaze lifted to meet mine.

My face felt like it melted a bit and I swallowed hard.

I was overcome with the urge to kiss him. To run my fingers through his hair. To salvage what was feeling like a meeting gone way wrong.

I swallowed again. Our eyes were still locked. I was sinking into a turquoise sea.

His annoyance and chill melted clean away. He smiled at me. And his smile was breathtaking.

He tucked my hair behind my ear. I shivered.

His smile went wider.

"Like that soft look on your face a lot better than the hard one, baby," he whispered.

My heart lifted, and my words tumbled out before I had a chance to measure them. "I'm sorry if I'm off today. I partied too hard last night, and you didn't show, and I was disappointed, and ... and I'd like to see you again."

He looked thoughtful for a beat.

"Is everything okay with your ... emergency?"

"Dunno yet. A brother is MIA. Hopin' it will be," he whispered and leaned over and his lips touched mine.

I let go of the door and he moved us back and had me pinned against the wall in my reception area.

"Who?" I asked, and our eyes were locked.

His left hand was on my hip; his right hand moved to my jaw.

"Scooter. Talk about that later," he moved in for a kiss.

His kiss was hungry, urgent, and mine was too, I think. I kissed him like I might never get a chance to kiss him again. My fingers were in his hair, and I let out a whimper or two. It'd felt, for a bit there, like that was a probability. That I'd fucked up. One of his hands went down to cup my behind and the other moved into my hair, holding me in place. I'd usually feel claustrophobic at something like that. I didn't. I felt the opposite. I wanted him to hold on tight and suffocate me with his mouth, his touch.

I let out a gust and it sounded needy.

"Tomorrow night?" he asked.

"Tonight?" I amended.

"I'll try. There's something on tonight that I might not be able to get out of."

"Not a date, I hope?" *God.* Me and my malfunctioning mouth.

"No, gorgeous. Not a date. I'll call you." He looked at me warmly.

"Okay." I smiled. And then I got up on my tippy toes and kissed him, supremely pleased that his height meant I got to do that instead of leaning over or simply being eye-level. It was a little thing, but to me it was one of the many things that made me very interested in this beautiful biker.

"Cuz if it was a date, I might have to fight her."

He chuckled and then he kissed me back with even more passion. And that was when Deanna, my next appointment, was coming in. Dee, twenty-three, was an auburn-haired beauty. She was also a dick magnet. She had two sons with two different men and they'd both fucked her over.

When Dick #1 turned into said dick and didn't bother to show up for the birth of baby number one, his best friend admitted his years-long crush on her and said he wanted her and her son. She left Dick #1 for the promise of him. Then, she got pregnant with *his* baby not even a year later, and he fucked off on her, thus christening him Dick #2. He was unable to handle the responsibility of her toddler; never mind the baby he'd put in her oven. So, she had to do it mostly alone. She had a disabled mom who tried to help, but no other family in the area.

Deanna was struggling. She worked at the cab office Ella worked at and sold make-up and household scented wax warmers, and did sex toy parties.

She worked her ass off since neither of the two deadbeat dad dicks of her boys paid child support on a regular basis.

She had a standing monthly appointment and always brought her two toddlers with her. They always tore up the salon like little terrors, but she was a single mom, so I didn't give her a hassle.

She was a pal, so I charged her just for the products I used and not my time and she made it up to me with free samples of all the stuff she sold. I regularly stocked up on the wax and had more than I could likely ever burn both here and at the apartment, but I saw how each sale helped her. I didn't buy her sex toys, but Ella regularly talked up some $200 purple vibrator and she was threatening to buy me one for Christmas.

I also let Deanna put her scented stuff catalogues in my waiting area for my customers and Pip would hand out her sex toy catalogues to women who got Brazilians. While she got her pampering, Pip and I did our best to keep her two toddler boys busy. Her older one loved to sweep the floor.

"Hey Jenna. Mornin'," Deanna beamed at me, taking in Rider from head to toe.

She bit her lip, with emphasis, her eyes locked on mine.

"Daddeeeee?" her 2 ½ year old son, Timothy, grabbed Rider's Dom vest and tugged.

Rider looked down at him and chuckled and then looked to Deanna.

"So sorry. I don't know why he keeps doin' this!" She ushered him away, beet-faced. "That's not Daddy, honey."

"So, anyway, I gotta take care of Dee," I told him.

"Try real hard for later, yeah?"

"Come pick me up? Take me for a ride on the back of your bike?" I asked.

His smile spread wide. "Yeah?"

I nodded, biting my lip. "Yeah. Maybe take me for a drink at the Roadhouse? Never been on a bike."

"No?" His lips were twitching like he was fighting a smile.

"Nope. I'd love for you to pop that cherry," I said.

"I'll text you," he whispered, giving me molten turquoise eyes.

"Sounds good."

"If I can't make it, you wait before getting on a bike. That cherry's mine."

Holy crap. I might've had a little bit of an orgasm right there.

4

I had a spring in my step throughout the rest of the day. I was scatter-brained and excited. I couldn't wait to get the salon closed and my last appointment was a no-show, so I was tickled pink to have more time to get ready to *hopefully* meet Rider.

But, as I was climbing the stairs to go back up to my apartment, I got a text from my mom, summoning me.

"We would like you to come over for dinner today."

Damn it! She hated texting. She only texted me when she didn't want me to have an opportunity to say *No.*

Me: "Can't do dinner. I have a date."
Mom: "With Daniel Sotheby?"

Double damn it!

Why did I say 'date'? Why didn't I just say I had 'plans'? Better yet, why didn't I wait to respond to the text tomorrow?

Me: "No. Daniel and I are still sorting out schedules."
Mom: "What time are you meeting this date?"
Me: "I don't know yet. He's going to txt."

My phone rang.

"You're seeing someone?" was how Mom greeted me. Before I got the Hello fully out.

"Hiiii Mommmm. How are youuuuu?" I drawled out snarkily.

"Jenna, please. I hardly have time for nonsense. Who are you going on a date with?"

Sigh.

"It's new. Brand new. You don't know him."

"Oh."

Loaded silence.

Another sigh from me but done away from the phone as she'd get irritated if she heard two in a row.

"What about Daniel Sotheby?" she asked.

"I texted him. We're gonna meet for a coffee. But it might not go further than that, Mom."

"So, you've kept your evening open; you'll be desperately waiting by the phone for some other man?" Her voice was laced with judgement.

She wouldn't ever allow any man to think she was waiting by the phone for him. My mother loved having the upper hand in everything. My theory was that it was one of the reasons why she works for a bank doing what she does. She likes to deny people money, make them grovel, repo their dreams.

"Not exactly. We just haven't set a firm time yet. I'll come by for an hour, though, before dinner? I'm sure me and Rider will probably be grabbing a drink later on."

"Then come for dinner, Jenna."

"You and Dad eat late and... "

"And bring the books."

"Mom, can we just do this another day?"

"We need to go over the books, Jenna. We'll eat early. For you."

She added the 'for you' in a way that was so condescending it made my scalp prickle.

As if we needed to do that today. As if something was *that* pressing.

No. This was punishment. It was her using the books as leverage. If I didn't love the salon so much, I wouldn't let her continue to have this leverage over me.

I closed my eyes and forced a quiet breath out, so it wouldn't sound like I was huffing.

"Okay, Mom. I'll come over now. How's that? We'll do dinner another time."

"Did you say, Rider?"

"Yes."

"Rider?"

"That's right."

"Does this Rider have a surname?"

"Well, ma... he's like Cher. He doesn't need one of each. He's just Rider."

"Genevieve."

Ugh.

"Rider Valentine." Shit. Here we go. She was like a dog with a bone.

"Do not call me 'ma.'"

Eyeroll from me.

"Valentine?" she confirmed.

"He's new in town."

"Yes, I know who he is, Genevieve."

Of course she did.

Silence. Loaded silence. God, this conversation was painful. No. Not silence. I could hear her typing.

"The son of Deacon Valentine Senior?" she asked with a shuffle of paper in the background and then more typing. Did she have notes on the Valentine family? It wouldn't surprise me. She was probably looking up Rider's credit score right now.

"I guess. Why?" I was wishing I'd kept my mouth shut. I didn't normally tell Mom about guys unless I was at the "introduce him to the parents" stage, which didn't happen much. Clearly, I wasn't thinking clearly. I must still be muddled by his kiss.

"Mom? Are you there?"

"Bikers, Jenna?" The disapproval in her voice? No, not just disapproval. Disgust.

"You know who they are?"

"I handled opening the father's business accounts a few weeks ago. His sons came in and opened their own accounts as well. I didn't handle that, but I saw them and had to have a talk with the girls who were inappropriately discussing those... boys afterwards. I don't remember which one Rider was, but they were bikers. They've all got healthy accounts, Jenna, but that's where the healthy ends."

"He had the longest hair."

"What?"

"Rider is the one who has the longest hair." I said this to identify him and show her that I didn't give a rat's ass about any of the shit she'd just said, including about their bank accounts. I wasn't surprised that all four Valentine men walking into my mom's bank caused a stir. Three gorgeous 20-something bikers and their still hot late 40s / early 50s dad? Plus, she'd hate that the guy I was dating had long hair. Another bonus.

Deke must've had a healthy account for Mom to handle it. She handled the branch's wealthiest clients and she also liked to oversee some of the foreclosure stuff. She liked wealth and she also had a sadistic streak.

"Genevieve." Mom's voice was filled with disappointment.

How could she be so prejudiced?

And how come I was being so forthcoming? I knew it'd buy me nothing but hassles with her.

"Come. Over." she ordered. "We'll eat early. I'll head there now. Do not forget the books, Genevieve."

So many Genevieves. Pulling out that name gave me the heebie jeebies. It never bodes well for me.

NO ONE BUT ELLA KNOWS my name is actually Genevieve. People think Jenna is short for Jennifer. Or that I'm just Jenna.

My parents named me after Dad's mother, Genevieve, and as a child, Mom never hesitated to complain to me at every opportunity how much she despised my father's mother and only did it because she had no choice. I never got to meet her, but my father has told me many times (though never in front of Mom) that he thinks I'm blessed with a bit of his late mother's spirit. He said she was loving, free-spirited, loyal.

I don't think my name is all that bad, but the association upsets me, so I prefer to be called by a name that doesn't make me think of someone my mother hates.

Case in point:

One day, I was eleven years old, and I was flipping through one of her decorating coffee table books, minding my own business, though reading upside down with my legs thrown over the back of the couch, my head hanging off the edge when she waltzed in and glared.

"Up. We do not throw ourselves on the furniture like that!"

I did a backwards somersault and landed on the Persian rug and looked up at her, apologetically.

"You look just like your grandmother. I can't stand the sight of you. Go to your room!"

I got to my feet and put the book back down, on an angle the way it had been before, and then as I walked by, I sarcastically said, "Yes, Mommie Dearest," having recently read the book of the same name, and she slapped me in the face. She slapped me so hard that my head hit the wall.

She just stared, nostrils flaring, and I just remember being stunned until she marched away.

I never told Dad. And things had always been strained between Mom and I, from as young as I can remember. But, from that day forward, things were almost always extra-strained or at least chilly between us.

She'd give me heck when I rode down the banister. She'd give me heck when I didn't cross my legs while wearing a skirt. She told me I laughed too big and unladylike. Imagine how awful it feels to be mocked for your laughter? Someone takes a moment of your joy and stomps on it.

She was like a table manners Nazi with me at the dinner table up until a few years ago. She was the definition of a WASP Tiger Mom. But, even when I did things according to her rigorous standards, I didn't get praise.

I WAS ARGUING WITH my mother. Dad was sitting there, quiet, letting her walk all over me. As per the norm.

She wanted me to start charging Pippa some rent. And she wanted me to up the rent for Debbie, who used to own the salon, too, and now rented a chair.

"We're locked in to an agreement with Deb. We made the deal when she sold me the salon."

"When she sold *your father and I* the salon," Mom corrected, reminding me that it wasn't really and truly mine yet. I had three more years to prove it profitable before it was fully signed over to me in exchange for a chunk of my trust fund, which I was supposed to get on my thirtieth birthday.

"Costs have risen. Utilities, products. All the stuff that woman uses. Your overall costs have risen seven per cent in the last five months. It only stands to reason..."

"We have a contract! I break the contract, she walks! And not only does she walk, but she takes her clients. Some of those clients bring their kids to me. Or buy my products after Deb does their hair. Or gets their nails and their Brazilians done from Pippa, who also pays rent."

"Rent on the salon but not on the apartment," Mom pointed out. And then she glared at my Dad. "Should have had me write up that contract, Paul."

Dad's expression didn't change.

I sighed. This was a repeated argument, once she found out I wasn't charging Pippa rent to live with me upstairs.

"The apartment is mine, as part of our deal I don't pay rent. So, why should I charge Pippa? She uses the spare room, so it's no skin off my nose, and she splits on utilities and groceries. She chipped in for the paint and everything when we redecorated, too."

"You paid for the carpet yourself and you carpeted her bedroom," Mom said.

"We're splitting hairs, here, girls," Dad finally spoke up. We both looked to him at the head of the dinner table, set with white linen and Mom's second-best china set.

We were eating take-out Chinese food, but in normal Mom-fashion, we were eating it on fine china out of serving dishes on a fully laid dining room table, rather than at the kitchen table with paper plates or directly out of the cardboard containers in front of the TV. We were even using fancy chopsticks that had gold-plated monogram m's on them. M for Murdoch. M for miserable.

Dad looked to Mom. "The books look relatively good, Karen. What we should do, Jenna, is discuss your marketing plan for the balance of this year and the start of next year. Have you thought of that at all?"

"Yes. We do need to discuss that, Paul," Mom said, "because she's not investing back into the business. She's spending any profit she makes," Mom waved her hand at the printout sitting beside her dinner plate.

"Actually, I have a plan," I said.

"Do tell," Mom said with a roll of her eyes. Mom would be attractive for her age. She took care of her skin. She exercised. She had dark hair like mine, but it was cut to her collarbone and her hair style along with her ultra-conservative wardrobe choices made her look much older.

Dad was tall and trim, too, with just slightly greying dark hair and blue eyes. He was always dressed either in a suit or in golf clothes, and he turned women's heads.

Dad didn't show much of a personality. He was all business. He was quiet. He seemed like he mostly glazed over when Mom talked.

My mother showed her personality all right, and it wasn't a nice personality.

"I have four weddings booked outside normal salon hours. I'll attend the bride's home and me and my crew will do hair, nails, and all of that for the bride and her bridal party. I'll hand out cards to bridesmaids and coupons and I'm sure some of them will come to the salon after."

"That's a great idea, Jenna," Dad said. "Isn't that a great idea, Karen?" He looked to Mom with far too much enthusiasm.

Mom sipped her wine. She didn't reply.

I continued, "I've talked to some wedding businesses within a five-block radius of the salon. Me, a florist, a DJ, a caterer, and a banquet hall are all networking and referring for one another."

"Excellent." Dad's face lit up.

"That's all fine, Jenna," Mom started. "But you need to find a way to..."

"There's more. I've had two meetings with a cosmetics and hair tools company," I said, cutting her off. She instantly began to seethe but I sallied forth. "They're going to send in some stock on consignment, so it's risk free. I'm getting good sales from the hair products and the few make-up products I'm shelving, so I'm adding more shelving so that I can display more. Make-up brushes, hair tools, some high-end skincare products." I went on and rattled off some of the brand names and if I wasn't mistaken, Mom looked a little bit impressed.

I continued. "I'm getting busier. The book is filled to the brim more than 85% of my opening hours. If it keeps up like this, I can hire a part-time stylist to work the days Deb doesn't work. When Deb's ready to retire in six months, I'll hire someone established full-time who'll bring their own clients and to replace her and do profit sharing rather than paying hourly or renting a chair. I'm also thinking about bringing in Ella to do reception on the busiest days, if she can work her hours out between the cab office and the salon, which'll help me get more people in chairs, and help sell stuff on the shelves when people pay. Ella can do sales as she cashes them out. It should buy me an extra one or two appointments a day and maybe mean I can take a lunch break occasionally. I'll have more income and won't give myself a raise. I'll be putting money into the business to upgrade the space."

"Well, Ella's hardly refined enough to sell expensive cosmetics. She looks too much like a cheerleader to appeal to high-end clientele," Mom put in with a sneer.

"Does she look like a cheerleader here?" I pulled out my phone and scrolled to show Mom the picture we took before we went to Deke's Roadhouse on Saturday night when Ella's hair and make-up had been done.

Mom didn't reply, but this was a good sign, because if she didn't think Ella looked transformed, she'd have said something.

"I'm thinking of getting our friend Andie, who's a baker next door but also a good photographer, to do photo shoots and do some befores and afters in a social media blitz for the flat iron and hair gloss, and I'm thinking about doing a Groupon for a flat iron bar, too. Ella fixed up my website a few weeks ago and it looks great." I passed Dad my phone, so he could see Ella. He made a 'wow' face.

I still had to talk to Ella about it, but I knew she'd be game, especially if she knew my parents were pushing me and holding the salon over my head, she'd do what she had to do to help me fight back and hold my position.

"And..." I straightened up and put my phone back into my pocket. "I talked to the local high school and a few students interested in cosmetology are going to do an afternoon a week as part of their credit, starting after Christmas, so it won't cost me anything. I'll do a flat iron bar those days and they can demo the product. I'm thinking Tuesdays as it's my slowest day and it could bring more people in. I'll market to the students for prom time, too."

"What a great idea," Dad said.

"If the hair irons do well, I'm thinking of bringing in this company that has an all-natural hair straightening treatment, too. My closest competitor does these Brazilian blow-outs that are filled with chemicals. People might like my alternative."

"All well and good in theory, Jenna. But, are you ready to stop acting like a teenager and..."

"Seriously?" I cut her off.

She raised her over-tweezed eyebrows up at me critically. She didn't come to the salon to Pippa for her brows. She also didn't let me do her brows or her hair. She also never recommended her friends come to me. And that kind of hurt.

"I work six days a week. My business is profitable. I've got a good and diverse plan for growth. What is this really about, Mother?"

Mom glared at me.

"I'm full. Thank you for dinner. If there's nothing else, I've gotta go get ready for my date."

"Then go," Mom folded her arms, "Out on a date with a...biker." She stared at my father pointedly. He didn't react. He rarely did.

I shook my head, dropped my napkin on the table, and took my plate to the kitchen, kissing Dad's cheek on the way.

I dumped the mostly uneaten plate of food in the trash and put the plate and fancy chopsticks into the dishwasher. I was trained. Not a single dish was allowed to sit in the sink. Ever. Even if I was pissed at her. And him. He wasn't as hard on me, but with the exception of the salon being his idea, he never stood up for me much, either. Yeah, it was his idea, but he allowed her to control me with it. She wanted to control me, controlling me made her giddy, so in a way, maybe he did it for her, to help her continue to lord over me so she would be on his back less.

Sometimes, I wished I could just walk away and tell them to stuff it. But, I love my salon. I love where it is and the rooftop terrace and my neighbors and working with Pippa and having fun making people feel great about themselves. I continue to recite the countdown in my head, knowing I'll be at the end of five years eventually. In a couple months, I'll be at the halfway mark. And then once I'm over that hump, I'll see the finish line in sight.

I grabbed my purse and jacket and went outside and crossed the lawn past my mother's perfectly manicured rosebushes, which were still in bloom alongside the pots of Fall mums that lined the property line, over to Ella's. I didn't walk the path. That was the extent of my rebellion...walking on the grass instead of down the path.

I went in through the side door and painted a smile on my face as I got a hug from Bertie, Ella's mom, and a bunch of waves and helloes from her dad, Rob, who tried to coax me out to the garage to have a beer with him and several friends and a couple bikers in Dominion Brotherhood vests. I declined, but said hello to everyone and grabbed two cans of Pepsi and as I climbed the stairs to Ella's room on the third floor of their old farmhouse, I thought about how welcoming it was.

The house wasn't dirty. It was cluttered, mis-matched, and lived in. Mom would be mortified at the sight of it. She'd never been inside, but she'd bitched about the exterior of it since I was six. Things didn't match. It wasn't perfect. There were all sorts of noisy windchimes outside and metal lawn ornaments everywhere, but it was a home. And it felt like it people lived there, loved there, laughed there.

There, I was offered affection, invited to stay for food and festivities. At my parents' house, Ella was never treated like she was even welcome unlike when I came over to her place and was treated like family.

I climbed up the attic stairs and found my beautiful petite curly-blonde bestie (who was built with double Ds). She was rifling through her dresser drawers, looking like she was on a mission. Ella's room was *the bomb*, too. The ceilings were sloped, and it was a total she-cave decorated in Betty Boop with a rustic yet frilly feel to it.

I put the Pepsis down and flopped onto her bed.

"Hey you," I greeted.

"Hey you," she returned, still rifling through her undie drawer.

"I tried to call you last night," I started, trying to think about how to broach the Deacon subject. I felt bad that I'd caused a misunderstanding.

I reached for her phone, which was lying on the bed.

"Don't touch it!" she snapped, pointing at me with accusation. I was famous for fucking with her phone settings, particularly her ring tones, which I'd always set to Gangnam Style just to be a little shit. This time, I'd just reached for it out of nervous habit.

"I was with Deacon," she told me as she pulled out a scrap of black from the drawer. Sexy undies.

She did a little twirly dance of excitement and threw the panties into the backpack that was there beside her.

She lifted and opened her can of Pepsi, took a sip, and made a Pepsi commercial "Ahhhh" sound.

"I know. I'm glad," I said. "I talked to Rider about his brother and he told me some stuff. About how Deacon got fucked over repeatedly so he's cautious about relationships and ... I'm gathering that you got that info from Deacon already, since you spent the night with him."

"Yeah, I blew him off and hid and then when cornered I threw what I'd heard in his face and called it quits and then he schooled me on the facts and then walked away from me. I had to grovel." Her eyes had a bit of a haunted look to them.

I winced. "That's some heavy shit he went through. Sorry, Elle."

"Don't be sorry for sharing facts. You were having my back. I'd have done the same. He told me that there was stuff, that I'd hear things, and I agreed to discuss them with him but then I jumped the gun. I just didn't think there could be reasonable reasons for that, you know?" Ella's chin trembled.

I knew. I agreed. And she *did* have my back that way always. She'd been the one who broke it to me when my high school boyfriend was cheating on me.

She took a big breath. "And with everything else? Getting held at knife-point, the shit I've heard about Jay, and now dating a guy who's going to war against the MC my uncle—-" She winced. "Forget that last part."

"I already know," I waved at her. "Rider told me to stay away from those guys and said we had to keep quiet about it. Said he figured you'd tell me anyway so he wanted to get in front of it. So last night? You groveled and all's good?"

She flopped onto her bed beside me. "He's amazing, Jen. I'm falling hard."

"His brother is amazing, too," I told her.

She rolled over and we were face to face. "Are you falling?" she asked.

"Little bit..." I said.

She smiled. "Look at us! Dating brothers. Biker brothers. Can you believe this?"

I laughed, filled with glee. "Did you... *do* it?" I asked in a whisper.

She nodded big, "Yes and oh my God! It was phenomenal. Is his brother phenomenal too?" Ella had stars in her eyes, the likes I'd never seen. I was so happy for her.

"Oh my God. Yes. The best I've ever had. Not to mention the biggest."

"Me too," she said, and we broke out into uncontrollable peals of laughter, ending in an excited hug.

"Oh my God, Jenna. I'm in so much trouble. So much." Ella shook her head, eyes filled with doom.

"What do you mean?" I asked.

"I'm so totally cock whipped it's not even funny! Deacon just, like, puts me in this cock fog..."

I laughed. "If you're gonna be foggy, that's the kinda fog to be in, I guess. I feel ya, sister." She was staring off into space and I knew by her face she was having some sexy flashback about Deacon's man parts.

I took the opportunity to slide my finger over to her phone and covertly re-assign her not-so-favorite song as the ring tone attached to my name.

Hehee.

She had this dreamy look on her face, staring at the ceiling. I snapped my fingers in front of her face.

"Earth to Ella, come in, Ella."

She gave her head a shake. "See what I mean? I just think about it and I go all..." she went cross-eyed.

I chuckled. "It's a good thing. Good you got some decent tail for once."

"But I've gotta dash, babes. I'm going to his place. Spending the night again."

"Ooh. I haven't seen where they live yet. What's it like?" I rested my cheek on my palm.

"I haven't seen where Deke, Rider, and Spence are. They live above the Roadhouse. Deacon has a trailer out in the back."

"A trailer?" I made a face and stuck my tongue out. My ex, the asshole who broke my heart now lived in a trailer. A run-down trailer.

"Nuh-uh, nope, Jenna. When I say trailer, it's like a rock star pad. All new and cherry wood and granite and modern. And it's spotless. Like, what biker lives in a spotless rock star trailer? It even has a dishwasher."

"Your biker?" I offered.

"My biker," she breathed in dreamy-eyed agreement.

She got up and reached for her phone, which was between us.

"Well, if you were ever gonna hook up with a biker, this sounds like *the* biker, the only kinda biker you'd have. Girl time soon, okay? And double dates soon, too."

"Absolutely."

I gave her a big hug. I loved my bestie. I loved seeing her like this. "You seem happy."

"I'm scared shitless," she said into my shoulder. "This is so far out of my normal comfort zone, Jenna. But I am falling hard and fast."

"Rider says he's had a lot of pain. A lot of it. But he is tough and loyal and smart. Rider says you couldn't ask for a better guy to have in your corner."

"That's really good to hear. Rider seems like a good guy."

"He does, doesn't he? It feels almost too perfect. He's gorgeous and sweet and funny and smart and amazing in bed. I'm so fucking scared, Elle."
I was. I was warring between letting my guard down and keeping my heart safe.

"Trust it. Maybe it doesn't have to be so hard."

If only.

Before I left, I went on to tell her about the part-time job I wanted to offer her at the salon doing reception as well as to help me with the upcoming weddings.

I'd offered Ella a job before, told her to go to beauty school and come cut hair, but it wasn't her thing.

She's smart, business-minded. She'd fit in perfectly at Mom's bank or at Dad's real estate office. But, she wouldn't fit in with their stuffy attitudes.

She agreed to take the job with me, temporarily, as her hours were being cut at the taxi company she answered phones for, and I was glad to help her out with some hours for now, suspecting she wouldn't be with me for long.

As I turned the key in my car, my mother looked through the front drapes. She shot eye daggers at me.

I looked at her with unguarded sadness. I didn't normally let her see that from me. But this time, I did. And she startled, and her lips parted.

I pulled away and headed back home.

I WAS GETTING READY for Rider and heard a text alert.

I grabbed for my phone, which was plugged in, lying on my bedside table.

"Been thinkin' about dirtying that duvet all day."

I smiled and chewed my lip.

Me: "It's spotlessly clean. It's very ready to get dirty."

Him: "Been thinking about your smile, your legs, that gorgeous hair, too."

Me: "Me too. Your smile and your hair. Your eyes. Not sure I've had a chance to develop a thing for your legs yet, but I seriously dig your gear stick."

I laughed at myself. How lame was that?

Him: "My gear stick? Funny babe. It's now twitching, thinking about you too."

Me: "See you soon. I look forward to you taking me for a ride... Rider."

Him: "Not as much as I look forward to it. Not sure I can get away yet. But I'm tryin'."

Me: "Lookin' forward to getting dirty with you. That's from my duvet. lol. I concur."

Him: "Can't wait. Text you soon."

Me: "Hurry."

I was ready. Hair and makeup. Casual jeans with a sexy top and heels and hidden away for (hopefully) unwrapping later: ultra-sexy undies. I got my bedroom ready for what I hoped would be a great night. Duvet off. Seductive scented wax melting in a warmer for a half an hour and then shut off, letting the aroma linger but not be too in-his-face.

I got a text from Rider.

"Sorry, gorgeous. I can't get away after all. Raincheck?"

Seriously?

"K"

He hadn't promised. But, I guess I'd hoped.

I put the phone down, changed into a pair of sweats, and ate my feelings in the form of three bowls of Ben & Jerry's in my room, avoiding the living room because Pippa and Joe were watching a movie, snuggled up like lovebirds.

5

It was Thursday morning and he was standing there with his glorious mane of hair loose and blowing in the wind, dressed in a denim jacket with his leather Dominion Brotherhood vest over it, faded jeans with those fawn cowboy boots. He was knocking on the glass door of my salon, holding two take-out cups of coffee in a tray in one hand, a paper bag hanging from his teeth, so he could knock.

I wasn't due to open for ten minutes. I was at the reception desk. I unlocked the door and opened it.

He handed me the tray of coffees and transferred the bag from his mouth to his hand and his lips touched mine.

I licked my lips, meaning I licked both of our lips.

He made an *Mm* sound.

"Good morning," I said softly.

"Mornin', beautiful. Sorry about last night."

"What happened?" I asked, trying to hide the hurt I was feeling.

"Found Scoot. He'd been attacked."

My eyebrows shot up. "Attacked?"

He let out a big breath and leaned against the tall reception desk. Scoot was Scooter, a.k.a Scott, the blond scruffy dirty-pretty prospect.

"Yeah. It was bad." His eyes held a darkness that chilled me.

"How bad?"

He shook his head, "He'll live. Not gonna sugarcoat it; it was bad." He opened the lid and sipped his coffee.

"Oh God. Is he in the hospital?"

"He's home now. We were there with him a good part of the night."

I winced. And then I noticed he had a scratch over his eye.

I touched it with my finger. "What happened?"

He shook his head. "No biggie. Cash my raincheck in tonight?" he asked, and he caressed my cheekbone with just the tips of his fingers and tucked my hair behind that ear.

I moistened my lips, feeling tingly.

His eyes moved to my mouth and then back to my eyes.

I gave a nod.

"Skeptical?" he asked.

"No." I smiled. "I understand. I hope Scooter is gonna be okay."

He clenched his jaw.

"Be careful, gorgeous. You see rabid dogs on leather you am-scray. Don't even make eye contact with those fuckers. Prospects are supposed to be off limits. These guys have no scruples, whatsoever."

I winced. I wanted to ask what happened, but I didn't. I watched him, waiting to see if he'd offer further explanation. He didn't.

"Gotta go. I'll pick you up at nine. Pop that cherry. Go to the Roadhouse for a drink. See where the night takes us?"

I smiled. "Yeah."

He kissed me again. This time his lips lingered.

I put my hands into his hair at the sides of his head and held on.

His body was plastered against mine and it felt good. It felt right.

Man, he was a good kisser. And he smelled amazing. Like fresh air and green apples.

He backed away, grabbing his coffee from the counter and he left, smiling at me.

I left the door unlocked, flipping my sign to "Open", watching him walk to his orange muscle car. He gave me a wink as he started it up. I bit my bottom lip and wiggled my fingers in a little wave.

I watched him drive away and then I opened the paper bag and it was a chocolate éclair donut in the shape of a heart, with a thick layer of whipped cream inside.

I texted him.

"What a sexy donut."

He replied about ten minutes later.

"Not so bad yourself..."

I laughed out loud and then took a selfie of me eating it, the donut tilted sideways, my tongue dipped into the whipped cream center suggestively. I put a dramatic filter on the pic and sent it to him. And then I ate the donut, while daydreaming about that night, hoping our date would actually happen.

I WAS GETTING MY MAKE-up done when Ella phoned me.

She was talking a mile a minute about Deacon moving in with her at her parents' house.

"Why are you so mad?" I asked.

"Did you hear anything I said?" She was acting like she was outraged.

"I heard it all," I told her.

"To recap," she started unnecessarily recounting, "We've been dating like four days, including the day that I sort of broke up with him, and he has moved in with me. My father is conspiring to marry me off. He and my dad discussed him staying here. Without me being in that conversation!"

She went on for a minute, continuing to recap all she'd already said but in a high soprano voice, assigning demerit points to Deacon and her parents while listing their infractions.

"So, from everything you've told me, Deacon has gone full steam ahead with your relationship," I stated.

"Double warp speed," she said. "Is Rider like this?"

I wish. I felt a stab of jealousy.

"No. And I gotta say, I'm a little jealous. Ten points against *you*, Elle. Everything I've heard points to him being protective. Let him protect you. He's giving you orgasms. He wants to be with you as much as he can. You like everything about him so far?"

"Everything. Except these controlling alpha male ways. He's amazing so far. But I haven't even practiced my signature with his name yet."

She was such an over-thinker. Well, I guess I was a bit of one, too, but I bottled it up. Ella needed to verbalize it.

She ranted some more until I reminded her to breathe and told her to roll with it. It was time for me to finish getting ready for my date with Rider.

If he actually showed up this time.

My text went off.

"Outside @ your back door."

"Oooh… dirty…got a diamond ring for me?" I wrote back and added a winking emoji.

"Get that sexy ass down here so I can pop that cherry."

I was excited. I was a tad downtrodden that he hadn't come to the door. I pushed it away and grabbed my bag, said bye to Pip and Joe, who were making fajitas together in the kitchen, and went out back to the roof patio and down the stairs. He was there, on his motorcycle, looking casual and so sexy.

"Hey, gorgeous," he greeted.

"Hey," I returned with a flirty smile. I was in jeans and high heeled open-toed Jimmy Choo boots with black nail polish on that had little silver stud embellishments (aka: biker girl toes), a leather jacket, and I was wearing a black bustier underneath. My hair was loose and wavy, and I had my irresistible blue-red lip stain on. He eyed me, head to toe, and I read approval on his face.

His hair was in a low man bun and he wore his Dominion Brotherhood leather jacket, dark jeans, and motorcycle boots. He had a black bandana around his throat.

He passed me a black helmet. I fumbled with it, so he got off the bike and put it on for me, getting the strap done up tight. It made me feel looked after, which was sweet.

And even with these high heels on, he still had height on me, which I really, *really* liked.

"Ready?"

"To get my motorcycle cherry popped? Yes!" I was exuberant.

"Can't believe you've never been on a motorcycle," he said. "You weren't shitting me?"

"Never," I confirmed.

He smiled, "That's what I was hopin' to hear." He winked, pulled the bandana up over his mouth, and he revved his very shiny, even in the dark, chrome Harley up.

He pulled away from the building. I put my arms around him and felt my smile go wide as we pulled away.

Being on the back of his bike felt awesome. My face hurt from the smiling I did on the way to Deke's Roadhouse. And Deke's Roadhouse was way too close. I wanted to do this for hours. I wanted to take it in, feel the power of the machine, feel *his* power in commanding it, absorb that through every single nerve in my body.

Too soon, we were getting off the bike.

My hair held up okay through helmet wear and somewhat windy weather. I fluffed it while catching my expression in the window of the Roadhouse on the way in. I gave him a huge smile.

"That effing rocked!"

He looked surprised and pleased. He held the door for me and I skip-walked ahead.

There were a lot of eyes on us as we entered and maybe it was because I couldn't wipe the smile off my face. And that I was skipping, sort of. He grabbed my hand and we went right to the bar.

Deacon was sitting there, drinking a beer and talking to Bronto, and another Dom in a prospect vest who had black hair, looked Hispanic, and was covered in tatts. He was kind of gorgeous in a Dave Navarro way. Deacon and Rider did a bro shake and then he did that with the other prospect as well.

"What to drink, gorgeous?" Rider asked and a different guy than the usual bartender, this one also a big man with a beard to his belly button, lumbered over.

"Corona," I said. "Hey, guys."

"Jenna," I said, holding my hand out to the dark-haired guy when Rider didn't introduce us.

"I know. Met you the other night when we took you two back to your place. Jesse."

I smiled. I guess that was why Rider hadn't introduced us.

"Ohhh, right. That was tanked Jenna you must've met. She's a forgetful thing."

He snickered and squeezed my hand just briefly and then he moved away saying, "Be back." and he moved to two Dominion Brotherhood bikers coming in the front door. Jesse's leather vest said "Prospect" on it.

I turned my attention to Rider, who was getting our drinks. He had our two beers and he looked so handsome, smiling with his mouth and with his eyes, that my heart tripped over itself.

"Wanna grab a table now or you mind if we have our first drink here with Deacon at the bar?"

"That's cool." I smiled, getting comfortable.

Deacon fished a phone with a broken screen out of his pocket and was texting someone.

I smirked, deciding I'd get ahold of his phone before the drink was over so I could program Ella's "favorite" ring tone on her biker's phone.

Tee hee.

WE WERE ON OUR SECOND beer and it was now just us two at a cozy little booth. We were both flirting shamelessly as he was starting to tell me about life back in Sioux Falls. So far, I knew he was a mechanic at his family's garage, he owned part of the three businesses that they'd just started (the bar, the garage, and a bike dealership), and he said he earned a cut of earnings from his MC, The Dominion Brotherhood, which he'd gotten his patch for when he turned 22. He and his brothers started prospecting at 21 and all three of them earned their patch at the one-year mark. He was 26. Deacon, 28. Spencer, 25. Their little sister, who was attending school in Sioux Falls to get her degree in teaching, was 19.

He also said that he and Spencer designed custom bikes. Spencer and Rider drew up the plans based on what they'd brainstorm together, and Rider built them. The other businesses and the MC took priority, but he tried to spend a day a week working on them on the side and had several orders to fill within the next year. Word was getting around and he had other potential buyers wanting to get in line.

"I'd love to see one sometime," I said.

"Got an album of pictures back at my place," he said.

"Yeah?" I asked.

"Yeah."

Maybe I'd get to see his place sometime. I sure liked the look in his eyes.

We were side-by-side in the half-circle booth, and my left leg was thrown over his right one when Paige Simpson walked by for the third time, shamelessly giving him 'fuck me' eyes.

He'd made eye contact with her the first time, but his face was blank. He ignored her the second. The third time, I could swear I saw irritation. And I couldn't hide my own, either. This time, he watched me as she walked by and I didn't stop myself from shooting daggers at her with my eyes.

Paige had been here trying to be all over Deacon the past Saturday night. We knew her from high school. She was a few years ahead of me and Ella and she might as well have had *skank* written in red Sharpie across her cleavage.

She'd been seen on many bikes since our teens, including Ella's Wyld Jackal cousin Christian and the president of the closest Wyld Jackals club.

Chris had kissed me once and groped me at a high school party. I'd been drunk as a skunk and thankfully it didn't go further. Ella would never have forgiven me if it had. And the fact that it happened was one of my few secrets from her. Maybe my only real secret from her.

The worst part was that it didn't stop because I'd stopped him, it'd stopped because the underage party got raided by the cops. I'd always joked with Ella that Christian was a hottie before that night and had to keep it up after that night, so she wouldn't know anything had happened. She hated him. And for good reason. He tormented her endlessly when they were kids going as far as cutting one of her pigtails off, once. I'd probably let it go as far as I did because I was in self-destruct mode post break-up with Michael, the guy who'd taken my virginity and then broken my heart.

In case Skanky Paige decided to do a slow swaying walk by, yet again, I moved in a little closer to Rider and touched his hair. I took it out of the elastic and fluffed it out. His eyes twinkled.

"You have zero split ends. I'm impressed." His eyes twinkled even more as I inspected the ends of his hair.

"Joelle turned me onto the right hair band. Comes out easy. I also trim it every month or two."

"Joelle?" I asked, on high alert.

"My little sister."

"Ah," I said, "And who cuts it?'

"Not had it cut for a while. It's due."

"Well, you can't let just anyone touch it. It could be a very bad idea if you don't choose your stylist carefully."

"I'll keep that in mind, baby," he said huskily and leaned in like he was going to kiss me.

And that was when she stopped at our fucking table.

Seriously?

"Hey, Riderrrr. How's it goin'?" She was oozing with sluttiness. She was dressed in a micro-mini skirt and her bustier had netting through the torso that equated to under-boob cleavage. Too much boobs. If I had boobs like that (though they were definitely fake; she didn't have those boobs in high school), I'd be tempted to flaunt them, but leaving something to the imagination. She looked like a porn star.

Her red hair was teased and stripper-hair big and it looked not far off from an 80's hair band groupie. She had on an inch of make-up. She was maybe 27, 28, but she looked ten years older than that. Hard living. Too much sun. Not enough moisturizer. And I could see her split ends from where I sat even in the dimness of the bar.

He glanced over his shoulder at her. "Hey. Good." He then dismissively turned back to me. He caught the way I looked at her. He gave me a heated look.

And I liked it *a lot* that he didn't let her engage him in small talk or give her any inclination whatsoever that he wanted to chat (or do anything else) with her.

"Don't I know you?" she asked me, instead of leaving.

Of course she knew me. She was being a bitch.

"Yeah, you know me, Paige."

"You seem a little familiar. Ohhh, you work at Walmart?"

What a catty cow. Not that there was a thing wrong with working at Walmart, but she'd been in my salon. Twice to buy hair spray. She knew I owned it. She's called me Jenna at the counter both times and the salon was called Jenna's House of Allure, for fuck sakes. She probably figured by the way I dressed that I was a label whore, and this was clearly her attempt to rattle me in front of Rider, who she clearly wanted.

"Nope, I don't. Is that where you got those shoes?" I asked.

She was wearing Jimmy Choo's. I should know. I was wearing $1400 Jimmy Choo open-toed boots right now.

She glared at me.

"Uh...actually, these are one-thousand-dollar Jimmy Choo's."

"Oh. You blow old Sal at the shoe store to get a discount?"

Rider snickered and put his hand on my thigh and gave it a squeeze. I glanced at him. He was looking at me intently. I didn't know how to read it. He looked amused. I think.

"Rider, I'm sorry I missed your call last night. I just wanted to say that."

My stomach took a dive.

"Didn't call you last night," he muttered, giving her a death stare.

"Pocket dial?" she suggested.

"Not sure how that'd be since you're not in my phone."

"Oh," she gave him a pout. "Weird. Well, call me anytime, sexy." She winked at him and placed her palm on the table. She moved her hand away and I saw a post-it with a phone number on it.

"Jenna," she sneered and then strutted away and idiotically so, since she'd used my name after having claimed to not know me.

Bitch.

Did I believe him? I didn't know. I tried to keep my face blank. I sipped my beer.

He gave my thigh a squeeze.

I faked a cramp with a wince and gingerly pulled my leg off his and squeezed my legs together, my hands folded between my thighs.

"I didn't call her, Jenna." He ran his hand through my hair, "I was with my brothers all night. Don't even got that bitch's number. Look. She left her number on the table. Would she do that if I had her number?"

I glanced at him and our eyes locked. It was a loaded moment and I didn't know how to respond to it.

I tried to brighten. "Whatever. I got her number, too. 1-800-Skank." I took another healthy swig of my beer.

I felt the heat of his gaze, which was burning into me.

"Like this," he muttered.

"What?" I asked.

"Possessive," he stated.

I didn't make eye contact. I reached for my handbag. "Little girls room calling," I chirped.

"You believe me?" he grabbed my hand, halting me.

"Of course. She's just trying to get me goin'. And she's making sure you know she's interested. Not that you would be, because, hello..." I gestured to the direction she'd walked like it was preposterous.

I slid out of the booth and I was kind of intrigued at the idea that he liked the idea of me being possessive.

And as for Paige's intentions? That's what I *did* think. That she was just trying to get me going.

Mostly.

A FEW HOURS LATER

He was leaving. Leaving.

He was pulling his boots on after giving me a lame excuse about an early appointment at the garage. My place was only a ten-minute drive from the garage. It didn't make sense to me.

What *did* make sense? He was being cold and detached. After sex.

And I was trying to hide my heartbreak. We'd had sex and now he was going. This hurt. This hurt a lot. This was a sure sign that he was only after sex, not anything long-term.

I had a sneaking suspicion the first time, when he left that morning and didn't come back up when he picked up his car, chucking my effing chin, but then he'd seemed like he was still interested...

I'd come twice. He'd come, too. And now it was five minutes later, max, and he was already dressed, so he could leave. Maybe he was heading back to the bar to fetch the Post-It with Paige's number on it.

He gave me a quick kiss at my kitchen door, and not the kind of kiss you give a woman you've just had sex with, unless you're not planning to come back for more. It wasn't the chuck on the chin I got last time, but it certainly didn't leave me thinking he was interested in thirds.

And then after he pulled away, I sat, in my pale pink lacy nighty in my big empty bed that still smelled like sex, and I tried to do a post-mortem on the night as the sound of his motorcycle pipes echoed in my aching heart.

What went wrong? I rewound the evening and thought it over.

After Paige had left, maybe I'd deflated, but I tried hard not to let it show. We stayed while I had another drink and he switched to water. I'd put my wall up, I guess, because the idea of seeing a guy seeing another girl was too déjà vu for me.

And we sat, and I talked to get rid of what felt like awkward silence, and he, in hindsight, replied mostly with *Yeahs, um hms,* and did more *yeah*-ing while he kept checking his cell phone. There was a lot of awkward silence.

"Are you waiting for a call?" I asked after he'd looked at it for the third time.

"Nope." He put the phone down face down and gave me a smile that didn't give me the warm fuzzies. At all.

Maybe he was checking the time. Maybe there was something up with his club to do with Scooter getting attacked. Maybe he wanted to go.

Maybe he wanted to see if he could catch up with Skanky Paige, who had been trying to catch that guy Jesse's attention after leaving our table.

"Do you, uh... wanna come back to my place?" I asked. And I sounded funny. I didn't like the way I sounded, because I sounded needy, and like I was afraid of rejection. And it *really* wasn't like me to tip my hand.

He leaned forward and looked me in the eyes and looked like he was unsure. He searched my face for a second.

And I wanted to erase any implication that I might be afraid of rejection. So, I touched the opening of his shirt, and then my finger glided from his throat down past the top three buttons, which were not fastened, to where the next button was done up. My finger then gilded back up and touched his bottom lip. I leaned forward and kissed his lips, letting my tongue touch that lower lip before my lips caught up.

He kissed me back, hungrily, and the look in his eyes changed to sexually charged.

He got to his feet, taking my hand, waving at a couple of bikers as we made our way to the door. Deacon was already long gone after we'd had just one drink with him and then Rider walked him out as they exchanged words in that huddle that ended in back slaps and grins by the door. Spencer was here, though, and I saw Rider shoot him a nasty look as we left. Spencer's response was to put a bottle of beer to his lips and glare back.

The ride back to my place felt too long. A sharp contrast to earlier, because I couldn't wait to get him alone. I wasn't drunk tonight. I was *very* looking forward to getting reacquainted with that piercing and that tongue. I pushed Paige out of my mind.

Literally. I envisioned shoving her over a cliff out into a great big black hole of nothing.

I'd already texted Pippa from the bathroom earlier and she confirmed that she and Joe were heading to his place after fajitas, so the apartment was all mine tonight.

Joe lived with two roommates, one had just moved out and the other was in the midst of moving, so they had some alone time. In a few more weeks, after the place was, in Pippa's words, "redecorated, fumigated, sanitized, and exorcized", she'd be moving in with him.

Why hadn't I told Mom that when she was going on about Pip living with me without paying rent? She'd mentioned a few times that if Pippa ever left, she could have that room rented out in a heartbeat. *Right*. To someone who worked for her, most likely, a someone who would report to my mother on all my business.

I had my mother on a need-to-know basis.

I'd find a new roommate myself before telling her that Pippa moved out.

I didn't *need* a roommate, but I wanted one. I liked having people around. My friend and neighbor Andie had six siblings and loved living alone in her little apartment. Me? I wish I'd had a bunch of siblings. Then maybe my Tiger / Helicopter Mom would've had more than just me to focus on.

When we got inside, I grabbed Rider's hand and took him straight to my room. I gave him a playful shove and he fell onto his back on my bed. The look in his eyes was ultra-sexy.

I grabbed a lighter from my dresser and lit a candle and then got out of my booties. He was on his back, watching me.

"Come here, gorgeous."

"One sec," I said and slipped into the bathroom and swished with mouthwash, rolled more deodorant on, and fluffed my hair, then turned on the bathroom's scented wax warmer.

I walked out, finding him lying there on his back, perpendicular on my bed, his feet planted on the floor at the side of my bed, staring at the ceiling, looking gorgeous in the flickering candlelight. I got closer and he didn't only look gorgeous, he looked bored.

"Sorry. I didn't mean to be so long."

"Way to kill the spontaneity," he mumbled.

I snickered and stood at his knees and then said, "Kick those boots off."

He did, using one foot to push the other boot off, then doing the same with the other boot, not taking his eyes off me.

I climbed up and straddled him.

His hands went to my waist.

I started to kiss him and work at his fly.

When I got his dick out, he reached into his leather jacket pocket and produced a condom. He passed it to me and slid the jacket off and tossed it to the floor.

Ugh. He wanted me to put it on. Flashback to our last night together.

"You do it," I passed it back. "It's too sticky and I can't get it just right."

His eyes flashed with something, maybe irritation, but then he ripped the corner of the package and got down to business.

I watched.

"The sooner that's on, the sooner I get to go for a ride," I wiggled my eyebrows. He wiggled his in reply. My eyes dropped and yep, he was as well-equipped as I remembered.

I rolled over onto my back beside him and waited.

A beat went by where he watched me, his eyes working actively and greedily over my body, and then he got to his feet and worked my jeans undone and hauled them off. He hauled my panties off next.

And then he settled on top of me and lined up. I felt the wetness gather between my legs. Just a look from him and I was ready. Very ready.

I opened my legs wider and wrapped them around his legs. He put a finger inside me and smiled. "You ready?"

I nodded and sank my front teeth into my bottom lip as his finger moved in and out a little bit. And then he crooked it, hitting that magical spot inside.

"You're ready." He took his finger out and then watched me as he *ever so slowly* advanced and slid inside.

A breathy moan escaped my lips and then I kissed him, putting my fingers into his hair.

He put his fingers to my clit and began to thrust harder and faster while working it. It took no more than a minute before I was panting into his mouth, ready to come, when he let go of my clit and grabbed my hips with both hands and started fucking me harder and faster.

"I was almost..." I whispered, "You stopped." My voice was filled with accusation.

"You want it?"

I looked at him thinking, 'duh'.

"Fuck, you're hot," he said.

I rocked against him.

"Hot for me, baby?" He asked.

"What do you think?" I asked.

"Say it."

"Say what?" I asked, not hiding my annoyance.

"That you want it."

I rolled my eyes and laughed.

He grabbed my face by the chin and stared, intently, stopping the thrusting.

"You want it bad enough, gorgeous? Ask. No. Beg. Beg for it."

I stilled. "Beg for it?"

"Yeah, baby. Beg for it. Beg nice and I'll give you the biggest climax of your life."

"I'm not begging for it," I said.

He stilled, "Then maybe you're not getting it."

I opened my mouth and then I closed it. I opened it again, "What?"

His expression changed, and he shook his head, "Jokin', Jenna." He put his thumb back and bit down on my throat while working that knot of nerves again.

My eyes rolled into the back of my head, but then I pulled back. "That hurts." I said, and he released my throat and began kissing me again.

I rocked into him, feeling him slide in and out and in and out as he twisted my clit and then, without warning, I hit a huge peak and let out a cry.

I floated back to earth again and he took a nipple into his mouth and sucked, then he changed positions and turned me to my side and was grinding against my backside, then sliding inside me.

I put my hand on his hand, which was on my hip and threaded my fingers with his.

He kissed my shoulder. "You are smokin' hot when you come, baby."

"Mm," I said. "Thanks."

"You could give a porn star a run for their money in the best orgasm face award," he added, sliding in and out.

I giggled.

He groaned like he liked the way that felt around his dick.

"Mm." He planted himself to the root and stayed there a second. And then he rotated his hips.

"Ah." Wow, that felt good.

He drilled in again and again, making my eyes roll back.

We were spooning, and it was a really nice angle he was at. His left hand reached between my legs again and he worked at me, hitting me inside in a way where the next orgasm that came was fast and hard, and it was coming from inside *and* from the outside.

Damn, he was good at that.

After coming the second time, I was boneless and hoping he'd come soon, because I just really wanted to curl up on his chest and sleep.

He was thrusting into me over and over. He moved, putting me on my belly.

"On all fours, beautiful," he whispered against my ear and then licked the ridge of it.

I moved up onto my knees and he pushed us forward so that I was pressed up against my soft padded headboard.

"Hold on." He grabbed my wrists and made me hold onto the edge. And then he started going really hard. I was glad the headboard was soft because I was being slammed against it.

"That feel good?" he asked.

"Mm," I grunted.

"Tell me."

"Mm. Yeah, Rider. It's good," I said.

"Did I make you come hard?" He asked.

"Mm hm."

"Talk to me, baby."

I froze.

"Talk," he kissed my ear, "to," he kissed my throat, "me..." another kiss, on my jaw this time.

"And say what?" I asked.

He slowed. His hand caressed up my belly, past my breasts, and to my throat. He held my throat in his grip, loosely, his fingertips at my jawline.

"Tell me what you want. Where you want me to touch you, what you want me to do to you."

I swallowed against his palm and felt a little claustrophobic suddenly.

I froze.

"For someone who's come twice, how come you're all tense? You're safe with me."

I couldn't exactly tell him he'd already done all the good stuff to me and now I just wanted him to hurry up and finish, so we could sleep.

"I want you to come, Rider. It's definitely your turn. Come." I tried, my voice husky. I put my hand on his and caressed it and used the caress to move his hand down to my breast, away from my throat, which felt too vulnerable for him to be holding in that way.

He was still a minute and then he moved backwards on his knees, taking me with him, until I was back on my belly flat on the bed.

His palm trailed up my spine, up to my hair, which he gathered into one hand and held tight.

"Ouch," I said.

He let go of it and was still a moment. He pulled out.

I waited.

He flipped me over to my back and then was inside me, looking into my eyes. I closed my eyes and put my arms around him.

He buried his mouth behind my ear and started to hammer into me. And he hammered. And yep... hammered. It was just skin slapping skin for a really long time.

"Tighten," he ordered, "Wiggle."

"What?"

"Fuck," he ground out, sounding frustrated.

It took a dog's age for him to finally moan into my hair. I ran my hands up and down his back.

Things felt... wrong. The affection of a few minutes before was gone.

I tried to bring ease back into the room.

"You want something to drink?" I kissed his shoulder.

"Naw, babe." He rolled to his back and ran his hands through his hair.

"Food? I could order a pizza. I have a big box of really good pastries in the kitchen."

"Naw, that's all right." He got up and walked, nude, to the bathroom and closed the door behind himself.

I stretched and leaned over to grab my purse from the place I'd discarded it on the floor when we came in. I pulled my cell out and plugged it into the USB port in my bedside table lamp. I checked the volume to make sure it was up for the alarm that'd wake me up in about six and a half hours.

He was back as I put the phone down. He reached to the floor for his jeans and got into them, commando.

My heart sank as it registered that he was getting dressed.

"You're getting dressed."

"Yeah, babe. Gonna hit the road."

"Uh... you can crash here." I said.

"Got an early appointment with a customer to fix the brakes in his pick-up."

"I don't live far," I muttered.

"Easier to roll outta bed in the mornin' and head right to the garage fifty feet away. But, cheers, babe." He leaned over and grabbed his leather jacket. "Walk me out so you can lock up?"

I got up and used the sheet to cover me until I could get to my closet where I found my nightie and robe. I was feeling all kinds of shy all of a sudden. And my chest was burning with a very unwanted emotion.

I tied the sash as he finished getting his boots on, and then I followed him to the door, my disappointment impossible to hide.

"Lock up. 'Night, babe." He kissed me on the lips and it wasn't a peck, but it also didn't feel like the other times he kissed me.

This was it.

We were done; I could feel it. I could see it in his eyes, which weren't the warm they typically were when he was looking at me. They were blank. Almost cold.

He got sex and now he was going. Done. Finito. And it felt like he was done in a way where I probably wouldn't hear from him again.

He gave me a smile, but it was a little bit of a sad smile. It felt like a goodbye smile. I was also pretty sure I was wearing my heart on my sleeve right then and he was reading it and confirming my suspicions.

I stood at the door and watched while he walked the length of my patio, climbed down the stairs, and then I heard him start up his Harley and ride away.

He didn't even glance back up at the doorway as he pulled away.

I went back inside, locked the door, and went to bed feeling empty and used.

I WAS NOT GONNA CRY. I was NOT gonna cry over a guy.

I cried over a guy once and he made me feel so small because of it that I'd vowed I would never ever do it again.

I was seventeen when it started and still seventeen when my heart got smashed. Michael was *the* bad boy of our high school. The James Dean.

He wasn't Mike. He was *Michael.* And he was deep. He was the champion of the underdog. He played guitar. He was soulful and smart, though he ditched class more than he showed up. He challenged the teachers when he *was* in class and sometimes he flustered them, because he was smart. He smoked and drank and drove a muscle car he'd restored. He also broke my heart right after he took my virginity, because I'd found out he was sleeping with half the other A-list girls in the school. Well, Ella found out and broke it to me.

He'd wanted our relationship secret. He'd given me a line about it being just about us and not about what society thought relationships should be. I'd bought it. I later found out, after giving up my V-card, that he'd been seeing a bunch of other girls, all secretly, at the same time, and at least three of them had given him sex, two had given their V-cards, too. They'd all bought his lines, too.

I'd told Ella about my secret relationship, so when she heard another girl telling her bestie about her secret relationship with Michael in the girls' change room, of course she had to tell me what she'd heard.

I had been madly, deeply in seventeen-year-old girl love with that v-card collector. I confronted him, tears in my eyes, and got so upset about it, behind the school by his car, that the confrontation drew a crowd. A crowd that meant other girls who were sleeping with him or fooling around with him also heard. It turned into a total Shit Show with multiple girls yelling and two of us crying. And he ridiculed me for it in front of a hundred other kids, laughing at my tears and calling me a traditionalist, saying it was sad and a total waste.

He had zero remorse for the lies he'd told about our future. He had no regrets about breaking the promises he'd made. Two weeks before graduation, he'd talked, with us naked under a blanket, about buying his older brother's VW bus and us driving across the country together, so we could live free. Together. Or so he'd said.

Me and two of the other girls he'd fucked over got a bit of revenge. We couriered a positive pregnancy test to him anonymously (one of the girls had a pregnant older married sister) stating he was the father and that as soon as 'Dad' found out who the father was, he was threatening legal action or murder. One of the girls was named Jill and with my name being Jenna, we signed it J. He could wonder. We watched him sweat for two weeks until we confronted him together and told him he was a loser and would always be a loser.

But, the revenge didn't stop me from spending the summer after graduation in a funk, a serious funk. Ella wanted to do Europe. I could barely lift my head off my pillow. Until the night I went to that party and made out with Ella's cousin, which I had so much remorse for that I'd wound up back on the pillow for days afterwards, out of guilt.

And I won't go back to being that lovesick and heartsick over someone who could potentially shred my heart into tatters again.

I told myself I'd never let a guy see me as weak again.

Telling Michael he was a loser wasn't just wishful thinking. I saw him two years ago. He was working at the Shell, pumping gas. He had a beer gut. He'd lost his looks. He was only 24 and his hairline was starting to recede. He had lost all his appeal. He'd probably never even been out of the state. And I'd been in designer clothes, looking hot, in my shiny new convertible VW Jetta. It'd been completely by chance and totally random, and it felt fucking great.

He recognized me. It was all over his face. I drove away feeling vindicated. A few weeks later, that gas bar transitioned to 'self-serve' only and he was on the unemployment line. Last I heard, he still lives in a trailer behind his parents' house, and it's not a rock star trailer like Ella's beautiful biker has, either.

And I hadn't cried over a guy since him. I'd had relationships, but I'd never let anyone back in close enough to be able to annihilate me again.

And it wasn't easy, because I really, *really* wanted to cry over what'd just happened with Rider Valentine.

What was I thinking?

I know what I was thinking. He was new and mysterious. He was sexy and different. He was not at all like anyone my mother would want me with. He was magnetically charismatic, and confident without being arrogant. He was amazing in bed that first time and even amazing the second time in spite of the hair pulling and trying to make me talk dirty. He was the kind of guy that could potentially give me the kind of big family *happy* that the Forkers had.

And I knew we'd look good together. I knew we'd be one of those couples that people look twice at.

And then he rode off five minutes after fucking me as if I was completely replaceable. Like my feelings didn't factor.

Well, fuck him. His loss. I'd beat back the tears and find a way to forget he existed.

And I'd hope that he lost his hair and grew a beer gut while I busted my ass to keep looking half-decent, so that when we ran into one another in ten years, I'd be again thinking I'd had a good escape while he got to kick himself, realizing that he fucked up.

6

The salon had been open an hour when my 11:00 appointment sauntered in, a sexy Clark Kent-looking type with a smirk on his face as he looked at me. Like he had a secret.

Wait. He was familiar.

"Can I help you?" I tilted my head.

"Dan," he replied and extended his hand.

"Hi Dan," I said and shook his hand.

He smiled and tilted his head, mirroring me. Waiting. For what?

"Dan Sotheby," he offered further explanation.

Oh. That was why he looked familiar. I'd seen his picture.

It'd just said "Dan. N (for new client). Haircut" in the book in Pippa's handwriting.

"Oh," I replied. "Hey."

He didn't want a haircut. He didn't need one. His hair looked perfectly styled. He wanted to go for a coffee and decided to be bold in blocking off a bit of my time. In a rare light Friday, I didn't have another appointment booked until 12:30, so I decided to take an early lunch.

He was great-looking. He looked at me like he was undressing me with his eyes. He was tall. Taller than Rider, even. Built like a personal trainer. And sexy. In a perfectly tailored suit, to boot. And, I just wasn't feeling it. I was still feeling the effects of the heartbreak the night before.

Me and Daniel were at a table in the window of the coffee shop, four doors from my salon. He was talking about his job or something, I don't even know, when I saw Rider get out of his orange old school Dodge Charger two spots over from the parking spot directly in view of where we were sitting.

I saw Rider's eyes as he spotted me. I pretended not to see him. I laughed at what Daniel said, because his voice had humor in it, not even knowing if he said something *all that* laugh-worthy. I must've had good timing, though, because Daniel laughed too, and then his hand came out and his finger twirled a lock of my hair. I lifted my coffee and took a healthy sip and it was just a little too healthy for the temperature, so I coughed and let out a gasp.

Daniel's face filled with concern. "Do you need water? Water!" he hollered to the barista who dashed over with a bottle of Fiji water. I cracked it open and took a sip, soothing the burn. He rubbed my back while I tried to recover.

He'd expressed a suitable amount of concern and chivalry, but my heart was not there. My heart was on the road, run over; biker road kill.

Rider didn't even look my way when he came back out of the bank he'd gone into. But his face was like thunder, making my heart rate spike, watching him get into his very nice orange muscle car and drive away.

When I got back to my shop, I saw that my phone had been forgotten. I'd missed a text from Ella.

> **"Gotta go to Sioux Falls with Deacon for a family emergency so I can't work today. Sorry! Call you when I know more. XO"**

I'd completely forgotten I'd asked Ella to come do reception that day.

I didn't think too much of it until much later, so far in my mental funk that it also didn't occur to me that a Deacon family emergency would also mean a Rider family emergency, too. Was everything okay?

IT WAS ABOUT 2:00 IN the morning when there was a loud knock on my bedroom door. I sat up, gasping, startled.

"Jenna... Big ginger biker at the door for you."

That was Joe. He must be sleeping over. I threw my robe on and went to the kitchen door, groggy, confused, greeting Bronto, the Dominion Brotherhood prospect.

"Hey Jenna. Sorry, I know it's late, but did you get Ride's text?"

I shook my head. "No. I was sleeping."

"Can I come in? It's important."

I opened the door wider and let him in. He shut the door and locked it. And then he put the chain on.

He was a tall curly-haired redheaded guy with a baby face, dimples, and a gut. He was doughy but also looked somewhat muscled underneath the dough, like he used to work out but had let himself go, or like he'd recently started working out but wasn't to the point of working the dough away yet.

I grabbed a beer from the fridge and distractedly handed it to him. "Be back. Getting my phone." I went to my room, grabbed my phone, and headed to my bathroom to pee while checking my texts.

There was a text from Rider.

"Hey. There's an emergency. My sister was in a motorcycle accident and badly hurt. I have reason to believe they may target you next so I'm sending Bronto. I want Bronto staying with you and keeping an eye until I get back. I'll explain when I see you. Let me know if it's cool for him to crash on your couch and shadow you until then."

What the heck?

I wrote back.

"Ok & I hope your sister is ok."

That explained Ella's text. And his thunderous expression that morning. It was also incredibly confusing. He was worried someone might hurt me, so he was having someone protect me.

This action certainly didn't jive with the events of the night before... him leaving after sex like he had just picked me up as a random hookup at a bar and didn't intend to ever see me again.

It also didn't jive with him giving me that cold look that morning when I was in the coffee shop.

What on Earth?

THE NEXT DAY, BRONTO, who was really named Ted, was still my shadow, and he was a helpful shadow.

I put him to work at the salon. He was tall, so he squeegeed my floor to ceiling windows and dusted all our ceiling fans. And then he did a lunch run, but he got that Jesse biker guy to relieve him. Bronto was a good guy. I didn't take advantage; he offered.

I didn't hear from Rider, though. And that was concerning. I asked Bronto what was happening, and he wasn't real forthcoming, but he said Rider's sister was reportedly going to be okay, but that another Dominion Brotherhood member had died in that accident.

My heart hurt for that. Bronto got me details, so I could have flowers sent to the hospital to Rider's sister.

After the salon closed, I followed Bronto (he on his Harley, me in my car) to his house so he could pick up some clothes. Bronto lived with his grandmother, who was a sweet old lady. She insisted I come in and then she made me tea and fed me homemade snickerdoodles while Bronto packed a bag and I gave her two coupons for free wash and sets.

She was sweet and highly appreciative. And I could tell it was a real treat for her, because she said three times that she never spent money on her hair. I told her I did a day a month at Ella's grandmother's seniors' home with free hairdos because I knew it'd brighten up the day of any of the senior ladies there to feel good about herself. Bronto's Grandma sent us off with two dozen more snickerdoodles from her freezer.

Bronto had said he'd gotten the offer to prospect for the MC from a cousin who lived in Sioux Falls who was prospecting there and ready to get patched in. Bronto had spent some time with "The Brotherhood" when he visited his cousin and he talked about how stoked he was to be prospecting for them. They recruited him because of his shooting skills.

I quirked my eyebrows up at that and the fact that he'd said all this in front of his grandma who beamed with pride, talking about how great Deke and his boys were. She'd said that Spencer had come over the week before and helped Bronto clean her gutters. This surprised me about Spencer.

Saturday evening, back home, I got a text from Rider.

"Hey. Everything all right with you?"

Me: **"Yep. I'm having a quiet night in with Bronto and Pippa. We're doing facials, manicures, and pedicures. Not Bronto obviously. LOL. How's your sister doing?"**

Him: **"She's doing better. Thanks for the flowers."**

Me: **"It was nothing. I hope she's gonna be okay."**

Him: **"Me too. Prognosis looks good."**

Me: **"Excellent. I heard someone didn't make it? I'm so sorry. Was he a friend?"**

Him: **"Yeah. Thanks babe. I'll check in with you tomorrow."**

I stared at the phone a while and then wrote,
"Ok. Very sorry about your loss. Have a good night."

Him: **"Will do. You too."**

Okay, suffice it to say... I needed Ella.

I needed Ella, because I now needed to analyze every single thing that happened, so I could try to make sense out of this. But, Ella was in Sioux Falls with Deacon. I'd had a text from her that day, but I needed to actually talk to her.

I took my phone to the bathroom and called her. It went straight to voicemail.

Pippa was crashed on the couch, her feet on Bronto's lap, separators still between her toes after pedicures, otherwise I could've talked it through with her.

He was eating popcorn and we were streaming *Breaking Bad*. His suggestion. We'd watched three episodes already, and polished off a dozen snickerdoodles. Pippa said she and Joe had had a fight and were taking a breather that night. But, she didn't want to talk about it. I wanted to talk about *my* issues, but I couldn't talk the Rider stuff over with Bronto, and it was getting late, so I decided to crash.

We tried to wake Pip, but as per usual, Pippa slept like the dead, so I took her toe separators off and Bronto carried her to her room and put her to bed.

SUNDAY MORNING, I WOKE up to hilarious drunk texts from Ella. And that told me that things were probably more than good with Rider's sister, otherwise no way would she be partying and texting me to tell me about what she ate and how she puked as well as the fact that she was in love with Deacon.

Me? This was braless Sunday, my new-ish tradition, and I was taking the day for me. I had no idea why Rider was having me protected. I had no idea how to de-code biker hot guy actions, and so I decided to just keep busy.

The salon was closed Sundays. Pippa had gone to her parents for Sunday dinner, and I cleaned my apartment after Pippa's early afternoon yoga class at a studio a few blocks away, with Bronto watching, and now I was home, in sweats, bra-less, and sorting out my make-up drawer, while washing my make-up brushes.

Bronto had shadowed me all day long, except now he was outside the apartment in some biker pow wow in the back parking lot with four other bikers, including Jesse and Scooter.

Scooter looked rough. Really rough. His face was purply and his lip was fat. He hadn't arrived on his motorcycle; he'd been dropped off by a cab. I waved at the driver, not remembering his name, but knowing Ella knew him and he'd definitely brought me home from the bar at least a few times. He waved at me as I'd come out to the rooftop terrace.

I'd been thinking about asking the bevy of bikers to put up the rest of the lattice so that the terrace would be fully enclosed, and no one would dangle anyone again.

While I was having that thought, my phone made a text alert noise and I didn't recognize the number.

"You with a dominion brotherhood biker? You need to watch this and know who you're in bed with. From a friend."

The phone made another noise and now there was a video attachment.

I sat down on the Adirondack chair by the chimenea and hit *play*.

My eyes were immediately assaulted by porn. Dirty rape porn.

I made a face of disgust at seeing a gang bang on my screen. A nude skinny chick with huge knockers and long straight blonde hair was roughly thrown over a double bed with the sheets half off in a shabby looking bedroom.

There were four guys in view, but just from the waist down. They were all advancing toward her and one grabbed his zipper and yanked it down and pulled out his dick.

I was about to exit out of the screen when I saw a black heart tattoo.

What?

And though he rolled on a condom fast, before I could get a good look, I knew. I knew there was a silver double stud piercing inside that condom. And I knew there was a name in that black heart.

No.

I blinked, trying to focus, but then the camera panned out a little and Scott...Scooter was one of the other guys. His face was clearly visible, and the camera zoomed in as he bent and grabbed the girl's hair and used it to hold her still while he jammed his dick into her mouth and glared at her with hate as he roughly yanked her hair.

Bile rose up the back of my throat.

I glanced down from my spot on the roof terrace at him standing there, holding his side like it hurt, his face all purple, his lip still fat, as he talked to Bronto, Jesse, and the other Doms that I didn't know.

My eyes moved back to the screen and another of the four guys was in view, very long dark hair, tattooed and bare-chested. Good-looking. A fourth guy moved in and was fisting his dick. He had his head shaved close, but not bald on the sides, his hair in a faux hawk. And then I got confirmation of what I already knew after seeing that heart tattoo and that piercing when Rider's face was visible on the screen, plain as day, as he moved inside the girl, his eyes focused on her ass.

Frozen horror is the only thing I can think of to describe my feelings.

The good-looking long dark-haired guy leaned into the girl's ear as he grabbed her roughly by the breast. "Yeah, you fuckin' whore, we're gonna fuck all your holes until they bleed."

Scooter was thrusting into her face and Rider pistoning inside her from behind. In her ass.

Scooter let her go so that the long-haired guy could climb under her. He stuffed his dick into her vag while Rider was still inside her rear. "No. Please no!" she called out and then Scooter roughly pulled her hair until he got his dick back into her mouth, stopping her protests.

I exited out of it. My heart was racing. Blood pumped in my ears. Bile was bubbling in the back of my throat. My hands were shaking. My whole body was shaking. I swallowed, fumbled clumsily, and forwarded the video to Ella. I dashed inside and grabbed my purse and my keys and then I was running down the stairs.

I got into my car and fishtailed out of there, my phone to my ear, shooting a look of absolute utter disgust at a shocked-looking Scooter, while dialing Ella's number.

"Hey Jen," she answered, "Can I call you back in like five minutes? I'm just getting out of the car."

"Kay," I sniffled. I was feeling woozy. I was in my car, driving. Reeling. My heart racing.

I shouldn't be driving. I'm too upset. This isn't safe. Shit. I drove straight through a stop sign.

"What's wrong?" Ella asked.

"I got... I got this video text and... and..." I dashed tears off my face and pulled over to the side of the road. I was on a side street. I needed to turn the car off and catch my breath. And stop crying. And figure out what to do.

"What was in the video?"

I put my phone on speaker and dropped it to the passenger seat, getting both hands on the wheel and trying to focus. I was parked, but I focused my eyes on the road ahead and chewed on my lips, gripping the steering wheel. My knuckles were white, I was gripping so hard.

"I... I...I just sent it to you. But maybe I shouldn't have. It's really horrible, Ella. Rider, he... he..." I choked on a sob.

Maybe I shouldn't have sent it. I was about to shout to tell her to delete without watching.

"Jenna, it isn't true!" Ella said, almost shouted.

"Ella, it is! The video shows it!" Then it dawned that she was making no sense. "Wait. How do you even know what I'm talking about? What the fuck?"

This didn't make any effing sense. How could she know?

"It's all unfolding here," she told me. "I heard this rumor. And it's not true. They're saying that it was just a scene. A consensual fake rape scene and it was before he met you."

"And you didn't fucking call me?" I could hear a lot of background noise.

Ella sounded out of breath. "Jenna, listen, there's a lot to talk about here. Things are unfolding. It has to do with the accident with their sister and the guy she was secretly seeing and that's why you're under protection and..."

"Jenna," a deep male voice cut in, "Deacon here. Where are you? Bronto said you took off and he needs to keep you safe. There's shit that you don't know."

No. Uh uh. I did not think so. Forget this shit! I hung up without answering him. I started the car back up and I drove to Ella's house.

When I got to her place, I saw her dad in the garage with two of his buds and I waved distractedly.

"Hey, Jennabean! What ya doin', where ya goin'? Elliebelly ain't home." This was a typical chant from Rob.

"Hey, I uh, need to borrow Ella's uh... belt." I waved my hand dismissively and ran in the house and up to Ella's room. I just needed a place to sit and gather my thoughts, figure out what to do next. I didn't wanna go back to my apartment where Bronto and *fucking Scooter* were.

Maybe I'd just crash here tonight, get some space. Call the cops. Or what? I had to gather my thoughts.

Rider ass-raping a girl while three other guys also raped that girl. Well, two other guys, but I'm sure the guy with the faux hawk would've gotten in there, too, if I'd kept watching.

My God.

I closed my eyes and tried to breathe through the emotions flooding me.

I'd had sex with Rider. Twice. I'd fallen asleep beside him that first time, trusting him.

A text came in and I twitched, worrying it was more videos. It was a text from Ella.

"Can you call me? We need to talk."

I put the phone down and got a bottle of water from Ella's mini fridge. I went into the bathroom and stared at my reflection, taking deep breaths. I heard my phone again. I went to her bed. She'd texted again.

"Deacon's gone. I'm alone if you wanna call."

I curled up on her bed, my head on her Betty Boop pillow, trying to get my bearings, trying to shut out the things imprinted on my brain. The guy I'd been fixated on for days and days, a guy I'd had sex with twice was a rapist. *A rapist.* I couldn't talk to anyone right now, even Ella.

How could I have been so totally wrong? And why hadn't Ella called me immediately to warn me about this?

Ella's closet door was open. I eyeballed it and saw all sorts of men's clothes in there with hers. Motorcycle boots and other pairs of guy shoes on her closet floor.

Yeah, he'd moved in with her in less than a week.

Shit. Ella needed to get the eff away from Rider's brother. With all we'd heard about Deacon and now this? They'd done some fast talking and fancy footwork to get Ella to overlook what Spencer had told us. I needed to get her and me away from them.

My mother's voice rang in my brain, "Bikers, Jenna?"

What *were* we thinking? These guys didn't care about the law. They wanted to ride fast, get drunk, and get laid. We'd grown up seeing lots of bikers around, knowing they caused havoc with bar brawls, knowing that some of them were outlaws.

Clearly, Dominion Brotherhood were a group of guys who didn't care about the law, or decency, or... evidently... female consent for fuck sakes!

She texted me again. It was a long one.

> **"I'm sorry if you're mad but I have had a lot going on and didn't know how to handle this rumor, certainly not by phone. I also know that it wasn't forced on that girl. I was talking it through with Rider about him talking to you about it. I can't say much on here because it's sensitive but it seems this is part of the rival between the two MCs and the bad guys are trying to make the good guys look like the bad guys. They've hurt people in retaliation for the feud and they're trying to use this to break up relationships since they can't enact the physical retribution because you are guarded. Know what I'm saying? You need to stay safe in case they try that. They tried to hurt me. Do the same as the girl in the vid. Only for REAL! They found out who my uncle is and that stopped them. There's a lot you don't know. We are coming home tomorrow I think and you and I can talk then but for now, please don't hide from bronto because he's keeping you safe in case they want to try to hurt YOU. Know what I'm saying?"**

I read it a second time and called her.

"Jenna!" she answered, relief in her voice.

"They tried to hurt you?" I demanded. And now I was shaking with anger.

"Thank God you called me!" she said.

"What happened to you?" I was choking up. I had to hang onto the anger. I could not fall apart now.

"They nabbed me and were gonna gang rape me. They sodomized Scooter on the side of the road because he doesn't have a girlfriend to get back at for Kailey, the girl in the video. But she *let* those guys gang bang her. She wanted it. It was a sex game. But then she started dating a Jackal and lied. They did that to Scooter, ran Lick and Jojo off the road. Lick's one of those four guys and now he's dead. The only reason they probably didn't steal Jojo and do that to her is because she and Lick were in a secret relationship, so they didn't know who she was. Jet, the girlfriend of another guy in the video, she got an email at work today because she's been under guard and now you. Jenna, there's so much shit swirling around it's like a damn hurricane."

"I'm not asking about any of that shit," I snapped, feeling slightly dizzy from her explanation. "Don't care about any of it; I care about you. They didn't hurt you?"

"No... They hooded me and tied me up, but then they found out who my uncle is, and Chris came and got me and dropped me back off with Deacon."

I felt sick. These sick bastards. For once, though, it was good that Ella's no-good uncle and alpha-hole cousin were bikers.

"Bronto was assigned to keep you safe in case those guys came after you, but Jenna, it's my fault."

"*Your* fault?"

How could this be Ella's fault?

"My fault they know about you. I started to plead with Uncle Willie, who said he'd put word out that no one was to touch me, that he should put that word out about you, too, and that's what put you on their radar."

"It's not your fault that these dirty fucking bikers are scumbags, Ella. I'm coming down there and getting you and getting you the fuck out of there. What's the address?"

"No idea. I'm at the Sioux Falls Clubhouse, but you don't need to come get me. Deacon—-"

"You need to fucking end things with that biker, Elle. This shit is whacked. First all that shit we found out about him and then all this?"

"You know that wasn't his fault. You don't even know all of it."

She needed to get out of her so-called cock fog.

"What I *do* know is that nothing but bad has happened since you met him!"

"I'll be home tomorrow. We can talk then. For tonight, let Bronto look after you. Rider and you can talk."

Pff. As if. I was so done with Rider Valentine. *So* done, I was beyond done.

"No fucking way any Dom is getting near me again. Bronto has been staying at my apartment, hanging out at the shop during the day. It stops now."

"Where are you?" she asked.

"Your room," I said.

"You're in my room? Have you spoken to my parents? Do my parents know any of this?"

"Your mom and Beau aren't here. Your dad is in the garage with Jase and Uncle Lou. They saw me and said you weren't here and I just waved and said I was borrowing a belt."

Ella's dad came into the room and smiled at me.

"Hey," I said.

He saw I was on the phone but moved closer, looking at me gently.

"Hey honey. Coupla Doms're coming and they're gonna need you to go with them. They'll be here in a sec and will take you somewhere safe, Jenny-girl."

Nope. I grabbed my bag and slung it over my shoulder and went to move past him. He blocked me.

"You need to wait. Go with them. Honest. Things are shakin' up and, wait a minute for them."

I shook my head vehemently. He reached for his phone in his pocket and then he was dialing. He was also blocking the doorway.

"Huh? What? No, I'm not." I tried to sidestep around him.

He blocked me again.

"What are you doing?"

"Wait a sec, sweetie. Who you talkin' to?" he asked.

"No. I'm not going with any of those motherfuckers. I'm talking to Ella. Why?"

"Jenna who's there?" Ella was asking in my ear.

Rob talked into his phone, raising his index finger to me to wait. "Use the outside stairs and come up. I'll keep her here till then," Rob said into his phone.

"Your dad is here and he's calling someone and saying I'm here and he's gonna keep me here until they get here. What the fuck, Elle?" I headed for the stairs, the inside ones that led to the second floor of the house. Rob grabbed my hand.

Bronto and that other Dom, Jesse, were at the fire escape door.

"Go with the boys, honey," Ella's Dad said, his face gentle, but his grip on my hand tightened so I couldn't get away. He walked me over to the door and unlocked it for them.

I tried to wrench my hand away. No way did I wanna go with these guys. He didn't understand. I had to make Rob understand.

I shrugged him off just as Jesse rushed past me and blocked the staircase leading down into the second floor of the house. Bronto was blocking the door leading to the fire escape.

I threw Jesse a challenging look. He returned it.

"You can either come nice, or we carry ya kickin' and screamin'," Jesse said.

I moved toward him, ready to push past him. He grabbed my phone.

I glared at him. "Gimme that back!"

"You comin' willingly or are we carrying you outta here?" Jesse demanded.

"You wouldn't dare!" I hissed. "Rob, do you have any idea what's going on, what kind of pieces of shit these Doms are? Gang raping dirty mother-fucking fuckers. I'm not going with them!"

I was losing it, I could feel how red my face was as I screamed in Jesse's face.

"Oy!" Jesse snapped and then motioned to Bronto, "Grab her, Bront."

"Don't you fucking dare touch me!" I pointed at the big galut.

"Jenny honey..." Rob put his hand on my shoulder, "I promise you, it's for your safety. I know these guys aren't out to hurt you."

"Oh, you know that, do you? Did you also know they're a bunch of gang-rapers, Rob? You need to get Ella the fuck away from these assholes. Gimme my fucking phone!" I snapped at Jesse and I was gonna let Ella's dad see, for himself, what some of these guys were all about, "I got a video and when you see it ..."

Jesse didn't wait for Bronto, he bent and threw me over his shoulder himself and I struggled until he took me out Ella's fire escape door. It was a wrought iron staircase that led to the driveway and I lost my nerve going down it upside down over Jesse's shoulder, so I grabbed onto his leather and held on for dear life. I was put into a pickup truck cab and sandwiched between Jesse and Bronto.

"I need to drive. Don't make us tie you up and throw you in the back," he threatened.

"Rob!" I hollered at Ella's dad. He waved at us as we backed out of the driveway. He had his phone to his ear. "Make them show you the video. You'll see! Call the cops and save Ella. She's at the Sioux Falls clubhouse!"

I started struggling harder, trying to climb over Bronto to get to the door.

"Hold her down!" Jesse demanded. Bronto gripped me in a bear hug so I couldn't move. I tried, but I was held tight against his chest. I fought like a crazy woman. This guy was immovable.

"Jenna, we're just gonna get you safe."

"Yeah, right! Safe. Bullshit! You know I saw that video and you guys are afraid I'm taking it to the cops. What are you gonna do? Take me into the woods, bash my head in and bury me?"

"Fuck, this bitch is rangy," Jesse muttered and pulled over. "Hold her." He got out, leaving the truck running. I was still struggling and Bronto had a solid grip on me.

"You're just gonna hurt yourself, Jenna," Bronto said, sounding all sad, not mad or annoyed.

"Fuck you, fuck you, fuck you!" I writhed and squirmed.

"No way any of us wants you hurt. We're keepin' you safe, babe," Bronto said and loosened his hold on me to look me in the eyes. "Swear to God, Jenna. No one wants you hurt."

I fought off the urge to start bawling. Bronto was tugging on my heartstrings with that sad look on his face and I couldn't let him.

Jesse had been fiddling in the back of the pickup, and now he was in and he had a roll of duct tape in his hand.

I screeched as he came at me with it and I tried to kick him.

He caught my feet, dropping the roll of tape. He used his arm across both my ankles to keep me still and lifted the tape.

"See this? Behave your fuckin' self or I wrap your wrists, your ankles, and your mouth!" He glared in my face and the guy was scary. I froze. His duct tape roll was an inch from my face. I was plastered against Bronto.

Jesse threw the roll of duct tape onto the wide dash of the pickup, slammed his door, shifted me so that I was sitting face forward again, shifted into drive, and we shot off into the night.

"Where are we going?" I demanded a few minutes later.

"Shut it," Jesse snapped.

"Fuck you!" I returned.

"Last warning." He lifted the duct tape and waved it in my face while driving.

I folded my arms across my chest and leaned back against the seat. Bronto snapped the seatbelt across my lap and I heard it click into place.

"We're taking you somewhere safe. Ride's on his way."

"Why is Rider on his way?"

"Talk to ya, I guess." Jesse shrugged. "Fucked if I know. I'm just followin' orders."

Talk to me? *Right.*

Threaten me, more like. Delete that video off my phone and warn me to keep my mouth shut, more like.

7

At least an hour or more later, we were pulling up to a remote cabin, and I was quietly flipping out. I'd had a long time to conjure up all sorts of scenarios for why they were dragging me off somewhere.

If they were gonna *off* me, this was a prime location to do it.

I should've kept fighting. I should've chanced the duct tape and kept fighting. I put my head in my hands and let out a sigh as Jesse turned the truck off.

"You watch her, and I'll run to the store for supplies," Jesse said, passing Bronto a set of keys from his glove box. "Take the tape and if she acts up, restrain her."

"Fuck you," I said, aiming a glare at him.

"Sticks and stones," he returned with a shrug.

"Jesse, man. Step outside," Bronto urged, his eyes big.

They both got out and shut their doors. I was wishing Jesse had left the key in the ignition.

I heard Bronto almost pleading. "Let me go to the store. You watch her. She's ... she'll listen to you more than me."

Shit. The giant biker galut was scared of me. I snickered.

Bronto gave me a look that made me feel a little bad for him, but I couldn't show it.

Jesse cussed under his breath and then he passed him the pickup keys and Bronto passed him the other set of keys and then the passenger door was opened.

"Out." Jesse motioned toward the cabin and then he lit a cigarette. He held onto my wrist while walking to the cabin.

If it weren't for Bronto, I'd still be shitting bricks. But, I felt like Bronto had been showing his true colors all along. No way was he gonna be here if I was about to be killed. I'd hope that if the other guy was going to do it, Bronto would save me.

The guy had introduced me to his Grandma! He was a prospect so maybe not a totally hardened criminal, but still. Jesse was a prospect, too, and he was bad to the bone. I could see it in his eyes and smell it in the air around him. I wouldn't be at all surprised if he'd killed for the Doms already.

I stood there while he took a few hauls from his cigarette before tossing it, and then I followed him to door of the single-story but wide and long cabin. It had a wraparound deck and was surrounded by trees.

Jesse unlocked and opened the door, looked inside.

"Wait. Doin' a walkthrough." He drew a gun from inside his coat and cocked it. "Don't even think about runnin'."

My heart stopped. A gun. Could this get any scarier?

He went inside. If I hadn't seen the gun I'd have made a run for it, but the gun? That gun made me stay put.

I held onto the door frame to brace myself and then slid against the outside wall of the house down to a squat, my heart racing, my eyes on Bronto, who was by the truck, his hand inside his coat like he, too, was holding a gun.

Of course he was. He was recruited by the Doms for his shooting skills.

FML.

Bronto aimed a thumbs-up at the doorway.

"C'mon," I heard Jesse say and I walked inside as Bronto backed out of the driveway and left.

Jesse no longer had the gun out. He'd turned all the lights on.

I walked in slowly, my arms folded across my chest. I took in the space. It was open concept and spacious.

There was a long parson's bench in the entryway with hooks over top filled with jackets, sweaters, hats. The living space had two big comfortable-looking plush chocolate brown couches, a long low light wooden table with eight backless barstools, three pendant lights hanging over top and behind that was a smallish but efficient-looking kitchen with wood countertops and instead of upper cabinets, there were shelves with colorful pottery. There was a white fridge and stove and they looked older, but in decent shape. The fridge had overhead cabinets and was covered in magnets holding up snapshots all over it.

This was certainly a man's cottage, but it had been given a few feminine touches.

The space had a big floor-to-ceiling gray stone wood-burning fireplace that meant you could view the fire from either side. There was a hallway that opened up at that back that led to several rooms, presumably a bathroom and bedroom(s) as well as an open staircase at the end of the hall that led down.

There was also a set of sliding doors off to the right, that led to a big screen-enclosed porch filled with some lounge chairs and a big hexagon poker table. Beyond that, was a deck. The whole place was honey stained wood walls. It wasn't dirty and didn't even smell dusty, so it must've gotten used and cleaned often.

"I have to use the bathroom," I snapped.

"Go," he waved. "But don't try jumpin' out a window or anything. It's dark, there's bears and wolves and other things with teeth out there, and we're a ten-minute drive from any kinda town, so you won't get anywhere but in deep shit if you try hoofin' it."

I stomped through the open area down a hallway and found three bedrooms and a bathroom as well as the basement staircase. I took a few steps down and saw a big room down there with a pool table and two more couches as well as another big saloon-style bar. The space was decorated in biker décor and man cave memorabilia down there. I headed back up the few steps and into the washroom at the end of the hall.

This cabin was rustic, but it was nice. I seriously hoped it wasn't going to be where I took my last breath.

I used the bathroom and then I stomped back out to the open living area and slumped onto one of the couches.

Jesse was standing by the window, drinking a bottle of water. He tossed me one. I didn't even try to catch it, so it landed on the cushion beside me. It looked frosty.

I shivered. It was nippy tonight.

He took that hint and moved to the fireplace and started filling it with wood from a brass basket to the side. In no time, the place was warming up.

I sat, saying nothing, just watching him getting the fire going.

He glared over his shoulder at me. "That video was bullshit. That girl wasn't raped."

I raised my eyebrows at him.

"Don't fuck up. Listen to Rider. Guys like him don't grow on trees."

I curled my lip at him and then rolled my eyes and opened the water and took a healthy swig.

He turned his back to me and went back to work on the fire.

He got it going and then put a DVD in a machine attached to the big screen TV.

Fast and the Furious.

Great. Not!

I sat, not really watching, more mulling over my situation, thinking about that awful video and what it said about these guys. What it said about Rider Valentine, even if it had been consensual, which I still couldn't wrap my mind around.

Some girls were kinky. Some girls were slutty. Some were both. But taking four bikers at once and pretending it was a rape? That just didn't sound remotely sexy to me. And that girl had looked and sounded terrified, not like it was consensual.

And Rider had such suave. He was this beautiful biker with sparkling turquoise eyes, a beautiful smile, a way with his charm.

He had this easy-going yet assertive energy that just drew me to him. I'd been like a moth to his flame and got my emotions invested almost from the get-go. I hated this. I was sad, mad, and scared and it was just too much to wade through right then.

Half way through the movie, Bronto came in with bags of groceries. Groceries is a term used loosely, because it was frat boy food. And my handbag, which he'd handed me.

"What now?" I asked after I watched him put away a pile of junk food that included half the frozen junk food section of a grocery store, two six packs of beer, a case of Coke, a four pack of Red Bull, and a bunch of other junk food, including four bags of potato chips, which he lined up on the counter.

He sat beside me, bringing a third six pack with him as well as a huge bag of Cheetos. He held the six-pack in my direction. I shook my head.

He pulled off a can. "Jess," he called, and tossed it to Jesse. Jesse caught it without taking his eyes off the TV.

Bronto held the Cheetos bag out. I took it and threw it.

"Awe..." he pouted, "Be nice to the Cheetos, babe."

"What's going on here?" I demanded.

"Just what we said. We're keepin' you safe," Bronto said.

Jesse glared at me, saying nothing.

"Until?" I tried.

"Until Rider gets here. He'll be here soon," Bronto fetched the Cheetos and opened the bag.

"And then what?" I demanded.

Bronto shrugged, filling his face with orange snacks.

"I need to go home," I said, trying to be unemotional, practical with them. "I have morning appointments. It's getting late and it's a long drive. Take me home. Rider can call me to 'talk' tomorrow."

"Sorry, Jenna. Looks like you'll be here the night," Bronto said after swallowing some beer. "When you took off, this is where Ride told us to bring you."

"I can't stay here tonight!" My unemotional / logical / practical mask was slipping.

"You're stayin'." Jesse clipped. "Now shut yer yap and either watch the movie or go find a bed to crash in." He gestured to the TV.

"Oh, am I interrupting some sort of high-intellect dialog? Vroom vroom vroom. Not exactly hard to follow!" I shouted.

Jesse threw his head back and laughed. He laughed huge. And flashing his perfect smile, his so-dark-they-were-nearly-black eyes sparkled, and his face transformed from broody-hot to insanely hot.

I huffed at him. Annoyed that he was so good-looking.

"Shut my yap? You're charming, aren't you?"

"Watch the movie or go to bed. Your call," he shrugged, "And I still got duct tape, so choose wisely."

"I need my phone." I held my hand out.

"Not fuckin' likely." He didn't even look at me this time. His eyes were aimed at the TV.

Bronto's eyes were on the TV, too. I glared at him. He shriveled a little bit, under my daggers, and wouldn't make eye contact.

He shoved more cheese snacks into his mouth instead.

So, I stormed down the hall.

Bedroom number one had two sets of stripped bunkbeds in it. The closet was big and had no door, just shelves. And the shelves were jam-packed with clothes, blankets, and towels.

Bedroom number two had a stripped queen-sized bed, two nightstands, and a dresser. The closet door was open, and it was filled with man's clothing. Biker man clothing. Flannels. Jeans. I'd guess this was Rider's dad Deke's room.

I went to the other room and it had a double bed, no closet. It was stripped, but there was bedding in a zipped up clear plastic bag. It was purple and pink galaxy patterned bed-in-a-bag bag on an easy chair sitting in the corner. On the white painted dresser were framed photos. Lots of them, of the whole Valentine gang. A photo with Rider, Deacon, and Spencer, all looking to be in their teens, a really pretty dark-haired younger girl held up by them, over their heads.

Another big framed picture of the three Valentine brothers and the pretty girl as well as Deke, were all outside what must've been this cabin, and looking recent, sitting together around a fire, all with sticks pointed at a fire. The girl and Spencer had marshmallows on their sticks. Rider and Deacon had hot dogs on the end of theirs. Deke held a fire poker in one hand, a beer in the other. There were other assorted snapshots of Valentine boys on their motorcycles.

The cluster of photos was sitting as if it was put there by a girl, likely the pretty dark-haired girl, who I surmised must've been Rider's sister. The one in the hospital because of that video, based on what Ella had said.

I closed my eyes, painful images flashing behind them.

The bedroom had a lock on the door knob, so I twisted it, made the bed and kicked my Converse off. I had a tank top on, so I took my hoodie off, too.

I lay there, in the dark, for all of five minutes, my chin quivering as I fought off the tears that threatened after all that'd happened that night, before I passed out, hearing the almost comforting hum of that car racing movie playing in the background, and hoping that the Dominion Brotherhood MC wouldn't hurt me or Ella.

That five minutes had been filled with thoughts that I couldn't go to the cops with the video. Nope. Threatening to call the cops wasn't a smart move. I needed to get through whatever conversation was coming with Rider, get home, having convinced him that I wasn't a threat. And then I needed to help Ella get away from Deacon, before she got hurt.

Maybe I'd drain cash advances off all my credit cards and clean out my bank account and Ella and I could take off for a month or two, go to Mexico or the Caribbean or something. Let Deacon move on. Let Rider forget I'd seen that video.

I tried to make my mind not see what I'd seen in the video, but I couldn't help it. I'd watched only seconds of it before exiting out and was sure of one thing: that minimal snippet of time was going to be branded on my brain anytime I thought about Rider Valentine. I wasn't looking forward to this conversation. Or setting eyes on him again.

"JENNA."

I opened my eyes to blinding light. I shielded them with my hand. It was only the bedside lamp on. And Rider was sitting on the edge of the bed I was in. He was dressed in a leather jacket, zipper done up, he smelled like outside, like the cold, and like he'd just come in.

I sat up and instantly jumped, scrambling backwards to get away from him. I slid off the bed and landed on my ass on the floor on the other side. He leaned over and reached for my hand. I rejected it and scrambled to standing. The problem was, I was on the side of the bed opposite the door. He was between me and that door.

My tailbone was sore.

I had a flashback of him fucking that girl's ass.

I was gasping.

So much for the lock on the door.

He was staring at me, his expression nothing I could read.

Eventually, I found words. "I need to go home."

His eyes flashed with irritation or something and his mouth was set in a hard line.

"I don't know why your lackeys brought me here, but please just take me home. I don't give a shit what was on that video. I just wanna go."

He shook his head and scratched his jaw.

"Rider, please," I pleaded, suddenly afraid. An icy feeling shot up my spine.

"Jenna, I didn't rape that girl. It was just a game. It's bein' played like it wasn't but honest to fuck, just a game. I'm not a rapist."

He had my phone in his hand.

"Delete it. Gimme my phone, and please, let me go home. Maybe Bronto can just drive me. Or, let me walk out of here and I'll find my own way. We can forget all of it. Just delete it and I'll forget I saw it. I didn't even see all of it, just a few seconds."

He rolled his eyes.

"I already deleted it. But, you can't go home tonight."

"Why?"

"I'm keepin' you safe."

"Safe?" I rolled my eyes and folded my arms.

"Told you there's a threat. Jackals think you're mine and they want back at me for this bullshit, which is just... bullshit. Just bullshit, Jenna."

I shrugged. "I..." I had to get out of here. I didn't trust him. After what I saw on that screen, I couldn't. "I'll go stay with friends. I have friends out of town. Bronto can drop me at the nearest bus station. I'll get a bus. Text me when it's safe to go back."

"Too risky. Not playin'," he said, shaking his head. "Get some sleep. I'm wiped. We'll figure out what's next tomorrow."

"No," I protested. And I was losing my hold on my cool. He crossed his arms over his chest like he wasn't going to listen to me. "No. I need to fucking go!" I was losing it.

"Nothin's gonna happen, Jenna. You're here tonight. Get sleep and we'll assess things tomorrow. It's too late to go anywhere. I'm fuckin' wiped. Sorry I woke ya; just wanted to clear the air."

He got up and left the room, shutting the door behind himself. Taking my phone. Taking my phone!

And... clear the air? The air was so far from clear it was like I was in the middle of thick soupy fog.

I stood there, my heart racing, staring at the closed door.

Maybe I should sneak out and steal Jesse's truck. Shit; I wish I knew where Ella was. I'd bust out of here and go get her.

Since I didn't know where she was, I had to just hold it together.

Maybe they weren't gonna hurt me.

But, maybe they were. Maybe they were out there discussing it right now. Rider could've just offed me in my sleep and he didn't. Maybe he wasn't a murderer, just a rapist. Maybe, not even a rapist, if that outlandish story could be believed, but a guy playing those games? Definitely not the guy for me. Not that he wanted to be the guy for me. He'd made that clear already.

I was pacing.

Maybe I could just wait it out until the morning and then go from there. But, what if things went really wrong before then? What if they talked it out and decided that I was too much of a wild card? The lock on this door hadn't kept him out; I'd even slept through him coming in. What if their enemies showed up here and shot the place up while we slept?

I didn't know what the heck to think. All I knew was that I didn't trust these guys and sleeping under a roof with them just did not feel like a smart choice.

I opened the door about an inch and peeked out. The fire was still going, but there wasn't much left of it. The television was off, and the lights were out. It was quiet out there, but I could hear the distant sound of a television.

I got my shoes on and threw my hoodie back on over my tank top and tiptoed out. I saw that the light was on in the basement. I tiptoed down a few steps and peeked over the banister.

Jesse was asleep lying on a couch. I couldn't see all of Bronto, but saw his socked feet. He was sprawled out on another couch. The TV was playing the original Star Wars movie.

Where was Rider? In one of the bedrooms up here?

I tiptoed to the mostly dark kitchen. The remnants of the fire and an outside light left on gave enough of a glow that I could sort of see. Were there car or truck keys lying around anywhere out here?

I didn't see any. I got to the front door and peered out the window to see which vehicle Rider had brought. It was his orange muscle car and it was parked right beside Jesse's pickup truck.

Okay, so no keys. I'd have to take my chances on foot. A ten-minute drive to the store? I could maybe walk it in an hour, hour and a half then.

If I went the right way. *If.* Ugh.

Better than lying in wait, wondering about my fate.

Decision made.

I spotted a big giant baton flashlight, like the ones the cops use, sitting on top of the refrigerator, so I nabbed it and got back to the front door. This was heavy. It'd light my way and if needed, be a tool to fight off anything that tried to come at me. I tried the flashlight. It worked, so I flicked it back off.

God, I hoped nothing tried to come at me. I'd find a payphone or a person who would let me use their phone and I'd call for help.

Call who, though? I didn't have my phone, so that meant I didn't know any numbers by heart. Cell phones made memorizing phone numbers redundant. Except in a case like this. I knew my parents' landline by heart, but I did not want to call them if I didn't have to.

"Bikers, Jenna?" Mom's earworm worked its way through my brain again.

I remembered Ella's house line off by heart, too, though. Her parents still had a landline, they'd had the same number since forever.

Okay, I'd call her house collect and beg Rob or Bertie not to tell the Doms about me calling. I'd impress upon Rob that these guys were not our friends. The Forkers would get me help. Or I'd take a cab and put the cab fare on plastic. It'd be better if I had my phone. I could use my map app. I could try to call a cab or an Uber. Book a room in a nearby hotel and hunker down and figure out what to do, how to get to Ella so I could get her away from Deacon.

Since I didn't have my phone, I'd just have to take my chances.

I turned the deadbolt and that was when I felt a hand clamp around my wrist.

I gasped.

Rider had my wrist. Where'd he come from? One of the couches?

"What're you doin'?" he sounded exasperated.

Unfortunately, I'm not well-versed in the combat stance and because I was opening the front door with my right hand, I had the ginormous flashlight in my left hand, which wasn't my dominant hand.

I swung for him. He caught the flashlight before it connected with his head and then it fell, and I jumped, but it landed on my foot and it effing hurt.

"Ow!" I screeched.

Lights went on and Jesse was sprinting up the stairs at the back hall and Rider had me, his arms around me. Bronto was coming up behind Jesse.

"C'mon. You can't go runnin' off in the dark, babe. We're in the middle of nowhere. What're ya doin? Tryin' to bash my brains in? What the fuck did I do to earn that?"

"Let me outta—-" I demanded, and he had me in a way that pinned my arms against my body. I bucked and struggled against his hold. I caught sight of Bronto, who was now blocking the front door with his big body.

I went lax in his hold and he set me on my feet.

"C'mon, Jenna. Just—-" Rider started, turning me by my shoulders to face him.

"Let me fucking go!" I screamed in his face, "I'm not staying here where your enemies can get to me or where you and your dirt bag biker buddies can decide I'm not worth the trouble and dispose of me yourself. Let. Me. Go!"

"You're not goin' anywhere. Enough!" he snapped.

I swung, and my fist hit his nose. But, it was kind of a girlie punch, so he startled, but it didn't slow him down.

He hefted me up and carried me, while I kicked and flailed, into the bedroom I'd come out of, and then I was on the bed, him on top of me holding me down.

"Settle the fuck down!"

"Fuck you," I struggled.

"Jenna!" he hollered, and I froze.

"Lemme go." My lip quivered.

He let out a breath and his voice dropped an octave. His anger looked like it was the same, though. "Jackals do not know about this place. No one's comin' tonight. You can sleep. Go to sleep. We'll get it figured out tomorrow. All right?"

"No. Eff you. You have no right to keep me here. And I don't trust you any more than I'd trust a Wyld Jackal."

He sighed and then shouted, "Jess!"

Jesse stepped in.

"Get me the cuffs," Rider said. "They're on the wall behind the bar downstairs."

Jesse disappeared.

"Jesse, no!" I hollered. "Don't you dare!" I snapped at Rider.

"Stop fuckin' around so I won't have to."

"Go fuck yourself!"

Jesse was back with handcuffs. Rider took them, and one clicked into place as he slapped it onto one of my wrists.

"No!" I screamed bloody murder and wrestled with him some more.

"Kill the light," Rider said to Jesse, who then gave him a salute with his index and middle fingers, and then flicked the light out and shut the door on his way out.

Now, I was struggling in the dark when he pulled my other arm up and I knew he wrapped the cuffs around the heavy white enamel headboard with all sorts of curlicues, managing to do that while still keeping a grip on me. My other wrist got shackled and I started to shout.

"No! You are not doing this to me! I'll shout bloody murder all fucking night long. I told people before your goons got to me what was what with you fucking people and if anything happens to me, you will go down! If you let me go right now, I won't tell anyone else you're a filthy fucking rapist pig."

The last part was a lie. No one knew about that video but Ella.

The light went back on and he was glaring at me. And my blood ran cold at the look in his eyes.

He leaned forward, way too close to me. So close I froze, in fear.

"I. Didn't. Rape her."

"Whatever," I challenged, matching his tone. "Ask me if I care."

"I didn't fucking do that, Jenna. It was a game. That's all. She was pulling one over on us. We were just drunk guys gettin' laid and doin' some role playing with a very, very willing girl. That's all."

Gross.

"Ask. Me. If. I. Fucking. Care!"

"Do you care?" he asked, softly.

I pulled against the cuffs. This headboard was solid.

Goddamnit!

"No! I don't fucking care. Take me home."

"I haven't slept a full night in three nights, maybe longer since I had a solid night's sleep."

"Then, Bronto can—-"

"Those guys aren't goin', either. It's four o'clock in the goddamn morning. Go the fuck to sleep."

He got up and flicked the light off.

And I was seething at not just this whole effed up situation, but also at the audacity he had talking to me like that!

"You won't get sleep tonight either, because I will shout, and I'll holler, and I'll sing Ninety-Nine Bottles of Beer on the Wall in four languages!" I threatened.

"I got duct tape," I heard from outside the door.

Jesse. Damn it!

"Want me to use that duct tape, Jenna?" Rider asked, in the dark.

I didn't answer.

Fucking Jesse.

"More shoutin' from you and I'll be tempted," he warned. And then I heard rustling noises.

"Let me out of these cuffs. I'll go to sleep," I relented.

"Can't."

"I'm gonna go to sleep," I sort of whined.

"Good." I heard more rustling. What I didn't hear was the sound of him unlocking the handcuffs.

"Then let me out."

"Can't," he said, through a yawn.

"Why?"

"Dunno where the key is."

Please tell me he was kidding.

"What?"

I felt the bed shift. And then his hair was tickling my face. He was leaning over me.

I tried to shrink into the pillow.

"I had to think fast to get you under control."

"And you didn't think about the fact that you don't know where the keys are?" I snapped.

"Nope," he replied and flicked the blanket out from under me and then pulled it over me. He yawned again. He was under the blankets with me.

No. Oh, hell no. He wasn't. He wasn't gonna try to sleep here with me. Was he?

"Uh... what do you think you're doing?" I demanded.

"Crashin'. If you'd shut up."

Whoa. He had nerve.

"If I'd shut up?"

He sighed.

"You're not sleeping in the same bed as me," I told him, shifting to try to get more comfortable, which wasn't easy with my wrists cuffed above my head.

"And what're you gonna do to stop me?" he challenged.

I glared in the dark. He sounded like he thought this was funny.

"You're not funny."

"Yeah, well you are."

"What about this is funny?"

"Maybe I'll share that with you if you let me get a few hours of sleep."

"This is not remotely funny. Find the key."

"Too tired."

"Then make them find the key."

"They've had enough of your shit for tonight."

"My shit?"

Silence.

"My shit?" I got louder.

"Baby, go to sleep."

"At least sleep somewhere else," I ordered.

He didn't reply.

"This isn't funny," I told him.

"Go to sleep, gorgeous. We'll see how funny it is or isn't, when I get at least five or six hours of sleep, please, Jesus."

"This bed ain't big enough," I told him. It was just a double and he was a tall guy with big shoulders and so it really wasn't, unless you wanted to cuddle, and I really didn't want to cuddle with him.

And then I tried shoving him with my feet. He firmly planted himself in the bed and grabbed my ankles and was holding them still. I kept trying to kick. He tightened his grip to the point of pain.

"Stop kicking or I'll find another set of cuffs."

"It's not big enough for two people, Rider."

"It also doesn't have a $1700 duvet," he retorted.

I had no response to that, mostly because it sounded like something he and I had used as a joke, as fun and sexy banter, was now being used against me in a way that made it seem like he was cutting me down for having an expensive duvet on my bed. And that was low.

"I can hand out low blows, too, Rider Valentine," I finally muttered, after way too long for it to be anything but obvious that I'd been lying there stewing on it.

He snickered, "Calling me a rapist pig wasn't a low blow, babe?"

I huffed.

"I didn't rape anyone, Jenna."

"Good for you," I bit off. "You want a medal?"

"Goodnight," he said. "I gotta sleep. I gotta sleep or I'm gonna be puking my guts out soon, baby. Okay? Almost seein' fuckin double all the way here."

I didn't answer. I wanted to ask, "Why'd you come?" I also wanted to tell him I wasn't his 'baby'.

But, I knew that if I did either, my voice would betray my emotions. Emotions I didn't have the strength or fortitude of mind to sift through right now.

Why didn't he just let me stay with Jesse and Bronto until the morning? They had things in hand.

I didn't ask. I also didn't roll the other way, because I couldn't. Our sides were touching on this double bed and I couldn't move away because my arms were cuffed over my head.

I had no choice but to try to go to sleep. Trapped on my back with my arms immobile, stuck beside and *touching* (due to proximity) a guy I did not want to be beside.

I WAS THERE, CLOSE to him, way too close to him, hearing him breathe evenly in sleep, and beginning to drift, when he cocked his leg over mine. And I shuffled to try to make him go away. And he didn't. His arm draped over my stomach, too, and I could feel his breath warm against my upper arm.

"Get off," I demanded.

"You want me to get you off?" he muttered, teasingly, sleepily.

"Move."

"Shh. Sleep."

"Rider..."

"Stop talking or I'll make you stop talking."

"You put duct tape anywhere near my face and you'll wish you were never born."

"Maybe I won't use duct tape. Maybe I'll find another way to shut you up."

He shifted and was leaning over me. His thumb, I think, moved up my neck, up my chin, then across my lower lip.

I drew a sharp intake of breath. How dare he!

I didn't speak. I jerked my head the other way.

He let go of my lip and then, after about a minute, he was breathing even and heavy, sounding asleep. And he'd thrown his arm over me again.

This situation? Man, I'd really gotten myself into a pickle this time.

I didn't know what the heck tomorrow would bring. I was feeling confident that he probably wasn't gonna kill me. If he was going to, he'd have done it. But, that didn't settle me much. I couldn't toss and turn, and I couldn't get comfortable. But, somehow, I eventually fell asleep. Being cuddled by him. And I was no longer mad. I was feeling something far more lethal.

Hurt.

8

I was dreaming of him. He was making love to me, whispering and calling me beautiful and gorgeous, his fingers in my hair, his lips on mine. I was licking his lower lip, then sucking on his tongue. I was feeling his cock sliding in and out, really slowly, all the way in, then all the way out, and that piercing kept hitting my clit on every inward glide. I was panting and saying his name. Tingles revving up between my legs. And then, as it hit me, I woke up.

I woke up mid back arch, mid gasp, mid-ORGASM.

Oh shit!

That wasn't a sleep-orgasm. He was here, outside my dreams, in the room I was in, holding me, making love to me, leaned over me and looking into my eyes, propped on his forearms, which were planted near my armpits, both hands holding my face, as he moved inside of me, his gorgeous turquoise eyes emitting heat. I cried, huge, straight into his mouth as he kissed me. He groaned and collapsed on top of me.

I was panting. Blinking rapidly. Attempting to process.

"What the fu-fuck?" I whispered from underneath a curtain of his hair, which was over my face, smelling like green apples. He was breathing into my throat, his heart hammering into my chest.

He gave me a lazy smile and kissed my lips. And then he was nibbling on my ears, my throat, nipping at my chin with his teeth.

I went to push him, but I heard the sound of metal against iron. Or whatever against whatever. I couldn't push him. My wrists were cuffed to the headboard still, and I'd pulled so hard I could feel my body protest, pain shooting up my sides.

"What the fuck?" I said, a little louder.

He frowned.

"Sleep-fucking, gorgeous. Fun stuff." He brushed hair out of my eyes and got up, pulling his dark blue track pants back up, as they'd been just down enough for him to fuck me.

I was in shock.

He'd fucked me while I was sleeping. And I came. And as I saw him put that pierced beast away, it registered that it was un-fucking-gloved.

He came inside me. He came——

"Uncuff. Un-c-cuff!"

He looked at me with curiosity.

"UNFUCKING CUFF! Find the key. FINDTHEKEY. Find the motherfucking key!"

He put a knee to the bed and leaned over me, touching my face. He was calm. I was absolutely *not.*

"You were grindin' on me. I was sleepin' and you whispered my name in my ear in that sexy fucking voice of yours. It was just sleep fuckin', gorgeous. It was a nice way to wake up. Never woke up like that before and gotta say, I liked it."

"Find the key, Rider!" I shouted, pulling on my restraints, my fists clenched. He smirked. Smirked! God, I wanted to punch him in the face. He was being so cocky.

My heart was pounding so hard I was afraid it would explode out of my chest and splat into the ceiling.

"Or a chainsaw or a fucking bomb. I don't care, Rider. I want out of this bed and I want out now!"

"Okay, darlin'. I'll see what I can find." He sauntered out of the room, no shirt, like he had all the time in the world, leaving me in the bed, freaking out. I started hyperventilating.

He just had sex with me while I was asleep.

And I came. Came! And how loud was I? Did the bikers in the basement hear that? Since when did I make so much noise during sex?

But, I knew *since when.* And I refused to think about that and what it meant.

I was so mortified. Why did I even dream he was making love to me when yesterday I saw a video of him gang-banging a girl with three other guys there? I was under the blankets and my jeans were at my feet. Sleep fucking, my eye... He'd gotten them undone and completely off. I doubt he was asleep when he did that, because no one had that kind of dexterity while they were asleep!

My panties were also gone. Nope, wait... not gone, but they were around one ankle. I was covered by the blanket, but most of my right leg was exposed, so I tried to shuffle for better cover.

Too long passed before he was back. But, at least he had two cups of coffee in his hands. He put them down on the dresser and then he turned back toward the door. I squeaked in protest as he left again.

Five or ten minutes passed before he was back with a red toolbox.

He rifled through it and then smiled.

"Bingo." He held up a key.

All the air left my lungs as I let out a gusty breath of relief.

"Now," He held it in the air, looking mischievous. "You gonna be a good girl?"

"Don't you even..." I hissed.

"Uh, uh, uh..." he wagged a finger at me, reprimanding, but with a playful smirk.

He leaned over and lifted a cup of coffee to his lips and took a sip.

"Open it. I need to pee. I need to move my arms. My arms are afuckingsleep, Rider. Don't play games."

"Say, please," he sang out.

I bared my teeth at him.

"P-l-e?" he spelled out helpfully.

My eyes narrowed.

"a-s......e?"

What a jerk.

"Waiting..." he sang out.

"Please," I said, emotionless, eyes fixed on the ceiling. But, inside, there were so many emotions. So many, I could barely contain them.

He leaned over and reached for the cuffs. His teasing manner vanished and he looked serious. "I open these and we talk."

"We're over. So, we don't need to talk. Ever. I forget I had to watch you gangbang that girl on the video with your biker asshole friends and you forget me. Done. End of story." I brushed my palms together in an 'all done' gesture. Sort of. My hands were still cuffed, so it was awkward, but I was sure my point was made.

"We're over?" He asked, but he was smirking. Not just smirking, looking like he was fighting off the urge to laugh.

What the heck?

"Duh. Obviously." I pointed out.

"Naw. Don't think so."

I glared at him like he was insane. Because he was insane!

"Naw, I don't like it. We're not done," he said with a sparkle in his eyes.

"Oh yes we are!" I insisted.

"Maybe I'll keep you here until you change your mind," he mused.

I looked at him like he was insane. Because he was still insane!

"You do anything naughty, you'll get cuffed again."

"Grr," I growled, glaring at him.

"Be naughty," he invited. "Please be naughty. Dare ya."

"I don't believe you," I said.

"Yeah, well believe, me, gorgeous. Try anything that puts you in danger and I will cuff you again. And I'll duct tape that gorgeous mouth, too. Which'd be a shame, because it and all that's been comin' out of it? Complete turn-on." He lifted a roll of duct tape out of the toolbox to show me and then dropped it. I stayed stiff, glaring.

All that was coming out of my lips was a turn-on? I've been cussing non-stop and spewing hate at him since he got here.

He then unlocked the cuffs and when they popped open, my arms felt like needles and pins went shooting through them.

"Ah!" I felt pain and relief at the same time. "We are SO over. And I can't even believe I was gullible enough to fall that hard for such an asshole." I let out a moaning noise of discomfort and relief woven together.

His eyebrows went up. I looked away.

I whimpered at the relief some more.

He leaned forward and aggressively grabbed my hands. Before I could protest, he was massaging my wrists and my arms. I was about to pull away, but he tightened his grip and if I was honest, what he was doing was actually helping.

I looked to the bedspread, though, letting him do it. He was helping, but I didn't make eye contact because I could feel his eyes on me. And it was as if they were generating heat on my skin.

Finally, I chanced a look up, since he hadn't let go, and I was right; he was shooting angry lasers from his eyes. Why was *he* angry?

I was the one who had a right to be angry.

But, my eyes looked everywhere but at him.

"You're a real piece of work, you are..." he muttered and let go, finally, and I carefully reached down under the blankets and pulled my panties onto my other ankle and, still not looking at his face, I lay back down and lifted my tush up to haul my undies back up and on under the blankets.

I was not dignifying that weird statement with a response.

He reached for his cup of coffee and sipped it, enjoying the awkward Jenna Show.

Having no other choice, due to his rudeness, I got out of the bed, in my tank top and undies, and I hauled my pants back on, nearly tripping as I did. I had a sock on my left foot. My other foot was naked. I threw the door open, blowing my hair out of my eyes. He stayed in the bed, leaned back on an elbow, and was watching me, sipping his effing coffee.

I glared over my shoulder at him. "Enjoying the show?" I snapped.

He snickered, "Yeah. A lot. And guess what?"

I glared, "What?"

"We're nowhere near over."

"What?"

"Thinkin' we'll have to stay here another day, explore all the ways we're not over. I think I'd like to know just how hard you fell for me. Then, we'll talk about whether or not you can end it."

My body locked tight. Shit. Not only was I 'that' gullible, but I clearly had a case of verbal diarrhea.

I stared, waiting for him to laugh or smile or tell me he was joking. He just stared at me.

"No. NO! We are so over, even farther than over. So far ... there isn't a word for it." I bit that sucky comeback out awkwardly and whirled and dramatically stormed to the bathroom. By the time I got there, I was mortified, because the whole way, I could feel him leaking out of me.

God, I couldn't believe he did that to me. He'd even been gloved in that video. I guess that was consoling, since he was up some skank's ass, but still. I couldn't think about it right now.

I paused. Skank *or* rape victim. I didn't know what to believe. If she was a victim, I felt bad for calling her that. If what he'd said was true, she was a total skank. But, that didn't change the fact that he and I were O-V-E-R.

Not over? That didn't make a lick of sense.

I opened the medicine cabinet over the sink and found decent lady face wash, four unopened toothbrushes, and other basics. I washed my face and went to town on my teeth with a new toothbrush.

And as I attacked my teeth, I tried to think of an attack plan to get myself out of here. And in one piece. So, I could rescue Ella. Even if she didn't know she needed rescuing. Because she did.

This shit was whacked.

I found a package of ponytail holders in there, too. Clearly, Rider's sister and / or mother spent some time here. Or some biker bitches. Not just because of the ponytails, because both Rider and Deacon had long hair, but there was even a jar of pretty damn expensive moisturizer, which I slathered on my face and neck. Generously. Screw him.

You kidnap me, I'll use up all your expensive shit.

I heard noises in the kitchen and when I stepped into the hallway, spotted that Bronto and Jesse were both there, so I went back into that bedroom and grabbed the untouched cup of coffee, so I wouldn't have to look at their faces and try to determine whether or not they heard us having sex, heard *me* moaning and groaning.

Ugh.

Rider wasn't spotted on my walk from the bathroom back to that bedroom.

When I closed the door behind me and sipped the coffee, I spotted his motorcycle jacket on the floor. I took another sip and put the mug down, then went for it, lifting it so I could rifle through the contents of his pockets. No keys, but his wallet, a switchblade, a strip of four condoms. Asshole. *He was packing condoms and still went bareback with me that morning!* A phone. Not mine, his. Not password protected. Jackpot. Ella's number was saved in it under 'Deacon's Ella".

Good. I made a mental note of her phone number, which I had to try to memorize. After last night's fiasco I'd memorize all my close friends' numbers.

I hit the button to call her, saying the digits in my head as it rang.

"Where are you, Elle?" I demanded when she answered.

I heard a vehicle start up outside.

"We just got home," she replied. "Where are you?"

"This asshole biker has me at a cabin and he took my phone and I just found where he hid his. I need you to find out where this place is and come fuckin' get me. I'm not spending a minute longer than I have to here with him." I rifled through the bed linens and found my missing sock.

"Rider has you there?"

"Yeah."

"Why is he keeping you there?"

"He doesn't like that I broke it off. He's trying to convince...oh fucking shit." Before I could finish explaining that he was trying to convince me he wasn't a rapist, he was taking the phone out of my hand, saying "Nuh, uh, uh." He had the cuffs in his hand. He clinked one around my left wrist.

"What? Why are you..." I demanded. The other end clinked against the headboard. He let go of me and was texting on his phone.

He backed away.

I pulled on the cuff, but it was pointless.

I plopped down onto the bed.

"Why the eff did you cuff me?"

He backed away as he kept texting.

"Rider!' I shouted.

He left the room saying, "'Cuz you're bein' sassy and not the kind I like. Be back with breakfast."

"I don't want breakfast! I want you to uncuff me!"

He was back ten minutes later with a plate of two toaster strudels and a bowl of some chocolate junk cereal. He put both beside me on the dresser beside the bed. He lifted my coffee cup, seeing I'd emptied it, and took it with him.

When he was back, putting the re-filled cup down, I tried to reason with him.

"I have to go. I have appointments at the salon that I've probably missed. I don't even know what time it is! And—-"

"Ella and your roommate got someone named Debbie to take care of the salon. She's covering your appointments today and tomorrow."

I glared.

"So, about us being done," he started, looking amused. I wanted to wipe the smug look off his face.

"We're done. No ifs, ands, or buts about it."

"You were grinding against me this morning, gorgeous. That doesn't say *done*," he teased, his eyes sparkling with mischief.

"You were just a warm body." I muttered, not making eye contact.

"You said my name," he said, voice low, not with humor, with accusation. "My whole name. Don't pretend you were asleep."

Damn it. Me and my mouth...

"I *was* asleep. It's over. Whatever I thought we had, I was wrong anyway, so just take me home and forget we ever did anything. You see me on the street, you don't have to wave or smile or say hello. Just forget all of this. I'll do the same."

"You told Ella, *he doesn't like that I broke it off*? Broke what off, Jenna?" he snickered. "What did you think we had? What do you think you ended?"

"Whatever I thought it was, I was off base. I didn't break it off. You did. Back home."

"I did?" He folded his arms and jerked his chin. "Explain."

"You ended whatever I thought we were building on when you left my apartment five minutes after fucking me the other night. You didn't want anything but what you got from me. So, it doesn't matter."

He threw his head back, laughing like I was absolutely hysterical.

"That's funny that you're only after one thing?"

"It's not funny *if* that's all I was after. What were *you* after?"

"Weren't you?" I asked.

"I didn't get a chance to figure out if I was after anything. Also didn't get a chance to figure out your motivations, either. Other than what you showed me."

"Huh?"

"You heard me," he stated. "I didn't get a chance to make an informed decision, because you were hidin' half the cards, babe."

"You used me," I said.

"Could say the same about you," he fired back.

I shook my head in confusion. "We went out. We had a bunch of conversations. How could you not know if you were after anything? You got sex. Twice."

"So did you," he said.

Duh. What?

I stared. He stared.

So I continued. "And the last time, you left like you didn't give a shit about anything but sex, so I figured we were done. Now, you've had me abducted and had sex with me again. Unprotected, I might add, which, after seeing what you get up to with other girls does not leave me feeling all warm and fuzzy."

"Well, I'm all warm and fuzzy after how we woke up. I don't mind putting all the work in once in a while, just so long as it's not all the time. Saw your pills in your bag last night, so knew I was good ungloved. I don't go ungloved, ever, so you've got nothing to worry about. Do I?"

I shook my head in confusion.

"You looked in my bag?" I didn't know what'd happened to it. I had it when he caught me by the door the night before.

"Yeah. And sleep fuckin' gives you a pass on avid participation, gorgeous." He left the room and returned with my handbag, tossing it beside the bed and gesturing toward it. "So, let's backtrack. What did you mean by 'I can't believe I was gullible enough to fall *that hard* for such an asshole.' How hard did you fall for me? Because you did a bang-up job of hidin' it."

I glared.

"You been playing it cool, playin' your games. I find out from Ella you're all doe-eyed over me, but I get somethin' altogether different from you. Once in a while, you let me see you, and I show you I like what I'm seein', then you put that wall up again. Naw. We're not over. This game we're playin' here is a fuckuva lot more fun than that game. We'll play this a while."

I was horrified. What did Ella say to him?

And what?

"This game?" I asked.

His reply was a big cat's-got-the-cream smile.

I gave my head a shake. "This is a game? A game? I'm suddenly under 'protection' because of the shit your biker gang has gotten into, getting my best friend kidnapped. And then I find out you're all being accused of gang raping a girl, of which the evidence does not paint you in a great light. I've seen it and I heard how your sicko buddy promised you'd all fuck all her holes until they were bleeding while she pleaded for you guys not to. And this is a game? Kidnapping me? Fucking me while I was asleep without a condom? A game?"

He just stared at me, looking unaffected.

I continued. "And I'm being held captive in a cabin in the woods, which is shady as fuck."

"Already said it; not gonna keep repeating myself about what was on that video. For the last fuckin' time, she was into it. She had a safe word and a hand-signal she could use if she couldn't use her mouth."

"Gross," I hissed.

"She's a Jackal old lady now, she wasn't then, and she's twisted that to give the Jackals reason to have another beef with us. The fact that there was a video tells me it was all part of some jacked plan. And it wasn't just hidden. The camera work tells us someone was hiding, filming."

"This is not my problem," I told him.

"No, it's not. It's my problem, gorgeous. That's why I've got you here. You'd be at home, at your salon, whatever, with Bronto shadowing you, keeping you protected, but you bolted, putting yourself in danger. And then you were unreasonable, which is why you were cuffed. And this is a fuckin' lot more fun than the games we were playin', so since you're obviously into the games, I pick this one. We'll keep playin' as long it continues bein' fun."

"Uhhh... what?"

"Think you heard me, gorgeous."

I shook my head, unable to wrap my brain around all that.

"And how do you explain fucking me this morning when I was sleeping, knowing how pissed I am at you? I could say *that* was rape-like, since

I didn't give you consent. Maybe you don't understand the concept of consent, Rider Valentine, but it's—-"

"No. Don't pull that shit. You gotta be here so you don't get raped or dead. I'm taking it upon myself to see that neither happens. And while I do that, I like a fuckuva lot the sparks that are flying between us, so I've decided to keep the friction up, so they keep flyin'." He wiggled his eyebrows.

"You knew I was pissed. Knew it! And you also knew I was asleep so even if I was doing that, you should've known better. That means that you—-"

"You started it," he cut me off again and did it with a shrug. "Maybe you're just pretending you were asleep."

"What?"

"Wouldn't surprise me the games you've been playin'."

"What?" I repeated. Was he out of his mind?

"Though gotta say... waking up, you cuffed and at my mercy, dry humping me. Fuck. Sayin' my name in your sleepy sexy voice. Seemed pretty consensual to me. You didn't say no. You came hard. And you kissed me. Fuck, but you can kiss." He bit his lip and his eyes traveled the length of me.

My stomach dipped. I ignored it. *Seriously, stomach?*

"I like this version of you better. This version, I can work with."

"What?" I asked, disgusted.

"You know." He rolled his eyes.

"No, I don't. Why don't you indulge me with an explanation?"

"The real you. Not the game-playing Jenna back in Aberdeen. This is you. The cussing, spitting mad, fightin' Jenna. Not the one playing games, being coy. Using me to get off."

"Using you to get off?" I asked.

He stared at me.

"Using *you*. To get off?" I repeated.

He shrugged.

"Maybe if you'd been interested in more than sex you would've gotten past those walls and seen plenty of the real Jenna, and not one who has decided she hates your lowlife biker guts."

He raised his eyebrows at me. "Why you gotta be two different Jennas?"

I gave him a sour look.

He continued to stare, challengingly, at me.

"I need to go. Uncuff me. Take me home or let me walk, but open the cuff."

"We need to get a few things straight before I take you home, namely that you need to let Bronto do his job. Let him shadow you and don't give him the slip again."

"No. All of you can fuck right off."

"Then no deal."

I glared.

"Uncuff me."

"Nope. You can calm down first, then we'll see what's next. Eat your breakfast." He wandered out of the room.

"I don't want this junk!" I shouted.

"It's what you get. Sorry, Starlet. Got no caviar kickin' around today. Maybe tomorrow."

I seethed. And seethed some more. Eventually, I ate tepid Toaster Strudel. And then I ate the cereal, which had gone mostly soggy but tasted like Reese's peanut butter cups and was so good, I decided that when I was home, I was hitting the nearest Costco for the biggest box I could find. I was gonna pour a gallon of milk right in the box and eat the whole thing. And then after what felt like hours of nothing, he was back.

He held up the key between his index and middle finger.

"Gonna be good?"

I batted my eyelashes at him.

"Behave yourself." He undid my cuff.

I pulled my wrist close and glared at him.

"I just want you safe. The other shit, what's real, what may or may not be over, we'll figure that out. Okay, babe?"

I blinked some more. Benign. Chastised. I winced at a cramp in my wrist.

He must've thought I was docile because he moved in and reached for my face.

"Hey," he said gently.

"Back off, asshole," I smacked him right across the face. Hard enough that my hand was stinging.

He looked incredulous. He grabbed my wrists and pushed back, pinning me to the bed, holding them above my head. His lip curled. My fingerprints were on his cheek.

"What the fuck? What if I'd done that to you?"

I glared at him. "Get your hands off me."

"No, really, Jenna. What if I smacked you? What is it with bitches thinking they can hit a guy, but he can't hit back? Reverse sexism is what that bullshit is."

"Did you just call me a bitch?" I hissed.

"Did you call me an asshole first?" He challenged.

"Oh, so what? You're gonna hit me? Typical biker piece of shit. Smacking their women around."

His eyes glittered with anger.

"You know nothing about bikers and you know sweet fuck all about me."

"I know you're a lying, cheating, piece of shit."

"What lie? Who did I cheat on? Are you my woman, Jenna?"

I glared.

"You and I aren't in an exclusive relationship, are we? Or are we and someone forgot to give me the memo?"

I huffed.

"Cuz if we are and I missed that notification, we have a problem, baby. And that means you're a hypocrite. I saw you on a fuckin' breakfast date with a guy the other day. So, if you thought we were beginning a relationship, did you cheat on a lyin', cheatin', piece of shit lowlife biker? What would that make you, Jenna?"

What?

"A date? I haven't—-"

"Was that not a date with that suit you were having a coffee with who touched your fuckin' hair, what, eight or nine hours after I fucked you? And news flash, I haven't slept with anyone since sleepin' with you that first time, so if we were in a relationship, or if we were starting one, I'd have a clear conscience. How 'bout you, baby?"

"I... that was... Dan is..." I huffed. Wait. I didn't owe him an explanation! "We weren't starting one, though. Were we, Rider?"

He eyed me sourly. "Naw, we weren't, Jenna. 'Cuz I can fuck a materialistic selfish hypocrite bitch a coupla times to get my rocks off, but that's my limit. Definitely my limit if I barely get off."

I blinked as I absorbed that. Hypocrite, materialistic, selfish? Wow.

Wait. *Barely get off?*

"What's that supposed to mean?"

He shrugged, "You're so good at drawing conclusions, go ahead and draw one."

"Barely?" came out in barely a whisper.

"Barely," he confirmed, his eyes were hard and cold.

My chin started to tremble. I was having trouble fighting off the tears.

"Oh. So, I'm not just a selfish game-playing bitch, I'm a selfish bitch who's lousy in bed?"

"You're the one that said it, babe."

"You weren't complaining."

"You weren't payin' all that much attention or maybe you'd have noticed that yeah... I kinda was. I wasn't sure I wanted to go back for seconds. I did, to see if maybe I could work with you a little, since you get my motor runnin' and fuck, you kiss better than any bitch I've ever kissed. Seriously hot fuckin' mouth on you."

I was breathing hard and my chest was burning. I was trying very hard not to burst into tears.

"And you talked a good game. Things were hot when we made out, but it fizzled out fast. Too fast. I've never done monogamy before, certainly don't plan to do it if it's also lookin' like monotony."

"Then why are you he-ere?" my voice cracked. I held my breath and willed my chin to stay still, to not tremble.

"Told you. I'm here 'cause there are people out to hurt me and the brothers. They might target you to accomplish that. I don't wanna be responsible for that."

"Well, I release you from any obligation."

"Don't work that way."

"Well—-"

"These guys can't get ahold of you. I won't let that happen. A good friend of mine, a brother Lick, he's dead. My sister almost got dead. She's gonna have scars. The kind you can see *and* the kind that keep her up at night that she *feels*. The only reason she survived is because they didn't know she meant something to him."

I frowned.

"They'd hurt you bad. You won't get off as easy as Ella did. And Deacon's girl was traumatized by what happened. Shoulda seen her." He shook his head in memory and my heart ached. "You won't even get off as easy as Scoot did. And Scooter was severely beaten and ass-raped by a coupla Jackals on the side of the road."

I straightened my shoulders. "Tell them I mean nothing to you, then. Send that message."

"Nope."

"Why?"

"That might not work. And did I say you mean nothing to me?"

I held his stare.

"And you mean a fuckuva lot to Ella and Ella belongs to my brother so now she's my sister, too."

"Let. Me. Go."

"I let go, you gonna hit me again?" he asked.

I glared at him.

"Hit me again, I hit you back," he warned and released my wrists and pointed at me.

He waited a beat, watching for my reaction. And then as he was getting off me, still pointing at me, I scrambled out of the bed, smacking his hand away and then I found myself spun, my back against his chest, his body pinning me face first to the wall.

"Fuck. You don't believe me?"

"Fuck you, Rider Valentine."

"You need a good old-fashioned spanking, you know that?"

"Let go of me." I wriggled and struggled, but couldn't move.

"Or what?" His voice vibrated against my neck. The scruff of his cheek was on it. He slid his chin across the area by my collar bone and then he tightened against me, against the wall.

My eyes bulged. His pelvis was against my backside and there was a definite erection pressing against my tailbone. I jolted. But, my body was out in goosebumps. His chin rubbed back and forth across my exposed shoulder.

"Throw you over my knee, jeans and panties tangled around your ankles. You'll be at my mercy," he whispered and then touched his tongue to my collar bone and then he sucked on my neck. Hard.

I shuddered. Or shivered. Or both. I don't know. I grunted with a bit of struggle and he knew the effect he was having on me, his tongue running over my goosebumps, making me quiver. And then, he clamped his teeth down.

"Rider," I said, meaning to come off bitchy but instead coming off breathy. He must've taken that as some sort of permission, because then he started grinding into my backside and sucking on my neck some more. Against my will, my neck rolled, and my head dropped back against his shoulder and a whimper bubbled up and out.

His hand dove into the front of my jeans and straight into my panties, his middle finger doing a curl right against my clit. He slid it down and put that finger inside me. He slid in with absolutely no resistance.

"Mm," he moaned against my throat.

"Ah," I tightened everywhere and felt the ridge of him pressed between my butt cheeks. My clenching had clearly extended back there by the sound he made. His free hand slid up my belly, over my breasts, to my throat and his palm rested over my throat at the front, his mouth suckling on my neck at the side. His fingertips touched my jawline. Then, his mouth released my neck and latched onto my ear a little bit roughly. "Fun playin' this game with you, gorgeous. I need to fuck you," he told me in a rough-sounding voice. "Need to fuck you hard and rough. Wanna spank you, then make you scream for me. Want a verbal consent this time so you can't throw out any more accusations. I have your consent?"

Rational thought was slowly seeping back in. What was I doing? I had to make this stop. I had to, despite the fact that I was out in goosebumps and my panties were drenched. I wasn't playing games. He was. I didn't know how to play *this* game.

"No."

"No?"

"No." I confirmed.

"No to some of that or all of it?"

"You don't have my consent, not for any of it," I said. And he let go of me and backed away.

My heart was racing. I was out in goosebumps, and I was, oddly, almost disappointed that he backed away. I turned around to face him. My face was hot.

"Why would you even want to, if I'm so bad at it?"

His gaze darkened, and he eyed me from head to toe and back to head again. He licked his lips and opened his mouth to say something, but then a phone started ringing faintly, from somewhere in the cabin.

He moved away. I followed. He went to the kitchen, reaching up into the cupboard above the refrigerator, pulling out his ringing phone. I wondered if my phone was hidden up there, too.

"What?" He answered and then his eyes narrowed as he listened.

And then his eyes were on me and his jaw was ticking as he continued listening.

He whipped his phone. It bounced off the stone fireplace and hit the rug. It was definitely broken.

I took a step backwards and backed into the wall.

My eyes focused on his face. His lip was curled, his eyes were fiery mad, and they were on me.

My heart was racing.

"You gonna let me keep you safe if I take you home?" he snapped.

I shook my head slowly. "You don't need to. I want nothing to do with you or your biker gang."

"Then I'm not takin' you home. You're staying here."

"Uh...no."

"Uh... yeah." He had a 'don't mess with me' look on his face. He looked 100% serious and ready to bite my head off if I argued.

"What was that phone call?" I asked, my back still plastered to the wall.

"That was Mantis, Prez of the Wyld Jackals Sioux Falls chapter, telling me how they can't wait to get their hands on my foxy fuckin' hairdresser piece. And how they can't wait to blow their loads on your heart-shaped ass before slitting your throat and watching you bleed out."

Oh, my fucking ... my hand came to my mouth.

"We're stayin' here and that's final."

"I'll let Bronto be my shadow," I whispered from behind my hand.

He crouched down and lifted his phone. The screen was cracked. He pushed buttons a few times and then tossed it to the coffee table. He moved back to the kitchen cupboard over the fridge and pulled one of those cheap phones out that was still in a package. He tore the package open and was fiddling with it. He pulled another phone out that looked like my phone. He plugged it into a phone cord that was already plugged into the wall beside the toaster.

"Rider?" I asked.

"I don't believe you're bein' straight with me, so no. You're stayin' here, tonight at least."

I opened my mouth to argue, but nothing came out. I was shaking. This threat was real. And what if they found us here?

The phone he plugged in lit up and made a bunch of noise. I knew those noises. It was my phone.

I heard a noise outside, a car was coming!

I screeched and started to run toward the bedroom. He caught me.

"It's Bronto and Jess. Look." He had his arm hooked around my neck. He pointed me toward the window and I saw them stop the truck. Bronto opened the passenger door and he had two big pizzas, boxes stacked. Jesse shut his door, carrying a bottle of Jack Daniels by the neck.

I was shaking. Hard. But, I felt my shoulders unclench and I involuntarily sagged against him in relief. A reflex.

"It's okay. You're safe. I'll keep you safe. Promise." He kissed my temple and let go of me. I stared at him a beat, frazzled at the show of affection and protection. Especially after those words he'd just spewed.

If they were coming here with booze and pizza then he'd already decided we were staying here, obviously.

I turned on my heel and went back to that bedroom. The bed was unmade. The cuffs were still linked against the headboard by one side, the other side dangling. I shook my head and my eyes rolled ceilingwards. But, I was still shaking.

I made the bed and then I curled up on it, staring out the lace-curtained window, which pointed at nothing but forest. I closed my eyes and chewed on my lips, willing my body to stop shaking. It wouldn't listen.

There was a magazine rack in the corner of the room. It was filled with my kinds of magazines, plus some crossword puzzle books, so I decided to leaf through some and try to keep my mind busy.

"STILL PIZZA LEFT IN the kitchen if you're hungry," Rider said, hours later, as he came in and closed the door.

It was also darkening outside, probably around dinner time. And I felt exhausted. I hadn't gotten much sleep the night before. My stomach rumbled.

I had to pee. And I was thirsty, too, so I stomped out and found my bag sitting on the coffee table. I took it with me to the bathroom.

I used the facilities, fixed my high ponytail, and found my birth control pills in my bag. I took it religiously every evening and was 100% relieved that I had my bag with me. I took one to the kitchen and washed it down with some water while I ate a slice of pizza over the sink. My phone was no longer on the kitchen counter. I opened the cupboard above the fridge and couldn't see all the way in, so I dragged a stool over and stood on it. The cupboard was a junk cupboard, filled with all sorts of miscellaneous crap, but my phone wasn't in sight. No other disposable phones, either.

I was still rooting around in that cupboard when I felt hands on my hips and startled. I was lifted off the stool and set on my feet and then spun around by my shoulders. Rider.

I stared into his eyes and my heart nearly stopped, because the way he was looking at me? Softness. And then something else. Lust? He was leaning in to kiss me. I stumbled back, to get away, my hands going up against his chest.

I heard laughter outside as the door was opened to the side patio. Bronto was heading toward us, eyes aimed at the pizza box stack on the counter.

I could see out the window that Jesse and some other guy, another biker, were lazing in lawn chairs around a campfire, Jesse with a beer in his hand, the other guy, a big blond guy that I could only see from the back, drinking straight from a JD bottle.

"Come out and hang with us, Jenna," Bronto called cheerily as he swiped another pizza slice. "I bought marshmallows and s'mores stuff."

I scooted around Rider, and marched back to the bedroom and slammed the door.

THE DOOR OPENED. I'D been lying there, deep in thought, not asleep. But, in the dark. I tensed, knowing Rider was moving to the bed and then my wrist was grabbed and there was the sound of a clink. The lamp was flicked on.

"You're effing kidding me," I moaned.

"Nope."

"I'm just minding my own business!" I pleaded my case. And I had been. This was hours after that kitchen incident.

"Not takin' chances you'll fuck off. I gotta go. I'll be back tomorrow."

"You what?" I demanded.

"Brady'll have the key. Be a good girl. He'll uncuff you in the morning."

"Brady? Who's Brady?"

"A brother. Jesse's comin' with me and we're not leavin' Bronto alone with you; you'll terrorize him." He snickered.

"You're leaving and you're leaving me cuffed? With a stranger? Rider, no."

"Can't trust you, gorgeous. Gotta go take care of something with Deacon and the boys. And it's not a stranger. It's Brady."

"I can't believe you. You're a fucking jerk."

"Then I'm a jerk. But I'm a jerk who's goin' to take care of your best friend's trouble right now, and I need to do that while not worryin' you're gonna be getting yourself into trouble, 'cuz I can only be in one place at a time. You being cuffed for the night is no different than if I was sleepin' here anyway. I'm goin' to take care of shit, I'll sleep a coupla hours at the clubhouse, then I'll be back."

"Trouble? What trouble does Ella have now?"

"No time to explain. Be a good girl." He moved to the door.

"I hate you."

"There's a fine line between hate and love, gorgeous."

I gasped in shock. "Not for me. There's a gap the size of the Grand Canyon."

"You don't hate me."

"Don't bet your Harley on that or you'll be walkin'," I huffed.

"I can deal with that if it means you're breathin' in order to hate me."

"Go. And don't come back then. Leave me with these babysitters until I can go home. I don't wanna see your face again!"

"Bullshit."

"Ever again. Fuck off and die."

"You don't mean that," he said, and he came back to me, leaned over and kissed my temple.

"I do mean it, Rider Valentine. Fuck off and die."

He shook his head at me, rolled his eyes, and then he left.

Left!

9

I heard his car start and then the noise faded away. It was only a moment later when the door opened, and the big light was flicked on. I jolted in fear.

Standing over me was a massive blond Nordic God-looking guy wearing jeans and a sky-blue t-shirt that was the same shade as his eyes. He had short blond hair and a blond trimmed mustache and beard, and his veiny arms were the size of tree trunks. They were also completely covered in black tribal patterns.

"I'm Brady. You need anything?"

I turned my back to him and put the pillow over my head with my free hand.

"Babe? You need to use the can, or you want somethin' to drink or anything?"

I ignored him.

"All right. Just holler. Hear you're good at that."

The light went off and the door clicked shut.

Was that a reference to my temper or the sounds of us having sex? Ugh.

This situation was fucked. FUCKED. I fall for a gorgeous guy who seems to be interested. We have great sex and fun banter, but he keeps standing me up due to drama with his MC. Ongoing drama that should've been my red flag, but I ignored it. Like a dummy all fogged by his pierced thick cock.

We have sex again and then he makes it crystal clear, in a way that can't be described as anything but a dick way, that it's not gonna be anything else. I'm suddenly under threat, only because of my association with him, and suitably pissed off because of what I've learned about him and out of that, he starts acting like he's crazy about me and that fighting with me is foreplay. He's had me kidnapped, keeps my phone, keeps cuffing me to the bed, and he had sex with me while I was sleeping. Even though he says he only barely got off the other times he fucked me. The sex that was the best sex of my life was bad for him.

How mortifying. But then I considered that video and the kind of sex he obviously liked. The things he tried to do. The dirty-talking he tried to get me to participate in. He was a pig. A pervert. Plain and simple.

A little voice in my head nudged that it was maybe kind of gallant that he was going all alpha caveman and keeping me here to keep me safe, but I didn't let that voice get any louder. Because it might not mean anything.

And even if I meant something to him, it wasn't enough. I couldn't let my guard down. If I let my guard down, he had the ability to stomp on my heart even worse than Michael did. Telling me I was lousy in bed hurt almost as much as what Michael did. That was an asshole move and I was not down with that. That was not the basis for a relationship. Being an alphahole and hating my sex skills?

I was older, wiser, more jaded, and better at hiding my pain than I'd been seven years earlier with Michael.

We'd had sex twice. This wasn't a relationship. This was barely an acquaintance.

And some guys wanted to slit my throat because of a guy I was acquaintances with. I was in danger of being kidnapped and sexually assaulted and then murdered. And Ella was in some sort of trouble right now that meant he had to drive off in the middle of the night to wade in, and I had no idea what it was.

I prayed that she was okay and that the Wyld Jackals hadn't gotten anywhere near her. How dare he tell me he had to help Ella and then not tell me what was up! He leaves me overnight to stew. Handcuffed. Asshole. Asshole who has me kidnapped to save me from being kidnapped! My head was spinning.

The reality of my situation had hit me and was hitting me hard. It pounded around in my brain half the night.

I WOKE UP TO THE CLINK of my handcuff being uncuffed.

"Hey." Brady leaned over. I rubbed my eye with my other hand and flexed that one, trying to get rid of the pins and needles.

"You don't gotta get up. I'm outside workin' out and didn't wanna not hear if you hollered for me."

"Couldn't Bronto have listened for me?"

"Bronto'll be givin' ya a wide berth," he said with a snicker and winked.

He was now in a skin tight white tee and track pants. Grey ones. That outlined his... whoa. I quickly looked back up to his face. The guy's arms were so muscular and veiny he looked like he was jacked up on steroids or something.

He walked away, and I could see his butt was just as buff.

I blinked twice. Who knew there were so many hot bikers?

"Wait. What's happened? Is Ella okay? Did you hear from Rider?"

"All's good now. They put her jackoff ex in the hospital."

"What? Jay? Why?"

He shrugged. "Don't remember the fucker's name. He's lucky he just got roughed up after the shit he pulled."

"Huh? What shit?"

He looked at me curiously.

"I'm Ella's best friend and I'm incommunicado. Out of the loop. Fill me in!"

"He was workin' with the enemy to try to abduct Ella and ambush the brothers at the same time."

My eyes boinged.

"They never got that far. Ride'll be here soon. He's just gettin' checked out with Deke at the hospital. I'll leave the handcuff off. So long as you behave." He winked at me and moved away.

"What? Why?"

"The enemy set the Aberdeen clubhouse on fire this mornin'. Burnt the bar out. Ride's fine. He fell out a window helpin' Spence get Chakotay out."

My body jolted in shock. "Cha-who?"

"Spence's dog. Spence, Ride, and Deke were sleepin' when they set the building ablaze. Molotov cocktail. I just talked to Ride. He'll be here soon. Just getting' the VP, er... his dad checked. His dad used to be my VP. Keep forgettin', he's Prez there now. Then he'll be on his way here. You want coffee? I can put it on while I mix up a shake."

"I'll get it. Go ahead and work out."

He gave me a smile and moved out of the room.

I ran to the bathroom. I'd been holding it half the night.

Holy crap. There was a lot that'd happened the night before.

Jay in the hospital after a kidnap ploy? Deke, Spencer, and Rider's clubhouse / apartment and their bar set on fire? I had to push away the feelings I had at the notion of Rider being burnt to death. My heart hurt.

I peed for what felt like ten minutes, splashed water on my face and brushed my teeth. I moved to the kitchen. Bronto was there, drinking from a Redbull can. He moved back and gave me room.

I ignored him and started rooting for coffee supplies. He passed me filters.

I looked up at him. When our eyes met I saw he was looking at me cautiously.

"Everyone's okay? The fire?" I asked.

He nodded. "Jess and Scott were already outside, so they saw. They called the fire department. They worked together. Everyone's breathing."

I let out a breath. "Where's Ella?"

"Far's I know, she was home safe with Deacon when it happened."

"Can I call her?"

Brady moved into the kitchen and leaned past me to reach into the fridge for a gallon of milk, which he mixed with his powder. The powder bottle said, 'All Natural'. If those muscles were all natural, not steroids? Wow.

"No phone calls, sorry, babe. You need somethin' you ask me till your old man gets here. Not Teddy Bear."

"My old... what?"

"Rider," he looked at me like I was dimwitted.

I rolled my eyes. "Rider and I are not together. And who is Teddy Bear?" I asked.

"Brontosaurus here." Brady was shaking a lidded cup with his powder and the milk. Bronto moved out of the kitchen, trying to look casual.

"Ella nicknamed him that or somethin'. It stuck, particularly since he's afraid of ya."

Bronto shot Brady a dirty look, "Teddy Bear isn't any worse than Cuddle Bear." He sipped his energy drink some more.

Brady threw his head back and laughed heartily.

Okay, whatever that meant.

And holy crap, when he laughed like that he looked like an extra-tall, extra-bearded, and extra-jacked Jax Teller.

Whoa. I shook off that thought.

"You and Ride aren't together?" Brady asked.

"Uh no," I said.

His eyes traveled the length of me. And I jolted. He looked at me like he could see me naked through my clothes.

"They're together," Bronto piped up.

Both Brady and I looked to Bronto.

"We are not!" I said.

Bronto looked to Brady. "To Ride, they are."

Brady gave a tight smile with a nod. "You are."

"To me, we're not," I snapped.

"Doesn't matter. If Ride says you are, then you are." Brady shrugged and sipped his shake.

"You know Ella?" I asked, changing the direction of this ridiculous conversation.

"Yeah. Met her at the clubhouse on the weekend. She was drunk as fuck, hanging outside my bedroom door about to pass out in the hallway in just her man's shirt. Sweet girl. She's a riot."

I gave my head a shake. Ella. God, I needed to talk to her. I needed to sit and go over everything, sift through it scene by scene, word by word. Even the devastating words. My heart hurt way too much.

I hit the button for the coffee and then followed Bronto to the family room.

"Not afraid of ya, Jenna. Just don't like you mad at me," Bronto mumbled, not looking at me.

"Rider fell out a window?" I asked, feeling my posture soften. This big biker was definitely a teddy bear.

Bronto's eyes met mine and he nodded. "Not a far fall. He and Spence both had to take a bit of a tumble working to get Deke and the dog out. Nothing's broken."

I shook my head and sat.

"Wanna watch more Breaking Bad? They have the whole series on Blu-Ray. Or you can pick a movie?" Bronto offered, gesturing to a bookshelf filled with DVDs.

I looked into the cabinet of movies and there were four shelves of guy movies, but surprisingly, one entire shelf of chick flicks. I grabbed Pretty Woman and popped it in. I needed something else to focus on for the moment.

Bronto didn't utter a word of complaint.

BRONTO AND I WATCHED the movie while Brady worked out, the whole time, outside, me having a front row seat on the other side of the picture window. To be honest, I might've watched Brady more than I watched Julia Roberts and Richard Gere.

Brady worked out with ropes, carrying tires back and forth in what looked like a relay race, checking his stop watch and timing himself. He did push-ups, pull-ups on a gazebo at the side. Watching his muscles move was mesmerizing. He was a beast.

He came in near the end of the movie and I asked, "Training for a competition?"

"Just a workout. Grabbin' a shower."

Wow. I could use a shower myself after watching that. A cold one.

I shook my daze off.

Bronto snickered, knowingly.

"Perv," he accused.

I gasped in surprise. "No!"

He laughed. "Yeah."

I shook my head and ignored him.

"Want some Reese Puffs?" Bronto asked.

"Yeah, okay," I said.

He got up to get us some. We both ate two bowls of it.

An hour later, I decided to get a shower, too. The bunkbed room's closet was stocked with towels. And it was a good thing, because I had to use some to mop up the lake Brady left behind in the bathroom. There was a rack of hooks on the back of the door. I hung them all up, and climbed into the shower.

After my hair was washed, in mid body-lather, I realized I wasn't alone. I jolted in horror, but saw it was Rider was in here with me, despite the locked door. Naked. In the shower with me.

I glared at the black heart tattoo, remembering that video.

"What the eff?" I grumbled at him. Mad, but relieved, in a way, it was just him.

He smiled at me and then his eyes moved down to my lathered-up boobs.

"Did you land on your head when you fell out that window?" I bit off.

He laughed while pulling me closer. I gave him a shove and pushed my way out, getting momentarily tangled up in the shower curtain, and he didn't help me, just watched me. I nearly slipped on the again soaking-wet bathroom floor, but caught myself.

I grabbed a towel and wrapped it around my nakedness and stormed into the bedroom, hair dripping water down my body. It was then I realized I had nothing to wear and zipped into the other bedroom, the bunk bed one. I pushed away thoughts of the big scrapes down his stomach, arm, and thigh that I'd seen. I had to ignore it, or I'd feel sorry for him and think about how terrifying it would've been to get caught in a fire and fall while climbing out of a window.

I rifled through a closet that was packed to the brim with men's clothes, blankets, and towels. I found men's grey sweatpants with a drawstring that I swam in, but I didn't care. I rolled the pantlegs up and pulled the drawstring tight.

I skipped undies, of course. Though there were two shelves of boxers and boxer briefs. I wasn't wearing some unknown person's underwear or putting my worn ones back on. I'd wear a pair if they were the underwear of my guy.

Kevin, the guy I dated before my last boyfriend Ryan, thought it was cute that I was always stealing clean underwear when I stayed at his place when we stayed in bed on Sundays. He loved it. Men's boxer briefs were super comfortable. Especially after sex.

But now? I didn't have a guy. Kevin and I had been going nowhere, so I'd ended things. He was always making comments about me being high maintenance. Besides, we didn't have much going for us other than stay-in-bed Sundays. Kevin was good with his tongue. But as good as he was, he never got the noises from me that Rider did.

I pushed that thought away, firmly. Over a cliff.

Ryan ended things with me, because I was too high maintenance, too.

And Rider certainly wasn't *my* guy.

I only hoped whoever owned these track pants didn't also go commando in them.

I carefully got dressed under my towel in case anyone else tried to come in. I threw a grey Adidas hoodie on top that was so big on me I could've swam in it. I had no bra on, because he'd had me kidnapped on Braless Sunday (the new name for the former Stay-in-Bed Sunday).

I also stole a pair of black tube socks and put them on and then grabbed my bag to look for a comb, sitting down in the living area.

He came out of the bathroom, a towel around his waist, looking hotter than should be legal. And I could see injuries from his fall even more clearly. And I felt like an asshole for my flippant comment about falling on his head. Not to mention when I told him to 'fuck off and die'.

He went into the bedroom with the bunk beds, presumably to get clothing, so I aimed my gaze out the window. The place was well-hidden in the trees and some of the leaves were starting to change color. I stewed in my self-torture until he came out, in jeans and a white t-shirt with a Harley Davidson logo on it. Bare feet. His long wet hair slicked back by a comb. He had a black hooded sweatshirt in his right hand.

He ran his fingers on his left hand to slick back his wet hair some more and leaned against the wall in the opening of the hallway, leveling a very serious gaze on me. And then he tossed the sweatshirt at me.

"Wear that instead." It was a Dominion Brotherhood hoodie.

"Yeah, no. I'm good." I glared at the shirt that'd landed beside me.

"Those're my sweatpants you've got on, but you're wearing Spence's sweatshirt right now. Take it off. Wear that."

I laughed. Wow. This was rich.

I ignored his dirty looks and folded my arms across my chest.

"Change the sweatshirt, Jenna." He said.

"Pfff. Make me."

That was the *way* wrong response.

He moved toward me quickly, grabbing me by the shirt while snatching up the shirt he'd thrown on me, making me scamper back. He held it in front of me.

"Gladly."

"Back off!" I barked.

"Put it on, or I'll do it," he barked back, not a trace of humor in his voice, nor on his face.

The look on his face, the intensity of his gaze, *so* serious, my heart stuttered.

I stomped down the hall, and closed myself up in the bedroom we'd slept in. I'd taken the hoodie with me, so I tossed it to the floor and climbed into the bed.

I seethed for a bit and then I guess I drifted off, because one minute I'm looking out the window and it was sunny and then it was dark, and I was flailing, panicked. And the shirt I had on was sliding up and over my face.

What the fuck?

"This is comin' fucking off." It was him. He pulled the shirt over my head, leaving my upper body naked.

"Seriously?" I hissed, covering my boobs.

"Seriously." He, straddling me, dropped the other sweatshirt over my head and then climbed off, heading toward the door with the other sweatshirt.

I pushed my arms through the armholes. It was only a little roomy on me. It didn't even seem like it'd fit him. And it had that soft feeling inside like a brand-new hoodie that hadn't been worn.

After ages, I wandered out and found him sitting on a couch, heard him talking on the phone.

"No. It's gonna need to be completely rebuilt. But it's not enough for a clubhouse. We need a clubhouse within a fortress, like there where we can keep all our women safe when shit amps up like this." His eyes were on me. I walked past him to the kitchen, opened the fridge, and took out a Coke, screwing my face up as I much preferred Pepsi. I sat on the couch opposite him and kept my eyes on him as I popped the tab open.

His eyes were still on me and they were burning a trail straight through me. Why was he looking at me like that?

He kept talking. "No. Chakotay's good. Spence took him to the vet before he even got himself checked out. Dad and Spence are staying at Ella's for now. Dad says they'll probably rent a house until they find the right place... Yeah, well if she shows, tell her nothing. She doesn't need to know squat. Naw, I'll call her when I get a chance. Got my hands full right now. Brady'll stay there the night with you. Boys'll patrol regularly throughout the night. I'll come get you in the morning. She shows, don't tell her we're comin' and that you're goin' or she might let that slip, too. Yeah...Okay. See ya. Love you, too." He ended the call.

I blinked at him.

"We gotta pick up Jojo tomorrow. She's comin' here."

I sipped my Coke, my eyes on him.

"Joelle. My sister," He clarified, as if I'd asked. I hadn't.

"Where's everyone else?"

"Who?"

"Bronto, Jesse."

"Prospects are takin' care of club stuff. Brady went to take care of my sister."

"When can I go home?"

He stared at me a beat, assessing me or thinking about his answer. I didn't know. I heard a phone. My phone. He pulled it from his pocket and looked at the screen. "Your mother again."

My heart skipped a beat.

"Again?"

"She's called a coupla times. I called Pippa and asked if she'd call her and cover for you."

"Pip?"

"Yeah. She said she'd call and smooth things out."

My head was going to implode. "Pippa can't handle my mother!" I grabbed handfuls of my hair on either side of my head.

Rider frowned.

"Mom'll chew her up and spit her out. Pippa's sugar and my mom is gasoline. What on earth was she gonna say?"

He leaned forward. My phone stopped ringing.

"Maybe she said you and your new man went away for a little romantic getaway." And then he smirked.

"Gimme the phone!"

It started ringing again. I looked over. It was Mom calling again.

"Give it to me, damn it!"

"What're you gonna say?" he asked, his voice a warning, holding the phone back.

"I'll think of something. I have to answer that!"

The phone stopped ringing again. Both times it'd only rang twice. That told me she was agitated. She was calling on purpose, not wanting to get my voicemail, but wanting me to see she was calling over and over and over.

I was flexing my fingers while pacing.

"Are there voicemails?" I asked. "I need to check."

He hit some buttons and put it on hands-free.

"You have... six... new messages. First message:"

"Gimme it," I ordered, wanting it *off* speaker.

He shook his head and held his finger up.

Mom's voice rang through and it sounded chipper. Strangely chipper.

> ***"Jenna? It's your mother. Call me back as soon as possible, please. Daniel Sotheby was very taken with you this morning. Sounds like you were, too. I'm thinking we should do dinner at the country club next Saturday. Let me know if I can book the two of you in for our table with us. See? I know what I'm doing..."***

I rolled my eyes. That was why she sounded chipper. She thought she scored on her matchmaking efforts. She was saccharine sweet and that only happened in situations like that one.

Rider's face was like stone.

He hit a button.

"Message erased. Next message."

> ***"Jenna, hey. It's Dan. Had a great time meeting you this morning. Sorry again for railroading you into it. But naw... not sorry. It was great we finally met. Just wanted to ... you know... call and tell you that. What do you think about dinner? Hit me up."***

Rider's jaw was clenched, and he was staring at my phone with a look that should've made the phone burst into flames.

I got a chill and I shivered. *Wow. Really?*

"You wanna gimme my phone?" I hissed, reaching out.

His burning gaze moved from my phone to me. And he stared, trying to scorch me with his eyes. Next came Pippa's voice.

> ***"Jen! It's me. Where are you? Your ten o'clock and your ten thirty are both here. Aaaand you're not. You didn't come home last night. Hope you were having fun getting boned by your beautiful biker and aren't drunk and face down in a ditch missing a shoe again. Haha! Told ya you'd never live that down. Call me. Or get your sexy ass in here. They both say they'll wait a bit longer."***

Shit. Pippa. Pippa didn't know everything. I said nothing on Friday, regarding the fact that things had gone bad Thursday night with Rider. I'd been quiet and in a funk and did not want to talk about it. She'd been fully booked that day so for all she knew, Rider and I were dating, having fun, and getting serious. I hadn't even gone into detail about Dan. I'd just said he was a friend of one of Mom's colleagues and rolled my eyes when I went for my early lunch.

Rider raised just his left brow at me and pushed the button.

"Message erased. Next message."

"Gimme that." I reached for it.

He lifted it and held it out of my reach.

More messages played.

"Jenna?

Mom. Damn.

"I called you last night. Return my call please. Immediately."

She no longer sounded like she'd been replaced by a Sugary-Happy-Mom-Robot. She sounded like her usual self.

"You have no right to listen to my voicemails, Rider Valentine," I hissed.

He hit the button.

"Message erased. Next message."

"Genevieve Maybelle Murdoch."

Great. Just great.

Rider choked on laughter.

I flopped on my back on the couch, palms over my eyes.

"This is your mother and I left you several messages already. Philippa's voicemail was laughable. I don't know what business conference you could possibly jet off to, but my sources tell me you're off with that biker. Lovely, Genevieve. Whoring around with criminals. Not returning my calls. Really. You either return my call yourself within the next few hours or you'll be sorry. I think you know that."

Sources. Her sources? Ugh. Knew it! Always felt like she was spying on me.

I kept my hands over my face. I felt the couch shift as he moved in. His arm went around me, and his hand landed on my hip and he squeezed.

No more noise came out. I heard the noise of him putting the phone down. Thank God we weren't going to listen to the rest of the messages.

"I was gonna say, you wanna call her, in case she's worried? But, it doesn't sound like she's worried."

I shook my head. Not looking at him.

"Your mother sounds like a royal bitch, Jenna."

I nodded, without taking my hands off my eyes.

I heard the sound of his phone dialing out. Ringing. I lifted my fingers and sat up straighter. No. My phone, not his.

Who was he calling?

His hand left my hip and moved to the back of my neck and squeezed. Reassuringly. And then he rubbed my back. Sweetly. A funny sensation prickled thorough me at this affection.

"Mrs. Murdoch? My name's Rider. I'm with your daughter and Jenna is fine." His eyes were on his hand as he rubbed my back from the top to the small of it and then his hand went up and down some more.

"No!" I whisper-shouted and tried to take the phone off him. He removed his hand from my back to grab my wrist and held it. I waved my other hand frantically, shaking my head. He ignored my warning.

"Yes, Jenna's with me. She wanted to call you, and it's my fault she couldn't. I apologize if you were concerned."

I deflated even further. This couldn't possibly go well. My wrist in his grip went limp. He didn't let go.

"There's an issue with my MC that has put Jenna in a bad position. Through no fault of her own. I take responsibility. I took her out of town to keep her safe while the heated situation simmers down... yes, ma'am, motorcycle club..." His fingers released my wrist, but he weaved his fingers with mine and squeezed.

And I couldn't give head-space to the fact that he was holding my hand, seeming like he was trying to reassure me.

And then as he listened, his eyes moved to mine and were a mixture of warmth and horror. He felt bad for me. He was experiencing an amped-up Karen Murdoch in all her bitchy condescending glory. His face twitched in a 'What the fuck' motion and then I saw a swallow move down his throat.

"Well, Mrs. Murdoch, it's a little complicated and I'd rather not go into specifics right now, but I wanted to let you know that she's safe and -—no, I understand. I'd imagine within a few days, but I can't say for sure. Pippa and

Debbie have things in hand with the salon... Well...we'll have to assess—-. Your daughter's safety is my prior—-. Right, well-—we're a club, not a gang, first of all, and—-actually I *am* gainfully employed." He looked at me with horror. "Okay then... no, that was my doing, not hers, and I apologize to you for th—-. Yeah, I'll tell her... Right... Right... Okay. Bye." He put the phone down and took a big breath and gave my hand, still in his, a squeeze.

"She said I should make sure to tell you that you need to call her by this time tomorrow or she'll have your father set up the listing."

I let out a huff and closed my eyes tight.

"Babe... sorry to say, but your Mom?"

I looked him in the eye.

"She's a bit of a cunt," he said.

I busted up laughing. I laughed so hard that I toppled off the couch onto my ass.

He looked at me like I was crazy.

He leaned over and held his hand out. I took it and he helped me up.

"The bitch who gave birth to me belongs to the same club, so I can relate," he said.

"Oh, I bet my Mom has your mother beat by a mile. My mother isn't just a bit of one... She's of the prehistoric meat-eating C-a-saurus Rex variety. Purebred."

He snickered. "Dunno which is worse, but eventually you'll see Shelly in action and you might eat those words."

"We'll see." I said.

"We will," he chuckled. "She might even motivate you to use the actual word."

I laughed, but then my laughter died when I realized that the air felt too light around us. I cleared my expression and looked the other way, pulling my hand out of his and tucking both hands between my knees.

"What's that mean, anyway?" he asked, tucking my hair behind my ear with his fingertips, making me shiver.

"What?" I asked, avoiding eye contact.

"Set up the listing?"

My shoulders slumped. My whole body did, actually. "My salon. It's in my parents' name. She's threatening to sell it out from under me."

He looked shocked. "Because you took off for a few days?"

I nodded. "They own the building that the shop and my apartment are in as well as the business. It's supposed to be my thing and we have a five-year plan and we've got three years to go before I can buy them out with early access to money my grandmother left me. She's not supposed to be my boss or anything, but she acts like she is. Like at any point, she can pull the plug. She doesn't hesitate to remind me of that when I displease her. She likes me on a tight leash."

"That's whacked," he muttered.

I lifted just one shoulder in a shrug.

His phone rang, and he lifted it, looked at me a beat, and then stepped outside with it.

My phone was sitting there on the table while he was gone.

And then it rang with my father's name on screen.

Yikes. I stared at it and let it go to voicemail.

I stared out the window, lost in thought.

Rider was pacing, on the phone, and I had no idea what it was about, but he was gone ages.

When he was back, he found me staring into the fridge.

"Anything good?"

"Just junk," I mumbled and shut the fridge door and opened the freezer again. Pizza pops, toaster strudel, frozen pizza, a box of frozen chicken fingers, and a bag of frozen fries. An unidentified red butcher paper package. Old-looking popsicles. Some ice. A half a bottle of Grey Goose.

"There's steaks in there," he said, and pulled the red butcher paper wrapped bundle out. "I'll set the fire up." He went to another cupboard stocked to the brim with canned goods, pasta, rice. He pulled out a can of peeled miniature potatoes and a can of baked beans.

He unwrapped the frozen steaks and put them in a Ziploc and filled the sink with water and dropped them in there.

I watched for a minute and then I went to the movie cabinet and the 'girl' shelf. I pulled out *13 Going on 30.* I loved that movie. And I needed a distraction.

But, I was watching him out the window more than I was watching the movie. First, he was making a fire and then he was putting a big grate on top of the fire pot.

When he got back in, he threw a sweatshirt on from the hooks by the door, and then went to the kitchen and was making all sorts of noise in there. I turned the movie up, trying to ignore him.

He was in and out a bunch of times. I tried ignoring the nagging emotions. How it'd feel if we were together and he was mine and making dinner for me. I'm a crap cook, but I'd set the table nice. Light candles. Wear something sexy. Do the dishes after.

It'd be nice to have a cabin getaway like this. Really nice.

Sadness fell over me like an itchy old blanket as I considered the fact that I'd never have that with him. Not for real. As soon as this danger and drama was over, that'd be the end. It was already the end.

We were just stuck together right now because of the circumstances.

I had to stop letting my mind wander to what might be. Because it wouldn't be.

"Dinner's ready, babe," he said, coming in with a plate with two steaming steaks on it. He put them on the long bar. I stared. He went back out and came in again with a frying pan that was also steaming.

I moved over and saw that he'd already set up two places for us. He'd cooked the canned mini potatoes in a way that had them all crispy. The steaks smelled really good. Even the can of baked beans he'd warmed on the stove smelled good. He plated everything and grabbed two beers and sat.

I stared at the plate, my eyes stinging.

I had to push it away.

"What's wrong? You don't like medium? I like rare, but I figure you're a girlie girl, so you probably don't wanna see much blood, but no way am I ruining that steak by cookin' it till you're left with nothin' but shoe leather."

I sliced into it and it was done perfectly.

"I like it medium," I said softly and took a bite. It was good. It had an interesting flavor. And it practically melted in my mouth. I swallowed.

And then I burst into tears.

He dropped his fork.

Fuck. I'm so stupid. Bursting into tears. Ugly-crying. Shit.

"Jenna, baby..."

"Your house was lit on fire while you were sl-eeping." My breath hitched, and I was full-out sobbing.

He shoved his stool back, making it screech across the floor and pulled me to my feet, wrapping his arms around me.

He held me tight.

Oh my God. The feelings that churned up in me. What could be. What wouldn't be. I was falling apart.

"You could've died," I sobbed into his chest and put my arms around him. He felt so good. He smelled good. Campfire and meat and Rider. He was so strong, enveloping me in his arms.

God, the feeling right there. Crying in someone's arms. I'd never had this, not since I was a little girl and scraped my knee trying to ride that first time without my training wheels, Dad lifting me up, comforting me, and then Mom barking at him, warning him not to coddle me.

Rider squeezed. "Just a coupla scratches."

"Your house burnt down."

"It's insured, baby. And it doesn't matter. No one got badly hurt. It was a flop house." He ran his fingers through my hair and kissed my temple.

"You guys saved Ella from Jay abducting her?"

"Maybe."

"Maybe?" I looked up at him.

"We don't know 100% but think that was his plan. It was an ambush. He was blackmailing her to try to ambush us, but we think he was gonna abduct her. He had rope and shit in his trunk that he bought on the way to meet her." His eyes were so gentle.

Eek.

"And your brother's dog got h-hurt?" I was blubbering.

"He's okay. Heard he's sleepin' with Ella's little brother. Dad said the little guy is pulling Chakotay around the place in a wagon. He's getting spoiled."

"And... and..."

"Baby... it's all gonna be okay." He rocked me slightly back and forth.

"You cooked me food."

He leaned back without letting go of me and looked down at me like I was crazy.

"You cooked me food and I've been a total bitch to you. I told you to fuck off and die and you could've died!"

"I'm breathin'."

"You could've! You even talked to my M-mom, so I wouldn't have to and bought me a day and she was totally a c-word to you."

A big gorgeous smile spread across his face.

"Not gonna starve ya. Even if you're being a bitch. And baby, I kinda dig it. Told ya that already. As for your ma? Well, I can relate."

I buried my face into his throat.

"I don't cry in front of guys," I informed him.

"Okay, gorgeous," he chuckled and squeezed me some more. "You wanna eat? Food's gonna get cold. I'll eat it cold if you'd rather just cry it out."

I pulled myself together, pulling away, because it felt just too good being wrapped up in him like that. "No, you worked hard while I just sat there pouting. It'd be a crime to let it go cold." I pulled away, sat down, and used the napkin he'd put there and wiped my eyes.

And then, despite the broken breaths I was trying to beat back, I ate every single bite on my plate, partly because it was really delicious, and partly because it meant I didn't have to look at him with my puffy red eyes.

While I ate my feelings, I was chastising myself for breaking Jenna Murdoch Rule #1 and having cried in front of a guy again.

But, where Michael laughed at me and walked away while there were tears in my eyes, Rider held me and comforted me. And I was having a really hard time processing it. It felt like there was a fist around my throat, squeezing just enough to make it uncomfortable.

He was up from his stool and at the sink before me.

"I'll wash up. You cooked. It's only fair," I said, and he looked at me with surprise.

"That was really good. Thank you. I can't believe how tender those steaks were after being frozen just hours ago."

"Yeah, Dad'll be miffed I ate the last of his stash. That's all right, though. He'll come bag another soon."

I gawked at him.

He lifted the empty beer bottles from the table and tossed them into a recycling bin beside the garbage bin.

"Bag another?"

He turned to look at me.

"What kind of meat was that, Rider?" I asked, my stomach flip-flopping.

His mouth opened as a look of uncertainty spread across his face.

"Venison," he said.

"Venison? As in...no."

He cracked a half a smile, but sucked in breath.

"Deer?" I asked.

He stared at me.

"You fed me a deer? Like... like Bambi?"

"Ah fuck," he rolled his eyes on his exhale, "Why am I not surprised?"

"The fuck is that supposed to mean?" I demanded.

"Babe. It's meat. You liked it. Fuckin' Disney."

"You lied to me. It was a deer!"

"It *was* steak, Jenna. It just happened to be a venison steak."

"I'm gonna puke." I pushed past him and ran to the bathroom and stood there over the sink.

I stood there. And breathed. And shook my head. And waited.

I wasn't gonna puke. Nothing was coming up. I conjured Bambi up in my mind all prancy and frolicky with fluffy little Thumper.

Still nothing was gonna come up.

I was thinking maybe I should make myself barf, so I could get it out of my stomach. No. I hated puking.

I looked at my expression in the mirror. I was still all puffy-eyed.

I couldn't believe I cried in front of him! Hugged him and thanked him for dinner when he was feeding me Bambi. After having me kidnapped, chained to a bed, and having sex with me in my sleep even after telling me I sucked in bed.

I stormed out and went back to the kitchen. He wasn't there.

I started washing dishes. Angrily.

I felt him behind me. He had my ponytail in his grip, his mouth went to my neck. I winced and shook him off.

"I take it our cease-fire has ended?" He ran his hand up and down my back.

"You're damn right. I can't believe you didn't tell me that it wasn't steak!" I faced him.

"It *was* steak."

"Not beef steak!"

"So, it's okay to eat a cow, not a deer. Ah. All right. I'll remember that."

I glared at him. He rolled his eyes at me.

"It's actually not okay to eat anything that's cute. If I think about Norman from City Slickers, I go off beef for months. I can't think of them as animals. I have to think of it as groceries. I think about Finding Nemo or Finding Dory and I can't even eat sushi. And I love sushi! And you just made me think of Bambi. After I ate him!"

"You can't think of venison as groceries?"

"Not right now I can't, because you didn't present it the right way!"

He looked like he was dizzy from my words.

"You do realize that it doesn't come from a grocery store. It comes from an animal."

"Shhhhhhhut uppp." I slapped his shoulder. "If I think about where it comes from, I can't eat it."

"You're funny, baby. And you're an elitist, too. Only eating ugly animals. I feel bad for those poor fuckin' duck-billed platypuses."

"No!" I pointed a sudsy fork at him. "Don't even try to make me laugh. I'm serious! Away from me. I'm so mad I could throw something at you! Go. Let me wash up in peace."

He backed away, shaking his head. "Whatever." But, he was smiling.

I washed up in peace. Sort of. He didn't bug me, but I made a racket. I was pissed. But I had peace, in a way, because I wasn't under his intense gaze.

When I was done, I looked over my shoulder and saw he was asleep on one of the couches, a fire crackling away in the fireplace. Despite the racket I'd made.

I stood there and looked at him a minute. He looked pooped. And he looked good.

All the driving back and forth. Up half of last night helping Ella. Getting woken because his place was on fire. Driving back here and fighting with me after spending what was probably several hours at a hospital. Cooking dinner for me. Making a fire. Guilt washed over me.

I found a blanket in the bunkbed bedroom closet. I put it on him, that fist feeling tighter around my throat. I checked to make sure all the doors were locked, which they were, and then I went to bed.

I WOKE UP TO HIM CLIMBING in with me. In the dark. He spooned me.

"Hey," he whispered into the back of my neck, gathering my hair and lifting it out of the way. He kissed the back of my neck, and I shivered.

I blinked in the dark a couple times.

"Rider, don't."

"Freezin' in here. I need your body heat." He kissed me again and wrapped both arms around me.

His fingers wove together with mine near my hip and that made me blink a couple more times. My ear was on his bicep.

I closed my eyes and snuggled in and dozed back off.

I WOKE UP AND THOUGHT he was gone, but then my hand moved around and landed on his arm. He was here. He'd just rolled away.

I rolled into him and spooned him and put my cheek against his bare back, then fell back to sleep.

I WOKE UP AT WHAT FELT like the crack of dawn. Alone. My phone's text alert was going off. From far away.

I dashed out to the living area and saw him standing there, bare chested, in just a pair of track pants, looking at my phone sitting on the coffee table, a muscle ticking in his jaw.

I picked it up. He grabbed it from my hand and pointed at me.

"Gimme my phone," I hissed.

He handed it to me and pointed. "Be good."

I slapped his pointy finger. "Don't point at me."

His eyes narrowed, and he slapped my butt. "Don't hit. I hit back, remember?"

My butt was stinging. I backed away from him and read the text on my screen.

A text from Daniel Sotheby.

"Sorry to text so early, but wanted to ask if you wanted to meet for breakfast today before work. What do you think?"

I put the phone down and walked to the kitchen to put the coffee on. The clock on the stove told me it wasn't that early; it was almost 9:00.

Rider was standing there, leaning against the counter. I could feel his eyes on my back.

"Not gonna text back?"

"I can't exactly text him to make a date if I'm not there, can I?" I retorted huffily.

I started washing yesterday's coffee out of the pot.

He pressed up against my back full-body. I locked tight.

"You're not making a date with him for when you're back, either." He moved my hair all to one side and massaged my neck and then kissed it.

My eyes widened.

"Oh. Aren't I?" I asked, busily cleaning the pot, trying (and failing) to ignore the goosebumps.

His teeth sank into where my throat met my shoulder. I hissed.

"Quit biting me!" I had an ugly hickey on my throat and several sets of bite marks from him. Like he was part vampire or something.

He let go of me. "You'd better not."

I spun around.

"Or what?"

"Or I'll find him." He moved forward, pinning me against the counter. "And I'll let him know you're not available. With a strong message, if need be." He put both hands on the counter's edge by my sides. Caging me in.

I rolled my eyes. "Since when am I not available?"

"Since here and now. Right now. Let's discuss it. You and me." He took a step back, folding his arms across his chest.

"What *you and me*?" I snapped.

"The *you 'n me* you wanted," he said. And he looked like he was serious.

I stared, my expression cold. "You don't want monogamy and monotony, Rider."

"What if I *do* want monogamy. What if you're showin' me it'll be anything but monotony?"

I glared at him. "What if I *don't* want it?"

"Because you saw some bullshit video? It was just a game and it was before we met."

"Okay, how 'bout this?" I said, dumping coffee into the filter and hitting the buttons to make it start. "Imagine I was the girl in that video. Would you want anything to do with me? Even if it was from before we met? If you saw that, or even saw a tame version of a sex video of me with a guy, would you want a relationship with me?"

His expression dropped. His eyes worked over my face. And then his shoulders dropped a little. Not a lot, but enough that I noticed.

And I immediately wanted to take it back. Against all logic. Because it was obvious right there and then that he wouldn't. Not ever.

"Oh, and I'm the hypocrite?" I challenged.

He moistened his lips. "So, you can't let that go? Even if it had nothing to do with you, because I hadn't laid eyes on you yet, and was just a game? What shoulda been a harmless game while I was unattached and wasted? I wore a condom. Never kissed her. And she wanted it. Got tested afterwards, too, to make sure. But seriously, if that's all you can think of when you look at me? Then maybe I'm kiddin' myself here."

My chest started to burn.

"Is that all you think of when you look at me, Jenna?"

I stared.

He stared back.

This was it.

Showdown.

His burner phone started to ring a loud, shrill, annoying ring.

"Better go answer that. It might be an emergency," I said softly, grateful, strangely, for the interruption.

He took a big breath and turned around and moved away.

I felt my shoulders slump. I closed my eyes.

He said *Hello*. And then he asked, *What*? And the *what* was said with alarm. He held the phone a long time. I watched from the kitchen and saw his expression drop, his eyes close, and his fingers pinch the bridge of his nose.

"Where's Joelle?" he whispered. "Brady still with her? Right. Be there in a bit."

He put the phone down and took a couple of big breaths. So big his shoulders moved up and down with his breaths.

Dread spiked in my belly.

"We gotta go," he said, moving toward the bedrooms. And then, he abruptly turned and headed back to the table, looking frazzled. He grabbed the phone and was dialing. "Spence. Call me back." He was dialing again. "Deacon? Where the fuck are you? Call me." More dialing. "Dad? Call me. Someone call me. Fuck."

I followed.

"What's wrong?" It wasn't good, whatever it was.

He stopped in the doorway of the bedroom and then I watched him take a big breath and then his fist struck the wood paneling with unleashed rage.

I jumped back.

He slammed into it again and again and again.

I backed up more.

His eyes cut to me. I was just standing there. Frozen. Scared.

"The Jackals got Jet," he told me.

I covered my mouth with both hands, eyes wide.

"Edge's old lady. They left her in front of the gates to our clubhouse." He braced himself on the doorframe with both palms. His eyes aimed at his feet.

"Left... her?"

"Her body."

I felt my knees give way. I went right down on those knees to the rug.

"They raped her, they wrote our names on her body. And they left her fuckin' dead on the ground at our gates. Her throat was purple."

His hand was bleeding. The wood of the hallway had multiple splits and a big hole in it.

"You have to let me protect you." He dropped to his knees in front of me and grabbed my shoulders. He was squeezing too hard. "You have to let me."

I nodded a little.

"We gotta go. I want to know my sister's safe. It's you and her."

"Me and her?"

"Scoot doesn't have a woman. They got Edge's woman. Lick's dead but Jojo isn't, though they almost took her out. They called off their hounds on Ella, but even still. D won't fall down on the job of keepin' her safe. And there's you. Because of me. I won't let them get you."

I stared, emotion clogging my chest, my throat, my brain.

"I'm sorry. I'm fuckin' sorry this shit is your problem, but baby, let me protect you. Please." He put his hand around the back of my neck and rubbed his thumb up and down my throat, staring at it.

I nodded.

"Let's go," he said.

"You have to clean that." I grabbed his hand. "You've probably got splinters."

He kissed my forehead and held my head there. Tears burned in my eyes. I wouldn't let them fall. If I did, they might never stop.

He let me go and then moved into the bathroom and I heard the water running.

I quickly tidied and got my dirty clothes that I'd worn when we got here. I stayed in yesterday's sweat pants and hoodie and put on a fresh pair of borrowed socks and my Converse. I grabbed a ponytail holder and two to-go mugs and filled them with fresh coffee. He was outside, talking on the phone. I popped my head out.

"One sec," he said into the phone, and his eyes came to me.

"How do you take your coffee?"

"Black. Thanks, gorgeous." His attention went back to his phone conversation. "Yeah Dad," he said, and I went back inside, finished up the coffees and turned everything off. I did a walk-through, turning lights off and met him at the Charger with my purse and my laundry bundle.

When I got in, it was already running, the heat on. It was extra chilly outside.

He moved back inside the house and I waited. And that was when my hands started to shake. I'd kept busy and focused between that scene in the hallway and now. And now, my brain had a chance to let the fear set in. My hands shook hard. My whole body was trembling. He came back out with a Duffle bag and locked up.

"There was another death," he said as we backed out.

"No," I breathed. This was surreal.

I'd only minutely been exposed to death. Dad's elderly aunt. A neighbor who passed. A couple of the people at Ella's gran's nursing home. And it'd always hit hard, but not like this. Not as a result of murder.

"Ben Costner. Jackal. Found in a dumpster back in Aberdeen."

I frowned.

"They're tryin' to frame us. Costner was Kailey's old man."

I gave him a confused shake of my head.

"Kailey. The cunt in that video."

I winced.

"He was a pawn. The Jackals are trying to take us down. This is war."

"Where are we going now?"

"Pickin' up Joelle from the house and you and her are getting locked down in the Sioux Falls clubhouse."

I bugged my eyes out.

"Um, I have to do hair and make-up for a wedding this weekend, and..."

"Jenna, honest to God, the last fucking thing I need is to fight with you about this."

I moistened my lips. "This is someone's wedding. The biggest day of her life, Rider. She's counting on me. I know what she wants. No one else knows, and if I could just..."

"No."

"Ri—-"

"NO!" He slammed his hand on his dash board and I jolted. His knuckles were already a mess from the wood paneling in the cabin. He'd wrapped them with gauze, but the gauze was all bloody.

I folded my arms across my chest and decided to give it a few hours. Let him calm down. People were dying. People were scared.

I was scared. Scared was an understatement.

10

Almost an hour had passed in the car with him and I was having a quiet but kind of intense internal freak-out.

A woman had died because of that video. Died. Brutally, by the sounds of it. Shit was real. Way too real.

A woman in a relationship with one of the guys (I didn't know which guy, the long-haired guy or the guy with the faux hawk) was dead. Scooter had been raped and beaten. And Scooter was a guy! This shit was real. And it was swirling around me.

Ella had been kidnapped and nearly raped. Rider's sister had landed in the hospital because of one of those guys and she could've died.

The only two people not affected so far were us two. Unless you counted that Rider was affected, because he was related to Jojo and in the same MC as the other three guys. And me affected by being kidnapped, but by the Doms instead of the Wyld Jackals (Thankfully). Would Rider or I get hurt before this was over? What would make the other MC call this feud off?

And I was anxious about the wedding, too. That bride, Kendra, was going to go ape-shit if her hairdresser didn't show up. She had a complicated up-do. And she wasn't a bridezilla, per se, but she was picky. As she should be. It was her wedding day! When my time came, if it ever did, I'd be a total bridezilla.

It took me four up-dos to find one she loved and not to be a brag, but I was good at the up-do. Not all hair stylists are created equal. It was going to be the most important hair-day of her life. She did not deserve to be flaked out on. She deserved those intricate braids, those curls, the pearls and gems in her hair that made her cry and hug me when I showed her.

And no matter what emergency I had, there was no way she wasn't going to see this as a betrayal.

She'd lose her mind if I texted her and told her I couldn't come, sending her the pics of our practice run and telling her to give them to some other stylist. It seemed petty to think about that right now when comparing it to rape and murder, but this was that girl's wedding day, and she didn't know about all this other stuff. Bottom line: I didn't want to let her down.

And would I even have a salon when all this was over? My parents could sell my salon, leaving me jobless *and* homeless. And that would also screw with Pippa's livelihood. And the promises I made to Ella to help her out with hours while she was looking for another job. The cab company had cut her hours, so she was relying on me.

I felt sick to my stomach. And neither of us had spoken the entire ride so far.

We were pulling up to a large ranch-style bungalow with a triple garage in a nice neighborhood. When we stopped in the driveway, a bleach-blonde late 40s early 50s woman wearing jeans, a pink tank top with excessive cleavage (and a black bra), and high-heeled boots (and what looked like yesterday's make-up), was standing there and talking to Brady, her body language looking angry. She dashed for the car, dropping a leather jacket on the ground. She looked like strung-out biker broad trash.

And up close, the lines around her eyes and mouth added another ten years, ten unfriendly years. She looked like she used to be beautiful, but had maybe been through a war.

"Fuck me," he muttered, and got out.

"My baby!" The woman threw herself at Rider before he even got his door shut. He caught and hugged her.

She looked in the car, eyeing me, critically.

I tried to give her a smile. It didn't change the look on her face.

And I saw that she had those same green-blue eyes as him. She was probably very beautiful back in her day, and could've still been beautiful. But, she looked like she'd been dragged through hell by heroin or something.

And at the way she looked at me, I knew he was right. She was also a c-word. I guess we'd see if she was as much of one as my mother.

He waved me out.

"C'mon, gorgeous. Inside quick."

"Who's this?" his mother asked, halting him.

"Inside. We're exposed out here." He was texting, corralling me.

"Hey Jenna," Brady said and crowded me, motioning toward the door.

"What're ya doin, Ride?" she asked.

"Inside. Now," he ordered.

She rolled her eyes and we followed her into the house.

I felt shabby. The too-big sweatpants. No make-up on, my hair in a haphazard ponytail that I'd thrown it into on the drive here. Not even wearing a bra or underwear. Old scuffed Converse on my feet. This usually wouldn't be the time to meet the Mom (*if* we were in a relationship).

He put his hand to the small of my back and moved us inside swiftly. Brady stayed outside.

A gorgeous girl was in the front foyer. I mean *gorgeous*. I recognized her from the framed photos back at the cabin, but she was even more gorgeous in person. She had the features and figure of Adriana Lima, the Victoria's Secret angel. She, too, had Rider's and his mother's eyes, but long dark gorgeous spiral-curly hair.

Her wrist was in a cast and she was in light and loose cotton pajamas. She was wearing bunny slippers. But, it couldn't be mistaken. Her killer curves could be in a burlap sack and she'd still be scouted to become a lingerie runway model.

"Joelle, Mom, this is Jenna."

Joelle's eyes lit up and she came to me and hugged me.

"Hey! Call me Jojo." she took me in from head to toe. I felt self-conscious. She didn't look judgy, though.

"Mom's Michelle. Everyone calls her Shelly," Rider added.

I looked to Rider's mother and she was assessing me, too, only she was looking at me like I was something she scraped off her stiletto boot.

"Forgive my clothes," I said. "We stayed at the cabin unexpectedly and I had nothing with me. And we rushed this morning after the bad news, so I couldn't even get a shower."

"What bad news?" Shelly looked to her son and demanded.

Jojo piped up. "Don't even worry about it. I can lend you something. You can take a shower if you want. But weird, I have loads of clothes up there," Jojo said. "Didn't Ride show you to them?"

I looked at Rider. He was smirking. So was Jojo. Like they had a private joke.

"No. Where?"

"The middle bedroom. The one with the double? That's my room. Under the bed there are two big drawer thingies that roll out. Jam- packed with cabin clothes. I go to the cabin a lot and I hate having to lug stuff back and forth, especially if I'm riding, small saddlebags on my Sportster. So, it's stocked with bum-around clothes. Any time you're there, help yourself. There's a washer and dryer in the basement, too. Closet behind the bar."

"Hm." I shot Rider a dirty look. "Your brother neglected to tell me that." And it would've been nice to be able to wash my undies. "I'm afraid there's a lot of towel laundry from us staying a few days. And bedding. And I used your facewash and your moisturizer." I felt guilty about how much of her moisturizer I'd used. Maybe I'd send her a new jar when all this was over.

"No worries. I'm sure I'll be back there soon. I'll take care of the laundry. But, anytime you're there, help yourself to anything of mine. And, I love your hoodie. It's way better than anything I have up there." She winked at Rider and his smirk widened to a smile.

I found that exchange sort of odd, but I wasn't about to ask questions or pull a tantrum here. It was just a Dominion Brotherhood hoodie and I'd bet that every woman connected with the club had one.

"You drive a motorcycle?" I asked her.

She smiled wide. "Yeah. Of course."

I blinked. "Cool."

"I'll get Jenna set up with a shower and clothes and then we'll grab food and head out. That okay?" she looked to her brother.

"Cool," he said, and we we'd moved into a spacious and modern kitchen. "Pack her a week's worth of clothes. Something for the funeral, too. But quick. Yeah? Boys'll be here in twenty or thirty. Mom, you tell no one I'm here, got me?"

A week's worth of clothes?

"Where are youze goin'?" Shelly inquired, arms folded over her ample fake-looking chest.

"Club business," Rider mumbled. "Go with Joelle, baby."

I was a bit thrown, probably why I didn't even shoot him a dirty look for his bossiness.

I followed Joelle.

This was a nice house. It didn't say biker, despite the fact that Rider's mom was clearly a biker broad. It was decorated nicely. It was comfortable. Tidy. It was a family home. But, it was missing something. There weren't any pictures on the walls and it had a bit of a haunted feeling to it. I walked away from him and heard his mother mumble, "Property? What the hell, Ride? You 'n yer brother go there and suddenly you've both changed that tune?"

I didn't know what the heck that meant. I glanced over my shoulder, feeling like there were eyes on me and there were. Rider was watching me walk away, a smile on his face, and his mother was eyeing me with irritation.

As I made my way down the hall to a wing of bedrooms, I noticed the walls were bare and it was the sort of hallway that should've been filled with family pictures. I'd have loved to see more family pictures. Little Deacon, little Spencer, baby Rider. I wondered if Ella had been here yet. Had she had a better experience with Rider's mother? What did it matter, though, right? This would likely be the only time I was here or in her presence.

On closer examination, I saw picture hangers on the walls. There had been pictures, but they'd been taken down. Maybe due to the divorce. I hoped all those memories didn't go up in flames when Deke's Roadhouse was set on fire.

I was led into a bedroom. A total princess bedroom. All soft pastels and a huge canopy bed with massive dressing table that matched. I looked around. She had to be a few years younger than me. But, when she opened her closet door, it rivaled even mine.

"Okay, so I can't believe he didn't tell me that there was a stash of girl clothes there!" I said as soon as the door clicked shut. "Or a washer. I'm goin' commando, here!"

She let out a little bit of a giggle. "I can. He wanted you to have no choice but to wear that."

"Wear what? No underwear?"

"The shirt."

"This?" I pinched the hem of the sweatshirt.

She nodded.

I rolled my eyes., "Yeah, we had a whole thing about me wearing this."

"A whole thing?" she asked.

I waved my hand dismissively.

She smiled knowingly. "He wanted you to wear it and there's a reason for that."

"And that is?" I asked.

"When you undress, look at the back of it."

I went to lift it. "Shit. I'm not wearing a bra, either. We left on braless Sunday." I shrugged. "If this was the second time we'd met, I'd whip it off without a second thought. I'll spare you."

"I have no idea what a braless day would be like." She gestured to her ample bazumbas. "How is it?"

I raised a hand, understanding. Not from personal experience, of course, but from Ella's complaints about lugging her ginormous knockers about and having to even sleep in a bra.

"Freeing. Um, what's on it?" I asked, jerking my thumb behind me.

Jojo passed me a hand mirror from on top of her dressing table. "Look." Her smile was big as she gestured to her mirror. I saw it in reverse.

The Dominion Brotherhood MC logo had been at the breast of the shirt on the front with a big motorcycle graphic taking up the rest. On the back, it mirrored the look of their biker vests. Only, instead of the city name, across the bottom of my shirt it said, "Property of Rider"

"Property of Rider? A rider?" I tried.

She shook her head. "*The* Rider. My brother. I made that shirt for all three of them. Gag gift, two Christmases ago. Him, especially, since he's allergic to commitment. Or he has been. I told him I wanted a sister-in-law from each of my brothers, and no bitches, either, please and thank you. Spence and Deacon have both brought girls around over the years. Bitches and non-bitches. Rider? Never. Not a one. And I knew he dated, but he never got serious enough to bring anyone home. Glad to see those days are done. That shirt has never been worn. I didn't even know what'd happened to it. Evidently it wound up at the cabin and he was saving it for the right person."

Wow.

That meant that every time I'd stomped away from him since the afternoon before, he saw "Property of Rider" on my back. My face burned with embarrassment at the idea of that. And anger. What kind of a joke was that to play on me?

That closet had been jam-packed with hoodies and t-shirts, and yet he *so* specifically wanted me to wear this that he physically forced me to wear it. But, of course I hadn't looked at the back of it. How many times had he sat and rubbed my back since he put it on?

Ohmigod. What?

I dropped my head and studied my feet. I wasn't sure I wanted to think on this for too long. I had a funny feeling in my stomach. An unfamiliar and *not pleasant* one.

"I take it this is a surprise to you. I could tell out there that you had no idea what you were wearing."

"It's been a... uh... rocky few days," I admitted, meeting her gaze.

She gave me a tight smile. "We're all havin' a bumpy ride right now. But, it means something that he gave that to you. Trust me."

"Oh my God. I haven't even said I'm sorry for what you're going through. I'm an asshole." I meant what I was saying, and it was helpful to be able to change topic, because I didn't have the ability to decode the sweatshirt thing at that moment.

She shook her head, but cradled her arms around herself. "The funeral's tomorrow. And I don't even know how to process."

"About that video," I said, unable to imagine how it would've felt for her.

"Video?"

Damn it. I closed my eyes. "I've said too much. I'm out of my element here with all this."

She huffed. "Don't worry, I'll make him tell me. I won't put pressure on you. It's not easy having three protective big brothers on top of my protective Dad. The whole club, really. It's like I have an invisible chastity belt and forty-five big brothers."

"I bet," I muttered, with a wince.

"I don't know what they're keeping from me about Luke, but I intend to find out." Her eyes went so sad it gripped my heart. I couldn't imagine how she was feeling. And how she'd feel when she got the whole story.

"There's towels in my bathroom. Wear whatever. There's about seven new pairs of new underwear, still with tags, in the top drawer of that dresser." She pointed. "I hit a sale just before the accident. Actually, I'll pack them all so since we're going on lockdown, you'll have plenty. I'll pack you some leggings and jeggings. I don't think my jeans would fit you with this J.Lo butt of mine. I'll throw a whack of clothes in bags for both of us when I find out what the fuck this video crap is." She stomped out in her bunny slippers, slamming the door behind her.

Uh oh. F-bombs and bunny slippers.

I stood, frozen a minute. And then I lifted the hand mirror I was still holding and caught the reflection of my back again.

Property of Rider.

He very intentionally wanted me to wear it. He physically put it on me when he saw I was in Spencer's shirt.

I blinked at my reflection some more and then quickly put the hand mirror down, deciding it was outside my capabilities to even think about the shirt.

I went to Jojo's closet and borrowed some yoga pants and a red tank top with a built-in shelf bra (better than nothing and I certainly couldn't borrow one of her bras unless I stuffed it with tube socks) as well as a black zip up hoodie. I grabbed a pair of black boy short undies with tags still on them, and went for a shower.

When I came out of the bathroom fresh as a daisy (she had some awesome body scrubs and top shelf shampoo), she was zipping up a black suitcase. It was beside a purple metallic suitcase.

"Black one's yours, purple is mine. I put a few dresses in there for the funeral."

I looked at her huge boobs. She chuckled.

"Oh yeah," I thrust my chest out. I was taller than her and felt like Olive Oyl in contrast to her. "I'm sure all your clothes will fit."

She laughed at me. But, it was good natured. I liked her already.

"Except bras. I dropped in a couple tanks with shelf bras. I packed you a wrap dress. It should work."

"Thank you so much. When all this is over, I'll mail you a gift card for the underwear, so you can buy new ones. I just left my clothes in your basket. They were all your brother's clothes anyway. Is that okay?"

She smiled. "Sure. But, you don't need to do a gift card. I have like four hundred pairs. I just have no impulse control when I see a sexy underwear sale."

"I feel ya. But, I do need to pay you back."

"Naw. It's my pleasure. And trust me, I don't need more reasons to shop. I could outfit us both for a month without having to do laundry."

I chuckled.

I'd definitely be sending her a gift card. But, hopefully we could go shopping together. I could tell, already, that Jojo Valentine and I would be friends. My heart sank. No. We would've been if I wasn't going to try to forget her brother existed at the first opportunity.

"Besides," she added with a shrug, her face turning sad, "No reason for me to have new sexy panties right now anyway."

Ouch.

"What'd Rider say?"

"He won't tell me anything. Wants to wait until after the funeral tomorrow. Oh. He told me to tell you that if you say anything to me about anything else, you'll earn yourself a spanking." She rolled her eyes.

"And you're telling me this?"

"He's probably right. I need to get through the funeral. I need to say Goodbye to him. After that, I'll get the rest of the details."

I sat on her bed. She sat beside me.

"I have no siblings, Jojo, so I don't know what it's like. But I do know that I'd have a very hard time in your shoes. Especially if there were people trying to control what information I had."

"They're protective."

I shrugged. We sat in silence a second and then I asked, "You wanna talk about it? Him?"

"We'd only dated a little while and it was secret, he didn't want my brothers to know."

"Oh, I know all about secret relationships. It's how they fuck us over."

She startled.

I realized my mistake. "Sorry. I meant me. It happened to me. A guy... it's a long story. I didn't mean... I don't know anything about your relationship with him. Sorry. I'm a jerk today. I'm in major malfunction mode over here."

She shook her head. "S'okay. We were gonna go public soon. It's just... he's in the club and he'd just got patched in. After a long, *long* stint as a prospect. My dad and brothers are protective, and he's known us most of my life, and... it was delicate. Anyway, we only spent time together alone a couple times. I've had a crush on him for years. He was close to all my brothers, wouldn't touch me. But, I knew he wanted to. So, I kept throwing myself at him. But then he found out my dad and brothers had plans to leave town and he started reciprocating a little. And even then... he was so careful with me. We've secretly had a thing a few months and no one knew except one person. He treated me like a delicate china teacup. He knew that any brother, mine or club brothers, they'd have his balls if they thought he was just out to tag some tail."

She shrugged. "We had only had a few dates. Secret dates. But we texted constantly, and we talked deep. Hopes. Dreams. The future. We'd gone farther than ever the night of the accident. I took him to the cabin. I wanted it to be him. You know? My first. He stopped before... you know. But..." her eyes filled with tears.

I reached out and grabbed her hand.

"Sad, right? Nineteen-year-old virgin. But with my brothers?" she shook her head. "Everyone's scared of them. They've all joked I'd be thirty-five before I was allowed to date. At this rate, it could be thirty-five before I find someone brave enough. I didn't wanna stay behind with the boys and Daddy moving, stuck with Psycho Shelly, but for the first time in my whole life, I didn't have a pack of bodyguards breathing down my neck and scaring off any guy who'd look at me. I figured I'd stay for a few months, enjoy the freedom. Mom barely notices me, so I do what I want. I figured I'd see if things with Luke would ..." she shrugged.

I gave her hand a squeeze. Her eyes were all misty.

"And he was so sweet, Jenna. Luke was just so..." She got all dreamy-eyed. And then the lovesick look died. "I don't even remember the accident. I guess I blocked it. I remember he was driving me home and then I woke up in the hospital." She wiped her eyes. "Ugh. I have to stop this. I gotta get a fast shower and then I'll get us breakfast before we head to the clubhouse. Go ahead and use whatever ..." she gestured to her dressing table.

"I'm so sorry, Jojo." I reached out and gave her a hug. She sank into me and then looked at me and gave me a little smile.

"I like you for him. I met Ella just briefly. I really liked her. Ride says you're her bestie?"

I nodded. "Since we were in kindergarten. But—-"

"This is gonna be awesome. Us three can gang up against them. We gotta find the right girl for Spency. He's a handful. He needs a strong woman. We'll work together on that once I move to Aberdeen."

"I don't mean to burst your bubble, but me and Rider..." I winced.

She laughed. "Right. You're as smitten as he is. It's all over your face."

I gawked. And then I shook my head. "No. I don't ... well, he and I aren't... I thought we might, but I was wrong. And, yeah, I was a smitten kitten, but I'm not now. Because I have to keep my head together. Because he made things clear. He's acting weird right now, but my guess is it's just this drama."

"You're wrong," she said, and with certainty. "And it's the only thing making me happy right now, so I'm gonna hang onto his little bit of happy. Okay?"

I kind of just blinked at her.

She gave me a still-teary smile and dashed to the bathroom, a blur of pink bunny slippers and curly hair.

I stood there a minute, frozen.

When I was finished quickly fluff-drying my hair and putting a bit of make-up on, I wandered back out and heard Rider arguing with his mother before I got to the end of the hall.

"You're the only one who gives a fuck about me, Ride. Your brothers are so cold. 'Specially Spency. Now you're taking Jojo? What about me? What. About. Me?"

"No, Ma. Joelle needs to be kept safe. We don't fuckin' know what else these bastards have planned. And Spence needs time. You gotta realize, all that's happened is gonna have some lasting effects. And it wouldn't hurt you ending your association with our enemies, Ma. Seriously."

"I gotta support myself and you know your father cut me off. I didn't know this'd happen. It ain't my fault the Jackals hang out at the bar I work at. This ain't on me. Your fucking father—-. And I love you, Ride. You know I love you the most. But, you gotta take responsibility that you and your buddies dipped your wick and didn't think about the consequences. Typical men."

I felt sick at hearing that. And I, strangely, almost wanted to defend him.

"Stop," he growled. "For the last time, that gash bullshitted. It wasn't rape."

"Sure as fuck looked like it."

"You saw?"

"'Course I did. I told Mantis I wouldn't believe it unless I saw it with my own eyes, so he showed me. They put it on the big screen in the bar. Lotta people saw it."

There was silence and I was flabbergasted at the idea of Rider's mother seeing that video. At people in bar seeing that video?

"It was just a game," he said. "A game that was Kailey's idea."

Ouch. Yikes. How could she watch that? And yet she still didn't believe him despite his explanation? Had I missed something pivotal by not watching the whole thing or was she just... a c-word?

I backed up, thinking maybe I should go back to Jojo's room to let these two have privacy, when I heard the horrible sound of a cat cry out. A tiny beautiful short-haired white cat with big powder blue eyes backed away, looking scared.

I squatted. "I'm so sorry, little kitty," I whispered. "Did I hurt your tail?"

It blinked at me and then rubbed against me, purring. It forgave me instantly.

I scratched its head and noted it had on a black collar with a bell and some silver studs. A badass collar for a tiny white blue-eyed kitty with a very feminine face.

"Baby," Rider called out, obviously having heard me. At the sound of his voice, the cat meowed loud and ran, faster than I could've anticipated, and I followed and saw her using her claws and climbing straight up Rider's jeans. He hefted her tiny body up into one hand and she rubbed her forehead all over his chin.

I stepped in with a tentative smile.

Rider's mother was leaning with her hip against the kitchen counter, her arms folded over her chest, a scowl on her face.

"I gotta go to bed. Haven't slept yet," Shelly muttered.

"It was nice to meet you," I said.

"Mm," she waved haphazardly in a 'whatever' gesture and looked to Rider. "Take that fuckin' fur ball with you if you're goin' more than a day. I ain't feedin' it."

Rider rolled his eyes, still scratching the purring kitty.

There was loaded silence. I looked at him and chewed the inside of my cheek, feeling awful about how she'd been toward him.

"How old is she?" I reached over and petted her head.

"Three or four."

"She's not a kitten? She's so tiny." She looked only about half grown.

"Nope."

"How are you so tiny? What's your name?"

"Marshmallow," Rider answered for the kitty.

I laughed. And then I saw him looking at me with warmth and the cat wriggled and then pounced onto me. Her tiny little claws were felt through the thin hoodie of Jojo's I was wearing.

I winced.

Rider carefully extracted her from my front and put her on the floor.

She did figure eights around my legs, purring her little heart out. And then she wound herself around his legs.

We watched her in silence a minute.

I heard the roar of motorcycle pipes. It sounded like multiple bikes. "One sec," he said and then he moved to the door.

Jojo was rushing to us, in a robe, hair wet. "Ay yay yay. Breakfast. I gotta..."

I touched her non-casted arm.

"It's okay. Why don't I do that while you get dressed? Just tell me what to do."

She brightened. "They're here now so maybe we should just toast some bagels and take them on the road. Or we'll skip it. There'll be food at the club."

"I can toast bagels," I said.

She pointed to a bread box. "Bagels are in there. There's cream cheese in the fridge. I like the dill. Ride likes the salmon. There's also plain and strawberry. Brady won't eat a bagel so just us three."

"Roger." I gave her a thumbs up.

Rider was back when I was half way through buttering the last bagel. He froze in his tracks and looked at me.

"Jojo is getting dressed so I'm on breakfast duty."

I put strawberry cream cheese on it and wrapped it in paper towel.

Rider grabbed a bag from a drawer and tossed some bottled water and bottled juice in and then called down the hall. "Joelle!"

She rushed out, dragging a suitcase, dressed in jeans, heeled ankle boots, and a black t-shirt. And I'd been right. She had seriously sexy curves. No wonder her dad and brothers were so protective. "Get the other?" she asked.

He went to her room and came back with the black suitcase.

"Your stuff, Jenna?" he asked.

"Oh. My purse is on Jojo's bed. I'll get it."

"Where's the clothes you had on?" he asked.

"I left them in Jojo's basket. They weren't mine, so she said it was okay." I gave him a glare and he looked like he was examining my face.

Jojo chuckled. "I repacked that hoodie with your stuff, Jenna. When we get to the clubhouse, I'll get it washed so you can get it right back on."

Rider's eyes hit his boots, but he wasn't even trying to hide his smirk.

"No need. I won't be wearing that again." I remarked, wiping the cutting board and putting the butter knife into the dishwasher.

Rider's eyes cut to me and then his brows went up.

"I saw what was on the back of it. Haha, very funny," I rolled my eyes at him, my face burning hot.

He looked at me with a deathly serious look on his face, but he said nothing. Though he said nothing, my heart was racing, because if I could guess at the expression, he was telling me, without telling me, that I *would* be wearing it again. I didn't hide my reaction very well. I looked away, feeling more burning in my chest.

"Time to go," he said. "Joelle. Drive the Charger. Jenna, we're on the bike."

"I, uh..." I didn't want to be on the back of his bike again. I didn't want to feel that feeling again. Why? Because it felt like something I shouldn't be allowed to feel after all that had happened in the past few days. The last night in my apartment, when we'd been on his bike was amazing. I wouldn't feel amazing this time. It'd make me feel the full weight of what wouldn't be.

"I'll ride with Jojo," I offered.

"No. You're on the back of my bike." He tossed keys at his sister. She caught them. He took both suitcases and the bag of breakfast stuff and left. Jojo disappeared down a hall and came back with a carrying case with little Marshmallow in it. She was blinking from the front of the cage, looking at me, as Joelle walked down the hall toward the door.

"What can I carry?" I asked.

"Oh. Shit. There's a bag with her food bowls and stuff. It's by the back door."

By the back door down a short hall from the kitchen was a big bag with a disposable litter tray that was prefilled, and half a dozen cans of kitty food, a bag of kitty kibble, plus pink and white *Hello Kitty* food and water dishes.

I grabbed those and my purse, and followed Jojo.

Outside, behind Rider's Charger, were several motorcycles parked with bikers standing in the driveway. They all had their eyes on me and Jojo. And their expressions were all hard.

With what was going on, I wasn't surprised. But, I felt very self-conscious. And I was also feeling very exposed. Where was Rider? I looked around and heard the sound of a gate. He was pushing out a very vintage but what looked like a meticulously loved motorcycle from the back yard. I knew nothing about motorcycles, but I'd say this was lovingly looked after. Every inch of it gleamed in the sun.

He went to an older man with long greying hair and a tidy beard and said something. The man gave a chin jerk and reached behind into a storage bag on the side of his motorcycle and passed Rider a helmet.

Rider set the bike on its kickstand and then moved to me, grabbed my hand, and moved me forward.

"Brothers, Jenna. She's mine."

My heart did a flip-flop. What kind of caveman statement was that?

All eyes were on me. And with all eyes on me at a time like this, I couldn't possibly disagree with him or tell him to *go to hell*. These men were dealing with the death of a member's woman. And the possible framing of another death. Only days after a member was murdered and a prospect butt-raped.

All the hard faces softened at his statement. This, for some reason, made my heart race even more.

"Jenna, Rudy, Prez of the mother chapter," Rider said and the man who'd passed the helmet shook my hand.

"Good to meet ya," he said softly and kissed my hand.

"Hi," I said. It said 'President' on the front of his leather vest.

"You know Brady and that's Axel." He pointed to a tall bald and bearded black man standing beside Brady who gave me a nod.

"Duckie." He pointed to an older man with a big belly, long curly grey hair, and a beard as long as the ZZ Top guys. "That's Bud." He pointed to another biker, this one short and stocky with a goatee, maybe in his fifties, with piercing green eyes.

"Hey, Jenna." Brady moved in and gave me a quick hug. It, thankfully, broke the awkward spell. He moved to Jojo and lifted her up off the ground and blew a raspberry on her cheek. She let out a little chuckle. He took Marshmallow from her and put the crate in the back seat of the Charger.

All the men moved in and gave me hugs, one at a time.

I sensed the heaviness in the air. Of course. A woman was left dead at their gates that morning. That they were here to escort two other females to safety felt kind of huge.

It was not the time for me to throw a hissy fit about being on his motorcycle or introduced as 'mine'.

I noticed that Brady and Axel were both actively watching our surroundings.

"Time to ride," Rider said and then he put the helmet on me. His eyes met mine and his expression was serious. My teeth sank into my tongue as I tried to hold myself together.

We rode with the president, Rudy, at the front. Two bikes were flanking him. Rider and I were behind him with Jojo driving the Charger behind us and then two motorcycles drove directly behind her.

The convoy drove only about ten minutes and then we were pulling up to gates. Gates that had police tape up around them and two squad cars parked beside the entrance.

We stopped, but kept idling, in front of the cop cars and Rudy waved at a cop. We then drove down a gravel lane beside the gate and a smaller gate was opened by a young biker in a prospect vest. The convoy moved in and I saw that we were in a yard with several big rig trucks that read *Dominion Moving and Storage*, several cars, and loading docks.

We drove around that area to a parking area in front of a big warehouse. The area in front of the place was filled with people. Bikers. Women. I saw people sitting on picnic benches under a covered patio area that was built off the side of the building. People looked like they were consoling one another. I saw people crying, people holding Kleenex boxes and passing them around. My heart grew heavy. Or heavier.

I also saw who *had to be* Edge, the faux-hawked guy from the video. He was sitting on top of a picnic table, with his head in his hands.

Rider turned the bike off. I got my helmet off and passed it to him. He passed it to Rudy and then walked us to the car where we met Jojo, getting out. She was looking around, looking confused.

"Jackals got Jet," Rider said, letting go of me and taking her by the shoulders. "Didn't wanna tell you till we got here. Dumped her body by the gates this morning."

She did a slow blink. Rider pulled her close and she looked up into his eyes.

"Why?"

"Tomorrow. After Lick's funeral. Tell you all of it then."

She shook her head in confusion and I could see in her eyes she was trying to work out how it was all connected.

"Are they just randomly taking us out?" she asked. Her lower lip was trembling.

He pulled his lips tight.

"No?" she asked.

Rider kissed her forehead. "Later, Joelle. Okay? C'mon."

She stood there, eyebrows furrowed. A young woman, maybe my age, with beautiful platinum blonde shoulder-length hair stepped up and put her arms around Jojo.

Rider took my hand and pulled me along and started to introduce me to people who were approaching. Bikers and women who were either with bikers at their sides, or who were maybe just there. And every time he introduced me, he said, "mine." "Jenna," he'd gesture, "mine." Or, "this is Jenna, she's mine."

How did I respond to that? I decided on the spot that I couldn't. I just said my helloes and my 'nice to meet yous' and eventually, I was introduced to a lady that engulfed me in a massive embrace after she'd kissed Rider right on the mouth.

"Aunt Delia, Jenna."

He didn't say, "mine" this time and I gave him a quizzical look.

She kissed me right on the mouth, too, and hugged me hard. I was a little bit taken aback, but she seemed so nice that I found myself putting my arms around her.

She looked like she'd been crying for hours.

"Patticakes is gonna give you some keys. I put you in the room I'd given your brother the other day since it has an ensuite. Joelle'll be down the hall."

"Thanks, Aunt Delia," he said. "How you doin'?"

She threw her hands up in the air. "I can't wrap my head around it. I can't. Blow and two other boys were comin' in early from a run and they found her. I didn't see her. I got here an hour later. Thank God. I don't think I coulda handled it, Ride. That girl was like a daughter to me. She woulda been if Edge ever put a ring on her finger. And he's a fuckin' mess."

He hugged her again. And then Rudy approached and pulled her to his side and I knew then, she had to be his wife.

I stood there, holding myself with my own arms, feeling the pain in the air like a living and breathing thing.

"Gotta give some sugar to your sister. How's she holdin' up?"

"She knows next to nothin' yet. Keepin' it that way till after Lick's funeral."

"Okay, well, I'll shadow her until we get her to her room. She's three doors down from you two. I'll pass word around that no one gossips."

Delia moved away from Rudy and then had Jojo, who'd been being hugged by a bunch of bikers ten feet from us, in her arms.

Rider took my hand and gave me a look. I didn't know how to read it at first, but it didn't take long for me to figure out what it was about. He moved us to the picnic table where Edge was sitting.

Edge looked up at Rider and his face? He was wrecked. Absolutely ravaged with grief.

I met Edge's eyes and my stomach roiled. I saw a flashback of the video. I don't know what his involvement was, because I exited soon after I saw his face, but I was glad for that. Now that I had to face him, I was relieved I didn't know.

He stood, and Rider pulled him into a hug and pounded on his back.

"We'll get them, brother. They'll pay. So fuckin' sorry, man."

Edge pushed out a long breath and nodded and wiped his eyes with the heels of his hands, and then his eyes came to me. "Hey. Good to meet ya." He moved in and hugged me. I went stiff. I couldn't help it. I doubt he even noticed, though.

"I'm very sorry for your loss," I said.

I felt him take a broken breath and then he moved away. The look in his eyes was communicating something to me, but I didn't know what. Rider grabbed my hand and pulled me to him. As I collided with Rider, Jojo was moving toward Edge, and she was red-eyed, and her chin was trembling. When she got to him, they both started to sob. My eyes welled up.

I didn't know these people. I barely knew Rider. But, I *did* know that this was real pain I was seeing here. And that a young woman was dead, murdered after being violated. It was awful. Beyond awful. I effing hated those Wyld Jackals. *Hated* them.

A tall dark-haired and tattooed older biker lady moved to us and passed Rider a key. She kissed him on the cheek and reached over and squeezed my hand, and then she moved to Jojo and pulled her into a hug.

Rider tugged my hand and we walked inside the vast warehouse, through an open area with exposed rafters and then down a hallway that had drop ceilings. We went down a series of more hallways and then he unlocked a door, taking us into a small windowless bedroom with a double bed, a plain dresser, a smallish TV mounted up in a corner, a wooden chair, and a door that led to an adjoining bathroom. This felt like a dorm room. It felt a little bit claustrophobic. Not only because of the windowless status, but also because of that scene out there. And the two of us being alone in here.

At least behind these tall gates with all these bikers, maybe I was safe. Maybe. Until when, though?

Rider's phone started ringing. He let go of my hand and pulled his phone out of his pocket.

"Yeah? Yeah. See ya in a minute."

He dialed another number and then put the phone to his ear. "Deacon?" He gave me a 'one second' finger and stepped out of the room into the hall.

I sat on the bed and pulled my lips tight.

A few minutes later, he was back.

He let out a breath as he tossed that black suitcase and a Duffle bag of his to the floor.

His eyes were on me.

I rolled my eyes.

"What?" he asked.

I shook my head.

"Got somethin' to say?"

"I might, if things weren't what they are because of what happened this morning with your friend's girlfriend. I might have a lot to say."

"Feel free," he invited, with a wave of his hand.

I shook my head, but glared at him. "No thanks. But, I reserve the right to save it for another time."

He crouched in front of me, so we were eye level. "Say it."

"Why are you introducing me that way?"

He smiled. "Because that's how it is."

"It isn't."

"Tell ya what. Try me on for size. We get through this, we'll talk about whether it's permanent."

How dare he.

"You know, I was tryin' to be cool with all you're dealing with, but how fucking dare you!"

He laughed a little bit and there was a sparkle in his eyes. He advanced, and I was pinned under his body. The playfulness was gone and in its place, was a look as serious as a heart attack.

"I dare."

I brought my knee up and almost got him square between the legs, but he deflected, spun me around, and then he had me pinned on my belly on the bed.

"Wanna wrestle?" he said, huskily in my ear.

I struggled.

"Fuck, forgot the cuffs," he grumbled.

I looked up and there was no headboard to cuff me to. Thank God.

"Get off me."

"Gonna have to get creative in makin' you behave."

"Get your hands off me," I ordered.

There was a knock on the door.

He stopped a second, most of his weight still on me, and then his mouth was on my neck. He kissed it affectionately and got off.

Weird. As if that was all a joke. All a game. This guy was a mystery to me.

He stepped out into the hall. And I sat up and tried to catch my breath.

I was pulled from my dark thoughts as the door opened and I saw Rider had let Jojo in, but he stayed out there, talking on the phone. Brady walked by, carrying the purple suitcase and Marshmallow in her crate.

Jojo put the bagel bag down on the end of the bed. "I'm just a couple doors down. She reached in and pulled a bagel out." I don't think I can even eat. People know what I'm not allowed to know so I can't be out there." She rolled her eyes. "Gonna be a long day."

I chewed my lip. "Come back and hang with me. Can we get a deck of cards or something?"

Rider entered the room.

"Good idea," she said. "We need some playing cards, Ride. Maybe you oughta just tell me. Let me deal. Then I'm—-"

"No," his eyes cut to her. He'd been eyeing me.

"You do realize that this is fucking with my head. This is making things worse."

"Jo—-"

"Tell me, damn it!" she shoved him.

He barely moved an inch.

"Jet's death is related. I know it. Explain. Please, Ride."

Rider sat down on the wooden chair by the head of the bed and put his fingertips to his temples.

"I can't take this back once it's out. And it might be better that you hear this after the funeral. Dad, Spence, Deacon, and me...we've all agreed."

"I wanna know what's going on. Me. I'm not a kid, Ride. Don't you see that this is torture? My mind is spinning. And if I know, I don't have to be cooped up. I can be out there helping get things ready for tomorrow and keeping my mind busy."

I felt like I shouldn't be here for this conversation. This was private.

"I'll just..." I pointed to the door.

"Stay." Rider said.

"Then, maybe you two should just..." I pointed to the door.

Rider shook his head at me.

Awkward.

Rider looked to me. "What do you think? If you were her, knowing what you know, would it be better before or after the funeral?"

I looked at Jojo.

"Jenna, be honest. If you say right now that he shouldn't tell me, I'll let it go."

"You don't know me, Jojo. That's a lot of stock you're putting into someone you just met."

"You're a sister. A sister'll know much better than a guy."

I looked at Rider. "She's gotta feel whatever she's gonna feel. I get you don't want her angry at him and then regret that later, and I haven't been to many funerals, but funerals are supposed to bring closure. I think either way, it's gonna be hard, but the sooner she can get started on working to coming to grips with everything, even the bad stuff, the better."

He stared at me a beat and then nodded and looked to his sister. "You ever meet Kailey?"

Wow. I was a little thrown by his confidence in my opinion.

"Kailey?" Jojo asked.

"Blonde. Hangs out with Gia."

"Gia's stepsister. Yeah."

"Gia's what?" Rider asked, anger glittering in his eyes.

"Gia's dad married her mom when they were kids. They split, but those two are still tight."

He gave his head a shake. "Skinny bitch, long straight blonde hair. Beauty mark on her upper lip? Harley tramp stamp?"

"That's her," Jojo confirmed.

"Didn't know they were related. This changes Gia's welcome status."

"Why? What's going on?"

"Kailey is an old lady to a Jackal."

Jojo blinked.

"She fucked around with a few guys, took four at once, secretly taped it, hooked up with a Jackal who made her his old lady, then she presented the tape as a gang-rape. Incorrectly."

Jojo's mouth dropped open.

"First, we thought she was lyin' because he heard rumors about her, that she was tryin' to save face, sayin' she was raped rather than admitting she was playin' with four guys at once. But once the tape came out, it was obvious. It was staged. She set up four brothers to play a sex game. She recorded it without their knowledge. She presents a good case, because that's how she staged it. It's bullshit. It was a game. Not the first time that kind of game got played in the back room at Charlie's. Not the first time she played it with brothers from our club. Jackals have come after us, using it as retribution, tryin' to get the other clubs on side with us to change teams."

Jojo blinked a couple times. "How does that get misrepresented when it's a tape?"

"It was a game. Role playing. Rough sex. She'd played it before and asked for it rougher."

I sat there, my heart racing, my stomach churning with something vile and acidic.

"Which four brothers?" Jojo asked softly, tears forming in her already red eyes.

"Joelle..." Rider said gently.

"Who! I already know at least one, obviously Luke, but who else? Edge?"

"Yeah."

"Who else?" she looked at me and then light dawned and her eyes cut back to Rider. "You?"

"And Scoot." His eyes moved to the wall and his jaw muscles were flexing.

"That's why Scott got beat up." Jojo's eyes were on her brother and they were haunted.

He nodded.

"When?" she asked.

Rider's face contorted.

"When did you guys and Luke fuck her?" she demanded.

"Mid-July."

She practically flew off the bed and was in the bathroom, door slamming hard. Rider closed his eyes.

Obviously, her relationship with Lick / Luke had already begun in July. We were now in early September.

Obviously, Edge had been with Jet at that time.

Scooter had been single. Rider: also single. But now Jojo wasn't just coping with losing her secret boyfriend; she was also coping with the fact that he'd been cheating on her. In dirty drunken four-on-one gangbangs.

I shook my head, feeling anger rise. I was jiggling my legs, trying to keep a lid on all of it. That poor girl in there.

His phone made noise. He looked at the screen and then leaned forward on the chair and put his hand on my knee. "I hate to ask you this, but can you just hang tight here and keep her here if you can? Keep her company? I gotta hit church. Be back as soon as I can."

"Huh?"

"I need to go to an urgent club meeting," he clarified. "Stay in here. I'll be back in a few. I know we got shit to work out, but don't fan those flames." He gestured toward the bathroom door.

"Go," I snapped, jerking my leg to make his hand slip.

"Jenna..."

"Go, Rider. I have nothing to say right now."

"Really?" he asked snidely.

"No. Not really. I actually have lots to say. But, I can't say any of it, because right now, all that matters is your sister's feelings. Don't worry, I won't make her feel worse. I don't even think that's possible."

He tilted his head curiously at me.

"Go. I'll take care of her."

He looked a little frazzled. He ran his hands through his hair and then abruptly hooked a hand around the back of my neck and brought my head forward and touched his lips to my forehead. He just as abruptly let go and went to the bathroom door.

"Joelle, I'm headin' to church. Stay with Jenna till I get back, okay?"

I heard a banging sound, like kicking the door, as a reply.

He turned and left the room, running his hand through his hair and shooting me what looked like an apologetic look.

And I sat there and tried to get my shit together. So, I could be supportive to a girl I'd just met whose heart went from crushed to completely annihilated.

There was a knock on the door. I got up and opened it.

Brady was there with Marshmallow. "Ride says Jo's in here. I was waitin' in her room. You want the cat, or should I drop her back in there?"

I reached out and took the carrying cage and the bag of cat accessories from him.

He gave me a tight smile and was gone, moving quickly down the long hallway.

I shut the door and put the crate on the bed and opened the door. She cautiously came out.

Not long later, Jojo cautiously came out, too.

"It's just us," I said, petting Marshmallow.

Jojo sat on the bed beside me.

"You okay?" I asked.

She shook her head. "No. We got started in June."

Shit.

"We'd only kissed a couple times by then, but..." she thrust her fingers into her hair and her chin started trembling.

And then she looked at me. "Emotionally, we were something. Were you and Ride seeing each other then? Is that why you're havin' a rough go of things?"

I shook my head. "No. We met the end of last month, I guess. We've only hooked up a couple times and his ... is this weird?" I asked, ready to spare her the details.

"No. I can deal. I need to understand this, make sense of all of it. That might not even be possible, but go ahead..." she invited.

"I kind of crushed hard," I said. "And he's totally not my type. But, it was almost like something snapped into place. And I tried to play it cool, because I've been hurt, so I have my heart shrouded in Kevlar, and... and he stomped on it anyway. And now all this is happening and I'm apparently in danger. He's trying to act like it's not just about hooking up, but yet... things he's saying don't add up. I don't think we're on the same page and doubt we ever will be."

I was not about to tell her that Rider told me I was bad in bed, so it made no sense to me that he was acting like he wanted to be in a relationship with me. I mean, why would he? He liked kinky rough sex and I guess I'm too tame in bed. Too selfish. Too materialistic. Too... me.

We spent the next few hours playing cards while she talked about her life, her family. She was solemn, but she was still good company. She had to have been dealing with all this the past few days and thought it wouldn't be any easier with the bomb that just got dropped, I knew already it was easier than not knowing, than wondering. At least now she could try to move forward. Not wait for the funeral to be over and then have a whole new set of things to cope with.

Listening to her talk about her family, about her life, it wasn't hard to conclude that the Valentines were held together with love that came from their dad and the club. Shelly didn't sound like she was around much and when she was, she'd done things to make herself an outcast. Jojo was the baby of the family, but she took care of the house the way Shelly should've. When Shelly and Deke broke up, she started working at the bar that was the local hangout for the Wyld Jackals. This was after she'd already been suspected of cheating on Deke with one of them on top of a bunch of other drama including stepping out on Deke with one of the Dom members, too. She was a shitty wife, a shitty mother.

Jojo told me her parents fought like cats and dogs and that months back, her mother had told her she wasn't even Deke's daughter. She blurted this at a family dinner for Spencer's birthday, causing a rip-roaring argument and it rocked the foundation of the world for all of them. A DNA test had revealed that Deke was, in fact, Jojo's father, but significant damage was done to the whole family.

Jojo went on to tell me more about her brothers and how their family (minus their mother) had unconditional love, telling me that Deacon and Spence fought a lot and that Spencer was a dick to Deacon and yet Deacon always forgave him.

Spencer had demons and Jojo believed a lot stemmed from his issues with his mother. She'd abandoned him as a toddler on regular occasions and cast him aside when Jojo was born and was verbally abusive to him. He'd had rough teen years, and then had turned angry, often turning to booze and drugs.

She talked about Deacon's history with women and I'd already heard a bit about it, but hearing more from Jojo as we played Gin Rummy, alternately giving affection to the little white purr machine, I felt sad for Deacon, hearing more about the story of his first girlfriend.

"How, then..." I started, feeling emotional, "could Rider be into that kind of scene, knowing what'd happened with Deacon?"

It made no sense to me.

She shook her head. "Rider is a live fast, ride hard and have fun guy. He avoids drama. Hates it. He's all about the fun. Always has been."

Rider sounded like me in male form.

She went on. "He uses humor as a weapon against stress, against drama he can't run from. When things go haywire he acts like it all rolls off his back. Things get crazy with the club. Maybe that's how he blows off steam. He'd never hurt a girl on purpose."

I made a face of disgust. But her characterization of him made sense. He'd been joking with me throughout all this. Was it his coping mechanism? Or did he really just not take much of anything too seriously?

She kept talking. "They all get liquored up and there are these girls that just stick around and wait. Like vultures. They're either all over them or they wait until the brothers are drunk enough. Dressed slutty, wanting to be with them, willing to do whatever. Some of those girls think that's the way in, the way to becoming an old lady, and they're wrong. Some girls want to get high or got nowhere to go. Some are just party girls, hang-arounds. I'm friends with Gia. She's a biker bunny. She's always around during the club parties. She's absolutely gorgeous, could be a model, but the way she found her way in means none of them would ever look at her as old lady material. And it's sad, because she's a great girl with a lot to give. And they'll never see her as anything but a piece of ass."

I shook my head.

"Gia's been with all three of my brothers at least once. I think she fucks Spence occasionally. She's probably been with every single guy under fifty in the club at one time or another. She's broken. And they don't see who she is. What she has to give." She shook her head. "I keep telling her to go somewhere new. To find herself a decent guy. She's convinced it'll happen for her with our club eventually. She loves this club. But in the meantime, she's lonely and she just takes whatever dregs she can get. That's probably another reason why my brothers are so protective of me dating. They didn't want me getting labelled biker bunny. That's the way my dad explained it to me when I was sixteen and complaining my brothers wouldn't let me date a biker." She snickered bitterly.

"Daddy said that one day, if I set my sights on a brother, that brother shouldn't have to worry I'd been with any of *his* brothers already. Daddy told me to date outside the club. Outside the life. But to keep my eyes peeled on club members in case any of them were worthy. I've never been attracted to a man who wasn't in a leather cut, so I didn't date outside the club. It's weird. My father drilled into the boys to not ever get serious about club whores. That they were better than that. That comes from his bullshit with my mom, of course. She was a club whore and she got knocked up with Deacon and trapped Dad." She shrugged. "But, I never got interested in any guy who doesn't ride. Never. To me, they're real men. They live by *their* rules. They go after what *they* want. They live large. We have a big awesome family that loves one another. We have a blast together. We'll take a bullet for one another. It's slightly dysfunctional in some ways, but aren't all families?"

We both must've gotten lost in our thoughts (me in my longing), because we played out the rest of the game quietly.

"How long did Jet and Edge date?" I asked after a long silence.

Her eyes went dark again. "Like...five years maybe."

I winced.

"But they've loved each other a lot longer than that. They'd dated when they were teens, too. She was in foster care and got transferred somewhere else, so they split due to distance. Found one another again years later. She was good people," Jojo whispered.

"I think she got the video I got."

"You got? You...you saw it?" Jojo's eyes went wide.

"Just a couple seconds. I thought I was gonna be sick. I closed it and took off. Bronto and Jesse took me kicking and screaming to your family cabin. The Wyld Jackals had already threatened to do something to me. It looked real. Jojo, if that's the caliber of the men in this club, why would anyone want that?"

She winced. "Not all bikers cheat, Jenna. My dad never cheated on Mom. Never. And she deserved it. She cheated loads. And Jet never said anything, but she and Edge seemed happy. I don't know if they had an open relationship or what, but..." she trailed off, looking lost in thought.

I didn't say anything to that, because her biker had cheated. Because, obviously Edge had cheated on the now-dead Jet. And his cheating had gotten Jet dead. Rape or not rape, open relationship or not, Jet was dead because of Edge sleeping with that Kailey girl.

"Did you see Luke?" she asked. "In the video?"

I put my hand up. "Please don't ask me about it. You don't wanna know."

She shook her head. "I can tell by your face that he was fully involved. It must've been hard to see my brother—-"

"It was."

"But it was before you two met."

I shrugged.

"My brother didn't rape her. Neither did Scott, Luke, *or* Edge. I know these guys. If they say it was a game, it was."

I had nothing to say to that.

Jojo got up with a sigh and a sad expression. "I'm gonna go grab my phone, call Gia and find out what the fuck. I also gotta warn her now that Ride knows she's Kailey's stepsister."

"This gives me a bad feeling," I warned her.

"I've known Gia for ages. She'll get me information about Kailey."

"Her boyfriend was found in a dumpster in Aberdeen his morning."

Jojo's eyes bugged out. "What the fuck?"

"Rider says they're trying to frame the Dominion Brotherhood."

"Who was he?"

"A Jackal. Ben something."

"I don't know him. I'll be back." She stepped out into the hallway.

I hung out with Marshmallow.

Rider stepped in a couple minutes later.

"Where's my sister?" he asked, looking around.

"She went to make a call." I kept petting the cat. "I need my phone."

"Why?"

"I have to call my mother," I grumbled. And then my gaze cut to him. "You know, I shouldn't have to ask to use my own effing phone." I thought I'd maybe left it at the cabin, but the look on his face told me he had my phone.

He folded his arms across his chest. "If I wasn't worried about what sorta calls you'd make, I wouldn't make you ask."

"I'm just gonna text her," I muttered. "Deadline, remember?"

He sat on the bed and took my phone out of his jeans pocket and passed it to me.

I found Mom's contact details and opened a text message.

"Can I help you?" I glared at Rider, who was looking at my phone screen.

"You're not calling; you're texting?"

"Yeah. So?"

"Chicken shit."

"You wanna call her?" I offered.

"Nope. I'm chicken shit, too."

I rolled my eyes.

"Call her."

I looked at him.

"Better to know where things stand than send a text that pisses her off even more." He shrugged.

There was wisdom in this. But, I often preferred avoidance where my mother was concerned. And, I wasn't keen to do what he said, even if it made sense.

I checked my email to procrastinate, and then re-opened my text messages, about to compose a message to my Mom when I saw Daniel Sotheby's text string.

I opened it. That morning's text had been replied to.

> **"This is Jenna's man. She's not avail for breakfast with you today. Or ever."**

I glared at him. "Really?"

He jerked his chin up in question.

"You texted Daniel?"

His lip curled.

I rolled my eyes and went to my mother's contact details and hit dial. Being pissed was being channeled into nerve...nerve to call Mom instead of text.

"You gonna stand here and listen, too?" I demanded.

He said nothing. He just stared.

There was a knock on the door. He opened it. My Mom's line was ringing.

I saw Jojo's head. Rider whispered something to her and then he stepped out into the hall with her.

"Hello," Mom answered, grouchily.

"Hey Mom," I said, my voice all scratchy.

Silence. But, I swear I could feel the animosity through the phone lines.

I cleared my throat. "I just wanted to check in, tell you I'm okay."

"Where are you?" she demanded.

"Sioux Falls."

"Why?"

"There's some drama. I'm hoping to be back soon."

"Genevieve, this is ridiculous. You have a business to run. You can't just run off with some loser and..."

"I have coverage," I defended, pacing the room. "And shit happens, Mom. I'm dealing with stuff and when it's dealt with, I'll be back. And he's not a loser."

I heard a noise behind me. Rider was standing there. He'd heard me defend him. His expression was blank. His arms folded across his chest.

"Don't you take that tone with me, young lady!" she snapped.

There was another rap on the door, so he stepped out again.

My eyes rolled ceiling-wards and I flopped back on the bed.

Marshmallow took that as an invite and climbed up onto me and stretched out across my belly.

"You get back here, and you get back here today or there will be consequences."

"I can't get back there today, Mom."

"And why is that?" she demanded.

"I can't tell you why. It's complicated. I just—-"

"Either you give me a good reason, right now, why you can't get back here today, or you'll force my hand."

"Mom! I'm an adult. I'm not a kid. And I don't have to answer to every damn thing I do! I can't get into things. I need you to just respect that I've got things under control with my business and that I'll be home as soon as it's feasible."

"Your business is clearly not your priority, Genevieve."

"You know what, Mother? I have a lot of priorities. My business. My friends and family. My safety. My happiness. And you and Daddy gave me the opportunity with this business, and I appreciate that, but sometimes I have to juggle things. You can't use the business to control me. I don't think I can take another three years of this."

Silence on the phone line.

I sighed. "I'm sorry if you were worried. I can't get into the details of why I can't come home yet. You're just gonna have to trust me."

"No. I'm just gonna have to go now. I'm busy. Some of us take our responsibilities seriously." And with that parting shot, she hung up on me.

Nice. I let out a growly sound in frustration and put the phone down.

Marshmallow was sleeping on my belly, her paws curled under her chest. She purred in her sleep. I put my hands on her head and felt her soft fur.

Mom had said she was allergic to cats, so we couldn't have one. I'd always wanted one. I didn't believe she was allergic. I'm convinced she just didn't want me to have one. My dad's aunt had two cats and we went there once for dinner, when I was a little kid, and Mom didn't sneeze or complain once.

I decided that when I got home, I was getting a kitten. Or maybe a big old shelter cat who needed a forever home. Whether I had a business, or an apartment didn't matter. I was a grown woman who could have an effing cat if I wanted to. Maybe I'd get a kitten *and* a shelter cat. And they'd have one another while I was at work, so they wouldn't ever get lonely.

Rider stepped in. Jojo followed.

"How'd it go?" Rider asked, his voice soft.

I looked away and shrugged. "Not good."

"I was just gonna get her and set her up in my room," Jojo said. I sat up and passed the sleepy kitty to her.

"You okay?" Jojo asked.

I shook my head. "I'm gonna get a cat. Maybe two."

Rider was staring at me curiously.

"You?" I asked Jojo.

She shook her head. "I'm gonna get drunk."

I smiled. "Day drinking. Best idea I've heard all week."

Rider's eyes bounced between the two of us, and then he said, "It's five o'clock somewhere. What do you girls wanna drink?"

"Pina coladas," Jojo said. "No! Strawberry daquiris. Jet loved daquiris. And shooters. We'll work up to the shooters."

"Sounds good to me."

"You two need to eat first," Rider advised.

"Cold bagels?" I screwed up my face. Jojo screwed hers up, too.

"I'll get you set up. Booze and food." Rider kissed his sister's forehead and then grabbed my hand. "What happened on that call?" I looked at his hand holding mine and felt something seize my chest.

Jojo reached for the bag with Marshmallow's things and left the room, telling us, "Bang on my door when you're ready for me."

Me and Rider were alone.

"You okay?" he pushed.

"No." I pulled my hand away. "But, I'm tired of her bullshit. She's more worried about pulling my strings than what's really going on that's keeping me away. I can't tell her the truth about why I can't get back and frankly, I'm sick of her treating me like this. If she takes my salon... I'll just figure something else out."

He was quiet a moment, studying me. "That what you've always wanted to do?"

"I got my business degree and I worked at her bank, at Dad's real estate brokerage. I just always wanted to do my own thing. I went to beauty school and got a loan for it and paid for it myself, despite their complaints about the business degree they paid for. I would've been totally happy working for another salon to start, but Dad insisted on giving me the salon. Well, I told them I wanted to pay for it. If it was gonna be mine, I wanted it to be mine for real, not a gift. And Dad came up with the plan to loan me the money and said if I did well, I'd only have to pay half and the rest would be early inheritance money from them. Morbid, kind of, but he insisted. She wasn't happy from the get go, especially since Dad came up with the plan without her. But, then she figured out she could use the salon to control me, which she loves to do. I'm just so sick of it. Maybe I should walk. Go work for some other salon. Say *forget it* to the hassles."

"You like having your own salon?"

"I love it. Love every damn thing about it." I sighed. "The spot. My customers. Making them feel good about themselves. Making plans for it to grow. Seeing it actually grow. My apartment upstairs. My neighbors."

He ran his fingers through my hair and I felt my insides freeze up. I was being real with him. I was being revealing. And it hit me that I shouldn't be. Why was I?

"There it goes again," he muttered.

"Huh?" I played dumb.

"The wall. Back up she goes. Read it all over your face and then saw it in your body language. If you and me are gonna work, we're gonna have to do something about that."

"If you and me are gonna work? What you and me? There's no you and me."

He smiled. And his smile wasn't sweet. It was cocky. And dangerous.

He leaned over and kissed my lips. "I think you know there is. I'll leave that for you." He gestured to my phone. "But, fair warning: you break my trust, it'll be hard to earn back." He pointed at me.

I jerked back away from him and shot him a glare. "Don't point at me." I reached to smack his hand away, but he caught my index finger in his grip and pulled it to his mouth and kissed it.

I was kind of speechless.

He smirked. "Text message there from Pippa for you."

He left.

I stared at the door for a long time.

And then I stared at my phone and lifted it and went to a message from Pippa from earlier.

> **"Hey.... I talked to Rider and not to worry. Doc Lola's sister Lulu is helping me with Kendra's wedding. Deb knows her. Met her teaching a class at the beauty school. Crisis averted. Lulu's fresh outta hair school but she has talent. 4sure. I sent Kendra her portfolio and told her to look @ it before I broke the news that you might not make it. I also got Lulu to do my hair in the style you picked for Kendra and she aced it. I showed Kendra and she was totally fine. You'll luv Lulu. I**

think we found our new stylist for when Deb retires, but we'll talk when you're back. Can I give her a couple of your appointments this week? Not to worry, I've been doing the daily deposits, too. Pay her by the split you talked about doing when you hire someone? Call or text me."

Rider called her about Kendra's wedding? I didn't know how to feel about that.

I texted back a heart and wrote:

"Thank you. My life saver! And sure. I trust your judgment. I'll msg when I can but all's ok right now. Love you. Xo"

I put the phone down. And I gave my head a shake. He'd acted like the wedding wasn't even on his radar, but then went and took care of it. And today was Wednesday and he'd covered me for Saturday, so clearly, there were no plans to get me home before then.

A couple minutes later, there was a knock at the door. I opened it and it was Jojo. She had a pitcher containing a pink frozen beverage concoction and two glasses.

"Strawberry daquiris," she announced. "I found a can of mix in one of the freezers. Likely from the last time Jet partied. I was gonna wait but he told me you were alone. He's getting us food and more daquiri mix."

Ten minutes later, Rider came in with a paper bag. He plopped it onto the wooden chair sitting beside the bed. I could smell whatever food it contained, and it smelled fantastic.

"Breaded veal parm sandwiches," he said.

I looked at him and blinked. "Veal? Uh.... I do not eat baby animals."

He took a big breath, pointed at the pitcher sitting on the chair, and said "Don't. I'll be back." He passed Jojo the bag in his hand, which she accepted, and then he turned on his heel and was gone.

Just like that, no complaints or smart-alecky comments.

But forbidding us to drink? Bossy.

Jojo glanced at the door and then her eyes darted to me. She shook her head in what looked like confusion.

"Pour me one of those," I said, feeling like 'fuck it'.

We toasted Jet when we had our first sip.

I'D ALREADY HAD TWO daquiris on an empty stomach, and I had no idea how much booze was in them, but I *did* know that those types of drinks didn't typically taste like booze -—but these ones did. In other words, whoever the mixologist was, they mixed with a heavy hand.

Rider came in with another bag. "Eggplant parm panini. You think eggplants are cute, babe, I'll just say, you can pull it out and eat a tomato sauce sandwich."

I laughed big.

He smirked at me, looking at me with warmth. I was feeling a buzz already.

Jojo got to her feet, holding the empty pitcher. "I'm gonna make some more..." she swayed just a little as she got to the door.

He tilted his head. "She eat?"

I nodded. "She ate both of them. She has no aversion to baby cow eating. The wench. Poor Norman."

Jojo laughed as she shut the door on her way out.

"How many drinks have you had?"

"Two. But, it feels like six."

"On zero food." He shook his head. "Jojo's cocktails are Molotov."

"Huh?"

"Lethal."

"I've never tasted eggplant parm," I notified him, eyes on the bag.

He passed me the sandwich.

"How was your meeting?" I asked, feeling chatty and thinking the sandwich smelled awesome.

"Rough. Lotta tough decisions have to be made. How you doin'?"

"My life sucks." I bit into the partly unwrapped sandwich. I chewed, swallowed, and then gushed about it. "Mm. This is really, *really* good."

"Their pizza is their specialty. I'll get us one before we head home."

"Mm." I kept eating. It was awesome.

Rider's phone made noise and he texted for a minute and then he left when Jojo had come back with another pitcher of drinks. Me and Jojo had been drinking and talking. We'd been listening to music with my phone while playing cards on the bed, the wooden chair beside the bed pulled close to act as our drink table.

We'd decided to try to get our minds off the heavy stuff. I told her about my salon. About Aberdeen. About my life before all this craziness.

She told me about her closest friends, about how they all had crushes on her brothers, but that she forbade them to date any of her friends, after Spencer had done the dirty with one and then the girl got pregnant. Jojo's friend had a miscarriage and it was a near miss... Spence was almost the first married off in a literal shotgun wedding. It had been a bad enough scene that Jojo made them all swear they'd never date her friends again.

Jojo kept losing her joy and sinking toward thinking about Luke, but when I saw it happening, I'd just start gabbing some more and change the topic.

She told me that a few of her friends met Ella at the hospital and were currently plotting to assassinate her for 'bagging' Deacon.

"Oh, Ella would win," I assured. "She may be little and all cute-girl-next-door, but she's fallen hard for Deacon. She'll end those bitches to protect her man."

"So, my *other* brother..." she said, pouring our fourth daquiris that felt like our tenth. "You fall hard for him?"

"Nope. We're not talking heavy stuff," I put my hand up.

She poured it too full, so I had to lean over and slurp some. My back was to the door and I hadn't heard the door open, unfortunately for me.

"He's off limits," I said, licking my upper lip, still hunched over the chair and my too-full drink. "I can't talk about him or how he's the best sex I've ever had and how I'm the worst sex he ever had."

"Err... Jenna..." Jojo started. But, I kept going.

"And how I could *absolutely* see a future with him. You know? The future I want. He needs a couple tweaks but he's definitely a canvas I thought I could work with. Not the future my mother wants for me. Which is fine by me. I think I saw my whole life in my head that first time on the back of his motorcycle, and what I saw was good. Mm. More than good. But I was wrong. He's allergic to commitment, as you said. And I'm just super vanilla. And he's not. He's... rocky road. Delicious rocky road."

I sighed and then kept going, shaking my head.

"And we're over before we got a chance to begin. Because I'm a selfish hypocrite materialistic bitch, apparently. It was over before I got a chance to see if I could trust letting my guard down. And fuck, I wanted to. It's just as well. I can't trust him." I looked up from my daquiri and noticed she had a horrified look on her face.

"What? Oh yeah, off limits. Let's forget about him. Sorry for talking sex about your brother. But, yeah. Fuck him." I put my mouth back to the glass and took another big slurp and lifted it off the chair we were using as a table. "Though I could go one more round, maybe. Show him that he's wrong. R-O-N-G wrong. Be the best sex he's ever had and then tell him Fuck You, Rider Valentine. Fuck you and your anti-monogamy..notony...monogo...whatever."

"Joelle. Go to bed. We gotta get up early," Rider said from behind me.

I jolted. I felt his hand on the back of my neck. He squeezed a little. Sweetly, maybe. Oh shit.

"Someone kill me. Please."

I closed my eyes. How long had he been standing there?

"Night, babes," she said to me.

"You got a gun, Jojo? Please. Shoot me," I pleaded.

"Nope. No way am I shootin' my future sister-in-law. Good luck, Ride." She took her full drink and moseyed on out.

"Oh God," I moaned.

He let go of my neck. "One sec. Hold that 'fuck Rider' thought." And then he disappeared into the bathroom. And I was thinking, shit.

Retreat? Retreat!

I jumped to my feet and went out into the hall and was about to shut the door. Shit. I didn't have my bag. If I found my way out of this labyrinth, I'd need it.

I ducked back in and he was coming out of the bathroom.

"Where you goin'?"

"I gotta go."

"Come here," he said.

He was in just a pair of jeans and a black muscle shirt. His arms looked amazing. His ink. I could see the nipple piercing straining at the tight fabric of his shirt. He kicked his boots off and yanked his socks off and sat on the bed.

"Come here," he repeated.

"Why?" I asked.

"I wanna talk to you."

"No." I shook my head, feeling like I was in mortal danger. Well, not me physically, but me emotionally. "Nope. I'm drunk, Rider. I need to just close my eyes and sleep. Not say more shit to embarrass myself while my Kevlar is malfunctioning."

I went to him anyway.

Why? Who knows. Kevlar malfunction. Evidently.

He got to his feet when I got close. I pushed at his chest.

"Don't. I wanna sleep. We're done, you and me. Okay?" And then I ran my hands up his chest until they got to his shoulders. My hands stopped there. And then I shoved and grabbed him by fistfuls of his muscle shirt.

I looked up into his eyes. His beautiful green-blue eyes.

"Are you sure that's what you want?" he whispered, kissing my temple.

My heart hurt so bad it felt like it was bleeding. "I'm sure." I touched his bottom lip with my fingertips. And then I pouted.

After a loaded moment of silence, me staring at his mouth, he stepped back.

"You don't wanna try? See if we can make fireworks together? 'Cuz I'd bet my Harley we can."

I stared at him. My throat was dry. "No." I took a step forward.

"Sure?"

"Yep."

I stepped closer again. My hands were on his chest again. Or still? I didn't know.

"Okay," he shrugged and backed up.

And that hurt. I chewed the inside of my cheek, feeling the burn in my chest and my eyes.

"Okay?" I asked. I still had my hands on his chest. Or maybe I'd moved forward again.

He smiled at me and looked like he was about to crack up laughing.

I flopped onto the bed and stared at the ceiling. He looked down at me and then pulled his shirt off and climbed in with me.

"Yeah, give up, Rider. They all do," I said, all maudlin.

"What?" he asked, lifting up on an elbow and looking down at me.

"Nothing."

He booped my nose with his index finger.

"Talk to me," he said.

"How bad am I?" I asked.

"Huh?" he asked.

"In bed. I'm that bad?"

He let out a long sigh, "Gorgeous..."

"I'm not bad in bed. I've never had any complaints," I defended.

I didn't like how my voice sounded. I sounded like a loser.

"Maybe you and me...we're just not compatible in bed." He was trying to be nice, but it was in his voice. It was written all over his face. And I could still hear those mean words he'd said about me being a selfish lay.

He was amazing in bed. He liked it rough, but the things he did with his tongue, his dick? He wasn't bad in bed.

I was pissed at this guy. Pissed. But, I had to change his perception of me. Even if we were over, which we *so* were, I couldn't let it end with him thinking I was bad in bed. He needed to have trouble getting over me because of how fucking awesome I am. He needed to think of me when he was old and gray and not nearly as hot, and think of me as *the one* that got away.

"Give me another shot. Let me show you you're wrong. I'm not bad in bed." I blurted.

His head jerked in surprise.

"We're over. Don't mistake me, Rider Valentine. But, I'm about to prove you wrong. Take off your fucking clothes!" I got to my feet and got the shock of my life when he got up too, and roughly grabbed my hips and backed me against the wall beside the bed.

I'd decided that though I was fed up with him and didn't want anything to do with a guy who got his rocks off in a staged rape gangbang, I didn't want to end this with him thinking what he thought about me. I was gonna walk away with him wanting more.

And not being able to get it.

His eyes were darker, hooded, and filled with intent. His hand cupped my jaw. "Since we're over, I'll give you a parting gift. I'll show you how to fuck. I'll show you how to rock the world of any man you wanna give that to. I'll take off my fucking clothes, but first..." He grabbed my tank top with both hands and shredded it, stopping at the hem so that the front was ripped straight down the middle, but it was still technically on my body. "Yours."

He looked angry. Very angry. My heartrate spiked. And then he leaned in and ran his nose up the ridge of my ear and then sucked my earlobe into his mouth.

I started breathing heavily and wetness had already hit the gusset of my undies.

But, my heart hurt at just the notion of rocking some other guy's world. I pouted. And then I pulled my lip back in, but he saw it. I know he did, because I hadn't hidden it and now he had a smirk on his face.

And I felt like he was playing me.

And I did not care.

I pushed it away and grabbed his belt buckle and worked his jeans undone. I went down with the jeans, sultrily, like a burlesque dancer, letting them sit on his thighs, then my hands rose, and I dug my nails into his perfect ass cheeks as I took him deep into the back of my throat. How I didn't gag, I have no idea. Pure resolve, maybe. But, despite that the round studs on his dick were hitting the back of my throat, I sucked.

"Teeth, Jenna. Fuck," he growled and pulled my hair back a little.

I deflated and pushed him away and wiped my mouth.

I got to standing and, looking down, avoiding his eyes, I tried to move away. This wasn't gonna work. He didn't even like the way I gave blowjobs. And I hated giving blowjobs. Why was I trying to prove something to him?

He wasn't having it. The *me pulling away* part. He grabbed my hair and used it to bring my mouth to his. And then he was devouring me with his lips, his tongue.

I whimpered, half with arousal and half with frustration. He spun me to face the wall.

"You want it the way I like it?" He licked my collar bone.

"Rider." I don't know why I answered with his name.

"I want it rough, baby. Just a little bit rough. You can handle it, promise." His mouth was at my ear and I was melting.

"Do it," I heard myself say, and I was too much of a ball of sensation and firing synapses to think it through.

The yoga pants and panties went down to my ankles and he went down with them and then he bit into my ass cheek.

I jolted. "Ow!"

And then my ass was slapped with a ringing startling slap that made me gasp. He stood and almost immediately, I felt him, sliding between my legs.

"You okay with no condom?"

He'd already fucked me bare so what was the difference? I'd taken my birth control pill that day. I never forgot to take it.

"Hurry," I demanded.

He slammed inside and then his hand snaked around to my throat and he held it.

"You're makin' me fucking crazy, gorgeous girl. Crazy like I've never been crazy."

I whimpered, feeling everything he was giving me. He bit into my neck and I went liquid. My legs were trembling. That little voice in my head was trying to tell me to push him away, to get a grip, but I ignored it.

"You know how crazy you're making me? I really fuckin' get off on fightin' with you, baby. I don't get off on fightin' ever. Till you. Never fucked without a condom. Love this. Feeling nothing but you around me."

I shook my head. "No-ho. Ohgodohgod oh...right there. Right. Fucking. Ah! There!"

"Never been jealous, either. Till you. No one touches you but me. We're not over, Jenna. We're just getting started."

I whimpered. "Uh uh."

He was slamming into me. This felt so damn dirty. His jeans zipper was cutting into my upper thigh and I didn't even care. Because, if I complained, he might stop what he was doing, and I did not want it to stop.

Maybe not ever. He was hitting my g-spot. His fingers were holding my throat possessively and then his other hand went to my clit and he was pinching it or something and it felt crazy good.

"You really mean it when you say you want us over?" He demanded.

I moaned.

"Answer me."

"Yes," I said.

"Then why do you want this?" he demanded, slamming hard into me.

"I... oh fuck..." I was gonna come. This fast.

"Beg me not to stop. Or I'll stop."

"Don't stop. I'm close."

"I should stop."

"No..."

"You turn lazy after you come. I think I should keep you on edge until I'm close."

"No. Don't stop."

"Beg."

I didn't even hesitate for a split second this time. "Please, Rider. Ride me. Ride me, ride me. Fuck. Don't stop..."

"No date with Daniel."

"Nope."

"Never."

"Okay."

"No dates with anyone."

"Fuck...ah...fuck you," I grunted, so close, so deliciously close to climaxing.

"Want me to stop?"

"No. Don't. S-stop. Don't. Stop."

He thrust in over and over and over; a punishing rhythm that matched the rhythm of my begging. I heard each slap of skin and grunted in time with it. And then he pulled out and spun me and as his lips crashed into mine, it was a tumble and a cloud of hair and arms and legs, clothes flying off, and cusswords ground out as we hit the bed, my legs thrown up over his shoulders.

He was intently staring into my eyes while driving forward. Hard. So hard. I came, hard. I grabbed his hair and pulled his mouth to mine, crying into it. His eyes looked hard, angry.

I jolted in surprise.

He threw my legs back down, moved closer to my face, grabbed me by the jaw, and then his lips crashed into mine.

"Like to get hate fucked, Jenna?"

I gasped. "What?"

He laughed and tried to kiss me again.

I was about to pull away.

He kissed me anyway, letting go of my jaw to pin both arms over my head. He got them into the grip of one hand. He rammed hard. Then again. Then again, then pulled out.

"Gonna come all over your belly. Gonna write my name on this sweet body with my come. Mark you. Make sure you remember how good dirty can be."

I was in such shock that I was frozen, mouth open, staring, reeling. Coming to grips with what was happening right here. In disbelief.

And then he stroked his cock with hard, long strokes until streams of his come were landing, warm, on my belly. He was staring at my stomach, not at my face, so he didn't see what must've been horror on it.

And then he leaned over and ran his nose along my jawline and kissed my ear.

He leaned back on his knees and lifted his gaze to me and a smirk on his face melted clean away.

I was just lying there, staring, in shock.

He flinched.

"Jenna..." His eyes softened.

"Hate fuck?" I choked out hoarsely.

I felt my face crumpling.

He shook his head, paling, "It was a joke. It's not—-" He reached for me. "Baby..."

I scampered away, not letting him finish, and yanked my underwear and pants on. I ran to the bathroom and slammed the door and locked it, getting away from him before he could see me fall apart.

I felt the vibration of him pounding his fist against the door twice, but I kept leaning against it. I slid down slowly until I was on the floor, my forehead buried in my knees.

"Baby, don't take that literally. It's a game. Angry sex. That's all. There wasn't an ounce of hate in that."

"Fuck you and all your games." I jumped to my feet and started wiping his jizz off my belly with toilet paper. I looked at my reflection in the mirror. Oh no. Shit no. He gave me another damn hickey! It was hideous and big on my neck.

"Gorgeous..."

"Fuck! Off!" I screeched and threw the toilet paper into the toilet and turned the shower on.

I stripped my clothes off, noticing I again only had one sock on. And Jojo's tank top was half on me, but ripped, ruined. And I got in the shower and bawled while I shampooed my hair and scrubbed my stomach.

I heard an ugly smashing sound. He got in, pulling me into his arms, against his body. I tried to push him away, refusing to meet his eyes so he couldn't see that I was crying. He tightened his grip on me.

"Talk to me," he demanded, rubbing his hands up my back. He turned the shower off.

"I don't wanna talk to you. I'm furious. That you would say that to me? I have a fuck of a lot more respect for myself than to let myself be treated like this. Fucking someone who hates me..."

"I don't hate you. It wasn't like that. You gotta know that what I'm feeling is a long fuckin' way from hate. Hate fucking is just a rougher version of angry sex. It's a good way to deal with frustration. We're gonna learn a lot about one another. What I like. What you like. I'm lookin' forward to it. What we did wasn't even that. I was only teasin' because of the way you yanked my hair."

"Not like what you and your biker shithead friends did to that girl? We're done, Rider. That hate fucking thing was the last of it. So, I hope you enjoyed that shitty Jenna Murdoch lay, because it was the last time you'll have to endure it."

He clenched his jaw. "I explained about that gash, Jenna. Is that something you're gonna throw in my face for the rest of our lives?"

"Do not call women gashes! And what?" I did a double take. "The rest of our..." I frowned.

He smiled deviously.

I shook my head. "Out. I'm pissed at you, Rider. Go." I pointed.

He took my face into both hands. "Not going."

"Then I will. I'm going to bunk with Jojo."

I pulled away and exited the bathroom, which now had a broken door knob, to the suitcase on the floor by the bed and dragged on hot pink cheeky panties with the word PINK in silver glitter on the bum. I hadn't even taken the tags off. I quickly threw on the first thing I could find. The hoodie. *The* hoodie. She must've put it back in the suitcase she'd packed for me. It was on and I was thinking it needed to come off. I was about to take it back off when he was coming out of the bathroom in a towel. I started dragging my purse and that suitcase out, heading to the next door to the right. In just the hoodie and panties. I banged on the door.

"Jojo!" I hollered.

I saw Brady and that tall bald black guy, Alex or Axis, standing a few doors down in conversation. No. Axel.

He looked at me quizzically. I think I must've said his name as I remembered it. Or maybe he was looking at me like that because I was in my undies.

"Hiya," I waved and then stomped on by them and banged on the door next door to that. Which door was hers?

The door opened and a sleepy-looking older biker eyed me. And then he smiled a big smile with only a few teeth in his mouth.

Yikes.

"Oops, wrong door," I muttered and moved along.

"Jenna?" Jojo was popping her head out of the door next to that one. She had red eyes. She'd been crying. I had misty eyes too, but I hadn't broken down and cried yet.

Rider was coming up behind me, in his half unbuttoned jeans. "You're in your underwear, baby."

"Can I sleep here?" I asked Jojo, slapping his hand away.

"But I like the shirt you're wearing," he whispered into my ear, sounding like he found me hilarious.

She opened the door wider and I pulled my suitcase and handbag in, seeing we had even more of an audience. Several more bikers were in the hallway. Oh shit, one of them was Deke, Rider's dad. I hadn't even properly met him yet and here I was in my underwear with a *Property of Rider* shirt on.

"No!" I shoved Rider back, "Go hate fuck yourself!"

"Why are you crying? I asked Jojo.

"Luke. It's just... I read our old texts." She wiped her eyes. "I don't wanna talk about it. Why are you crying?"

"Hate sex with your brother," I said, and she looked like she was going to laugh but then she stopped herself. I realized we still had an audience. I shoved Rider back as hard as I could. "Go!"

He stepped back, and I shut the door.

"Why would he... why did I... oh fuck." I started to bawl.

"Oh honey..." she hugged me, and we were both bawling in one another's arms.

"I wasn't crying. I was holding it. I can't hold it anymore."

She nodded.

We both sat and cried a bit, drank some water, and I told her I didn't want to talk about Rider. She didn't wanna talk about Luke.

We were in her bed, which was smaller than mine and Rider's, Marshmallow between us (purring up a storm), and I fell asleep, tears wetting the pillow.

11

It was morning and Brady had already popped by with coffee and breakfast plates loaded up with bacon and eggs for us, waking us up far too early. I had a mild hangover, so he went and got me a couple of ibuprofens.

Jojo and I took turns showering and I was trying to put my crap aside and just be there for her. I'd decided it was my mission that day. To be supportive to my new friend. I'd also decided that even if I hated Rider's guts, I was going to be Jojo's friend. If Ella stayed with Deacon, that'd make it even easier to be friends with Jojo.

She'd lent me a very nice black wraparound dress and black heels. I wore a black shelf bra tank top underneath. She wore a black pencil skirt and black blouse with sheer sleeves.

The heels she lent me were a little snug, probably a size too small. I'd survive. They did look pretty fantastic with the dress I had on.

I left my long dark wavy hair loose and put on waterproof mascara and eyeliner as well as my blue-red lip stain that I had with me, in my bag. I put my sunglasses on, just as there was a knock at the door. I answered, because Jojo was in the washroom.

Rider. Wearing dark black jeans, black biker boots, a black dress shirt, and his Dominion Brotherhood black leather vest. He had a black band on his arm and his hair was pulled into a ponytail at his nape. He was clean shaven. Completely. Not a whisker on his face. His eyes pierced into me. He looked absolutely beautiful. So beautiful it hurt. His eyes traveled the length of my body and then back up to my face. I guess my eyes had done the same to him, but at least I had the sunglasses on, so he couldn't see it.

"Sleep okay?" he asked.

"Yes," I said, trying to be emotionless. "You?"

"Like shit. Missed you."

I had to hold firm and not react.

"We're gonna talk, me 'n' you, Jenna. After the funeral. Get to the bottom of all this shit. Okay?"

"We don't need to," I said.

His brows rose.

"There's no me and you, Rider. There won't be."

A lump in my throat sat, aching. I stepped aside so he could come fully in. People were walking by, eyeing us. I was thankful I had the dark glasses on.

"There is and you fuckin' know it," he snapped, then loudly called "Joelle!"

He'd cleared the door, so I closed it.

She came out of the bathroom, putting silver hoop earrings in.

"Hey," she said.

"You're in Jesse's pickup. So's Dad. Jenna's on the back of my bike."

I opened my mouth, about to protest, but he shot me a look that I read as threatening. It was a "don't argue" look. I wasn't about to argue with that expression on his face. That look on his face was almost blood-chilling.

Jojo reached for her purse and passed me mine and we left, leaving Marshmallow to her self-grooming on the bed.

When we got into the hallway, Rider grabbed my hand. I went to pull away and his hand tightened.

"What are you doing?" I demanded, through gritted teeth.

"Bunch of brothers saw you in your panties last night. Lucky for you my name was on your back, but you better believe they're also gonna see you holding my hand."

Okay then. I had no reply.

Shit, but my feet were already hurting from these tight shoes. I was in for a rough day ahead. For many reasons.

THE CONVOY TO THE FUNERAL home from the clubhouse was a long one. Dozens of motorcycles. Local Doms, Aberdeen ones, and ones with other city names on them, too. And some of the biker jackets had other club names on them. I saw at least five different emblems beyond

Dominion Brotherhood and I wondered if that meant that all these clubs would be against the Wyld Jackals.

I'd gotten a quick hug from Deacon and then from Spencer outside when Rider grabbed a helmet from him and pulled me away from Spencer, shooting him a dirty look. I almost tripped at the jolt backwards. I collided with Deacon, who steadied me.

I saw Spencer shoot Rider a weird look and step back.

"Where's Ella?" I'd asked Deacon, to break the loaded silence.

"She's outta town safe with her Ma and Beau. 'Til shit calms."

I was thankful she was okay. And far away from the nonsense. That said something about Deacon, at least.

Rider had grabbed my hand and pulled me to the vintage bike we'd ridden on the day before.

That was when Deke came over to us. "Hey, Rider's Pink Lady." He winked.

"Hi." Oh God. Talk about mortified.

"We haven't officially met yet." He kissed me on the forehead and gave me a hug. "Though I thank you for your patronage at The Roadhouse. You gave the place a boost just showin' up that few times. Lookin' forward to gettin' to know you better, Jenna."

"Hi," I repeated again, stupidly, feeling embarrassed that he was one of the ones who'd seen me dragging a suitcase down the hall the night before, drunk, angry, and in underwear. Of course he did. Just my luck that Rider's dad would witness that. I shouldn't care what Rider's dad thinks of me. Yet, I couldn't help it.

"Hi." He returned, his mouth twitching with humor, and he moved to Jojo and put his arm around her and led her to Jesse's pickup truck as Rider secured the helmet on my head.

He was President of the Aberdeen chapter, so I wasn't sure why he wasn't riding a motorcycle himself.

THE ALMOST TWO HOURS at the visitation before sitting down for the service weren't easy.

First of all, when we walked into the funeral home, there was a wall of photos and I saw the many images of a long-haired, tall, dark, and incredibly handsome Luke 'Lick' Hanson. And I had video flashbacks of him. Of Scooter. Of Rider. I tried to push it away. There were loads of pictures of him with the brothers of the Dominion Brotherhood. There was one picture of Jojo with him in a headlock and my heart seized at that. She was staring at it, too. I grabbed her hand. She leaned into me. She started to move toward the front of the room, toward Deacon and Spencer, so I let go of her hand. They flanked her and followed her up. There was a large poster-sized photo of him on an easel, beside a closed coffin.

I heard a female voice stage-whispering behind me.

"Couldn't do open casket because he got himself decapitated in that wreck."

I felt my body seize. Rider's body moved closer to mine and I couldn't help but lean into him. My knees had buckled at that comment.

"Ma, fuck," Rider snapped. "Get her outta here," he clipped, and two bikers I didn't recognize moved in. Shelly glared at Rider while they ushered her out, away from a bunch of other older ladies. She was dressed in a black leather strapless dress, way too much black eye makeup on. Fishnet stockings. So *not* classy it wasn't funny.

Jojo was up front and she was in Deacon's arms, bawling.

My heart hurt seeing her shoulders shake, hearing that painful sound coming from her.

I looked at Rider. He was staring up at the front and his jaw was ticking.

"I can sit if you wanna go up," I whispered. There were a few empty chairs against the wall.

"Come?" he asked softly, and with the look on his face, I couldn't help but nod. He took my hand and we slowly made our way to the front. He was walking so slow that my guess was that he was delaying the inevitable. Rider was not looking forward to being at that coffin. And he wouldn't. Who would?

When we got there, amid flowers and many other bikers, I saw another mural of photos. I saw Rider and Luke both in a field, on ATVs both covered in muck with big smiles on muddy faces. He was in several of the group shots. I guess he and Luke "Lick" Hanson had been close. I looked at his face as his eyes moved around the photos and I saw pain there.

A lady and man were standing there, by the coffin, faces pale, eyes haunted and on Rider.

"Mrs. Hanson. Mr. Hanson." Rider reached out and shook his hand and then moved to the lady and gave her a hug.

"My girlfriend, Jenna," he introduced, and I shook hands with them both.

"About time," Mr. Hanson said to Rider, softly, a little bit of a smile tugging at his lips while he motioned to me, and Rider gave him a tight smile.

"Thank you for coming," Mr. Hanson said to me. And he had kind eyes. Sad, but kind.

Mrs. Hanson just stood there, looking almost zombie-like.

"My condolences," I said, or more croaked, trying and failing to ignore the emotions Rider's introduction had churned up.

Rider's free hand landed on the casket and he stood there and closed his eyes. I just stood there, holding his other hand. Why was I here? Why did he want me by his side for this? I didn't agree to be his girlfriend. Why did he want me to be after all that'd happened so far?

He took a breath and his eyes tightened. And I, for some reason, squeezed his hand.

His eyes moved to me. And I saw the bleak stark pain at the loss of his friend.

Something snapped inside me at seeing that pain on his face and so, before calculating the move, I moved in and put my arms around him. He buried his face into my neck and squeezed. I felt weak in the knees. He was a little shaky. And holding me a little too tight.

I just stood there, holding him, feeling for him. For all of them.

I was chewing the inside of my cheek raw in an effort to keep the tears away. I had no right to cry. I didn't know Luke Hanson. I only barely knew the Valentines.

Rider grabbed my hand again and we moved out of the room, thankfully. He grabbed a pair of dark glasses from his pocket and put them on and we went back outside. We stood in a circle with a bunch of bikers, most of which were smoking cigarettes or standing there vaping. Some Doms, some from other motorcycle clubs. Some men just in suits and not biker gear. The parking lot was crawling with motorcycles.

I saw Scooter, who was still looking a bit beat up, but much better than the last time I'd seen him. He saw me and quickly looked the other way, looking embarrassed, maybe. He lit a cigarette and I knew he was hoping I'd look away.

"Cherry," the large bartender from Deke's Roadhouse approached and gave me a jolly hug, pulling my attention away from Scooter.

"Hi," I greeted.

"Cherry?" Rider growled at him, looking ready to throw down and fight him.

"Yeah, she likes cherries in her drinks," the guy said, innocently. "Like...14 of them."

"Name's Jenna," Rider said, almost snarled.

"All right," he waved his hands defensively. "Guess I picked the way wrong fruit for a nickname."

"I'd fuckin' say you did," Rider snapped.

I gave the bartender, I think his name was Little John, an apologetic smile. "I'll ask for extra limes or olives next time."

He laughed. A few others in the group laughed. Rider's face was still hard.

Deacon approached us and then Rider's body tightened, and he seemed like he was even angrier.

What now?

"Can you take care of her for me for a sec?" Rider asked Deacon. Deacon gave him a chin jerk and put his arm around me. I watched Rider stride purposefully across the parking lot and stop at an absolutely gorgeous blonde girl, around my age.

She was dressed in a black dress, she had loads of beautiful blonde hair that fell to her waist. He grabbed her by the wrist and pulled her around to the other side of a big passenger van, out of sight.

My scalp prickled in response.

"You okay?" Deacon asked, jiggling me with the arm that was around me.

I nodded and looked up at him. He was even taller than Rider. And then I shrugged. "No. But how's everything for you?" I asked.

"It's amped." He gave me a squeeze and kept his arm around me.

"Is Ella all right?"

"She's good," he replied, and he got a twinkle in his brown and amber eyes.

"I can't remember the last time I've gone this long with not talking to her, seeing her."

"She misses you. She'd been worryin' about you. My brother taking good care of ya?"

"No," I said softly.

He looked angry. "Why? What's up?"

I shook my head. "I don't... I can't..."

"Listen," he said, the anger melting away. "Whatever you two are dealing with, it's gonna be harder with all this shit goin' on. Hanson's death is gonna fuck with him, but he's gonna have trouble showin' it. Just take things a breath at a time and let him keep you safe." He gave me another squeeze.

"There's no us two, Deacon. He's not... this is just a game."

He shook his head. "Nope. He's playin' for keeps, Jenna. Never seen him like this." He gave me a pointed look.

I blinked.

He gave me another squeeze, as if to drive the message home.

"Ride and I are close. I'm not just his brother, I'm his *brother*. Trust me. He says he wants to be with you, he fuckin' well does. Introducing you as his woman? He's a joker, but he wouldn't joke about that. Believe it."

I blew out a breath. We were talking low, but I noticed Deke had his eyes and ears on us. My eyes met his and he, Spencer, and Deacon all had the same eyes.

Deke gave me a nod. He was wordlessly agreeing with Deacon.

I chewed my cheek.

And I decided right there that regardless, I liked Deacon. And Deke. I also didn't know how to feel about those words from Deacon, the confirmation from Deke.

Spencer moved closer to me, "Hey," he said. He lit a cigarette and leaned against the wall and leveled a gaze on me. "You been takin' care of Joelle. Thank you."

I shrugged. "We've been keeping each other company while being under lock down or whatever you guys call it."

"Naw, you've been doin' more. Thank you," Spencer said, with feeling. His eyes told me he knew how rough all this was on his sister.

Maybe Spencer wasn't a complete jerk.

Rider was beside me again, the blonde mysteriously gone. Deacon let go of me and Rider put his arm around me and kissed my temple.

I stood still.

"She's been taking great care of Jojo," he said, pulling me tighter against his side, obviously having heard Spencer.

Jojo was off to the side with Brady and they were making their way toward us. She was pale and puffy-eyed.

"The service is starting in five minutes. Let's go get seats?" she suggested. "Luke's parents had space reserved for our family."

I linked arms with her, giving me an opportunity to move away from Rider. I moved inside with the rest of the Valentines. But, then I saw, across the parking lot, the other Valentine. Formerly.

Shelly was standing there, smoking a cigarette and talking on her phone, an absolutely venomous look on her face as her eyes followed the family she'd thrown away.

I saw Rider throw her a look and then we were inside. We moved into a chapel and sat in the row behind Luke's parent's. Jojo was on my right, Rider on my left, at the end of the aisle and I'd held Jojo's hand during the service.

We sat through the twenty-minute service, the minister speaking, saying prayers, and I hadn't had much experience with death or funerals, but it felt like he was giving a fairly generic service.

After saying a series of prayers, he said, "Lucas's friend Rider would like to say a few words."

Jojo's hand started to shake. I squeezed it and watched him walk up to the podium.

And I was transfixed by it. By his face. His body language. His gestures. His voice. He spoke well. Clear. Composed. But with feeling. So much feeling that I felt more guilt at Deacon's words sinking in, thinking about all the photos of Rider and Luke, realizing he'd been carrying the pain of this loss quietly the past few days.

"Lucas Arthur Hanson was a recently patched member of the Dominion Brotherhood Motorcycle Club. No one called him Lucas. Some, his parents, coupla girls... called him Luke. To the rest of us, he was Lick. Or Hanson. But, despite only recently getting his patch, he was one of us for over a decade. He was a brother to many men in this room. Looked up to many of you half his life. He was there for me through many rough times the past twelve years. Some of which, he was there without being there, because he couldn't be. But he was where he was because he *was* such a good friend. He was around for a whole lot of good times, too. Lick was the reason for a lot of good times." He stopped and moistened his lips, then continued.

"Lick liked to have a good time. Lick loved his brothers and Lick was an only child, and he was tight with his folks, but he always wanted the big, loud, obnoxious family you get when you're in an MC. He wanted that his whole life. He had to prove he was ready, so he waited a long time to be brought in as a prospect, but he proved he was committed, and once he got his shot, he took to the brotherhood like a fish who'd finally got put in water where he belonged. He woulda got his patch much earlier, but he had to do a stint with the state until a few years ago when he started prospecting for us.

He was the kind of guy willing to give you the shirt off his back. The kinda guy willin' to do time for a brother, even. That time he did was a prime example of the kind of brother he was. Many of you in this room get my drift. But..."

He took a breath and smiled a beautiful smile that stole my breath for a second.

"He was also the kinda brother who'd shave your head and draw a unibrow with a Sharpie if you passed out before he decided the party was over. He was always the last to pass out, always. And many in this room have faced the fallout of fallin' asleep too early."

Chuckles broke out in the room.

"And you were lucky if it was a Sharpie, because the alternative was his tattoo gun. Brady knows."

There were louder chuckles through the room and a lot of people looking over their shoulders to Brady, who was laughing, standing against the wall at the back of the jam-packed chapel. My eyes moved from the sea of biker vests, tattoos, and beards back there to the turquoise eyes at the podium.

Rider's expression went sober again. "He told me, years ago, he'd always known he'd die young. Lick knew it. He just felt it. He wanted to live his life *full throttle*. And that was what he did. He found his way. And he was taking steps to put down roots, too, though he hadn't shared that directly with me yet. And knowin' the man he was, I gotta believe he had his reasons. Anyway... Lick wanted something, he went for it, fuck the consequences. He loved his family, he loved his club, and he loved to ride his motorcycle. We'll miss you man. You were an amazing artist and I am thrilled to have so much of that art on my skin. I carry it with pride." Rider looked to the large photo of Luke off to the side. It was a photo of him leaning against the side of the clubhouse, dressed in full biker gear, a big smile on his face.

"And now, I've finally got the best hair in the club. Thanks, man." More chuckles. "Thanks, man. For everything. You know what you've been to me. At least I hope you do. Love ya. See you on the flipside." He stepped down, rapped twice on the coffin with his knuckles, and moved down to our spot the second row back. I thought he'd sit, but instead, he reached for my hand and jerked his chin. He lifted his sunglasses out of his pocket and gave a flick to open them up and put them on his face. I rose and took his hand and he walked, with me, through a room packed to the brim, and out the door.

I followed my aching feet in silence until we got to his motorcycle. I couldn't read his face with his sunglasses on. His mouth was in a tight line as he buckled my helmet on.

"You good for a long ride? I need it," he asked. But, it wasn't a question, because there was no way I could say no.

I gave my head a jerk, a little confused.

"Tap my left elbow if you need me to pull off."

I blinked and then I nodded.

He climbed onto the bike and waited. I stood a second, and then shook myself free of my daze and climbed on behind him and put my one arm around his middle, using my other hand to hold the dress closed (wrap dresses were not recommended for motorcycle riding, FYI). We were off before anyone else came outside.

12

The ride was obviously a 'clearing of the mind' ride. We must've ridden for an hour or longer, and though it started off feeling heavy, I can honestly say that by the time we stopped at a dead end, I realized it was probably cathartic for me, too. Something about the open road was just, I don't know, helpful.

Lick was an only child...he wanted the family you get when you're in an MC.

I'd been thinking about how I'd spent so much time at Ella's because I wanted to be in a big family. And Ella was an only child until a few years ago; her baby brother was born when we were in high school. So, Ella's family was the same size as mine. But, it never felt lonely over there. There were always people in and out, always big meals. Always lots of laughter. They invited people without family for Sunday dinners, for family game nights, for Christmas dinner.

If Paul and Karen Murdoch had more than just me, would my house have felt any different than it did? I doubted it.

I always told myself I'd eventually, when I found the right guy, have a big brood, lots of kids so that my kids wouldn't ever be lonely. Once my parents were gone, it'd be just me. I didn't have cousins. My mom had a sister, but she didn't have kids. My dad was an only child. I wanted a big family, so I'd need to make one.

We stopped by a guard rail and I could see that beyond it was a little bit of a clearing. A trail.

He turned the bike off and I got off. He got off.

"Can you do this in those shoes?" he asked, taking the helmet from me and setting it on the seat. "I need to go somewhere that, somewhere..." He didn't finish. I couldn't read his face behind his dark glasses, but I didn't need to. His mouth was in a tight line.

I nodded. I shouldn't have; my feet had already been killing me.

Ten minutes of walking along behind him on a worn-in trail, I could take no more. I took the shoes off and was walking in stockings. The ground was cold.

He was just ahead of me. He looked over his shoulder.

"Shoes are a bit small for me," I said, noticeably limping.

"Shit," he said. "Hop up." He crouched and crooked his arms.

"Naw..."

"Hop. Up." he insisted.

So, I did. And Rider piggybacked me.

"Shouldn't have said you were okay in those, Jenna."

He was right. Though I didn't know how long we'd be walking or what the terrain would be like.

"You need this," I whispered.

He didn't respond verbally, but his body halted for a second and he was just standing there with me on his back. It was loaded silence. I was wondering how long he was gonna stand there when he started moving forward again.

After a long while, we were in a clearing with a view that was staggering. We were on top of a hill, looking down into a beautiful valley. We were by a fire pit dugout and there were trees and not-very-well-made wooden benches surrounding it. It looked like a place that had seen loads of bush parties.

I saw empty beer bottles, a broken glass pipe, and some condom wrappers. Yep. That's exactly where we were. But, the view of the valley below was incredible.

He put me down on the grass, took off his biker jacket and put it on the bench and gestured for me to sit.

"I would've expected a biker would never give up his leather for some girl to sit on," I mused.

He smiled and took his sunglasses off. "Depends on who the girl is. She's his, he'll give her anything."

My heart stopped. I looked away.

He sat and patted the jacket beside him, spreading it out so that I wouldn't sit on the pocket, which I could see had stuff in it.

My heart managed to start up again. I sat down.

I stared out ahead. Leaves were beginning to turn. In a few weeks, this view would be breathtaking.

"He did your tattoos for you?" I broke the silence after a while. After a long while. But, it wasn't awkward silence. I could tell that Rider was here because of his friendship with Luke. This place had meaning to that friendship.

"Yeah. All of 'em."

"You were close," I stated.

"We used to party here. We used to hang here when we had to get away. Spent a lotta time up here. Felt like a good place to go after... that. His ashes should be scattered from up here. I'm gonna ask his parents if we can have some of them."

He reached for the inside pocket of his jacket and pulled out two airplane bottles of Jack Daniels.

He passed me one.

I looked at it and then looked at him. He opened his and held it up in a silent toast to the sky.

I quickly opened mine and raised it.

He downed his. I downed mine, first fighting to breathe against, and then relishing, the burn.

I felt more than a bit bad. I hadn't factored the dead friend into my thoughts the last few days. He'd been carrying that, along with everything else, around the past few days. But, he hadn't let on. I thought about how Jojo said Rider let stuff roll off his back.

But, despite that, I could see he was affected right now.

"He was talented with the tattoos," I said.

"He did time for me."

"Oh?"

"Fucked up. I was eighteen. We were doing a stupid b and e. Just bein' assholes to this bar owner who pissed us off, 'cuz he wouldn't serve us. Shit was whacked. We just wanted to steal a couple bottles. But, we tripped the silent alarm and the security guard who showed got hurt. Shouldn't have gone so bad. I fucked up. We took off on foot, but he got caught. Never ratted me out even though I was just as guilty as him. They offered him a deal. He was sixteen almost seventeen. They tried him as an adult. They woulda given him a lower sentence. He wouldn't rat."

I winced.

"My Dad and Rudy said they wouldn't let him in the club when he got out. They said he was too much of a liability. He'd wanted it. He fuckin' needed it. I fessed up about my involvement in that b&e. Dad gave me a kick in the ass and schooled me on not being a stupid ass. Then, when Lick got out, they greeted him with a prospect cut. Most prospects do it a year, two max if they're gettin' in. He did it for three before they gave him his patch. He had to finish probation, prove himself. Fuck, but he wanted that patch. Just glad he got it before he died."

We sat in silence a minute.

"Wish I knew what the fuck he was thinkin' about my sister, though," he said.

"He treated her like she was precious. He never... They never... She's still a... virgin." My face got hot.

He blew out a breath, his posture loosening.

"I could get kicked out of the sisterhood if you say I said that. So... keep that under your hat."

He let out another breath, and stared straight ahead.

"He must've held back because he cared about her. Cared about all of you," I added. "You did really well with the eulogy."

Rider looked at me and then his hand came up and tucked my hair behind my ear.

"You look beautiful today," he said.

My lips parted. He was giving me some intensity with his eyes.

"You're showin' me what you're made of, too," he said.

My eyebrows furrowed.

"Pissed at me, but not bein' a bitch. Bein' cool to my sister, my family. Not contradicting me around the brothers. Bein' there for me up at that...that fuckin' coffin. Tryin' to keep up and walk through the bush in nylons when your feet are sore because I needed it. Tryin' to get me to talk about him up here, 'cuz you think it'll help me to let some of it out. Dad's always told us you can tell a lot about a woman by how she deals in the middle of a shit storm."

My face reddened. I was surprised that he'd paid such close attention. I shrugged, staring at my hands, which were fiddling with the empty airplane bottle. "Just because things are screwy with you and me, I shouldn't take it out on her. I wouldn't. Or anyone else. Anyone can see you're all in pain over what's happening."

"Okay. So, when you gonna stop punishing me?" he asked.

My eyes moved up to meet his and they were more than serious. But they were also warm.

"Punishing you?"

"If you're this good to me when you're pissed at me, I can only guess how things'd be if you and me were solid. You know I want you. You know I want us. You're holdin' me back as hard as you can."

"Of course I am."

"Why?"

"I'm protecting myself," I said in a rare moment of transparency.

"From what?"

"From..." I swallowed. "This isn't the time to get into this. You're emotional. You've lost a good friend. Another good friend's girlfriend got killed. People are after you. Your family business and clubhouse burnt down. I should be the last of your concerns."

"But yet you're not. You're not." His eyes pierced mine. "You're first."

"I don't know what that means."

"Yes, you do. For fuck sakes, Jenna." He glared at me.

I shrank back and closed my eyes.

"I'm just a distraction for you," I said.

He started at me, incredulously. And then he shook his head. "No. You're not."

He grabbed my hand and held it to his thigh, moving his lips to right by my ear. "I want us. Can't even tell you how fuckin' good I feel seein' my name on your back. Havin' you by my side. I want what I see you're capable of giving. I take back what I said about you being selfish. You're not. I was wrong. I've seen behind the wall the past few days. A few of us have. What

I've seen while you're holding back, can't wait to see what I'll get when I get that wall down."

I chewed on my cheek, thinking, *that's never gonna happen*. But, almost wishing that it *could* happen.

"Except the 'in bed' part. You're selfish there. But I can work with you. Teach you."

I glared at him.

He smirked.

I rolled my eyes.

He was mourning his friend. It wouldn't be nice to do this now.

But, it also wouldn't be fair to either of us to *not* do it. I needed to put a stop to the madness. It hurt too much, this game he was playing. As much as I was trying to fend him off, I was failing. And I couldn't put my heart on the line for a guy who acted like this was a game, a joke. He might not be acting like that now, but that's how he'd been all along.

"You're allergic to commitment, I've heard," I said.

"That's what they say."

"But?"

"But, I wouldn't say I was allergic to it. Just never met anyone I wanted to try it with. Never liked the drama and bullshit. The takin' and no givin' back. Saw it all around me. My parents. My brothers. Buddies. Club members. Drama...fuck..."

"Well, I'm all about the drama." I folded my arms across my chest. "So..." I was about to say I was a bad pick, but he cut me off.

"Don't give a fuck. You make me wanna give it a try."

I stared at him.

He stared at me.

"This is a heavy day," I said finally. "Not the time to think about this stuff."

"Having you with me through this *has* helped. Helps me see that there's a lot to a relationship. A lot both people can get out of it."

"Besides shitty sex and monotonous monogamy?" I mumbled.

"Hey. I was an asshole. I'm sorry about that. We were fighting. I fight dirty. And I'll say again, I didn't have all the facts."

I rolled my eyes.

"You fight dirty, too, baby. You've slapped me, punched me, tried to bash my brains in with a Maglite, wished me dead... should I go on?"

"Exactly. And you act like it's all a joke," I muttered.

"Having you up there when I had to see that coffin, know it was him inside. Broken. So fuckin' broken it had to be kept shut? Havin' you helped. Smellin' your hair, feeling you reach for me? To give me what you knew I needed? Fuck."

There went that burning feeling in my chest again. But, this was an even deeper burn than I'd had so far. Because the idea of having someone for me, for when I needed them to lean on? That would be huge. But, I didn't know that I'd ever let myself show that I needed that. To anyone.

I was Jenna Murdoch -—good time girl. I'd have anyone's back, if they needed me, but I rarely showed the need for that. Other than Ella, and I was sure even Ella would describe me as strong, independent, and not needing anyone or anything, unless it was a partner in crime to have fun with.

But the way he'd had *my* back a few times so far? What would that be like to have all the time?

"How's that for a joke? I ain't playing. Not gonna be like the rest and give up on you," he stated.

I had to ignore that. I had to ignore that because it felt like my eyes were filled with broken glass all of a sudden. And if I blinked, it'd be all over. I'd be fully exposed. He heard me say that last night. Why the heck did I say that out loud?

We sat in silence for a minute as I did the best I could to beat the emotion back. And then he was using his phone texting or something, then said, "We should get back to the club."

He got to his feet and took the bottles from the bench and stuffed them into his jacket pocket. He grabbed my shoes and passed them to me. I squeezed my sore feet into them, then stood and lifted his leather jacket from the bench and passed it to him. He shrugged it on and then leaned over, motioning for me to hop back onto his back.

I did, feeling something pretty powerful inside of me the walk back to the bike.

I LOVED THE FEELING of riding on the back of his motorcycle. Something about it was so soothing. And I shouldn't be on the back of his bike because of how deeply I loved it. It wasn't just the mode of transportation. It was him and me on that bike. Together. Like we were a unit. A *Rider and Jenna* unit. But all the way back to the clubhouse, I reveled in it. I let myself feel it. I let myself muse with *What If*. What if this was real? What if I was really his? And what if I didn't have to guard myself?

He had my back with my mother. He helped sort things out for the salon while I was away as well as Kendra's wedding. He was dealing with all my abuse toward him in order to make sure no one raped and killed me.

How would riding his bike with him feel if I had let go of my fears? How amazing would it be to be with him, carefree?

Far too soon, we were back at the clubhouse gates and I noticed the yellow tape was gone, as we went in that way. Two prospects, one that I'd seen back in Aberdeen, but couldn't recall where, maybe Deke's Roadhouse, opened them for us.

When Rider turned the bike off, the other guy stepped up and shook his hand in what looked like a complicated bro-shake.

"Great job on it," he said.

"It's sick!" Another few bikers approached. "Swear to God you'd never know it wasn't from sixty years ago. Dress your babe like a pin-up, buddy. Do a photo shoot and you'll sell a shitload of these."

I got off of it, looking at the bike, seeing what the fuss was about. I'd thought it was a great bike, figured he'd maybe had a classic, or restored it himself. I didn't know it was a custom-made new bike. He'd told me he did custom bikes. This was one of them? He was talented.

"Thanks, man," Rider said somewhat solemnly and moved me forward. "My babe's gotta get outta these heels. They're hurtin' her feet. See you guys in a few."

He moved me forward toward the building.

I was really looking forward to getting out of these shoes. But, all I had with me were the Converse I'd had on my feet when I got kidnapped from

Ella's room. Would it be frowned upon if I changed clothes? Maybe I could just hang out in the room and skip this luncheon.

"Blow," he said to a guy inside the door and they hugged with back slaps.

"Just got here. Ran late. This her?" The guy asked. He was a tall, muscled fair-haired guy in his mid to upper 30s with piercing grey eyes. He reached for me and lifted me up off the ground, making me gasp as he hugged me.

He gently set me back on my feet.

"Yeah," Rider said, and I glanced over my shoulder and saw Rider had a little smile on his face.

"You Aberdeen girls are legendary!" the guy said. "Chaining unchainable Valentines? They're droppin' like flies. First Deacon, then Ride? Spency!" he hollered.

Spencer made his way over from a crowd of bikers who were sitting at picnic tables smoking and talking, drinking beers, over to us.

"You hitch your wagon to an Aberdeen star yet?"

Spencer snickered, taking a haul off his cigarette. "Not yet. Gonna up my game, though. All the good ones're getting snatched up fast."

"Jenna. Blow, also known as Sean O'Grady. He'll be our VP at home..." Rider started the introduction.

"If he ever gets his ass in gear," Deke added, and approached Blow and they did the biker hug back slap and bro-shake thing.

"See you guys in a minute. Jenna needs more comfortable shoes."

"Eh..." Deke said and approached Rider. He hooked a hand behind Rider's neck and kissed his forehead.

"Love you," Deke said to Rider.

"Love you," Rider replied, gruffly.

I choked up. Audibly. Shit. I had to hold it together.

Deke put his arm around me and gave me a kiss on the cheek and then squeezed my free hand.

I gave him a bit of a watery smile, almost losing it. What an emotional day. It was taking everything in me to hold tears in. I wanted a hot bubble bath, a bath bomb with sparkles, and to sit and cry it out.

I had no idea when that'd happen.

"I set you up, honey," The lady, Delia, I'd met the day before, the mouth-kissing one, said, moving past the doorway, which was propped open. She had a steaming lasagna tray in her hands, just a towel around it; she wasn't wearing oven mitts. Eek. "Another pair of shoes on your bed."

"Oh. Thank you," I said. How did she know?

"Go take time to rest those feet and then come give us a hand in the kitchen," she informed me and moved along.

I saw that long tables were set up with all sorts of food and many funeral garb-wearing biker women were coming in and out, bringing more food.

Rider led us through the throng of people, most of which gave him a wide berth or just a chin lift. His exit from the funeral home would've spoken volumes and it was heartwarming that they seemed to respect that and were giving him space.

As soon as we were down a few hallways and no one was around, I said, "Wait." We stopped, and I used his arm for stability as I got Jojo's shoes off. My poor, poor feet.

"Texted Delia to find you something for your feet."

"That's how she knew. Thank you," I said softly.

Wow. He was showing himself to be pretty thoughtful. I'd been hoping to use my sore feet as a reason to stay in the room and avoid human interaction, but I guess I'd have to make an appearance.

At least I'd been summoned to the kitchen, so I'd get some distance from him. From him and all he was making me feel. I didn't know how much more sweetness I could take before I just threw myself into his arms and surrendered. No, not just surrendering -—declaring myself his love slave.

Inside our room, I saw a pair of new black thong flip flops on the end of the unmade bed, tags still on them. They were thick, like memory foam, the part that went between the toes was velvety, and I was sure they would feel wonderful.

He pulled his glasses off and grabbed a bottle of vodka sitting on the chair at the side of the unmade bed and took a swig and then flopped back.

I guess he'd gotten that after I vacated last night.

I saw that my stuff, or rather the stuff Jojo had lent me, was back in here. That made me want to fume a bit, but my angry resolve was fading.

I went into the bathroom and pulled the now-ruined stockings off, checked my make-up, used the facilities, and then I came back out and was trying to separate the flip flops, which were held together with one of those plastic loops. It was proving difficult and I didn't want to break them. I heard a click and saw he was holding out a big knife, that he'd switched open.

I lifted the shoes over the exposed blade and brought them down and it cut through the plastic loop like butter.

"Thanks," I muttered and separated them. He closed the switchblade and dropped it onto an opened black gym bag on the floor.

I put the flip flops on, glad that my pedicure from Saturday night pedicures with Pippa and Bronto was still fairly intact and that I wasn't rocking Frodo feet or anything.

"Come here," he said.

I looked at him.

He was lying there, on his back. He opened up his arms.

I stared.

"Please?" he asked.

I sat on the side of the bed instead of climbing on top of him, like I wanted to do.

"I wanna talk about this," he stated, eyes serious.

"This?" I asked stupidly. Wanting, wishing I could touch his smooth face, which he'd shaved for the funeral. It looked so good.

"Us."

I blinked. "Who was the blonde?"

He gave his head a shake, annoyed with me.

"At the funeral home. The one you left me with Deacon to cart off," I clarified.

"I knew what you meant."

"And why did you—-"

"Are you interested in being with me?" he cut me off.

"That's not answering my question."

"If you're with me, you can ask me questions like that. If you're not, then it's none of your business."

"If something about you is none of my business, then *I'm* none of your business and therefore you have no reason to keep me here," I fired back.

"You're playin' it that way?" he challenged. "Like you're fine goin' out there and putting yourself at risk knowing there was a direct threat against you? Mantis, Jackals' Prez himself, called me personally to tell me just what they wanted to do to you. And I told you what they did to Edge's woman, so you know he's not blowin' smoke."

I was being unreasonable; I knew I was. I was stubborn, though, and was feebly trying to hold my ground. My ground that wasn't solid ground, it was quicksand.

He must've seen it in my eyes and come to a decision. "Gianna, Kailey's stepsister. She wasn't welcome at the funeral now that I know she's got family ties to the woman responsible for all this. I let her know that and got her out of there before she got in there."

"Jojo says she's a great girl. Loves your club." I was fuming because I was also thinking about the fact that Jojo told me the lovely Gia had been with all three of her brothers at least once each.

He shrugged. "That may be true, but until all this shit is sorted, I'm not takin' chances. Won't be putting Joelle or you at risk. There's shit goin' down all around us. Moles in Aberdeen, even. The only good thing about the Roadhouse being closed right now is that it's forcin' us to keep to ourselves, rather than being under microscopes out in public. My dad's not even thinkin' about re-opening until things die down with this feud. Now, about us..."

"Did you build that motorcycle?" I asked.

He smirked. "Jenna."

I swallowed. "It's beautiful."

"Thanks, gorgeous."

"I thought it was a classic. Something vintage. I don't know anything about bikes, but it's beautiful. You must be talented."

"Thanks, babe. Me and Spence. Not just my design."

"I'd better go help your Aunt Delia."

He watched me for a beat. "You okay to go help in the kitchen?"

"Yeah," I said, feeling relieved, thinking I was getting away with not having an 'Us' talk.

"So, to give you the lay of the land, things're not 21st century feminist-friendly around here. Especially right now. The women like to baby us at times like these. It gives them something to do when they feel powerless about loss. But, if Aunt Delia's invited you to help, it means she likes you. She shoos off bitches if she doesn't like them. She's like a second mother to us. No, like a first mother. She's done more for us than Shelly ever has other than giving birth. Delia wants you in there with the women, it's an honor for her to invite you."

I nodded, feeling a little warm at the idea of being accepted so readily.

"There'll be food and people shootin' the breeze. And then kids'll disappear and it'll go full-on wake."

"Okay."

"It'll get rowdy. It always does."

"Okay."

"You've been introduced as mine. No one should try anything with you. To be safe, you stick close to me until you've had enough and then I'll walk you back here. If I think things're too rowdy, I may decide to bring you back here earlier."

I tilted my head curiously. "You might decide to bring me back here."

"Yeah."

"Before I'm ready to be brought back here," I confirmed.

"Right. Gonna need you to trust my judgement on that. It'll be a good time. We feel that loss through the funeral and then we celebrate his life. Have the kinda party he'd wanna be at. That's how we roll. It gets rowdy, you call it a night."

I shook my head. "Me."

He looked at me like I was dim, so I clarified.

"Me, but not necessarily you?"

His lips twitched a little bit, but he didn't reply.

"All right Captain Caveman, we'll see."

"Not, we'll see. I tell you it's time for bed, I don't want lip about it." And now he looked like he was messing with me.

I glared. "Well. I guess I'd better not give you lip then."

He looked at me with amusement. "Your eyes are huge right now. And angry. And your body language tells me you'll be givin' me lip."

"Good you can read my body language this soon in our acquaintance."

"Jenna. I fuckin' get hard at your lip. And your lips. And your hips." He reached over and put his hand to my hip.

I backed away. "Whatever. Show me to the kitchen so I can go be useful."

I headed toward the door. He grabbed me and spun me around.

"You reflect on me here today. You been doin' good so far."

I laughed. "I ran away from you in the middle of the night drunk in my underwear. And your Dad saw me. How on Earth is that 'doin' good so far'?"

"That was last night. Today is today. Things're different during a funeral. And different still at the after-party. This next few hours are important."

"I wouldn't reflect on you if you hadn't incorrectly identified me as your woman."

"It's what you are," he said.

I shook my head. "No. That's you being delusional."

"How do I change your mind?" he asked.

I scoffed.

"Be serious here for a minute."

I rolled my eyes. "Like you are? Like you ever are? It's all just a big joke to you."

He took my face into both hands and got close. Super close. "I'm serious."

And I couldn't challenge that, because he looked serious.

"How? How do I change your mind?" he asked.

"This isn't the time for this."

Oh God, I'm gonna cave; I know I am. And I want to. I want to so badly. But, is that smart?

"Baby, it is the time. You're helping me through this and gotta say, it'll help me a whole lot more to know you and me are starting from here as a you and me."

"This is emotional blackmail, Rider Valentine," I breathed.

"Is it working?" he asked, his thumbs caressing my cheeks.

It was. It *totally* was.

He moved even closer.

"So, you good about what I've said about out there?" he asked.

I shrugged, sinking into his eyes.

"Tonight, it's anything goes. Just want you prepared," he said softly.

"Nothing could've prepared me for the whirlwind that has been my life since meeting you, Rider."

He smiled and took one more step forward, backing me against the door. Still holding my face, he softly said, "Yeah, but stick with me, gorgeous, and you'll get the reward. The winds'll change and life'll be a joyride instead."

My lips parted and between his words and the look in his eyes, I was moved.

"Gimme a chance, baby," he said leaning in. "I gave you your first ride and you loved it. You climb back on and hold on tight and I'll rock your world every fuckin' day. Give you that future you saw that first ride."

I blinked at him. My body was covered in goosebumps.

He moved in for a kiss. He hesitated a half an inch from my mouth, giving me a chance to want it.

And damn, but I wanted it.

I licked my lips and then he moved in and his lips touched mine softly, sweetly. And I opened up and kissed him back.

His hands moved back, into my hair, and the kiss turned hungry.

My fingers dove into his hair. I pulled the elastic out and had handfuls of it.

His face, still smooth from that morning's shave? It felt amazing.

His hands went to my hips and he pulled me into his crotch. I let out a little whimper at the contact. And then my dress was sliding up and his hands were on my thighs, moving to my ass. "We gotta get out there. I want to bury myself in you for days, hear all about our future in that sweet voice, but we gotta get out there, so this is gonna be fast," he said this against my mouth.

"Fast," I agreed, and then he was fiddling with his jeans and pulling my underwear to the side and then he was filling me.

I gasped.

His eyes burned a hole in me. A beautiful hole.

He hefted me up by the thighs, so my legs were wrapped around him.

"Need you, gorgeous. "

"Okay."

"Want you to be mine."

"Okay."

"Okay?" he asked, rotating his hips.

I gulped and nodded.

He slammed harder and his eyes went hard with this look of...what? Possessiveness.

He turned us around and moved us toward the bed. We went down, mouths connected, pelvises connected.

He went fast and hard and I did nothing but lie there. I was kind of in shock.

What was I doing? Okay? I said okay?

He moved hard and fast, and I knew he was holding back, waiting for me, because when I hit the climax, he hit it a millisecond later, coming inside me, groaning into my mouth, letting out a little moan that was super sexy-sounding.

"Baby..." he breathed.

I blinked.

I swallowed.

I blinked again.

I just agreed to be his girlfriend. While having sex. Against the door. During a funeral.

Oh my God... I was cock fogged like Ella. What was it about these bikers?

He kissed me again and I didn't finish my thought, because I melted into the kiss. He pulled back a few inches and his eyes searched mine. That was when I got scared. I grabbed him by the shirt and couldn't decide whether to push him away or pull him closer.

I had to catch my breath. I needed air. Or him. Or maybe he was air.

"What's the matter?" he whispered.

"I don't know if I can do this," I admitted, breathless.

"You can," he whispered. "I'll help."

"I—-" I was feeling panic rise. I needed air. This room felt so small and closed in. "But, you've never done it."

My heart was racing.

"Never felt like it was right before. But with you, it's like I was built for it."

I was gasping, panicking. I tried to get away from him.

He tightened his grip on me.

"Baby, don't. Don't do that. Just breathe."

"I'm freaking out."

I was. I was freaking *right* out.

He got off me and sat on the side of the bed and then pulled my panties the right way and fixed my dress as he pulled me onto his lap. His belt was still undone.

He put his arms around me.

"You're shakin'. Hey. It's okay."

I tried to breathe, but I was having a full-on panic attack.

"Put your ear to my chest," he said.

"Huh?"

"Do it."

I did.

"Hear that?"

"What?" I felt his warmth seeping through his black dress shirt. I closed my eyes.

"Focus."

I tried. I heard his heart beating.

"Hear that?"

"Your heart?" I asked.

"Yeah, just listen."

"Rider, I..."

"Shhh. Listen." He cradled my head against his chest and I did what he'd asked. I listened to the steady tempo of his heartbeat. I absorbed the feeling of him holding me, comforting me.

I did that for a few minutes. And my pulse was slowing down.

"Solid, steady," he said. "It's there, just doin' its thing. Thumping away. Right?"

I nodded.

"That's what you gotta do. Take one breath. Then another. I'm steady, baby. Solid. I want this. I want us. Just hold onto me. Like you do when you're on the back of my bike and I'll get us there."

"But so much... in such a short amount of time, Rider. And drama. I—-"

"Shhh. Listen." He kissed the top of my head and kept playing with my hair.

I listened. I closed my eyes. He slowly reclined until he was lying flat on the bed and my ear was still to his chest.

He ran his hand through my hair.

"Life can be short, babe. I'm learnin' that. Life can be hard. Life can be sweet, too, if you open yourself up to possibilities. Never wanted a club girl for more than a little fun. You're not a club girl."

"No. I'm definitely not," I whispered.

"You're different. You're gorgeous. You're high fuckin' maintenance. But, shit, you're gorgeous. Your apartment is the shit. You work hard, and you care about that. You give a shit about people. People gettin' their dream wedding day. Old lonely grandmothers who you give fuckin' coupons to. Doin' old lady hairdos at the retirement home for free."

How did he know I went to the retirement home and gave free hairdos? Bronto.

"Your parents might be snobs, I don't fuckin' know, haven't met them yet but your ma was a piece of work on the phone. I know that you work hard. You're not looking for your folks to give you a hand-out. You're willing to work for it. And you're generous. I also know that what I see from you so far, you constantly fuckin' surprise me. I'm sorry. I was wrong about you. And I'm fuckin' glad I've had a chance to realize that before you wound up with a banker or a lawyer or some shit who gives you what your mother wants but not what you need or deserve. I am lookin' forward to a whole lot more of seeing what you're hidin' from me."

"I am high maintenance," I said. "I have expectations. And expensive bedding that's just for show. And I can be demanding."

"That's all right. I'm game. And I can be demanding, too."

"Right. Sex." I muttered.

He chuckled.

"And you think I'm bad at it."

"Naw, baby. You're lazy at it. You took those orgasms like you were entitled to them and then you were done. You were fuckin' like a guy."

I gasped and lifted my head off his chest.

"But, fuck. I see potential. You're a canvas I can work with." My face burned with embarrassment at him using the words I'd used the night before. "Few tweaks, I'll get you there. And you'll love every minute of it." He put his hand on my ear and pushed my head back to his chest.

I listened to his heartbeat some more, trying not to feel mortified.

"We should get out there," I said.

"In a minute," he replied. "Wanna hold my woman for another minute."

I was melting.

"Night before last night, you cuddled up to me when I rolled away."

I lifted my head again to look him in the face.

"That was nice," he said. "Never slept with a girl all night unless it was just a mess of drunken bodies passed out. No cuddling or any of that shit. Fuckin' loved it those few nights with you. My head was fucked when I rolled away. You rolled in and it helped. Last night...without you... it sucked."

I made a face.

"Though you made me really fuckin' hard watchin' you struggling down the hall with that suitcase, your ass in those little fuckin' pink panties. And seein' my name on your back while me and half a dozen other guys watched that sweet ass? That helped. If it weren't for my name on your back, I would not have been down for that. Would've paddled your ass until it was pink like your panties. That says something, too, because I don't usually get possessive. And knowin' you were keeping my sister company when she was gonna have a night of crying herself to sleep? I figured I could sacrifice and sleep alone, so she could have that. Let Jojo borrow you for the night. I needed you, but she needed you more."

I was not gonna cry. I was not gonna cry.

"But just sayin', don't leave me at night like that again. You sleep beside me or I'll find you and bring you back to my bed. I need you tonight."

Shit, if he didn't stop, I was gonna effing cry.

His voice had gone husky and that threat had turned me on, for some reason.

He slapped my butt. "We should get out there."

I sat up.

"You good about this?" he asked.

"This?" I asked.

"You and me."

I shrugged. "I'm not sure...um, no. I'm probably not good about this."

He leaned forward and kissed my lips. "What do I gotta do for you to be good about this?"

I shrugged. "I'm just...skeptical."

"Stick with me and I'll bust my ass to make that uncertainty evaporate. Okay?"

And those green-blue eyes were like endless pools. "Okay," I whispered, "But... I don't trust easy. I have these walls and it might take..." I let out a breath. "I'm high maintenance and you might get sick of that. And it might take more than a little bit for them to come down. And you'll probably give up before you get through it."

"I got a pick axe. I'll pick away. Watch and see. I'm more stubborn than you. And you're stubborn, gorgeous..."

I was trembling.

"You want this," he stated.

I stared at him with big eyes.

"You want this, or you wouldn't care so much. And baby, that means a fuckuva lot."

I put my forehead to his chest. He put his arms around me.

"Open up. Give me you. I won't make you sorry," he said.

He kissed the top of my head.

And I just wanted to get lost in him all over again. I was afraid to speak, to breathe. The promise of him that I felt after that first night was nothing compared to the reality of him. I couldn't kid myself that this would be easy. But, I had a feeling right then that it might be worth however difficult it'd be to get there with him.

God, but what if I was wrong?

His phone made a noise and he reached into his pocket.

"We headin' out?" he asked.

I nodded. "Need the little girls room first," I said. I went into the bathroom and got cleaned up and looked at my reflection in the mirror.

I had the look of a woman who'd just gotten fucked fast and hard. And I had the look of someone who was petrified. And I was. I wasn't sure I wanted to roll with this. I also wasn't sure I was capable of doing anything *but* rolling with this. I took off the undies I had on and stepped back into the bedroom and he went into the bathroom. I put a fresh pair on and then he was coming out of the bathroom with a smile. He took my hand and took me toward the door.

"Wait. I just wanna make the bed."

"Huh?"

"I hate leaving the bed unmade." I went back to the bed and motioned for him to come help. He did, but he was looking at me weird.

"It's not nice to get into an unmade bed when you're tired. Or drunk. And if we're partying later..." I shrugged.

"I agree that stopping festivities to deal with bed shit is not fun."

I fought a smile, feeling my face go pink, because of the disaster of my duvet that first night.

He chuckled and helped me tidy the bed and then we left the room and headed to the kitchen, finding Delia, with two other women.

13

"We're good, you two. Just heading out now to eat. Go have some food. Jenna, you can be on clean-up duty. Okay?" Delia was shooing us out of the kitchen.

"Sure," I agreed, and Rider took my hand and we headed to where everyone was, to an area that opened to the outside. There were tables both inside and outside, and people sitting, standing, walking in and out. Some were getting plates of food from the massive spread. There were close to a dozen long tables that had to have twenty or so chairs at each. The place was crawling with bikers. Biker wives. Kids. People that didn't look like bikers, too. The photo collages from the funeral home had been set up on one side.

Some people were dressed up and others were dressed down, so my flip flops with my funeral clothes didn't look too out of place.

Jojo waved at me and I saw that she was sitting with Deke, Spencer, Deacon, and a few other people from the Aberdeen charter. They'd saved us seats.

Jojo's eyes were now make-up free and a little puffy, but she gave me a small smile.

Rider waved at them and then pointed toward the food, gesturing we were grabbing some. Deke gave us a thumbs up.

The two long food tables were filled with lasagnas, crock pots filled with meatballs. All sorts of appetizers, salads, cold cuts, veggie and fruit trays, and buns.

And I was suddenly famished.

And I was going to sit and eat with my new boyfriend and his family.

My boyfriend. A biker. A biker who... no, Jenna. Don't look back right now. Look forward.

He didn't know me when he had a gang bang. He only had me kidnapped to protect me. He had never wanted an exclusive relationship with someone, not even spent the night sleeping beside someone all night cuddling like that. But, he wanted it with me. *Me*. He liked his name on my back. He looked out for me in multiple ways. A life with him could have lots of fun, laughter, good times.

But, if he'd never been in a relationship before, how did he know he wanted it? How did he know if he'd be capable of being faithful? Would that be a struggle? I didn't want to be with someone who would ever be able to even fathom cheating on me. It shouldn't take effort to be faithful to someone.

Normally, I led a cat and mouse chase with a guy and *I* decided how far to let him in. I was always careful with my heart. Some got in more than others. Never did they get in very far. Not since Michael. But, Rider Valentine had ploughed in despite my advanced defense system. Was I really gonna do this?

Shit. I wanted to.

I made a decision. I'd try. I'd be cautious, but I'd try. And hope that when all the drama was over, he didn't change his mind and decide I wasn't worth the trouble. And hope that this wasn't a 'thrill of the chase' game. I'd have to try to stop myself from falling head over heels in case this fizzed out fast. It might be too late for that already, though.

We sat and ate with everyone. And people told stories. And showed their tattoos that'd been done by Luke "Lick" Hanson. And I sat beside Rider, his arm around me or on my chair. He was attentive. He got me a drink refill. He brought me a red velvet cupcake with that drink refill without my asking. He touched my hair. He introduced me to more people. He was demonstrative.

It felt nice. It felt promising.

I was still scared, but I was trying to 'roll' with it.

"I gotta have a bathroom break." Jojo rose from the table after we'd been sitting for well over an hour with Axel and his woman Leah, the pretty platinum blonde I'd seen with Jojo the day before.

She'd told me that she'd partied with Ella the weekend before, the night of pudding shooters and pulled pork (according to the texts I had from Ella). They'd partied with Jet, initiating Ella into the Dominion Brotherhood Sisterhood with a shooter consumption challenge. She passed with flying colors.

Not surprising.

"That explains those texts I got from her," I'd said with a laugh.

Leah was nice. She was feeling the loss of Jet of course, as they'd been tight, but Rider was right. This party here was to celebrate Lick. Leah promised me that there'd be a shooter initiation night for me as soon as possible.

I hadn't seen Edge, other than for a very brief appearance at the funeral home. I overheard some people saying he was heading to Jet's hometown to see her parents and be there for the funeral.

The club was planning to have a party for her when he got back.

She had a rough relationship with them, had minimal contact, but as she and Edge weren't legally married, he had very little say in her final arrangements. I'd heard them say it wouldn't be a 'club' funeral, because her parents were very anti-biker.

"I'll go tinkle, too," I said to Jojo's bathroom break comment. "Bring you back a drink or anything?" I asked Rider.

"Beer would be nice, gorgeous."

"Anyone else?" I asked.

I got a bunch of 'nopes' and 'no thanks'.

I saw Bronto by the door when I went inside.

He was smiling at me.

"Hey Jenna. Jojo." He said.

"Hey Bront..." Jojo said and gave him a high five.

"Teddy Bear," I said low and gave him a mock punch in the arm." He winced and grabbed the opposite arm, teasingly.

I smiled and gave him a look that I hoped spoke volumes. By his resulting smile, I think it did.

"Feet feeling better?" he asked.

"Yeah. Much," I said. "Were you sent out for these?"

He gave me a nod. "They were squishy. I thought they'd be good."

"Squishy *is* good. You did good. Thank you. How much do I owe you?"

He shook his head. "Nope. Nothing. We have a fund."

"A sore foot fund?" I laughed.

"A fund to take care of guests of the club. But, looks like you're an old lady now, so you never offer to pay back a prospect or a member for doin' something for you. Your old man takes care of all those expenses. Okay?"

"Old lady? Bleck."

"Not bleck," Jojo said. "It's an honor. Trust me. Lotta women want it and never get it."

I winced. "I need biker broad lessons."

Jojo laughed. "I got you. Let's go. Ima pee my pants."

"Thanks, Teddy Bear," I said.

"Anytime, Jenna." He smiled.

Not far from the door was a ladies' bathroom with several stalls.

Washing our hands at the sinks after using the facilities I asked, "You okay?"

She shrugged. "It's hard, but this is helping. People telling stories, celebrating his life. Everyone is treating me like I lost him and that helps, too, because it's the first time I've been able to show my feelings for him. Makes me sad, though. Makes me want him here, so I can be on his arm, unembarrassed. But, we never got that."

I nodded, sadly.

"But, he fucked that girl."

I gulped.

"And I know he and I were early on, but I don't know if he'd have kept doing things like that or if it was just 'cuz he knew I'm a virgin, so he had to get off, because he couldn't get off with me." She dried her hands and then her hands went into her hair at both sides and she looked tormented. "If I wasn't and we'd been having sex, maybe he wouldn't have been with Kailey. And if he hadn't fucked her, maybe they wouldn't have had him killed."

"No. Don't you take that on your shoulders." I grabbed her hand.

She pulled her hand back. She was struggling. She was struggling hard. She needed space, so I took a step back.

She cleared her expression at my look of worry and fluffed her hair.

"Yeah. I just need... time."

She jerked her head toward the door and I followed her back out, feeling worried about her state of mind.

She should *not* feel responsible for his death. At all.

But, unfortunately, guilt and, I'm guessing, grief, don't work that way. I did not have a good feeling about Joelle Valentine's road toward getting over this.

"SHOW US!" I GOADED Brady.

It was dark and there were campfires burning in three big firepots. The booze was flowing, and the tunes were blaring. Lick's favorite band had been Aerosmith, and someone had put together a huge selection of their songs to play on a loop.

Some people had left, others were obviously here for the night. I'd changed into a pair of black jeggings and a long drapey black and blue tee that Jojo had packed for me, washed a truckload of dishes with the other ladies, and now it was turning into a good time.

Someone turned off Aerosmith and put on some dance music.

There were a few grumbles, until a bunch of girls got up and started dancing and the complaints died down as the men were watching the girls. That guy from The Roadhouse who'd begged us to dance with him was in there with them. He spotted me and wiggled his finger at me to invite me into the group. I stood, and Rider grabbed my hand and tugged it, so I landed on his lap.

"Hey?" I joked.

He shook his head. "No."

"Huh?" Was he serious? He looked serious.

"You dance way too sexy for these fuckers. I'd have to fight them off."

I laughed and smacked his arm. His lips went to my ear and he sucked on my earlobe, giving me goosebumps.

"Serious, gorgeous. I clocked you that first night and thought you were damn gorgeous. But when you danced? Fuckin' pulled me in like a tractor beam."

"Tractor beam?"

"Star Trek?"

"Huh? You're a Trekkie? Ewwww."

He shook his head. "Don't diss Star Trek, Jenna, or we'll have problems."

I laughed. "Ella likes that show too. I don't get it."

"You're gonna learn to like it."

I giggled and then he kissed me breathless.

When he finally let me up for air, I saw Spencer staring at us and I didn't like the look on his face.

I smiled at him. He seemed to shake himself out of whatever angry thoughts he was having. He smiled back and took a sip of his drink and the ugliness seemed to disappear.

After three songs, the third of which I found myself moving and grooving to from Rider's lap and getting Rider a little bit hot and bothered (not unintentionally) when Aerosmith got put back on and at the firepot we were at, people started telling more stories about Luke.

There'd been quite a few stories about how he was a practical joker. He sounded like the life of the party. And so did Rider. The stories of antics and practical jokes often included the both of them.

But, Spencer had told a few stories that had some of us grinding our teeth. He was well on his way to pissed drunk and wasn't hesitating to throw in comments about women who'd been present at certain things. A story was told about a teenaged Lick getting caught with a girl, having sex, by her older brother, who tried to beat Lick up. Rider had been getting lucky with the girl's friend in a bathroom, and he and Rider had beat the snot out of the older brother.

Rider had glared at Spence.

"I know it wouldn't've been two on one if the guy fought fair. He pulled a knife on Hanson, so Ride had to put his dick away and jump in."

"Spence," Rider said, his tone laced with warning.

Spencer chuckled and sipped his beer.

Jojo stayed quiet during that. But, the group felt the tension. Except Spencer. He carried on, drunkenly half-repeating the story, emphasis on the highlights, as if the rest of us hadn't already heard or as if we'd laugh the second time he told an inappropriate story when no one laughed but him the first time.

Someone changed the subject. Spencer brought it back around to some other story that began at a strip joint and ended with a party at a house rented by four of the strippers that worked there.

And that was when I cut him off and changed topics and asked Brady what tattoo he'd gotten that was brought up that day in the eulogy Rider had delivered.

This story was explained to tell me about the time Brady passed out first at a party and was so drunk, he slept straight through his ass getting tattooed by Lick. Spencer didn't seem bothered that I'd hijacked his story. He laughed at the Brady story.

Brady refused to tell us what the tat was of.

I got a reprimanding squeeze from Rider when I'd again hollered out "Come on...show us!"

Brady had a *seriously* fine ass, but I was more curious about what that mystery ass cheek tattoo might be than I was seeing his bare butt.

Finally, Brady glanced at Jojo and said, "Fuck it", then dropped his drawers on one side and showed us.

And me, Leah, and Jojo laughed our asses off, because bent over, in the firelight of the campfire, we saw a cute little teddy bear that looked like Ted from the *Ted* movie, with a Viking helmet in black ink and below it, it said "Hlökk Cuddlebear". And I wanted to kiss Brady for dropping his drawers, because of the beautiful sound of Jojo giggling on such a sad, *sad* day. I knew that he did that to give her a nanosecond of laughter.

"Cuddlebear!" Leah howled in laughter.

"Warrior cuddlebear. Hlökk," Brady corrected.

"But Hlökk was a chick warrior," Spencer said and there was more laughter.

"He cuddles," Spencer said. "Everyone knows it. You don't wanna camp in the same tent as this guy."

Brady got a serious and somber look on his face. "I was always gonna cover it. Some day when I get hitched, figured I'd cover it with somethin' for my wife. Now, it stays. And I'm gonna have to find a girl who's got a warrior spirit."

"Good relationship goals, Brady," Leah said with a smile.

Everyone at the firepot we were at went quiet for a moment and there was just the flickering flames and crackling sounds of the campfires, with the music and distant hum of people talking at the other fire pots.

"To Lick," Brady raised his beer to the sky with a sober look on his face.

Everyone else raised their bottles or red Solo cups. Including Jojo, whose eyes were bright, whose chin was trembling.

I glanced at Rider and he was staring into the flames with a faraway look. I knew he wasn't mentally here. He was in his mind, with Lick, somewhere in one of their many adventures together.

I put my hand on his thigh. He looked at me and his eyes went sparkly and he put his hand on mine.

"You. Hitched? Like that's ever gonna happen," Spencer snickered, ending a nice moment by making a wisecrack.

Brady looked at him with seriousness. "Why you say that?"

Spencer threw a hand up in the air animatedly, as if it was self-explanatory.

"Spencer?" Brady folded his arms across his chest and waited, his face like stone.

"Man, I see you with two, three women at a time after every party. Being married typically means committing to one woman. One."

"Maybe she'll be into threesomes," Leah offered. "Or foursomes."

I smiled, hoping the tone would lighten, but yikes. Maybe Leah didn't know about the video. And the look on Brady's face was scary. He was looking at Spencer like he wanted to wipe the floor with him.

Spencer looked at him with a cocky smirk. "Maybe you need to move to polygamy land and get hitched three or four times. Do we need a rural Utah chapter?"

"Spence," Rider clipped with a warning look.

Brady's nostrils were kind of flaring.

"Bray..." Deacon mumbled, and Brady's eyes cut to Deacon. Deacon gave a shake of his head.

"What?" Spencer asked. "Am I lyin'?"

"When I'm ready, I'll be ready," Brady informed him.

"All right, man." Spencer raised his hands defensively. "Clearly, we're slowly droppin' like flies. Getting addicted to one pussy. I'm lookin' for my one. Didn't know you were, too."

"Didn't say I was lookin' for her. But, when I meet her, I'll know. Right Ax, Ride, Deacon?" Brady asked.

"Absolutely," Deacon said, sipping his beer.

"Oh yeah," Axel kissed Leah's neck and she beamed with joy. "Sometimes it sneaks up on ya. And you just know."

Rider gave a non-committal smile that didn't touch his eyes. And I was uncomfortable.

I pulled my hand away from him.

"Until she stops puttin' out, then it's *game on* with club whores, right?" Spencer said, with a sneer.

My eyes moved to Jojo, staring into the flames with more tears in her eyes and my heart sank.

She sucked in her lips. "I'm goin' to bed." She got up and Rider's eyes were now on her and they were hard. So were Deacon's. I could see Deacon's jaw clenching.

I reached for her hand and gave it a squeeze. She squeezed it back, but didn't make eye contact, and then she left our group, getting stopped by Deke, who was at the next firepot. He kissed her temple and I saw him say something to her. She waved nonchalantly and then faked a yawn. She went inside.

Rider abruptly lifted me off his lap by my hips, setting me on my feet. He got up and stood in front of me.

"Why do you gotta be such a fuckin' shithead?" Rider hissed this at Spencer and then whipped his beer bottle and it smashed on the concrete several feet away. I startled.

"What?" Spencer asked. "What I say?"

"You need it spelled out?" Rider lunged for Spencer. "I'll fuckin' spell it."

I looked to Deacon, thinking he'd intervene. But, he didn't. Instead, he used his foot to shove his chair back, out of the way, and watched, as Rider's fist collided with Spencer's mouth.

Spencer toppled over in his lawn chair and then both men were on their feet.

"Fuck you, Ride. What's your fucking problem?"

I was in shock. I went to move forward out of reflex, but Brady sidestepped and got in front of me.

"Stay back," Brady warned.

"Stop them," I breathed and looked pleadingly at Deacon, from around Brady's back.

There were still sixty to eighty people, minimum, here. And they all watched as Rider and Spencer had a fist fight near three lit fire pots.

It just didn't seem smart.

"Do something!" I pleaded at Deacon.

He gave a shake of his head and rose and came over to me.

Spencer swung for Rider and Rider dodged it and punched Spencer in the throat.

Spencer choked and doubled over. Rider straightened and bounced on his feet a little, like he knew Spencer would recover and come at him. And it was a good call, because Spencer did, with a surprising spinning kick and the toe of his boot grazed Rider's left eye. It could've been much worse if Rider hadn't bent back.

"Oh shit!" I shouted and tried to go to Rider, but Deacon's arm clotheslined me, blocking me from moving forward. Rider stumbled and then he was on Spence again, punching him in the face.

"He needs this," Deacon gestured, steadying me and keeping me back, and I didn't know if he meant that Rider needed to beat up Spencer or that Spencer needed a beating.

Spence punched him back. Right in the mouth.

Even Deke, their *father*, was just standing there watching. Rudy, too, the president of the mother chapter of the MC. Standing there, avidly watching.

"Is someone gonna sell popcorn? Fucking stop them!" I hollered.

I was ignored.

And Rider and Spencer seemed evenly matched with their height and size, Spence might've been an inch taller, a teensy bit broader, but I think Rider was angrier, and that might've meant he had the advantage.

"It's all right," Leah was beside me suddenly, hand on my arm. "They just need to blow off steam. Funerals always end in at least one brawl in this clan."

"Brawls and orgies," Brady muttered, and I startled at that comment.

"Yep, life affirmations," Axel agreed.

I shivered, hoping this was the end of it, as they were both backing away from one another. And I was caged in, which I guessed was intentional. I had Brady in front on the left, Deacon in front on the right, and Axel standing behind me.

"You shoot your fuckin' mouth off with no thought for what's simmerin' underneath, you fuckin' fuckhead," Rider ground out. They were both catching their breath. Spence's nose and lip were bleeding.

"Sayin' shit to Jenna. Shooting your mouth off around Ella. What the fuck do you think you just made Joelle feel?" Rider spat on the ground and there was blood. His lip was bleeding.

Spencer looked at Rider like he was speaking Greek.

"Stop your fuckin' shit, Spence. You're killin' your liver and burnin' a fuckin' hole in your brain," Rider lunged and stabbed his index finger against Spencer's temple, "with that shit you're puttin' up your nose. And every fuckin' one of us is sick and tired of it."

Spencer looked at him like he was out of his mind. "Fuck you."

But, Rider was still in his face and Spencer didn't swing for him.

"Ding ding. That's it. To your corners, boys," Deke finally spoke up.

Finally, I felt my lungs deflate.

Rider looked around. "The fuck is Jenna?" he snapped.

Brady and Deacon stepped aside from being the wall in front of me. I'd been peeking between their elbows.

Rider's eyes were on me. "Now."

I followed him, assuming 'now' meant *come with me*, feeling all eyes on us, seeing Spencer's eyes on Rider with venom shooting out of his eyes. My eyes met his and his eyes were filled with the kind of venom that was reminiscent of Shelly Valentine, watching us at the funeral earlier that day.

"Good luck with that one, Blue Eyes," Spencer called out to me. "You don't even need to thank me for wakin' his shit up. I told him how good you felt on top of me and how if he didn't nail you down, I would. Next thing, he's cuffin' you to a bed. You get tired a that... feel free to come jump my bones again."

Rider turned around and advanced on Spencer and clocked him in the face so hard that Spencer went down like a felled tree. T.K.O.

And then Rider grabbed my hand and I had to jog to keep up with him, which wasn't easy in squishy flip flops.

We were walking too fast, down the endless hallway maze, when I saw a biker and a woman having sex against the wall. I was sort of mortified, but they paid us no notice at all as we went by and Rider didn't even seem like he'd noticed them.

They had to be in their 40s, minimum, and they both had it goin' on. Her skirt was hiked. His hands held her up against that wall, by her butt, and her legs were wrapped around his lower back.

Yowza. I guess the rowdiness had started. A brawl and now it was time for all the orgies. I was glad we were heading back to our room.

When we were back in our room, as I shut the door, he let go of my hand and kept going until he slammed the bathroom door behind himself.

I stood there, staring at the closed door for a minute, unsure of what to do with myself. The doorknob had been fixed, at least.

I heard the water turn on, so I sat down on the bed and was still sitting there, pinching my lower lip between my thumb and forefinger, when he came back out, in a towel only, his hair wet, his eyes immediately on me.

He had a bit of a shiner, by the looks of things, and it'd probably be angrier by the morning. He also had a slightly puffy upper lip. He still had scratches and bruises from the fall after the fire. He looked rough. And he still looked fiery mad. And yet beautiful.

"You pissed at me?" he demanded.

My eyes bulged, and I shook my head. I could let the alpha-hole behavior slide today, I figured.

"No?" he asked, his voice and body language like he didn't believe me.

I shook my head again and swallowed.

"Why're you acting scared?"

My mouth dropped open and nothing, no sound, would come out.

"Get over here," he ordered.

I got up and moved toward him.

He pulled me against him and wrapped his arms around me. "I'm sorry," he said into my hair.

I put my arms around him, too, feeling relief that he wasn't as mad as he'd looked a second ago. "Why are you sorry?"

"Sorry Spence is an asshole. Sorry you had to hear some of that shit tonight. Sorry we're starting over on a day when emotions're runnin' high and shit is so fuckin' amped. But, baby, it helps having you. It fuckin' does for some reason."

"What would you rather?" I asked, looking up at him.

He let out a long breath and then his expression softened. "To go back to the cabin. Be alone with you. Shut everything else out."

"Yeah?" I asked.

"Yeah. Take you for long rides. So many places I wanna show you. Fuckin' need to ride when I'm dealing with shit and today, havin' it while also having you wrapped around my back? Just what I needed."

I put my head against his chest.

I heard his heart beating strong and sure. I lifted my head away, looked up at him, and asked, "You wanna listen to my heart?"

He smiled a gorgeous smile at me and it was a lot like the carefree smiles I'd gotten in the very beginning. I smiled back.

His mouth came down softly on mine and he was kissing me slow, sweet, but thoroughly. And then his hands were in my hair and he was moaning into my mouth, walking me backwards to the bed. I fell, him falling on top of me.

"I'll give it a listen when I'm ready to sleep. Not ready to sleep."

"No?" I asked, giving him a flirty expression.

"Need something," he said.

"Hm?" I looked up at him, thinking *life affirmations*.

He kissed the tip of my nose. "I wanna fuck you while you're wearin' that hoodie."

I giggled.

"You still wearin' those pink panties?" he reached for my button and undid it and then pulled my zipper down.

"Nope," I told him.

He shimmied Jojo's jeggings off me. I had the same style of panties as yesterday, cheeky panties with the word 'PINK' on the back, but these ones were turquoise and not glittery. Earlier, when we'd had sex, he hadn't even looked down. I'd been wearing black underwear. He hadn't taken his eyes off my face the whole time.

This time, he was looking down.

I rolled over to show him the back of them and his finger traced the letters.

And then he leaned over and bit into my butt cheek and I squealed and laughed.

How could things be this lighthearted after that scene out there?

I didn't wanna spoil the moment by asking. And I liked that we could be this for one another. A place to laugh. Good-time Jenna and Good-time Rider.

I could see all sorts of emotions swirling in his eyes and I just wanted to take care of him. So, I decided that's what I'd do.

I opened up the towel he had on and rubbed his cock. He flopped onto the pillows and watched.

"Do you own any underwear?" I asked. I'd never seen him wear them.

"Don't like bein' confined. And easy access is way better."

"Hm. That's a thought," I said, stroking him.

"Don't you get any ideas. I fuckin' like seein' them on you. It's like unwrapping a present covered with pretty paper."

I smiled and started to kiss his throat, kiss his chest.

"Put it on," he said.

"Hm?" I asked.

"The hoodie."

"It needs a wash," I said. I'd slept in it the night before. And I'd worn it to sleep and to his mother's house the day before that.

"C'mon...just for a bit."

I crawled backwards and then got off the bed at the foot. I fetched it from the suitcase, climbing back on top of him. I put it on. It didn't smell funky, thankfully. His hands went to my hips.

I leaned over and kissed his eye, which looked a little bit sore and bruised, and then I ran my hand up his side where he had that long scratch, reached down and kissed it. And then he had my face in his hands and brought my lips to his. His tongue chased mine and he groaned.

"Fuck, you're sweet," he told me, and I smiled against his lips.

I drove my fingers into his hair and I rubbed my crotch along his shaft. He sat up, me straddling him, and yanked the sweater and tank top up to rest over top of my boobs. His mouth moved in and he licked a nipple.

I got lost in that for a second, my head rolling back. But then I pushed him to his back and yanked the panties to the side and guided him to my entrance. I moved slowly, letting him ever-so-slowly sink inside.

He gripped my hips and watched as my body sheathed him.

His eyes were ablaze. I'd bet mine were, too.

His hand moved away from my hip and his thumb slid past the elastic of the panties to my clit.

"No," I grabbed his hand and put it back to my hip. "This time, it's all about you," I said.

His lips parted, and his eyes were ablaze.

And I gyrated slow, tightening on the inside, making it all about him. Watching his reactions to see what he liked. Loving the look on his face, the way his lips were parted and how his chest rose and fell as he watched me, as he felt what I was doing. And liked it. I slid my hands up his torso as I kept rocking and swaying my hips, and toyed with his nipples, his nipple ring. I started kissing his throat. I sucked, and he groaned. I tightened my inner walls and he groaned again.

I was getting so turned on by seeing the effect I was having with what I was doing to him.

"You markin' me as yours?" he asked, huskily, his pelvis moving in time with opposite gyrations, his hands tightening on my hips.

"Mm." I released his neck, seeing a bright red mark where I'd sucked. "Is that what you've been doing to me? Hickeys and teeth marks, sweatshirts with your name on them?"

"Mm hm. Never wanted to do that before."

"No?" I asked.

"Uh uh. Can't even tell you how I felt seeing my name on your back. Fuck, baby. Want my name on everything you own."

Wow.

"Tell me what you want, how I can please you..." I invited, goosebumps all over me.

"Deeper, but slow, baby. Nice 'n slow. Squeeze my cock with your pussy again." He moved my hips with strong slow movements, showing me what he wanted.

And it felt so good, I made a whimper noise, feeling like I might come. I had to *not* come, I wanted this to be about him. As I did Kegels with him inside me, I got close, dangerously close.

I slowed a little, so I could stop my body from doing what it wanted to do, and he flipped me over onto my belly and took over.

"Hey," I said, "Wait..."

He gave my neck a hot, wet long kiss, and then grabbed my hips.

"Wanna see the back of this shirt while I take you."

"Rider..." I breathed.

"Gonna come with you," he said. "Let go, gorgeous."

"I—-"I shook my head. I was trying to find the words to protest.

"Come for me," he ordered, "I want you to. Let go. Don't hold back with me. Ever."

"I hold back with everyone," I admitted.

"Give me time. We'll get you there," he said softly.

His fingers moved fast, cupping me, rubbing my clit. His pelvis moved fast. The shudders started. My legs were trembling.

"Gonna take you hard," he told me, and holy cow, I got wetter.

I was flipped, and the shirt whipped off my head and tossed, then the tank top. His mouth was on mine and I felt it hit. It hit so hard I thought I was splitting in two.

"Riderrrrrr..." I breathed out as I let myself be split wide open.

"Baby..." he groaned as he spilled inside of me while my body bucked against my will.

And then he rolled us, so I was on top of him. I shifted half off and kept my head against his chest. His heart was beating in double-time. And it was a beautiful sound.

I closed my eyes, snuggled in, and fell asleep listening to it as it went back to that steady beating.

I jolted out of my slumber a few minutes later when he flipped me and put his head to *my* chest.

"Thanks, gorgeous," he said, and kissed me on my lips, then kissed each of my nipples, then put his head back to my heart.

I ran my fingers through his hair in answer, as he used my chest like a pillow, until my hand flopped when I gave in to sleep.

14

When I woke up, I was alone.

I reached for my silenced phone to check the time and there were two missed calls from my Dad. It was 8:33. Where was Rider?

I got up and went to the bathroom.

When I got back, he still wasn't here, so I decided to listen to my voicemails.

There were a few more angry voicemails from my mother from before I'd spoken to her, so I erased them. And then I got two voicemails from my Dad.

"Jenna, call me, please." Was the first one.

The second one was a longer one. And it had been left a half hour before.

> "We've seen the news and ... call us as soon as possible. Your mother is out of her mind with worry, as am I. I need to leave for Nevada for a business trip. Please call me as soon as you can, so I'll know you're all right."

I called him back immediately, feeling guilty. They'd seen the news; Jet's murder would've been on the news!

My father answered on the first ring.

"Jenna," he breathed.

"Sorry, Dad. I didn't mean to make you guys worry!" I said quickly.

He took a big breath.

"What are they saying on the news?" I asked, figuring that might be a good way to approach things, rather than answering blindly.

"A thirty-year-old woman was found murdered at the gates of Dominion Moving and Storage in Sioux Falls yesterday. The news didn't identify her, but went on to talk about how the location isn't just the moving and storage company, that it's also the headquarters for the Dominion Brotherhood Motorcycle Club. Where are you, Jenna?"

"I'm ... uh... at that same Dominion Moving and Storage location," I said.

"Excuse me?" My father's voice went hard.

"I'm safe, inside the gates. The place is locked down like a fortress. I wasn't here when Jet was found. And she was hurt elsewhere and dropped here. I'm safe, Dad."

"And what is it you're doing there?"

"Well..." I swallowed. Shit. I really should've gotten myself caffeinated before this conversation. And thought about how I'd handle this conversation.

The bedroom door opened, and Rider was coming in, wearing a blue t-shirt and faded blue jeans with his black motorcycle boots. Gray wool beanie on his head. Smiling. A black coffee mug with the MC's logo on it in his hand. He jerked his chin up when he saw me on the phone. I was chewing my lip, a look of uncertainty on my face.

He passed me the cup of coffee.

"Jenna?" Dad pushed.

"Thank you," I mouthed. He leaned over and kissed my lips just briefly. "Morning, gorgeous." He didn't mouth that, so I winced.

"Who was that?" Dad asked.

"Well Dad, that was Rider. My new ... boyfriend."

Rider's lips turned up slightly. His eyes sparkled.

"And he has you there, why? Your mother said he wouldn't give a straight answer, said something about your safety, and then we see the news, and Jenna, we saw it last night, so it was a long night here and you didn't answer your cell phone."

I winced. Rider gave me a questioning chin jerk.

"Help?" I mouthed.

"Put it on speaker," Rider commanded.

I did, wincing and feeling panicky.

"I put you on hands-free, Dad."

"Mr. Murdoch?" Rider asked.

Just like that. I mouthed help and he helped. I could fall in love with this man.

"Yes?"

"Dad saw the news," I said quickly, "Jet's murder was on the news and they were worried about me. All night." I made a face of horror.

"Mr. Murdoch, my apologies," Rider said, putting a hand on my back and rubbing it, soothingly. "We have had some difficulties with a rival club and they've gotten violent. Jenna's safe and will continue to be safe."

"Well, Rider, since we've never met, you can imagine how I felt hearing the news after Jenna's mother told me that Jenna was with a Dominion Brotherhood member who spoke of her being in danger, up in the same city as a murder that appeared to be connected to the Dominion Brotherhood."

"I'm so sorry, Dad. I didn't think," I said.

"No, it doesn't seem like you did," my father said, sharply.

Rider's body jerked back and then his eyes were angry.

"Sir, Jenna's under 24-hour guard. She and others who are deemed at risk are all safe and will continue to be safe. I'll give you my number so that you can check-in direct with me any time."

"Rider, no offense, but nothing you've said has made me feel any less concerned."

"Well, sir, would it help if I put you in touch with the lead investigator on the murder? I'll get you his contact details. Our club is working closely with the police not only to get whoever did this behind bars, but also to ensure that no one else gets hurt. The rival club threatened my sister and Jenna directly and this was why I put her under protection."

The phone was silent a moment.

"I see. All right," Dad said, finally.

"I'll send you my contact details and I'll get you the name of the homicide detective. I'm happy to check in daily until this is over, should that put you more at ease."

"That'd be good, son. You need my help making anything happen with the authorities, you let me know and I'm happy to wade in."

I was staring at my phone. My mouth had dropped open.

Son? And offering his assistance? To a motorcycle club? My dad had met two men I'd dated and had been indifferent to them both.

Son?

"Dad, I'm sorry," I said. "I'm good. I told Mom that the salon is in good hands and—-"

"Don't worry about it, sweetheart. Glad you called. Now, I've gotta head to the airport or I'll miss my flight, so I'll watch for those texts. You need anything done for the salon before you get back, let me know."

"Uh, okay," I said.

"You'll have texts in a few, sir." Rider said.

"Right. Paul; call me Paul. And Rider?" Dad asked.

"Yes, sir?"

"Take good care of her."

"You have my word. Myself, my family, and my club are all keeping her safe."

"Thank you. Bye for now. Bye, honey. Love you." His voice changed when he started addressing me.

"Uh... love you, too, Dad. Have a safe trip."

Wow. He didn't throw *I love yous* my way, too often. A lump formed in my throat.

"Bye," Rider said and disconnected the call and gave me a look.

I was wincing.

"I didn't think," I defended.

"What's this?"

"I checked my voicemail and he was worried. They were up all night worrying after seeing the news, and I just dialed out of reflex. I didn't even think about how I'd have to answer questions. I should've known. My Dad never fails to watch the eleven o'clock news."

"It's good they're in the loop."

"Um, maybe not. Dad was being cool and all, surprisingly cool, that was probably my first 'Love you' from him this millennium. But not sure your assurances will help with my Mom."

"Don't worry about it. I'll keep him in the loop. He can deal with her. You wanna come out and get some breakfast? Some of the women put on a big spread."

I nodded, feeling a relief I'd never felt before, having someone take my back like this, shielding me from stress with my parents. Could I get used to this? Emotion surged through me.

"Your eye looks a bit sore. But, I thought it'd be worse," I said.

"You should see the other guy," he said, with a chuckle.

"Eesh. Have you talked to him?"

"Yeah. He's acting like nothing happened. Hopin' I got through."

"Well, I think you made your point."

"Been a long time since I decked him. Hopefully it makes him realize how far gone he's been. I've usually got a lot of tolerance for his shit. But, he messed with Jojo and he was messin' with you and that was not on. Especially not on a day like yesterday."

"My hero." I leaned over and puckered my lips. He leaned down to kiss me.

"Sleep okay?" he asked.

"I slept great," I told him, sipping my coffee. "You?"

"Yeah, me too. Loved waking up to you curled into me. The cute little snorin' thing you do."

"The what?"

He snickered. "It wasn't loud. It was kinda cute."

"I don't snore!"

His eyes sparkled with mischief. "I'll record it tonight."

"Don't do that." I put my hand up.

"How else do I prove it?"

"You don't. You go on thinking it's cute, but you don't mention it ever again, *you do not* record it, and you never ever tell a soul about it."

He moved in and kissed me breathless. I went weak in the knees, even though he quickly got me vertical.

"So, what's on for today?" I asked, what felt like fifteen minutes later, my lips sort of swollen and tingly, my knees wobbly.

"Today, we work more on takin' those fuckers down."

"Oh?" I asked.

"Yeah. You and Joelle'll hang out here and stay safe. We have a billiards room, a TV room. A gym. Between all that, you two should be able to keep busy."

Fear lanced through me. What if he didn't stay safe?

"What are you gonna do?"

"Nothin' for you to worry about," he said.

I raised my eyebrows.

"No offence, gorgeous, but you want plausible deniability."

"Yikes. That sounds like..."

"Like we're going on the offence, yeah. We don't lay back and take this shit. They broke a cease-fire. Their name is mud. They killed one of our women, ripped a prospect's ass open, murdered another brother, put my sister in the hospital, took Ella, the list keeps on goin'. Not to mention what Mantiz threatened about you. That alone is enough for me to go to war. And we *are* declaring war. Let's go get breakfast so I can get on with this shit today and get back here to you," he said, like it was just as simple as that.

And I didn't like being shut down like that, but I didn't wanna react immediately, after all that was going on. I needed to process things. I was in foreign territory what with being a new member of this biker woman club. I needed my *biker broad* lessons.

"Gimme a sec to make the bed and get changed," I grumbled.

"Aberdeen boys are goin' home soon. You want one of them to fetch you some of your stuff?"

"Is that an option?" I asked, perking up.

"Yeah. Get Pippa to pack you a bag. I'll get someone to run it back."

I reached for my phone, so I could text Pippa.

"Oh. I need your other number," I said. "So I can text you Dad's contact details."

"The burner numbers never get shared outside brothers. And I never use it for long anyway. I'll get a new phone today. I'll text your dad from your phone and send a prospect out for a new phone I can put my SIM card into. You need me, you text or call my regular number."

He started to make the bed, so I dropped my phone and helped him.

My mind was reeling.

"Do me a favor?"

I looked at him.

"When a prospect tells ya my phone is up again, send me that pic of you with your tongue inside that sexy donut again?"

I tilted my head.

"Lost it when I trashed my phone. It's gonna be my screensaver."

My face split into a smile.

And then I went to get dressed, in yoga pants and a t-shirt, figuring I'd find that gym he was talking about. He pulled out a business card with the Sioux Falls police logo on it, so he could text my father.

BREAKFAST CONSISTED of a mountain of fried food and a good number of people, including all the Valentine boys. Spencer had an ugly shiner and his jaw looked a little swollen on one side, but he was acting like nothing had happened. He'd even been trying to tease his sister, but she was subdued, not paying much attention to anyone.

After breakfast, the bikers all disappeared to go to 'church', their name for a club members meeting.

About an hour later, doing yoga, and in the middle of downward facing dog, I felt hands on my hips and some hardness pressed up against my butt. I jolted.

"Hey, gorgeous."

I breathed relief and stood up. His mouth went against the back of my ear.

"Puttin' on quite a show, aren't ya?"

"Hm?" I asked and saw that a bunch of men were walking by the area, which was in an open bit of warehouse space. This place had rooms, halls, open spaces, a combination of them, using a lot of modular walls and dividers. I guess my workout had coincided with the end of biker 'church' and they'd passed by on their way wherever they were going and saw me.

"Turn around and kiss me."

"I'm all sweaty," I told him.

"Mm hm. I like it." He sucked on my neck at the side.

I twisted so that we were face to face and put my arms around his neck and got up on tiptoes to give him a hot and heavy one.

He made a growly sound. "Mm. Good."

"Is that enough of a show that I'm yours for your biker buddies?" I teased, nibbling on his jawline.

"You're figuring me out already?"

"It's kind of obvious," I said.

He slapped my butt. "Need to get you yoga pants with Property of Rider on your ass so anyone who finds their eyes heading in that direction will know their eyes don't belong there."

"All right, but I get to start putting "Property of Jenna" on you, too."

"Deal," He kissed me again. "I'll tattoo it on my chest. Gotta go, gorgeous. Be a good girl. Go find my sister when you're done here and hang with her? Try to get her smilin'?"

"Will do," I said.

He squeezed my butt again and then he left.

I found my way back to our room (asking directions when I got lost) and took a shower and changed and then banged on Jojo's door. She and I headed to a TV room. Bronto hung out with us, being a gopher, rather than a bodyguard, since we were inside the compound.

I spent the rest of the day with Jojo. And not doing much, because she was not up for it. She was in her head mostly.

The TV room had windows, at least, but our view was of a parking lot and the gates around the place. She gave short answers and mostly stared at the screen, so we didn't have much conversation. I got the impression that if I hadn't been there, she'd be in bed, under the covers, crying. Or staring into space the same way she was staring at the TV, that's to say not absorbing what was happening in front of her eyes, because she was in her head.

I would've liked to have played foosball or ping pong or something, and suggested it when Jojo shrugged with just one shoulder and continued to stare at the TV. We watched *Finding Dory* and then all the Twilight movies, and I was more than ready to stretch again when Rider turned up, five minutes before the end of the third movie.

Bronto had gone out and gotten burgers for us at around six. I had no idea where Rider was or what he'd been doing, but it was a long day and I was overjoyed to see him when he finally walked into the TV room.

My heart skipped a beat at his angry-looking expression as he walked in. But, then he brightened when our eyes met, and he moved in. I got to my feet and he bent and lifted me up and kissed me, holding me in his arms. *Swoon.*

"Rough day?" I asked.

"Mm hm." He squeezed me and buried his mouth into my neck.

Jojo took his arrival as a cue to go to bed.

"I'm tired. See you guys tomorrow," she said.

"Night," I said.

She waved and wandered out.

"How is she?" he asked, setting me on my feet.

"Not good. She was very quiet all day. I tried to be good company, but..." I shrugged. "She's gonna need time for healing."

"Thanks, gorgeous. You have some food?"

"Yeah, Bronto got us burgers. You?"

"Yep. Grabbed some pizza from that place I told ya about. Dug in when we got back. Starved. Still more than half left; it's in our room."

"Cool. Late night snack."

"Mm hm."

"What's up for the rest of the evening?" I asked.

"Just you 'n me, gorgeous girl."

"Sounds good," I said, "Can we get outta here? Go for a ride?"

"'Fraid not. Some wheels are in motion and it ain't safe outside these walls tonight."

"Oh?"

"Don't ask."

I grimaced. He took my hand and led me back to our room, which was a good long walk through a bunch of hallways. This place was humungous.

His phone was ringing before we got to our room.

"Shit, one sec," he said and opened the door and let me go ahead. He stayed in the hall.

I scrunched my face up at that and then decided to take a shower.

He wasn't back when I was done. I peeked out into the hallway, but it was empty, so I shut the door and waited on the bed.

He wasn't back an hour later when I decided to eat a piece of that cold pizza out of boredom. It was pretty damn good pizza.

He also wasn't back an hour or so after that when I was tired of staring at the ceiling and fell asleep. I couldn't get signal on my phone for some reason.

I woke up not knowing what time it was. The light was on and I was disoriented. I looked at my phone. It was 4:45 AM. Had he been gone all that time? Where the heck was he?

I got up, went and had a pee, brushed my teeth, and threw on yoga pants, flip flops, and my Property of Rider hoodie. (I'd done a load of wash that day, in between Twilight movies). I needed coffee. I'd fallen asleep before eleven and I wasn't someone who needed eight hours, usually.

I often went to bed late and still woke at dawn without an alarm. Unless I'd tied one on the night before, in which case I usually set two alarms. That day, we'd done nothing much of anything, so I was awake and feeling well-rested, and ready for coffee.

The previous day, Jojo and I had gone from our rooms to the kitchen twice, so I was fairly sure I could find my way.

I wandered out. The hallways were quiet.

And I made a wrong turn. The door numbers were getting higher than I'd recalled seeing earlier, so I tried to find my way back.

Every time we'd left, we'd gone from rooms in the low 400s to lower numbers. I was now in a hallway with rooms in the 500s. And I could hear music. Since I was lost, I figured I'd might as well find the source of the music and get directions back to room 424, our room ... or directions to the kitchen, which was in the 100s section.

The music got louder, and then I found myself in an area where the hallway opened up into a big open warehouse-like area with a bar and a bunch of La-Z-Boy chairs, a pool table, and a flat screen TV mounted on the wall. This was like a dive bar in the middle of a warehouse. The area was littered with people. Partying people. Half a dozen men, three women. The air was thick with cigarette smoke and the scent of pot.

I spotted another man. *My* man. Rider was standing off on the other side of the open area where it branched into another hallway and he was standing there talking to a girl with long blonde hair. No. Not just a girl. That Gia / Gianna girl. She had her back against the wall, looking up at him, her lip pouty. He was speaking to her, his body language... I couldn't tell for sure, but it looked relaxed.

Others all had their eyes on me, the party crasher. I felt the vibe change. The music volume went down and I heard, "Ride."

The voice? It was a prospect, the one who'd commented that he should put me in a photo shoot with his vintage bike. Rider looked over his shoulder and then his eyes landed on me.

If I could shoot daggers out of my eyes at him, I would've.

I felt my face get hot.

What on Earth?

"Hey, baby. What're you doin'?" Rider asked, making his way toward me.

It felt like steam was coming out of my ears. My nostrils. Even my toes.

I didn't know whether I wanted to scream, cry, or gouge his eyes out with my nails.

I spun around dramatically, and marched out of there.

Back the way I came. I think. This place was confusing.

He caught up to me in no time. "Wrong way, beautiful."

Of course.

I spun and changed directions.

"Hey," he grabbed for my hand. I smacked his hand.

"Jenna."

"You!" I hissed, for lack of a better reply and he blinked.

The numbers were getting lower again. Good. Okay. I found our door and opened it. He was in behind me.

"Jenna? What's wrong?"

"Are you effing kidding me?" I hissed.

He blinked, and his head jerked back.

"I... I... I can't even believe you have to ask me this!"

"Back it up, gorgeous. Explain."

"Me? Me explain?"

"Jenna, calm down."

"Calm? Calm isn't anywhere in sight, Rider Valentine! You leave me alone all day yesterday and then all night without telling me you're even leaving, and I wake up and go looking for the kitchen and find you in the equivalent of a bar, talking up that girl? At almost five o'clock in the morning?"

"Whoa. Wait a second..."

"A girl that I know for a fact that you've had sex with!"

He clenched his teeth and leveled a glare at me. He took a deep breath.

"So, what? The thrill is gone? I agree to be with you and a day later you're chatting up some girl at five o'clock in the morning after leaving me alone all day and all night?"

"Slow your fuckin' roll there, baby. You've got it wrong."

"You left me here. All day. Am I right?"

"Yeah. And that's because we're in a war with people who wanna rape you and kill you."

"And then you tell me it's just us tonight and then you leave me. You don't tell me where you're going. You're just gone. And hours and friggin' hours later I find you with a girl you've had sex with."

"Who told you I fucked her? Who's been shooting their mouth off?"

"Wh-what? That's what matters here? Who told me?"

"Club whores aren't supposed to shoot their mouths off to the women."

"Club whores? Nice. Really nice."

"Settle down and let me talk to you."

"No. I'm going." I started zipping up my bag. "I'm done with this shit."

"Jenna."

"No Rider. It wasn't a club whore. You people really don't think much of women, do you? It was your sister that told me. And not to rat you out, she told me the other day about Gianna the poor biker bunny who wants nothing more than to be a biker's *old lady,* and no one takes her seriously. They just use her for sex. Move."

He was standing against the door, looking at me with irritation.

"You're going nowhere."

"Right. My safety. Thanks so much for giving a shit. Just get me another room. I'm not staying here with you. We're done."

"Jenna, listen to me..."

"No. I'm done listening to your bullshit."

"Fuck," he bit off. "Sit the fuck down and listen to me, goddamn it!"

I glared. "Or *you* find another room. Does Gianna have a room here? Does she like hate fucking?"

"I just got back half an hour ago. I thought we were in for the night, but there was an emergency. A brother needed some cover with a situation, so we had to roll out fast. My phone was dead. No one else had your number. I figured I'd be back before you woke up. Shit got twisted and we were longer than I figured we'd be."

I folded my arms across my chest.

"I got back here, heard Gia was here, and she's persona non-grata right now, since we don't want to put anyone at risk with someone who might be a double agent, so I had to ream out the brother who brought her and find out what she was up to. I came here, opened the door, which you forgot to lock when you went to bed..." He let that hang.

"I didn't know I was gonna be alone all night!" I hollered. "You were supposed to be here. And aren't I supposed to be safe here?"

His nostrils flared. His voice went lower, gruffer. "I saw you sleepin', then decided to go deal with the fact that she was here, spoke to her for like five minutes, gettin' her side of the tale between her and Kailey, and that's when you were there, tryin' to strike me dead with lasers from your eyes. Now we're here. And yeah, it's safe, and next time I'll tell you if I gotta go, but just sayin'... lock the door. I don't want my girl sleepin' somewhere vulnerable unless I'm there to watch over her."

That last comment was trying to penetrate my shield, but I fought it off and kept glaring.

"So, no. You're not going anywhere." He took a step forward.

The wind was out of my sails a bit, so I felt my posture loosen.

"Don't assume, Jenna. Not cool."

"It's also not cool to feel abandoned and then see you chatting up a beautiful girl that I know you've had sex with."

He rolled his eyes.

"Did you just roll your eyes at me?" I demanded.

He smirked. "You're really fuckin' riled, aren't ya? Fuck, but you're beautiful when you're angry." He took another step toward me.

I shoved him with both hands. He went back on a foot and then laughed at me and advanced and then I found myself pinned to the bed, beneath him.

"Maybe I should fuck the angry right outta you."

I gasped in shock.

"And when you're possessive. Makes me really fuckin' hard."

"You're kidding me right now, right?" I snapped. "I can't believe—-"

He cut me off with a kiss. He was hungrily ravishing my mouth.

And for some reason, I started kissing him back. With some sort of unleashed anger slash passion.

And then my shirt was going up and over my head and then it was gone. And then I pulled his t-shirt over his head.

His mouth was on my one boob, his hand on the other, and then the other hand was down the front of my pants. And I wasn't protesting. I was feeling. I was feeling, and my mouth was in a big O.

"Soakin' wet," he said against my mouth and holy crap, that made me wetter. "Knew I saw some promise in you."

My back arched and then my pants were coming off and then his mouth was right between my legs. I let out a squeal of surprise.

My legs were up and over his shoulders and he was feasting on me. He had way more than a five o'clock shadow with a two-day growth that felt like sandpaper on my inner thighs. And it was phenomenal.

One of my hands went to the top of my head and I had a fistful of my hair. The other went to the top of his head and I had that fist filled with his hair.

"Rider," I breathed.

"Mmmmm," he made noise against my clit and it vibrated straight through to a place that make my soul sing.

"Fuck, you taste good, gorgeous. My bubblegum fucking lollipop."

"Ah!" I was trembling. I was coming. I was coming this fast! It hit hard and I let out a grunt that didn't sound *at all* pretty, but then he stuck his finger or maybe his thumb into my butt just a little and holy crap did that feel good. Primal. Dirty. So effing good.

And then I was dead. Yep, I might've died. I couldn't move. Was I breathing? Yeah, I was breathing. Okay. Phew. *Okay.*

He rose up and then flipped me over onto my belly.

"Up. Knees, baby."

"No. You get dead lay Jenna now. Because you're a jerk. You might've just gave me a Top 5 ever orgasm, but I'm angry. So, you can do the rest of the work, too."

My face was half-smushed into the pillow.

My ass was slapped, hard. I squeaked.

"I said knees. Right now. Up!" His voice was guttural. And I jolted in fear for a second and looked over my shoulder. But then he winked. And I knew it was just a game. And I was *so* down to play it wasn't even funny.

I got up on my knees and he entered me doggy style. He started to drill into me hard and fast.

"Rider," I moaned. Holy crap that felt good.

"Mm, good girl," he said and grabbed my hips with both hands and started hammering even harder. "Now... you get your reward." His angle was fan-fricking-tastic.

"Oh my God." I moaned, and collapsed onto my face. He started going faster, holding my bottom half up, faster *and* harder.

And then he collapsed on top of me as he let out a husky, masculine groan and kissed the back of my head.

He got up and flicked the light out and got back in beside me.

"Like fightin' with you, baby."

I grunted a half-angry sound.

"I was only there five minutes. Honest, beautiful. And Gia doesn't mean a thing to me. She's bein' walked out. She understands. She might be innocent, dunno, don't care. Not takin' any chances right now."

I tensed up a little.

"You mean something to me."

I loosened.

"And when I say *something*, I mean something I've never felt before."

Omigod.

"Okay," I whispered.

He turned me so that we were on our sides, facing one another in the dark.

He kissed my lips. I kissed his, too. I ran my hand up and down his arm, snuggling in to his chest. He put his arm around me and held me close.

I fell asleep, blissfully sated, naked, tangled up with him.

I WAS WOKEN UP BY HIM.

"Jenna. Baby."

"What time is it?" I rubbed my eyes.

He was leaning over me. "Nine. Gotta go take care of business, beautiful girl. Forgot to charge both my phones. Bronto's here with you guys today. You need me, he can get word to me. I'll be back as soon as I can. Okay?"

I was frowning. "You hardly slept, Rider."

"I'm aware. Thanks for givin' a shit, though."

He sounded more than tired.

"What's going on?" I reached for his hand.

He gave mine a squeeze and then let go.

"Taking the Jackals down takes work." He leaned over and grabbed for his Duffle bag. He unzipped it and had a gun in his hand. I gasped.

He stuffed it into the back of his jeans. He put his leather jacket on and zipped it up, then put his gray wool beanie on his head.

He leaned over and kissed me.

"Rider!" I gasped.

"Gotta go, baby."

"You have a gun."

He tilted his head at me.

"A gun!" I repeated.

"Yep."

"Uh, we need to talk," I said. I was shaking.

"When I get back."

"When?"

"Tonight, probably. Gotta go. Boys're waiting."

I watched him go. I was shaking like a leaf.

IT WAS 24 HOURS LATER. It was Sunday morning, and I was woken by a text. From Pippa.

> **Sending to you both J&E. Wedding yesterday was a hoot. Here are pics. The bride was thrilled with the results so no worries. Hope you're both safe & getting SOME in scary bikerland. Xo. Love yas.**

I put the phone down.

I was glad Kendra's wedding went well. I'd look at the pictures later.

Rider was asleep beside me. He'd gotten in late. Very late. Like, three o'clock in the morning. I woke when he came in, but said nothing. I was kind of seething. I was kind of freaked out all day. I mean, he left with a gun!

When he came in, he undressed, climbed in with me, spooned me, kissed my bare shoulder (I was sleeping in a tank top and panties), and then he was out like a light.

He'd been gone all day. He'd texted me a few hours after leaving to say his new phone was charged and to text if I needed him.

I didn't. Instead, I was in my head all day.

Jojo was a bit perkier that day. She was slightly better company. But, I probably wasn't. I didn't bring up the gun. I didn't bring up any of my concerns. Not even Gianna. I tried to keep my shit to myself so maybe she'd be slightly less gloomy.

It was a nice day outside, so we walked around out there and got some air. And then we'd played cards and helped Delia put away all sorts of groceries as well as stocking the numerous bathrooms in the place with supplies. The girl bathrooms had pads and tampons and shower stuff. The men's washrooms also got stocked with a Costco-sized box of condoms each.

And then I borrowed a vacuum (the cleaning supply room had four of them) and vacuumed our room and then vacuumed some halls. Delia was thrilled about having my help.

Later, Leah came by and hung out with me and Jojo, and I think that perked her up a bit, too. We played some video games and some foosball, and then a few of the other ladies, an older lady named Connie and that Patticakes lady from the day before the funeral came by, and we all sat and watched the Fifty Shades of Grey movie and had a laugh talking about sex. Well, they talked. I laughed.

The older ladies were not *at all* shy about it and Patticakes talked about how her 'old man' liked to have sex with her in a swing that they'd put in their room since he had some medical condition that meant he couldn't handle any weight on him, but the swing helped because he liked her on top. Luckily for Bronto, he'd been turfed out of the room for the movie and subsequent girl talk.

Ella would love this conversation. My bestie was a bit of a perv. She often made me blush with her sex talk. I'd never considered myself a prude, just considered Ella a little bit oversexed. But, whoa. If I told her about some of what Rider and I had gotten up to, maybe I'd make *her* blush for a change.

How was I feeling about things?

It hadn't sat well. The whole Gianna thing. And the whole, *being left alone for that length of time*, thing. But, things were bad right now. And I hadn't seen him do anything with that girl. He was just talking to her and he didn't look guilty when he saw me, didn't seem like he'd been caught with his hand in any sort of cookie jar.

Yeah, I was making excuses, but I'd decided I had to give things time. We were new. We had to set expectations with one another. And things weren't exactly normal around us with the MC war, and me being under a deadly threat.

I also wasn't used to sitting around doing nothing like this. It felt a little bit like a prison. I didn't want to complain about it, because it was better than being raped and dead, but it wasn't easy to sit around knowing things were happening outside these walls.

Kendra getting married. Someone else doing her hair. I hadn't talked to Ella in forever. There was knowing my salon was ticking along without me, but not knowing what my mother's revenge would be for my blatant disobedience. I'd texted my Dad that day to say *Hi* and let him know I was just checking in. He replied with:

> **"Good, Ryder messaged me and I called the officer in Sioux Falls. I feel a bit better after talking to police but won't rest easy until this is behind us. Let's have dinner together when you're back home. I look forward to meeting him."**
>
> **"Will do, Dad. Rider, not Ryder. He's a rider, not a truck. Ha. Love you, talk soon."**

Dad texted me back a happy face. This was so weird. My father and I did not have a jokey texty relationship. Maybe we could, though.

I'd bet my mother wasn't going to be looking forward to it. He wasn't Daniel. He wasn't country club material. And she'd blame him for all that was amiss right now. Me not there at her beck and call. Me not there for her to torment.

I was *not* cool with him leaving with a gun and not addressing my concerns about it. I mean, I was obviously flipped out at the sight of it.

I felt my hair being tucked behind my ear.

I looked up from the wall of beautiful chest in front of my eyes and saw he was looking down at me.

"Hey," he said.

"Hi," I said.

"Your eyelashes were tickling me. You a million miles away?"

I guess I was blinking against his chest.

"Sorry."

"Nothing to be sorry about. Gimme a kiss."

I leaned up and kissed him and went to roll away. He caught me and pulled me back and flipped to his back so that I was on top of him.

I put my hands between us and tried to push back.

"How're you mad at me already? We're not even up yet."

"How am I mad?"

He flipped me over onto my back and pinned me.

His erection was against me. He was in track pants.

"Yeah. Why?" He was grinding against me.

"I saw you leave here with a gun yesterday," I said, trying to ignore the grinding. And failing.

"Yeah?" He reached down and freed himself from those track pants and was pressed up against my underwear.

I tried to roll him. He didn't allow it.

"Rider, be serious for a second."

"Baby, I carry a gun when things are at a level where I could get killed. If it's me or them, you better believe I'll take care of me."

"You just discounted my feelings and—-"

"I had to go. Time is important in this situation. I'm sorry I left you with concerns, but I wouldn't have done it if it weren't necessary. I can handle a gun. I wouldn't use it unless I had to use it."

I pursed my lips.

He kissed them.

I stayed still.

He licked my lower lip.

I tried to jerk my head the other way.

"Let me in, beautiful." His tongue pushed in and then he was grinding against me with more friction. "Open up."

His knee nudged my legs open.

"Rider, I'm serious. We need to get a few things straight."

"Oh yeah, like what?" He kissed my lips again.

"I don't like being kept in the dark, for one thing."

He grasped around my knee and wrapped my leg around the back of his leg.

"Rider. Stop for a second."

"Mm, no way. You're already wet. I can feel it through your little panties, baby. We'll talk after, when I've got you all sweet and loosened up."

"No. Now." I dug my nails into his bicep.

But, he was right. I was wet. *Why? How would I ever gain the upper hand in this relationship if he used his penis as a weapon?* Maybe I wouldn't ever have it. Maybe I was okay with that. Surprisingly.

"Usin' your nails? Even better. Fight me, baby."

I jolted in surprise. And irritation.

"Get off."

"Oh, don't worry. I will. We'll both get off."

"Rider! If you don't get off of me right now, I'm about to lose it. Like, really lose it!"

He stopped and looked down at me. "Maybe we need a safe word. I don't know if you're joking right now or not."

"I'm not joking!"

He rolled off. I sat up.

"I don't wanna be kept in the dark. I can't sit here and—-"

"You need to be in the dark, Jenna, about some of the shit happening, because that's just the way it is. All you need to know is that I'm keeping you safe and going after these fuckers for what they've pulled. What they've done will not stand."

"But... you could get hurt."

He stopped and looked at me.

"You could get hurt and I could be Jojo. Or Edge. Gutted. Wrecked. Without you. Yes, this soon, Rider. I'd be such a wreck."

He climbed back on top of me and put his forehead to mine and let out a slow breath.

"Fuck, baby."

I scored a point. Good. I let my wall down just enough to get that out and it worked. He was taking me seriously.

"Okay, here's the thing, babe. I can't tell you much, because a) I can't put you at risk and knowledge ain't always power in my world. Sometimes knowledge can get you in trouble. b) I don't want you to worry about me. Here's what you gotta know and I hope it'll put you at ease. We're smarter than they are. Way smarter. We've got multiple clubs in our corner, helpin' us. And we've got cops helpin' too. The cops do not want these fuckers to continue to do what they've been doin'. They've been pissing a lotta people off. Pissin' on turf that ain't theirs to piss on. They've gotten a lot of the wrong people upset, including The Brotherhood. A lot of the wrongest people around are involved with them and their bullshit. They're not just small-time outlaws selling drugs, sellin' tail, or even just runnin' weapons. They move flesh. For human trafficking rings. They deal in kiddie porn. They killed Lick, put Joelle in the hospital, fucked Scoot up, raped and murdered Jet, and they've threatened to hurt you. Of course I have to go after them armed. And I'm not gonna put you at any sort of risk by telling you anything more than I have to. I know time stops when you're on lock-down and it can be stressful. Today's for you and me, okay? We're gettin' outta here."

I blinked at him.

"After we fuck," he added, and then yanked my panties aside and slammed forward until he was rooted in me.

I let out a shuddering breath.

"Use your nails, gorgeous." I blinked again and dug them into his back. He seemed to really like that.

"And don't try usin' that pout too often to manipulate me. It's good, gorgeous, but if you overuse it, you'll find yourself with a pink ass from my hand."

I glared at him and dug my nails in harder. He liked it. He showed me how much he liked it, by making me come really hard before spilling into me.

15

There was a secret back way out of the compound that we took, with a gravel road, but we had to take another vehicle instead of the bike or the car. With all that was happening with the club's war against the Wyld Jackals, Rider didn't even want to take his orange muscle car. It was far too recognizable. And on the bike, we'd be too exposed.

So, we took a borrowed member's black SUV with tinted windows and we drove to the cabin. But, we did this after someone else left in Rider's car to distract any potential followers. It was a good call, because five minutes after *we* left, his phone rang, and he talked to someone on speaker who either was a bud or who was named Bud, who told him the Charger had been followed by a white cargo van, but that he'd lost them.

I kept watching to see if I saw anyone following us, but it didn't seem like it. I was tense almost all the way to the cabin, despite Rider trying to reassure me.

We were going to spend the night there. I was feeling both lighter and more worried. Worried about our safety, but it was nice to be out of the clubhouse / compound bubble for a bit.

I was happy that I'd soon have some of my own belongings, too. Some Aberdeen prospects would be meeting Bronto and some other member or prospect and the next day back at the clubhouse, some of my clothes would be waiting for me.

Rider said most of his stuff at the clubhouse above the bar had been ruined in the fire. He said he'd had enough clothes at the cabin to get by for a while before he'd have to shop for new clothes.

"Can I shop for you?" I asked.

"We sell clothes at the bike dealership, so Trina, our office manager, she's gonna order some new jeans and tees in for me, Spence, and Dad so we don't clean out the stock. She's put some stuff aside already. I'm all right for now with what I got from the cabin. But as for shoppin' for me, have at it. Anytime I can avoid a trip to a clothing store, I'm game," he told me, on our drive.

I was stoked about that.

"Trina's leavin' soon," he continued. "Ella might be takin' her job."

"Really?" I asked.

"Yeah. Dad offered. She's thinkin' it over."

"What would she be doing?"

"Reception. Handling the buying for parts and stock. Bookkeeping. Marketing. Shit like that."

"She's gonna rock that."

He smiled.

"Are you sure no one knows where your family's cabin is?" I asked.

He sweetly assured me again that it was a well-guarded secret and that we would be safe. We stopped at a grocery store on the way there to grab some food for dinner.

"What you want for dinner tonight?" he asked, as we were wandering the aisles.

"Umm, you could cook me steak? *Beef* steak," I said and gave him a smile.

He kissed me with a chuckle. I picked up a package of beef tenderloin steaks and tossed it into the basket he was holding. He grabbed some vegetables while I picked out some cupcakes for dessert, and we grabbed some beer, too. I also grabbed a box of that Reese's puff cereal and some milk, because *yum*.

He teased me for it, too.

"You gonna eat that junk?"

I smirked. "Yeah, I sure am. It makes the milk taste amazing."

"I look forward to havin' some with you."

"After you make me steak."

"After I make you steak. Even if the cow was cute."

"Shhh," I put my hand over his mouth. "Groceries, not cows."

"Groceries," he said, and then he kissed me and booped me on the nose.

We got to the cash register and I reached for my debit card, but he gave me a dirty look and hip-checked me aside and handed cash to the cashier.

"Equal rights, equal responsibility," I informed. "I'm not one of those chicks who wants equal rights but expects her boyfriend to pay for everything."

"Yeah, well, feel free to burn your bras, but I'm payin'."

Maybe I did that partly because he'd assumed I was selfish before. I didn't want him to think that. And I wasn't selfish with money. I was always picking up tabs, buying gifts for people *just because*. My mom hated how frivolous I was with money.

True, I am a spender, but wasn't that what it was for? I'm 24. I didn't need to worry about retirement quite yet. I didn't have to put money away for my future kids' college. I had a trust fund coming when I hit thirty and I didn't know the exact amount, but I knew it would be in high six figures, since my grandmother planned for any children of my dad's and I was the only one, so I thought of it as my future money. Down payment on a house. Opening accounts for college funds for my future kids. I was going to work and earn more money with my salon, too, so I was free with cash, because I felt like I could be.

The cashier, an older grandmotherly-looking lady snickered. "Let him pay, sweetie. We put up with a whole lot for our men. Least they can do is put their hands in their pockets once in a while."

I smiled at her. "He does loads for me, believe me."

She looked at him. "Bless you. And you're nice on the eyes, too."

"Why, thank you, ma'am," Rider winked at her. "My daddy raised me right."

She blushed and handed me the receipt. "He sure did. Now, sugar," she looked to me. "He pays, but you keep track of the receipts. Men always lose 'em."

I smiled at her. "Got it. Have a great day."

She waved us out. "You two will make some beautiful babies. Mark my words."

I laughed. Rider chuckled and kissed me affectionately on the side of my head on our way out.

On the way back to the SUV I informed, "I won't burn my bras. Oh God, bras. I actually miss wearing bras. I've been living in tank tops for a week."

"Not to worry. You'll have your over the shoulder boulder holders tomorrow. Shame, though." He opened my door for me, looking at my chest. I smiled and got in, saying, "I've got some very pretty bras and you like unwrapping pretty wrapping paper, so..."

"Good point," he said and rounded the vehicle and got in. Ten minutes later, we were at the cabin. And it was definitely getting chillier. It'd been just a few days since we'd been there, but I saw more leaves turning color.

He put the food away and I found the washer and dryer downstairs and tossed in a load of towels from what we'd dirtied when we were there last, and then I found him chopping wood outside, so I joined him, bringing us each a beer.

"Show me how to do that?" I asked.

He did. I chopped for a bit, so bad at it, but he looked highly amused. And then he pulled a big target out of a big garage that I hadn't noticed, a ways behind the cabin, and set it up on a big tree near the garage. We threw axes at it.

I'd heard axe-throwing leagues were getting popular, and this was a hoot.

"Got good aim," he told me. "Real surprised to see you interested in choppin' wood and throwin' axes."

"I have varied interests and talents. I play a lot of darts," I advised. "Way too much time getting up to no good in bars."

"You any good?"

"Little bit." I smiled.

"Yeah?" he asked.

"I'm actually very good," I amended.

"Yeah? We've got a dartboard here. You wanna play?"

"Do I want to emasculate you, you mean, by kicking your very nice ass?"

He threw his head back and laughed. "You're gonna put your money where your very sexy mouth is, gorgeous."

"I always do," I said, sipping my beer, teasingly swirling my tongue around the bottle opening and then sticking my tongue inside and wiggling it, before swallowing back some.

His eyes were on me and they were heated.

And then he was moving toward me. He bent and hauled me over his shoulder and I dropped my beer. He slapped my ass and carried me inside. I was giddy all the way.

He went straight downstairs with me over his shoulder and sat me on the bar while he opened up a dartboard case on the wall.

"Stakes?" I asked.

He grinned. "I win, you let me take your ass." He passed me three darts with red flights. He had three blue ones.

"Ho-no. Nuh uh. Four carat diamond, I told you. And don't think I haven't noticed you getting a little bit too familiar with that area." I wagged my finger at him with admonishment.

"Breakin' you in slow. And you like it. You fuckin' know you do."

"Yeah, well, your beast of a cock ain't getting in there, believe me."

He got the biggest smile on his face.

Yeah, he liked that. He straightened and strutted proudly right up to me. "Beast?"

"Mm hm," came from me.

"I win, you do what The Beast wants. *Anything* The Beast wants."

I smiled. "Except my ass."

He shrugged. "We'll see."

"What if *I* win?" I asked.

"You win..." He looked thoughtful, "You can do anything you want with The Beast for the rest of the day."

I laughed. "Sounds like a win-win for *The Beast*."

He wiggled his eyebrows.

And I didn't wipe the floor with him, it was a close game, but I *did* win.

He put the darts away and asked, "So, what do you wanna do for your win?" He adjusted himself crassly, and I laughed at him.

"I want *The Beast* to pick," I said.

His teeth sank into his bottom lip and then he moved to me, put his arms around me, and then he put his lips to mine.

I wrapped my arms around his neck, and pulled his elastic out of his hair and held him to me while I kissed him.

"What does he want? Tell me what he likes."

"Better not. Don't think you're ready for that," he winked.

"I'm ready," I assured.

He looked uncertain for a second.

"C'mon, Valentine. Tell me. What does my beast want?" I poked his chest.

"Your beast?" he smiled.

I gave him a sly grin. "Yeah. Mine."

He gave me a heated look.

"C'mon. Tell me."

"You really wanna know?" he asked.

"I'm asking, aren't I?"

He grabbed me by both ass cheeks and pulled me tight to him, got to my ear, and whispered, "Act like you're scared. Beg me not to."

"What?" I giggled. "But I want you to."

"Beg me to stop. Then when I don't stop, fight me off."

"Rider, seriously." I giggled.

"I am serious, gorgeous." His voice went lower. "You wanted to know what I like? What gets my motor runnin'? I want you to fight, scratch, bite, and know that no matter how hard you fight, we end the chase with me sunk deep inside that beautiful body. And Jenna, the harder you fight, the harder I'll get."

I swallowed hard.

"You want it hard?"

I'd wanted it slow and sweet. Passionate. Tender. But the look in his eyes and the visible bulge in his pants at just this conversation? Maybe it was time to try things his way. After all, it had gone well the few times I'd sort of gone with it. If you didn't count me taking off after the 'hate sex' comment.

I put my lips to his throat and kissed it. "Okay," I whispered.

He looked at me, both surprise and promise in his eyes.

"You're gonna need a safe word."

My eyes bulged. *Maybe I wasn't ready for this.*

His thumb caressed my cheek. "If it gets too intense, if you get scared. Okay? I'll go easy this time, since we're new, but the places I wanna take us? The places I fantasize about taking us? We'll go easy today, but you get too scared, or you want me to stop, you say the word. I'll stop."

I nodded.

"Your eyes are huge. Am I scarin' you?"

I smiled. "I thought you wanted me to act scared."

He closed his eyes and blew out a breath. "Fuck me, you're fuckin' sexy."

I smiled again. And then I cleared my expression, using my hand flat in front of my face and pulling down to reveal a serious face.

"What's the safe word?" he asked.

"How about 'safeword'? Keep it simple."

"Okay. You use it if you need to."

"Okay."

"You sure?" he asked.

"I'm sure."

Was I, though? I wanted to be.

"Okay, baby. You don't go any farther than the garage that way. Or, we stick to inside the house, if you prefer. What?"

"Wherever *The Beast* wants. Except my ass. Or anything too weird."

"From the SUV to the garage are the boundaries. Go, upstairs, do some busy work, distract yourself. And soon..." he eyed me from head to toe. "I'll come for you. We'll save the weird stuff for next time."

My belly wobbled, and I giggled nervously.

He winked.

I went upstairs and cleaned the bathroom sink and mirror. And then I was wiping the kitchen counters (that didn't need it). I wandered outside onto the side deck and was just about to sit down on one of five wooden rocking chairs that were out there, when a hand came around from behind me and covered my mouth.

The rocking chair was knocked over and then I was pulled against a hard body. For a split second, I actually panicked, thinking someone had found us, but then his mouth was by my ear and I heard his voice.

"Hey there, pretty girl. I'm gonna fuck you now. And you're gonna like it."

And I felt a mixture of relief and adrenalin surge at the exact same time. I turned ultra-competitive and stomped hard on his foot and elbowed him in the gut. I heard him grunt and then I took off running, toward the garage.

It didn't take long before he was right on my heels. He caught me and took me to a pile of leaves on the ground.

My heart was racing. My heart was racing so hard it felt like it'd fly right out of my chest.

I had a safe word. This was pretend. And, I wanted to be exciting for him. The idea of turning him on? It was turning me on.

I kicked and scrambled as he tried to flip me to my back. He either let me get away or I legit got away, and was scrambling to get up, but then he grabbed my ankle and dragged me backwards and then flipped me.

I swung a fist and caught his shoulder and that's when I saw his face. His eyes were heated, determined. I slapped with the other hand and caught his jaw with just the tips of my fingers. He subdued me, getting my wrists pinned over my head and then his lips were on mine.

And suddenly, I felt like I had to fight harder. Like this was real. Like I had to make it stop. Because it was hitting me, like a ton of bricks, how twisted up this was.

God. What was I doing?

People were dead because of a fake rape game. A fake rape game that got a man dead. A girl hurt. Another girl dead and raped for real. And here we were... playing a fake rape game.

"SAFEWORD!" I shouted.

Instantly, he let go of me.

"This is fucked," I said, breathless. My heart was racing. Hard.

"This is fucked!" I repeated, crab-crawling backwards, putting about five feet of distance between us. I collapsed onto my ass in the dirt.

He leaned back.

"How can this be hot? How? Jet died like this. What's wrong with us?"

I couldn't believe I'd even let it get that far.

"Jenna," he closed his eyes and moved back and sat on his ass in the leaves. "I was gonna go easy. But, you were..." he stopped talking and stared at me, looking like he was searching for words, or maybe trying to figure out what'd just happened.

"How does this turn you on? How did I allow myself to even...I'm turned on, too! Or I was, and now I'm not. I'm so, *so* not, Rider."

I was shaking my head. "I got excited, too. The idea of being something other than a dead lay? Being something you wanted? But, Rider. This isn't right. Especially not now. Maybe some other time, but with everything going on right now?"

He nodded. He looked remorseful. "I was gonna go easy. You were so into it, I guess I... got too into it."

So, this was my fault? Maybe it was. My shoulders slumped.

I got to my feet and dusted leaves off my jeans. I felt bile rising in the back of my throat.

I walked back toward the cabin. But, I heard something up ahead and Rider tackled me back to the ground.

"Fuck. Wait a second," he said.

My eyes were wide. We were hunkered down while he listened.

I heard a voice that sounded familiar and his body relaxed.

"It's okay," he said. "Just Jess."

He helped me up and kept my hand in his as we walked toward the cabin.

Spencer and Jesse were both there, by a silver pickup truck.

Spencer spotted us and then grabbed a black and pink glittery overnight bag (mine!) and a large suitcase (Also mine. Wahoo!) out of the bed of the pickup truck and headed toward us.

"Hey," Rider greeted.

"Stopped and saw Pippa and Joe. Brought your girl's stuff. Thought we'd hit the cache and grab a few weapons. I need some clothes, too. Running low since most of my shit got singed."

"Shoulda texted," Ride informed him.

"Yeah, see that." Spencer smirked and reached over and pulled a leaf out of my hair and tossed it. He reached again and pulled out another one.

My face went hot.

Jesse chuckled and lit a cigarette. "Sorry, Ride."

Rider put his arm around my neck and pulled me closer to his side. "Get what you guys need and take off. We need some time."

Spencer smiled and shrugged. "Gotcha."

Rider had my big bag and I took my smaller one, and they headed toward the garage. We headed back to the cabin.

Inside, he put the bag down and then took the bag that was in my hands and put it down. His thumbs went to my jaw, his fingers into my hair. "You okay?"

I nodded, and face-planted into his chest.

He put his arms around me.

God, that felt good.

"I'm sorry," he whispered into my hair. "Didn't think of it that way. It's not the same, any games we play, okay? What's between you and me has nothing to do with anything bad. I just like to play. I get why it flipped you out, and we won't play again like that until you're ready. Okay? You seemed into it and I got carried away. That's why there's a safe word. It was just too soon."

I looked up at him. "What if I don't wanna play that way at all?"

His face went blank. And I felt it like a kick in the gut. This was what he liked. What if we were fundamentally too different?

The silence between us went awkward, so I pulled away.

"I wanna see what Pip packed for me." I picked my smaller bag back up. He lifted the bigger one and carried it into Jojo's room. I followed.

"Is she okay with us sleeping in here?"

"Yeah, she's cool," he said, looking irritated.

"Rider..." I said, feeling all awkward.

"Baby, don't. Forget what happened outside, okay? I just want us to have a good night together. I'm gonna go get rid of these guys and start up the fire to cook our steaks. You wanna do the sides?"

"Do the...?"

"Make the salad, do the spuds?"

"I don't cook," I said.

He tilted his head and smiled. "You can't make a salad? Wash the potatoes and wrap them in foil so I can throw them on the fire?"

I scrunched up my face. "I can open a bag and dump it into a bowl. You bought individual salad ingredients. That requires slicing and chopping, and julienning, and fancy knifework."

He chuckled. "Shit. Okay. Yeah, after seein' the way you hacked at that wood, I can't imagine what you'd do to a cucumber."

I laughed and playfully smacked his arm. He was good at erasing the tension.

"I'll take care of the food then," he said.

"I'll wrap up the potatoes," I offered. "Then I'll see if Pippa packed me any lingerie and put it on under my clothes for you to play 'unwrap Rider's present' later. Does that help?"

"Deal," his eyes went heated and he moved in and kissed me. The kiss was sweet, though, almost chaste. Not hungry. And I wasn't sure how I felt about it, or all that'd happened since getting to the cabin, when he wandered out of the bedroom and left me in there.

I HAD JEANS, MY OWN sweats, bras (hallelujah), and a lot of sexy underwear and lingerie. Way more than Pippa had been asked to pack. This was a massive suitcase and my overnight glittery Duffle bag. She even packed me a little black dress. I was happy to have four of my own pairs of shoes, plus more make-up and skincare products.

I'd brought the suitcase that Jojo had packed for me with mostly clean clothes in it since we'd done laundry at the clubhouse, but I'd be happy to be back into my own stuff.

A few minutes later, I heard voices, so I went out and saw Spencer heading out the front door. Jesse and Rider were out front already, looking deep in conversation by the truck.

"Thanks for bringing my stuff," I called out.

"Not a problem, Blue Eyes," Spencer said, heading out with a filled massive hockey bag. "See ya soon." He gave me a smile and then walked to meet Jesse and Rider.

And I thought about what Jojo had said about finding Spencer a girl. A strong girl since he was such a handful. He was a really good-looking guy and I'd seen some humanity from him a few times, but he certainly had some demons.

I waved out the door as Jesse got in the truck. He gave me a two- finger wave and slammed the door as Spencer stood by the driver's side.

Spencer and Rider spoke for a second and then Spencer laughed at something Rider said and got in the truck. I guess they were over their squabble.

Rider walked back toward me, a little smile on his face.

"You two cool?" I asked.

"Huh?" he asked.

"You're past your fight?"

He waved his hand. "Yeah, countless fights over the years. Me and Deacon, D and Spence. It's all good. Brothers." He shrugged.

"Did he really make reference to nailing me?"

He glared. "Don't bring that up again or he and I won't be cool."

My eyes went wide.

"That was over the line. Don't wanna discuss it."

I waved my hands defensively. "Can we go back to the fun portion of our one-night getaway?"

He let out a breath. "Sounds good to me."

"Pippa packed me loads of lingerie."

"Yeah?" he raised his brows and the tension vanished from his face.

"Loads of visual delights in store for you," I said, with a wink.

Mission accomplished. My tension erasing game was strong, too.

IT WAS LATER THAT NIGHT and we were cuddled up, watching a movie. It was a little scary, though, and I kept burying my face in his shoulder. I showed the extent of my culinary skills by wrapping raw potatoes in foil and leaving the rest to him. I did the dishes, though, and then before our movie, I only half-burned the Jiffy-pop popcorn I'd found in the pantry.

Dinner was good. Steak with mushrooms and baked potatoes and salad. After the movie was over, he said, "Watch another?"

"Naw, let's go to bed," I said.

"You sleepy?" he asked teasingly, stoking the fire in the fireplace.

"Nope."

He smiled again, but it didn't look like his heart was in it.

And I was feeling a bit frustrated.

"I'm trying here, Rider, but work with me. Show a little enthusiasm?"

"What?" Now he looked irritated.

"You're stuck on what happened earlier and my saying 'What if I don't wanna play those games?'"

"Ah fuck, let it go, will ya?" he grumbled.

I glared. "Obviously, this is an issue. So, no. I'm not gonna effing let it go!"

"We don't need to figure everything out in one day, Jenna. You don't wanna play today, you might feel differently when this shit is behind us, I get that. We don't need to beat that horse to death today. Let it go."

"I'm going to bed. Goodnight," I snapped and headed toward the bedroom.

"Get back here, Jenna."

"Don't call me Jenna!"

"What the fuck?"

He looked at me like I'd lost it. And I guess maybe I had.

"You never call me Jenna unless you're pissed at me. You have no right to be pissed at me right now for wanting to fool around with you. I'm pissed at *you*!"

"Huh?"

"I'm pissed at you!" I repeated.

"No, back it up to calling you Jenna. What the fuck?"

"I don't like it when you call me Jenna."

"Uh, would you like me to call you Genevieve Maybelle instead?" He spat.

"Don't you ever say those names to me again!" I hissed.

He threw his hands up defensively. "You might wanna start explaining and start explaining now, before I call the fuckin' loony bin to come lock you down. You're near the end of your birth control pack, aren't ya?"

I gasped. "Don't you even!" (But he was right; I was only a few pills away from the end of my pack).

"Start explaining, then," he invited.

"A) Don't call me Genevieve. Ever. I'm not ready to tell you why, but trust me, you manage to get those walls you want inside of down, you'll find out why."

"Fine," he agreed, and he looked less irritated already.

"B) You only call me Jenna at specific times. You call me gorgeous, or beautiful, or babe, or baby. You only call me Jenna when you're being bossy or when you're fighting with me. And right now, you're fighting with me."

He looked a little thrown for a beat and then he started to laugh.

And then I felt embarrassed. Because I sounded like a lunatic.

"Okay, gorgeous, how 'bout you get over here right now?"

He was still by the fireplace. I was by the hallway.

"And why should I do that?"

"Fine, I'll come there." He put the fire poker back into the holder and stalked toward me. I backed up at the intensity coming from his eyes. He backed me into the wall right beside where the hallway opened up.

He thrust his hands into my hair. "I told you I get off on fighting with you."

I blinked.

He brought my mouth to his and touched it softly. "No more fighting back tonight, though. The rest of tonight, you do what I say. The Beast wants to finish our game."

I just stood there.

He grabbed my hand and walked me into the bedroom, past the holes in the walls, and he shut the door.

"Drop your jeans," he ordered.

I stared.

"You wanna play or no?" he asked, with more than a hint of condescension. But strangely, I found it sexy.

I swallowed and then I unbuttoned them and pushed them down and stepped out of them.

"Shirt off," he told me.

I threw my t-shirt over my head and tossed it at him. He caught the balled-up fabric and tossed it to the floor.

"Take your panties off," he ordered.

I hooked my thumbs into the sides and peeled them down. I stepped out of them.

His eyes traveled the length of me.

"Get over here."

"Can I take my socks off? *So* not sexy in just a pair of socks."

"Yeah," he said with a smirk, his eyes on my red pair of fluffy socks.

"Unless they're thigh-highs. Now those look sexy," I informed him.

"Get some of those," he demanded.

"I've got some. I jerked my thumb behind my back. "In my suitcase. They're white and sheer with little red hearts on them." Pippa did good with the packing. Those socks had been packed with matching cheeky red panties and a matching bra.

"Fuck sakes..." he shook his head. "We'll get to those later. First, get over here."

I pulled my socks off and walked to him.

"On your knees, gorgeous. You're gonna learn how The Beast likes to get his daily sesh of head."

"Daily?" I choked.

He shrugged. "A guy can try."

I giggled.

"Not jokin' about getting on your knees, beautiful girl."

I went down.

"Take him out."

I undid his belt buckle and then his jeans, and there it was.

"Hey Beast," I said, lifting it.

"Hey, beauty," Rider said.

I looked up and smiled.

He winked.

"Kiss him right there." He pointed to just below the crown, right at the studs.

I placed a kiss right there.

"Open your mouth.

I opened it.

"Look up at me. I wanna see obedience in your eyes."

I looked up.

He shook his head slowly, with a look of approval though, and chewed his bottom lip.

"Flatten your tongue. Curve it up a little. Take it in, slow, grazing along the flat part of your tongue."

I obeyed.

He moved forward and put the tip in my mouth. He glided in part way.

"Eyes up and on my face."

I obeyed.

His hand moved to the back of my head. He went slow, half way in.

"Suck. Gentle. No biting."

I obeyed. He was thrusting into my mouth a little bit, slowly, gently. And his face was lit with such sexiness, I felt the wetness increasing between my legs.

I reached up and grabbed his ass cheeks with both hands and went deeper.

"Yeah, baby." His head went back and I saw a swallow move down his corded throat. "Ah. That's good."

I was doing good. And I was turned on.

I tried going deeper still, but then I gagged and he pulled back.

"Okay?"

I nodded and tried again. He took my hair into his fist and held it in a ponytail and moved my head a little. I was bobbing a bit, sucking a bit, and feeling it move in and out. He started to go a little bit faster.

"Open your throat. Try. Feel it open up."

I stretched the muscles just under my jaw and I think it was working.

"Touch yourself," he said.

I blinked.

"Put your fingers between your legs. Are you wet?"

I reached down and did as I was told. I was definitely wet.

"Rub your clit."

My eyes rolled back as I did what I was told. Holy crap, this was hot.

"Don't come."

I jolted.

"Don't come, gorgeous. Not yet. But keep rubbing."

"Hm?" I asked around his dick. He kept pumping into my mouth, gently, his hand holding my hair.

"Keep rubbing."

I whimpered. I was gonna come. I didn't know how to *not* come with how worked up I was.

I started to tremble. He leaned over and grabbed my hand and pulled it away from between my legs, and this meant his cock wasn't in reach of my mouth. And between my legs was practically buzzing.

I was so ready for that orgasm and to have it yanked away? I was trembling. He pulled me toward the bed and we tumbled down together. He flipped me and lay down on his back.

"Ride my face while you finish sucking off The Beast, baby. No directions. Just do what you wanna do on my face while it's in your mouth. Lick, suck, bite, whatever. I'm ready to feel what you're gonna give me. I want it all."

I shakily climbed up and he sucked hard on my clit. Really hard. I started to shake.

"Get my cock in your mouth." He slapped my ass.

I did what I was told. He sucked some more, and I rocked against his face, my knees dug into the mattress, and my mouth filled with Rider. And it only lasted about a minute before I was having what would've probably resembled a seizure. Because the orgasm was absolutely massive.

He came in my mouth and was so deep in there when he did that I didn't have a chance to do anything but swallow it down.

Swallowing? Not my favorite. I usually wound up with it in my hair as I'd pull whoever out just as it started. If I wasn't fast enough and ended up with a mouthful, I generally spat it onto the guy's belly. That was why I'd recently adopted the suck a little / jerk off a lot mode. Less chances of a mouthful of jizz.

But, Rider had been so deep in my mouth that it literally just went right down. I had no choice but to swallow. And the sound he made? I decided maybe I didn't hate giving head after all.

And then I told him that.

"Maybe I don't hate giving head after all."

And he laughed out loud. Really loud. And then he pulled me up, kissing me hard, deep, and passionately.

And we curled up together.

I wasn't tired. I was awake. Sated. Way sated. But awake. With a bazillion things roaming around my brain.

"Lots of fun games, gorgeous. Not just the kinda game we played in the woods."

I nodded, feeling a little bit better.

"Don't keep doin' that."

"Doing what?"

"Looking for reasons we won't work. Jenna. We're workin' great."

"You hate drama."

"Not with you."

"And you don't like vanilla."

"You're a whole lot more fun than vanilla, baby. And vanilla ain't terrible. I just like more than the same flavor all the time."

I sighed.

"And so do you, evidently."

Yeah. Maybe. This was my thought, but I didn't say it out loud.

He kissed my temple. "I'm gonna get in."

"In?"

"Inside your walls, gorgeous."

I cuddled into him and didn't say anything in response. But, it felt really, *really* good that he said it.

"Sweet dreams, Rider."

"Sweet dreams, gorgeous."

"You too, Beast." I cupped him between the legs.

He chuckled. "Don't wake him up, unless you wanna deal with makin' him tired again."

I laughed. "Thanks for the warning."

I guess I was a little bit tired after all, because I fell asleep soon after.

And when I woke up, he was spooning me.

I TURNED OVER AND STARED at him for a few minutes after waking, thinking I needed to pee, but wanted to look at him for a few minutes before he woke.

He was sleeping naked. As was I. I looked over his ink, thinking about Luke "Lick" Hanson drawing all those tattoos on his skin.

He had a defined stomach. A sexy happy trail of dark hair that led downward to a very happy place that he appeared to spend some time grooming. He hadn't shaved his face since the morning of the funeral, so his face was definitely sporting more than scruff, and it looked damn good, surprisingly based on my usual taste.

His ears were pierced but he had no jewelry in them. I could see his eyebrow was pierced, too, but he wore no earring there, either. Deacon had a barbell in his eyebrow. Spencer wore black studs in both ears.

Rider had a ring in his left nipple, though, and other than his dick piercing, it was the only jewelry he'd worn since we'd met.

I touched the ring protruding from his nipple with my finger. He stirred. And then I did it again. He grabbed for me, startling me, and then flipped me and filled me.

He was inside me before his eyes opened.

"Ah!" I gasped and then pulled my knees up, relishing the feeling of depth.

"Are you sleep-fucking me?" I asked.

"Mm," his mouth moved to mine.

His phone was ringing from the floor, probably his jeans pocket. He ignored it and kept at me.

Five seconds after it stopped ringing, it started ringing again.

"Shit," he grumbled, and sliding out of me, reached down to the floor and then answered it after saying, "Sorry, gorgeous. One sec."

"This better be important," was how he answered. And then he listened for a minute and then clipped an angry, "Fuck!" And I was on high alert, wondering what the heck was going on now.

"Yeah. Okay. I'll be there as soon as I can," he said and threw the phone to the bed and buried his face in my chest.

"What's wrong?" I put my hands in his hair.

"Fuck," he grumbled. I let go of his hair and he lifted up onto his knees.

"We gotta go to my mother. She's been beaten up. Coupla brothers are there, but I'm the closest Valentine so I'm up."

"Oh no. Who did it?"

"She's not sayin'. She refuses to talk 'till one of her kids get there."

"Oh no. At least she can talk."

"Yeah, it'd take more than getting slapped around for Shelly to be rendered speechless."

Yikes.

"Where's everyone?" I asked.

"Spence headed back to Aberdeen last night. Deacon's in the Falls, but he's in the thick of something. Dad's not goin' near Shelly right now. He asked me to go instead."

I winced and got to my feet and we quickly got dressed and closed things up at the cabin and then we headed to his mother's.

16

There were two cars and a bunch of motorcycles in the driveway when we got there, and when we got inside, I heard Shelly shouting.

"No! I want my sons. Alla them." Shelly was practically screeching in her scratchy two-pack-a-day voice. It did *not* sound pretty. I rushed in behind Rider.

Blow, the one who'd be moving to Aberdeen to be VP, was there, as was Axel, and three other members I had seen, but couldn't recall names of.

Shelly was in the family room, on the brown leather couch, two black eyes, bruises on her face, and she was holding her arm funny. The bikers were all standing, Blow standing right in front of her, looking like he was the one trying to reason with her.

The place had been spotless when we were here a few days before. Now, it looked like a cyclone had been through it. There were beer and booze bottles all over the coffee table. Overflowing ashtrays littered the place with the scents of stale cigarette smoke and skunky beer in the air. A big hole in the wall glared at us, and broken glass littered the hardwood floor outside the range of the area rug.

Blow, standing there in jeans, cowboy boots, and a denim Dominion Brotherhood vest, jerked his chin up at Rider and continued trying to reason with her. "Your arm is broken, Shell. You gotta go to the hospital." He folded his bare arms across his chest, highlighting some seriously big 'guns'. The guy had full colorful tattoo sleeves that reminded me of Rider's, but they were in color. I wondered if Lick had done Blow's tattoos, too.

"Ride," she whimpered as we were moving into the room. Her whimper melted into a bit of a glare when she saw I was behind him.

"C'mon, Mom. Hospital first. We'll go from there after."

"Where're your brothers? Are they comin'?"

"Me and Jenna were closest, so right now you got us. Let's go." He lifted her up carefully into his arms. She winced and held her arm protectively.

"My purse. My cigarettes," she whined, motioning toward the table.

"I've got them," I told her and lifted up the pack of cigarettes and the lighter. "Where's your purse?"

She jerked her chin toward the big brown leather couch. I saw a black silver chained big hobo bag sitting on the floor beside it.

I grabbed it and we headed out the door. Rider put her in the front passenger seat of the borrowed SUV we had and buckled her in. I got into the back seat.

There were men getting on their motorcycles behind us and two of them followed us, two more got into a car and headed in the opposite direction.

"Who did this, Mom?" Rider demanded, seething with anger.

"Mantis," she mumbled.

"When and why? Tell me the story."

"There's no story. I was having a little get together last night. He showed up, beat the shit outta me, and threw me at the wall, then left. I called Deacon. He didn't answer. Called you. You didn't answer. Obviously, you were caught up in *her*."

The venom with which she said 'her' was...wow. This woman hated me, and she didn't even know me.

She went on. "Spency has me blocked. Jojo answered her phone and sent Blow, till one of youze'd bother answerin'. Did yer father tell you all to ignore my calls?"

"No, Mom. He didn't. We all have a lot goin' on. In case you hadn't heard."

"You're with your new piece, though, she's not on lock down with yer sister, so obviously—-"

"Do not fuckin' call Jenna my *new piece.*"

My brows shot up. I stayed quiet in the back seat.

Shelly was quiet.

"Who else was there?" he demanded.

"Huh?" she asked.

"You said you were having a get together. Who was there when this went down?"

"No one," she said kind of loud.

"What?" Rider was showing he was irritated. "Explain."

"Explain what? Can I have one a my cigarettes?" she called over her shoulder, not very politely.

I scrambled and leaned up and then passed her the pack and her lighter.

She took them without acknowledging me and then struggled with one hand to get one out of the pack, her other arm sort of dangling uselessly.

"Want some help?" I leaned up between the seats.

"I got it," she grumbled.

"Seatbelt on, gorgeous." Rider ordered, reached over, took her pack, and tapped one out of the pack, lit it, and passed it to her.

I'd never seen him smoke. The easy way he did that, it was obvious he used to smoke.

I sat back and buckled in, then I cracked the window.

"Party was over. My friends'd gone. The Jackals must've been watchin'." She puffed on her cigarette.

"When?" Rider demanded.

"Last night."

"What time?"

"Around... I dunno; late. What the fuck, Ride? I wasn't watchin' the clock. I was getting' thrown into a wall in my livin' room!"

I could see his eyes in the rearview mirror and they were so angry it made my blood chill.

We pulled off a main street onto a side road and then down another side road and finally pulled into hospital parking lot.

Two motorcycles had followed us. They pulled off towards a parking area while Rider pulled up to the door at the emergency entrance and said, "Can you get in there okay?"

"I can walk, yeah," she muttered.

"Jenna," Rider said, "You good to take her to the desk? I'll park. Gotta make a few calls, talk to the brothers. Be in soon?"

I gave him a nod, grabbed my bag and Shelly's bag, and jumped out.

I opened the door for her and held my hand out to assist her in getting out. She half glared at me, but took my hand and then let it go once she was standing. I glanced at him and his expression? Yikes.

I did not have a good feeling about this. Things were obviously about to be taken to the next level in this war between the Wyld Jackals and the Dominion Brotherhood. I closed the door and he drove off.

She took a few more puffs off her cigarette by the door and then dropped it on the ground and didn't even bother crushing it with her heel before stepping in through the automatic door. I stepped back and stepped on it and then rushed in behind her.

IT WAS FIFTEEN MINUTES later, and I was sitting in a waiting area, watching her through the window while she smoked and seemed to be arguing with her son.

She'd talked to the triage nurse and I heard her say she "Just got beat up". The nurse offered to call the police and Shelly waved her non-injured arm impatiently and said, "Just put my arm in a sling or whatever you gotta do so I can get outta here. Hate fuckin' hospitals. Spent way too much time here lately."

She was so scowly and angry that the triage nurse just got on with things. I was quiet, at her side.

"Are you next of kin?" The nurse had asked.

"No, she ain't. My boy is out parkin' the truck. He'll be here in a minute. You wanna go sit?" She huffed at me. "You don't need to hear my personal details, do ya?"

Awkwardly, I jolted. "I... I'll just—-"

"Leave my purse," Shelly snapped. I'd put it on her lap and walked to the waiting area and sat.

The waiting area was big and filled with chairs all around the perimeter as well as a few clusters of chairs in the middle. It had a few televisions on, muted, but with news channels with subtitles on it. I could see out the windows that two of the bikers that had come with Rider were by a smoking shelter with him. They were smoking, and he was on his phone, pacing, while talking into the phone.

A minute or two later, Shelly went out there with them, lighting up.

Rider got off the phone and was talking to her, his arms folded across his chest. She was waving her right (working) arm while smoking. Her left arm was now in a sling.

I sat there, sort of frozen, watching her rant at him while he stared at her angrily. I didn't know what I was missing, but he looked skeptical. Like he didn't believe whatever she was saying. And he wasn't hiding it. He pointed toward the door and turned his back on her and was dialing a number on his phone. She took another few hauls and then threw her cigarette on the ground and crushed this one with her high-heeled black leather boot and waltzed back in.

She sat down in a chair across from me.

There were only two other people in the large waiting room and one was near us, the other was way on the other end of the room.

"They call my name?" she asked me.

"Not yet," I answered.

She made a disgruntled sound.

"Need somethin' for the pain. Assholes makin' me wait."

"Do you want something from the vending machine?" I asked. "I have a bunch of change."

She shook her head, annoyed, and didn't look at me. She was looking out the window at Rider talking with the other two bikers.

"You think you know him? Think he's the best thing since sliced bread?" She still had her eyes aimed out the window, but she was obviously talking to me.

"We've only been dating a little bit so we're still getting to know one another," I said.

"He's got a taste for wild. A taste for rough." Her eyes moved to me and traveled the length of me. "Don't look like a girl who likes a rough life."

I had jeans and a nice top on, a pair of heeled ankle boots. My hair was a bit disheveled since we'd rushed, and I'd only slapped on a bit of mascara and eyeliner in the car on the way to Shelly's from the cabin, but I'd had a good hair day the day before and it didn't totally look like bedhead. I didn't look as rough as the day she met me, but I certainly didn't embody "Uptown Girl" right now, either.

"You like gettin' your rocks off with bad boys? You like bikers?"

I shrugged. "Never dated a biker before Rider."

She laughed. Laughed like it was hilarious and shook her head at me with a snide sympathetic look.

"You're in for a rude awakening. These men like to share women. Like breakin' the law. Expect their pieces to overlook a lotta shit. Did you know this whole war thing started because of his sex drive? Him and his buds gangbanging some ho bag? Doubt you can keep up with him, honey."

I gave her a tight smile. "He told me about it, yes. An unfortunate misunderstanding." I wanted to defend him. I didn't want to argue with her, though.

Her eyes narrowed. "You don't believe me. You'll see. If you stick around long enough, you'll see. He tell you about his kid at least?"

I startled.

Her eyes brightened. She snickered. "Didn't think so."

His kid? *His kid?*

"He tell ya that Lick went to jail for him?"

"He did, actually." I replied, shakily. My heart was now racing, and I was in a cold sweat.

"Oh. He told you he beat that security guard with a steel pipe? Hurt him real bad. Guy had brain damage. Lick went down for that. Did five years. Five."

Rider was doing a bro shake with the two guys and then they wandered off in the other direction. Rider had his phone to his ear again.

"Ride's ex, Melanie, keeps sniffin' around with the baby, tryin ta get Ride to buy diapers, but he kept tellin' her to fuck off. He ain't about doin' a test to prove or disprove whether that boy's his baby. Looks just like him. Spittin' image. She was over yesterday, lookin' for him. Askin' where she could have him served with papers. Asking *me* for diaper money. My ex cut me off, so I don't even got the money to buy my grandbaby diapers. Ride's all about fuckin', fightin', and ridin'. He ain't about consequences of his actions, that's for damn sure. A high-class rich bitch like you won't put up with that shit for long. No one can tame that boy so don't think it'll be you. He might be enjoyin' some designer pussy right now, but it won't last for long. Don't let yer heart get involved, Jennifer. Enjoy the dick, but keep yer heart outta it."

I was staring at him, talking on that phone, pacing. He ended the call and then started heading for the door. I didn't bother to correct her on my name.

She was sitting, watching me, a smug smirk on her face.

I swallowed and blew out a breath.

A moment later, he was coming toward me, a muscle still ticking at the hinge of his jaw. He sat down beside me and threw his arm around me and pulled me close and then kissed my temple. I was stiff. A little bit dumbfounded.

"Michelle Valentine," a nurse called out from behind a half-opened door at the other end.

She got to her feet.

I got up, too.

"Be there in a minute, Mom." Rider tagged my hand and stopped me from advancing.

"You don't need to come in with me. Neither of ya." Shelly informed us. "You watch my purse, though?"

I nodded woodenly, and Rider reached for it and put it on the empty chair beside him.

She went in the direction of the nurse.

I sat.

"She's full of shit. Mantis wasn't at the house last night. I don't know what the fuck she's playing at. Don't know who beat her up or why she's trying to escalate things with the Jackals like this."

I rocked back, confused.

"Sorry we're stuck here right now, babe. Gotta stay and see what's what. We'll get her home and then drop you at the compound. Then I'll head back to the cabin, grab our stuff myself and be back to the clubhouse as soon as I can. Gotta get this shit figured out."

I opened my mouth, about to reply, when his cell started ringing. He glanced at the screen and I saw it had Spencer's name on it.

"Be back." He headed toward the exit.

I sat there, reeling. Numb. Dizzy. Emotion making my chest hurt.

A kid. A little baby boy the *spitting image* of him. An ex. So much for never having been in a serious relationship. Had he lied to me? If so, what other lies had he told me?

I SPENT THE NEXT HOUR in that waiting room and I'd spent it mute and mostly alone, while Rider was in and out on phone calls, talking to his mother in one of the exam rooms.

He was striding toward me, looking tweaked.

"Let's get you dropped off. She's gonna be another hour at least. She's getting a cast on her arm. Just saw a Jackal ride by so don't like how exposed we are here, especially you. I'll drop you at the compound, come back, take her to the house, then I'll run back to the cabin and get our stuff. Here. Let's drop her bag off to her." I passed him the purse, then he grabbed my hand and I followed him in through to the examination rooms. He let me go, went behind a curtain and handed the bag off, then grabbed my hand and we left.

When we were inside the SUV and heading out of the parking lot, he reached across to grab my hand. I pulled it away.

"What?" he looked at me, confused. I glared at him. He reared his head back in surprise.

We were at a red light.

"Who's Melanie?" I whispered, staring into the intersection, my chin quivering.

His head jerked in surprise and he stared at me, letting my words register. He shook his head. "That fuckin' bitch," he muttered. "Her scam is backfiring so she's punishing me by sayin' shit to you."

"Huh?" I looked at him.

"Melanie's nobody. My mother's really fuckin' spankin' me this time, ain't she?"

"She said Melanie was there yesterday. Trying to get money for diapers for the baby boy that looks exactly like you. Spitting image, if I remember her words."

Rider's eyes shut tight and he shook his head.

The light turned green and we moved forward.

"You have a son?" As soon as I said it, my heart started to hurt harder.

"He's not mine."

"She says he's the spitting image of you." I swallowed down what felt like a ball of broken glass.

"He's not. He looks like Mel. She's full of shit."

"Did you do a test?"

"I don't need to. I know he isn't my kid."

We were quiet. I was aching. He looked like he was seething. He was driving fast. Sort of angrily, recklessly.

"She's such a fucking bitch. Jealous. I'm the last of the family, boys anyway, payin' much mind to her and now she sees you as a threat, so she decided to poison you so that you drop my ass and I've got more time for her. Bitch is venomous, Jenna. Don't take all this shit in."

I said nothing. I stared out the window.

"Jenna?"

I shook my head.

"Fuck," he grumbled.

We rode in silence the rest of the way.

He walked me to our room and when he shut the door, I folded my arms across my chest.

"You never had sex with that baby's mother?" I asked.

He grimaced.

"Did or didn't you sleep with that baby's mother around nine months before he was born?"

"Jenna... It's not my kid. Just trust me on that."

"Did you fuck his mother?" I got louder.

"It's complicated." His phone made a noise. He glanced at the screen and then his face went harder. He shoved the phone into his front jeans pocket.

"It's comp—-what the fuck? Did you or didn't you fuck her?" I shoved him. He was grinding his teeth.

"It's not my kid. I don't need to do a test."

"If you fucked her... What? Can't you remember?" I was right in his face.

"I fucked her up the ass, Jenna. That's it. Last I heard, a girl can't get knocked up that way."

My mouth contorted with disgust. I stepped back.

"She's got mental problems. She'd been stalking both me and Lick for months before I moved. That baby is six months old already. She was hasslin' us when she was pregnant, too."

"Your mother called her your ex."

"She wasn't. We hooked up. Once. My mother doesn't know dick about my love life. Never has."

"You never fucked her the regular way?"

"Never. The baby is possibly Lick's. Though it could be anyone's."

"Wh-what?"

"Yeah. We had a threesome with her. He was in front, I was in back. We were all on E, but she was on other shit on top of it. She was fucked up. We were both gloved and she swears we weren't and says it was the other way around, that I was in front. Now knowin' Lick's dead and she can't get nothing out of him, she's probably gonna lay it on thicker. Try to turn the heat up and make it my problem."

"Oh my God."

"I know. It's fucked," he grumbled. "Can't believe my mother told you about that shit."

"You're the one that's fucked!" I accused.

"What?"

"So many things. First. This problem is a baby. It's a little boy. A person."

He gritted his teeth.

"Second, an Ecstasy-fueled threesome?"

He looked at me and rolled his eyes. Like I was ridiculous. How was I being ridiculous?

No. *Fuck this.*

Fuck.

This.

"I can't. I can't do this shit." I had handfuls of my hair in both hands. I was shaking my head.

No. No more of this.

"What shit?"

"You have threesomes and gang bangs and rough sex and roll your eyes when I find it disturbing. You carry a gun like it's no biggie. I'm just ... I'm me. I like nice sheets. I like having sex indoors, in a bed, like... 95 % of the time. I don't think we're gonna work."

"Jenna."

"No. It's better to stop now," I said.

"You fuckin' with me?" he shouted.

Sadly, I wasn't. I was not kidding. I was scared out of my mind that if I got in any deeper with him that I would not be able to recover when he walked out on me, when he cheated, or when he gave up trying because I wasn't truly his *type*. This was all evidence that it was inevitable. I had to get off his roller coaster. Like now.

"No." I shook my head.

"This is bullshit."

"I'm Jenna, the good time girl. Not the crying miserable scared girl. I don't like what feeling things for you have turned me into! This early on, even. This isn't me! Unsure of myself. Letting you plow over my walls and decide everything. I'm not good at this. I can't do this. I won't."

"We've just gotta ride out this storm, Jenna. The rainbow's comin'."

"It's seeming like it's gonna be a never-ending storm, Rider. Golf ball-sized hail is just pelting me over and over and...I'm done. I have to be." I wrapped my arms around myself.

"I can't fuckin' do this now. The brothers are pollutin' the street waiting for me. We need to go and take her back home and then—-"

"Then go." I shrugged.

"I'll call you later."

I didn't say anything.

"We're not done," he informed me.

I held my lips tight.

"We've barely gotten started. We're not done."

"You'd better go. Stop polluting the earth and all."

He grabbed me and pulled me to him and took my face into his hands.

"Let me go." This was killing me. My hands went to his wrists and I tried to pull his hands away. He didn't let me, yet still managed to hold my face tenderly. His eyes. His proximity. The way he was holding me. This was killing me slowly.

"Not happening." He kissed me. A bruising, punishing kiss that wasn't gentle, though his hands still kind of were. "You're mine."

"Yeah, well you're not mine," I returned, bitterly. Pain twisting something in my chest up tight.

"I am," he insisted.

I shook my head and tore my eyes away from his. "Go."

"Don't do this."

"Rider, please."

"Jenna."

"Go."

"I'll be back soon, baby." He caressed my cheeks with his thumbs.

"Don't."

"You're just scared. I'm in this. For the long haul, Jenna. I'm not giving up on you. Fuckin' forget the bullshit about before we met. I don't want that life, don't need it. Been there, done that, and I want and need you. You."

Ouch.

I think my face betrayed my emotions. He kissed my lips, my forehead, and then he gave me a look. A look of depth, of promise, of warning all at the same time. And then he was gone.

And I was gutted.

TWO DAYS LATER

He wasn't just gone. He was gone, gone. It'd been two days. Two long and excruciating days. He hadn't shown up. He'd left me at the clubhouse and sent not a text, not a single word. Forty-eight hours to marinate and stew in my pain.

A few hours after he'd left, a knock on the door brought my bags via Bronto, so I knew he'd already taken his mother home, made it to the cabin, came back, and then what?

And now, out of nowhere, forty-eight hours later, he was approaching me in the TV room. Looking tired, worn out, wearing jeans and his leather jacket.

My eyes met his and I immediately looked back to the television.

"Joelle, give us a minute?"

Jojo got up and left the room. I'd been sitting, cross-legged on a recliner. We were watching a Tiny Houses marathon.

Jojo was in slightly better spirits today. She knew her mom had been beat up and was all riled up about it, but not in a 'Who hurt my mom?' way, more of a "What the fuck is she doing now?' way.

Good that Jojo was in slightly better spirits, but I wasn't. I'd been faking it, though. I didn't want to stress her out. I didn't want to add to her mourning process by telling her that I wasn't going to be her future sister-in-law, that I wasn't joining the Dominion Sisterhood. I was biding my time until this crap was over and then I was going to see whether my parents had sold my salon or not. If they had, I'd leave town. To where? No idea yet, and I couldn't think that far ahead. All I knew was that inside, I was destroyed.

I'd given up on the possibility of any sort of 'us'. There was no Jenna and Rider. There wouldn't be. It was bad enough what his mother had said to me. Okay, maybe he wasn't that baby's dad. Maybe Melanie was just a hook-up. And he'd already told me he fucked up and felt all sorts of guilt about Lick doing time when it should've been him. And he was a stupid teenager. Teenagers fuck up.

It wasn't just what Shelly had said. It was adding all of it together, all of it, the gang bang, the attitude at the beginning, the telling me I was bad in bed, the games he tried to make me play at the cabin because... would I have to change who I was to fit him and his sexual appetite? And to top it all off, knowing what I'd said to him after the hospital and then vanishing for two whole nights and not even texting me once. Not once. I hadn't seen him in 48 hours.

To me, those actions spoke louder and clearer than any words would've. I'd always ended things at the first sign of alpha-hole-ism and I'd let things go on way longer than a sane me would've. Way longer.

And now here he was, squatting in front of me and putting his warm strong hands on either side of my face. He looked deep, impossibly deep, straight into my eyes with those green-blue eyes of his.

And my heart seized. I was gonna drop dead from a broken heart right here. Dead. Gone.

"How you doin'?"

I blinked. I blinked again. My lips parted in surprise. *No.* in shock.

Was he really saying this to me? After a two-day disappearance right after I told him we were over?

"We're gonna head home. Things are simmered for a minute. Some shit went down. We're goin' home. We're all gonna be watchful. You'll have a prospect on you at all times for the foreseeable, but we've gotta get back to life."

I blinked again, dumbstruck.

"Let's go pack."

I got to my feet, feeling a bit zombie-like. He grabbed my hand and we headed back toward our room. When we were inside, he grabbed his Duffle bag, which I'd already packed and zipped up the day before yesterday, figuring as soon as he was back, I'd throw it at him.

He tossed it on the bed and then grabbed my bags from the floor by the bed and put them on the bed.

"Go grab your stuff from the bathroom," he ordered and started piling my shoes from the floor into my bag. Haphazardly, as if it didn't matter how he packed them.

I glared at him, arms folded across my chest.

"Put my stuff down. I can do my own packing. You're putting shoes on top of clean clothes."

His eyes moved to me.

His expression was hard. It'd been sort of hard even back in the TV room, but now we were alone and face to face, and *fuck him.*

"My stuff from the bathroom already in here?" he asked, gesturing to his bag.

"I packed it the day before yesterday."

He pursed his lips.

"In case you showed up. So, I could throw it at you."

He raised his eyebrows.

"Give me five minutes to get ready and then you can drop me off."

"Drop you off?"

"Yeah."

"I'll be stayin' at your place with you," he said.

I felt my face go screwy. "No, you won't."

"My place burnt down. I'm not stayin' at Ella's when you've got your own place. This way, you're safe at night, too."

"No."

"No?"

"No. if you give a shit enough, feel free to ask a prospect to drive by once in a while, but I'm having an alarm system put in my apartment when I get home and there's already one at the salon. I'll accept your help with a prospect during the day for now, since you got me into this, but that's all."

"Jenna, what the fuck are you goin' on about?"

"You can't be serious," I informed him.

He made to make a move toward me. I put my hand up, warning him to stay back.

"Sit down a sec. Talk to me," he invited. He sat down and patted the bed beside him.

"Nope. Done talking."

"You're done talking?"

"Done with all of it, Rider. Just done."

I held my face stoic. He wasn't going to get any more emotion from me. I'd been publicly numb since the hospital the other day. I was going through the motions with his sister, but when I was alone, I was a mess. I was all tapped out on emotion right now.

Okay, actually, I was lying to myself. I was fighting back the emotion. And him, after leaving me alone for two days without even a text after how we left things? That was going to make it easier.

Or was it?

I didn't like how he was looking at me. It was threatening to crack my armor. He'd been gone 48 hours, and while the first 24, I'd been wallowing, the past 24? Fortifying my armor.

There was a knock on the door.

He glared.

"Answer that," I said, snidely.

He huffed and went to it.

Spencer was there. "I'm heading out now. I got Jojo. I'll see you when we get there. You're staying with your girl, I take it?"

"Wait," I called.

Rider opened the door wider and Spencer leaned in and looked at me.

"Hey, Jenna," he said.

"Hey. Can I get a ride back with you?" I asked.

Spencer's eyebrows furrowed. "Somethin' change with your plans?" He was asking Rider, not me.

Rider's expression was like stone.

"*My* plans," I corrected.

"I don't fuckin' think so," Rider glared at me warningly.

"It's not up to you," I snapped. "Spencer?"

Spencer just stood there.

"Can I get a ride with you, Spencer?"

"No. You can't," Rider answered for him.

Spencer just stood there, looking uncomfortable.

"I asked Spencer!" I spat.

"Sorry, Jenna. Ride's not cool with it, I can't."

Fuck. Now he has to go and stop trying to stir shit. I would've thought he'd be all over this one.

"Fine. Fuck." I threw my hand up in the air and stormed to the bathroom and slammed the door. I gathered all my stuff and went back out. Spencer had gone and Rider had his back against the door, his arms folded, his eyes on his feet.

"Sorry I didn't call you the past two days," he said softly. "A lot of shit was fuckin' with my head."

I started tossing my stuff into the bag and didn't reply.

Unfortunately for me, he kept going.

"I had a lot of shit to deal with on top of that. We got a lot done with the Jackals. Things aren't 100% clear, but we worked hard to get to where you and Jojo don't have to be locked down, just watched. I should've called you, though."

"It doesn't matter," I said.

"It does. I took some time to think, too. After the blow-up before I left. About us." He took a step toward me. "Being away from you for two days, I know I want us. I know it down to my fuckin' bones, gorgeous. I'm sorry I didn't call, but a lot was fuckin' with me. My head's clear now. And I want you."

"No!" That came out as if it was an angry, tortured sound that had been ripped out of me.

Shit.

He winced.

"No." I steadied my voice. "You left me after that scene for two days without even a text and..."

"Did you text me, Jenna? Or are you being hypocritical here?" he demanded.

I ignored him and kept talking "It gave me a lot of time to think, too, and I've decided I'm sticking by what I said when you left me here two days ago. I'm still done. Just done, Rider. If you don't wanna drive me home, let your brother bring me. Avoid hours of awkwardness stuck in a car together when there's nothing left to say. Let it go. You're you. I'm me. And I know I'm done. This isn't a game. This is me saying we're over. We're finished."

He sucked on his teeth a second, looking supremely pissed. He lifted his phone out of his pocket. "Spence."

I stood there.

"Drive Jenna home?"

All the air left my lungs. I was going to have to fight hard to stop myself from collapsing to my knees.

"Yeah," he added and ended the call, grabbed his Duffle bag, then turned away and left, slamming the door.

Done.

Okay.

I took a big breath.

So, he was done, too.

Well, good.

17

On the way home, with Spencer and Jojo in Spencer's pickup truck, I was informed that Rider, Deacon, and Edge had *all* been sent the video of Jet's rape and murder. It was videotaped. All of it. The men in it, wearing masks.

I didn't allow that to permeate. I didn't know if that played a role in him not calling me for two days, but I couldn't let it get to me. I had to push it out of my head, not think about how horrible it would've been for them, particularly for Edge, to have seen that.

Spencer was more than informative about other stuff, too.

Deacon had a gut wound; he'd been stabbed by Ella's Uncle Willie. A bunch of Wyld Jackals were in jail, including their second in command, for crack, meth, and weapons charges.

A couple Wyld Jackals had died. Details on how or by whose hand was not offered. I didn't ask. Neither did Jojo.

Deacon and Ella had reportedly gone away for a few days for a getaway and were probably back by now.

Spence told us he'd wiped out on his bike during some Jackals drama and was still feeling a bit sore from it.

Apparently, Blow had even taken a bullet to the belly at some stage before Shelly was beat up, so he'd been sporting that injury that day at Rider's mother's house.

I'd missed a whole lot of drama. I still didn't really understand where this rivalry had even started. I didn't want to ask. Didn't want to know. Even when it was happening all around me. Rider had been keeping me in the dark, *majorly*.

"They have shit on us, we have shit on them. So, we're at a stalemate. We're hoping for peace for a bit," Spence said, but then added. "But, we'll see. You girls be vigilant, you hear me?"

I was looking forward to being on the other side of this thing.

Jojo had asked why I was riding with them and Spencer had muttered that me and Rider had 'had a fight'.

"You okay?" She looked over her shoulder at me in the back seat.

I nodded and looked out the window.

I didn't say much. Spencer and Jojo picked over all sorts of details of the feud and about their mother the whole way home, talking about how the Valentine boys had done some sort of intervention with her, with even Spencer attending and trying to talk sense into her about her association with the Jackals and how she'd gotten hurt a couple days later. Rider hadn't told me about that, either, and that was before we were apart, before we'd gone to the cabin for our overnight.

I began to tune them out, but I knew Jojo was coming to our town, staying a couple of days. They were starting at Ella's house, and then possibly moving into a new place, then she'd be leaving in a few days to go to New York, where she was going to stay with a friend for a bit. She said she'd be taking a semester away from school to get her head together.

Deke was reportedly having their Sioux Falls house put up for sale after "That shit Shelly pulled" according to Spencer. I didn't ask questions. Because, again, it all had nothing to do with me. Spencer told Jojo their dad was looking at two potential rental houses in my parents and Ella's neighborhood so that they could grab something for now until figuring out their longer terms plans for living arrangements and a clubhouse.

When Spencer pulled in to the parking lot behind my salon, Jojo gave me a big smile, as we got out. I saw Bronto's little car there.

"Can't wait to see your place and your salon!"

"Salon's closed," I said. It was dark out, after eight o'clock. "But, come up and I'll show you my apartment."

Bronto had been assigned to me, Spencer informed me, saying that Pippa had let him in to wait.

Spencer, insisting on carrying my bags, had a look of concern on his face as we climbed the stairs.

"You're real pissed at him, aren't ya?" he asked, as we climbed the stairs.

"Nope. Just done," I said, and kept walking.

"Done?" Spencer asked, looking angry.

"Shh," I said, pointing at Jojo.

He looked strangely at me and then at his sister.

Jojo missed the exchange and was commenting about loving my terrace. I introduced her to Pippa, who grabbed me and gave me a huge hug. And then her eyes met mine and she winced. My heart must've been on my sleeve. I had to put it away.

Pippa tried to turn it into a hangout thing, offering to order Chinese food or pizza and wanting Spencer and Jojo to stay, but I made a face and Jojo caught it.

"Jenna probably needs a quiet night after all the excitement. And I need to get to see Dad and Deacon. I haven't seen them in days and need to get all the news on where everything's at, so... raincheck? Maybe I'll pop in to the salon in the next day or two before I head to The Big Apple and you girls can make me pretty?"

"Like you need help," I muttered.

Jojo beamed at me and then gave me a hug, whispering, "Thanks for becoming one of my best friends in a matter of a week. I'm sorry you and Ride are in a fight. I'll see you before I go. Okay?"

I nodded, holding back tears. "You are *so* in my girl posse no matter what happened with him and me. Okay?"

"Happened? You guys are gonna be okay." She gave me an alarmed look.

I shrugged. "I'm dying for a bubble bath so I'm just gonna..." I jerked my thumb toward my bedroom. "Thanks for the lift, Spencer."

"Yeah, sure, Blue Eyes. Any time." He ruffled my hair and headed toward the door. "Later, Sunshine," he said to Pippa. She wrinkled her nose up at him and stuck out her tongue. He snickered, amber eyes sparkling mischievously, and left.

What was that about?

I watched him and Jojo go. Bronto was sitting on the couch and I saw Walter White and Jesse Pinkman frozen on my screen. Paused.

"You guys continued without me?" I accused.

"No," Pip defended. "I fell asleep during the last one and a half and you two kept going, so we're re-watching so I can catch up. We were gonna wait for you after that. Go get your bubble bath and then we'll watch the next one."

"Honestly, I just wanna crawl into my own bed and sleep after too many nights away from it. If you guys wanna keep going, I guess you can..."

"No. We'll wait." Bronto said.

"If we can't wait, we'll re-watch with you tomorrow," Pippa amended.

I gave them a half-smile and wearily wandered into my room, dragging the bags that had been dropped by my door in with me.

I closed my door and put my back against it. I reached behind my back and twisted the lock on the doorknob. I needed privacy. I needed to shut everything else out.

My room. My home. Above my salon. For now, at least. My bed. I threw myself on it and cried like a baby. All over my $1700.00 pure white duvet.

I'D HAD MY BUBBLE BATH. I'd gone out and watched one episode with them while making myself eat a slice of pizza. I hadn't had much of an appetite the past 48 hours. Usually, I ate my feelings. Not this time. This felt different.

Back in the kitchen, getting a drink, I got cornered by Pippa.

"We have a lot of catching up to do, me 'n' you."

We sure did.

She gave me a look and rolled her hand, urging me to get on with it.

"I can't tonight. I-—I can't." I choked up.

Her brandy-colored eyes went wide, and she pulled me in for a hug. She'd never seen me cry.

I stiffened. No. I wasn't gonna do this. I wasn't going to cry over him. I pulled back and got myself together.

"Rider and I are finished. We're done. I don't wanna talk about any of it tonight."

Bronto was walking into the kitchen, looking remorseful for hearing that. Or remorseful at that news, I didn't know which. I also didn't care.

I continued talking to Pip. "I just wanna go to bed early and then open the salon in the morning and get on with my life. I have to face my mother, too, eventually, and that won't be pretty. Tonight, I just want a little bit of peace, to sleep in my own bed, and try to forget about the nightmare of the past week.

"Okay," Pippa said and gave my hand a squeeze. "When you're ready, I'm here."

She was a good friend. The second-best friend I had.

I slipped past Bronto and went to my room, shutting the door behind me. I pulled the duvet off, letting it drop to the carpet, and then crawled into my bed and turned out the light.

BEING PULLED OUT OF a deep sleep, I felt lips on my neck.

It felt nice.

"Jenna," Rider said, softly.

He was in my bed. With me.

What?

No.

Hell no!

I jolted awake and shoved him, and I must've been on the edge of my bed, because I started to fall. He reached for me and tried to catch me, and I teetered for a second, and then I fell anyway. I landed hard on the carpet. Fuck.

Poetic.

"You okay?" He was in a squat beside me, trying to help me up.

"No! What the eff are you doing here?"

"Goin' to sleep," he said.

"Why are you trying to sleep here?"

"We already went over this, gorgeous."

I was aghast. "Over this?"

"The part where I said I was stayin' with you to keep you safe at night. If my place hadn't burnt down, we coulda stayed there. But since it did..."

"What about the part where I said we were over?"

"Jenna."

"Don't Jenna me!"

"Sorry. Not Jenna. Gorgeous." He sounded amused.

"I'm not joking."

"Baby?" He tried, teasingly.

I flicked my lamp on and pointed to the door.

"Get out."

He raised his eyebrows at me.

"You're naked!" I gasped.

He smiled at me. A big smile.

"Get the fuck out!" I pointed. "We're over. You're not welcome in my home, certainly not naked, and extra-certainly not welcome in my bed. So, go."

"You don't want me to go," he said cockily.

"Go."

"You don't want me to go."

"Oh. Then why am I telling you to go?"

"Because you're upset. Your head is fucked up and you're tryin' to push me away, like you told me you would, like I told you I'd deal with. I'm *not* goin'. I've missed you the last two nights. I wanna sleep beside you. You're upset at me, so we don't have to fuck, unless you think that'll help you work out your anger?" He raised his eyebrows questioningly.

I scowled at him.

"Okay, then. But, I wanna wake up beside you. You're still angry in the morning, feel free to dig those nails extra deep into my back when we fuck."

"Get out."

"Let's get some sleep."

"Get out."

"Jenna, let's—-"

"Get out, get out getoutgetoutgetout!" I was fuming. How dare he not take that seriously. How dare he!

"Baby..." he tried, having the decency to look a little bit contrite.

I saw his clothes on my carpet. I lifted his jeans up and whipped them at him. They missed and landed on the floor. I threw a button-down blue and grey flannel shirt at him. I'd never seen him wear this. It would go amazing with his eyes. *Asshole.* It hit him in the face. But he didn't budge, and it floated to the rug.

I threw a grey t-shirt at him and the two black socks that were sticking out of his boots. He just stood there. The shirt fell on my bed, nowhere near him.

I picked up a heavy black motorcycle boot and then I heaved that at him, with a grunt, and he dodged it. I threw the other one. He didn't manage to dodge that one and it hit him in the shin. He grunted and then advanced and got me and pinned me to the bed, just as I was reaching for the lamp on my bedside table.

"Gorgeous, settle down. Talk to me."

I grunted and fought. He had me pinned. Just like that first night at the cabin. I went lax, knowing that struggling would just make him get sexual.

He loosened the grip.

"Baby, please, settle down. I'm not goin' anywhere. We have to talk this out. If you don't wanna do it now, we'll do it in the morning. Let's just sleep on it. Okay?"

"No. You're not welcome here." I raised my voice. "Pippa? Pip! Call the cops!"

He put his hand over my mouth, "Bronto, don't let her call the cops!" he yelled.

"She's crashed," Bronto sounded like he was just outside the door. "That girl can sleep through anything. Don't worry, Ride."

Damn. He was right, too.

I slapped his hand away from my face.

"Get out," I demanded.

He shook his head.

"Get out. Get out. GET OUT!"

"I told you I wouldn't give up on you. I'm not giving up on you."

"I thought that was sweet, yeah. When I didn't want you to give up on me. Or when I wasn't sure. Now I'm sure. Give up."

"No." His face was serious.

"Get out. I told you I was done. You left. Why are you here?"

"Jenna."

"Get out of my apartment."

"I was giving you a few hours to cool your head. For me to cool mine."

"Mine isn't cool. It won't ever be. So go." I pointed at the door.

"Shoulda brought the cuffs," he muttered.

"Oh, fuck off," I sneered.

"You don't want me to go," he said and got up off me.

I sat up.

"I do."

"Want me to tell you how I know you don't?" He asked, looking smug. "Right after I spank your ass for tellin' me to fuck off?"

"Fuck off. Fuck off, fuck off, fuck off! Right now. You and Bronto, both go. I'm done. I'm gonna fly out tomorrow, get the fuck outta Dodge. Ella can call me when all this shit is over."

"You can't go. You have a business to run." He was smiling.

"I probably don't. My mother's probably in the middle of selling it right now. And I need to get the fuck away from you. That's all I want right now."

His expression dropped.

I stormed out to the living room. Bronto was on the edge of the couch, looking stressed with his head in his hands.

"Go home, Bronto. You're done here," I said.

"You can go, Bront. I'll be here at night, so you can sleep in your own bed." Rider was behind me. I whipped around and glared at him. He was doing up his jeans.

"Actually, I *do* need to go, Ride. My gran called and reminded me she needs me to take her to an early appointment. I was talkin' to Scoot. We were thinkin' of switching for the morning."

"That'll work," Rider told him.

"But, Scoot's crashed at my place. He can't go back home tonight. Somethin's gone down there, and my gran doesn't let anyone sleep on her sofa."

"Text Scoot. You run home, and he can come here and crash on the couch."

"Do not tell him someone can crash on my couch!" I snapped. "Go, Bronto. And tell Scooter I don't give a rat's ass where he sleeps. He can sleep with you for all I care."

Bronto's face went sad.

I rolled my eyes. "Fuck this shit. Both of you get out!"

"Settle, Jenna." Rider was looking annoyed with me.

I whirled around and went into my room and slammed the door and locked it. And then I started dragging my dressing table. It was effing heavy. Bottles, jars, everything scattered to the floor as I dragged it.

I put the table against the door. And then I dragged suitcases and boxes from my walk-in closet and piled all of them under the table and in front of the table, barricading myself in and him out. And then I went to my bedside table and downed the rest of the bottle of water I'd brought to bed with me. I climbed in and shut the lamp off.

Fucking jerk stupid shithead asshole. I couldn't believe his nerve. Climbing in bed with me, like our conversation today didn't happen. Did he take anything seriously? And naked! Stupid jerk.

I fluffed my pillow up. If he dared try to come back in here, I'd lose my shit.

And then it dawned on me. What I was wearing.

I was wearing that stupid, *stupid* effing sweatshirt. I'd put it on with little jersey sleep shorts to sleep in, deciding I'd sleep in it one more time and burn it in the morning. I had this whole plan to take it out to the chimenea and torch it. I just decided to wear it one more night. That was why he'd been so cocky saying that I didn't want him to go.

Mortified.

I *did* want him to go. I was just being stupidly sentimental about this sweatshirt like an idiot. I tore it over my head and threw it and then stomped to my dresser and yanked out a tank top.

I heard the doorknob jiggle.

"Jenna, lemme in, babe."

"Fuck you!' I shouted. "You fuck with that door I will call the goddamn cops. I have my phone in my hand!" I reached for it and held it up. Like an idiot. As if he could see through doors.

He didn't answer. I waited. Nothing.

Okay, good. Maybe he left. I heard a door close. I strained to hear and heard two car doors slam from out back. That was promising. Maybe they'd both left. I looked out the window. Rider's car was still here. Bronto's wasn't. Maybe they left together in Bronto's car. I rolled over and tried to get more comfortable.

God, I was never so effing angry in my life. How the hell was Pippa sleeping through this?

If they both did go, I certainly hoped I wasn't being watched by their enemies. And I hoped they'd locked the door. Fear prickled up my spine.

I tossed and turned.

I tossed and turned some more. I reshuffled the pillows around and pulled my blankets up some more and a scent hit my nose.

Was he back here? It was his scent. It was a faint fabric softener, male body wash, and green apple smell mixed with the smell of leather and outside. Yes, I could smell all those things.

Why?

I flicked my lamp on and saw the source of the scent. The gray t-shirt I'd flung at him. It was draped half over the pillow beside the one my head had been on.

I flicked the lamp off and reached for it and held it up. I was about to give it a toss. I didn't. I held it up in the air for what felt like an eternity, before bringing it to my nose.

My eyes closed as I inhaled it. It was super-soft and it was also warm, and that made it worse.

My heart was bleeding.

I had to hold firm with him, because this wouldn't ever work. Not ever. We weren't right for one another. Even if I wished with everything in me, that we were.

This hurt ten times worse than Michael in high school. A hundred times worse. Because even though I thought I'd kept up a bit of a wall, evidently it wasn't nearly enough.

I silently cried. And cried some more, until my eyes drifted shut, the t-shirt still held to my face, visions of all the things I loved about him streaming on a loop in my brain.

MY ALARM CLOCK WAS blaring at me to get up. I got up and got right into the shower. And then I got into my bath robe and shoved the door blockade stuff out of the way enough to get out of my room.

In the living room, I saw Rider sitting on my white couch, in his jeans, and Scooter was crashed on the rug, using a toss pillow and a throw from the couch as his blanket. Rider was using the pillow and the blanket I'd put out for Bronto before things went mental last night.

I glared at him.

"What are you doing here?"

"Told ya I wasn't leavin'," he said, sleepily. "Scoot. Wake up." He nudged Scooter's back with his foot. Scooter's eyes opened, and he smiled. "Mornin'."

Pippa was coming out of the other bathroom. She was in her little black sexy short satin robe, hair up in a top knot, sexy librarian black-rimmed eyeglasses on, and looking fresh as a daisy and all smiles.

"Lookie here. Full house," she smirked. "Want me to make pancakes?"

"I like pancakes," Scooter said, getting to his feet and stretching.

I went to the kitchen, deciding to ignore them, and made myself a coffee.

Rider was behind me, slipping his arm around my middle, pulling my back to his front. I froze.

"We'll talk tonight. I gotta get to the garage. Scoot's gonna shadow you all day. He's carryin'. Boys'll do drive bys regularly. Okay, baby?"

I didn't answer him. I was too angry.

"Tonight, we'll talk, Jenna." He kissed my neck and then he left via my kitchen door.

And I didn't know whether to throw something, to scream, or to throw myself on the floor and have a toddler tantrum.

Scooter was in the kitchen with me. "Got coffee on the go yet?"

I growled at him. Right at him. He reared back and went, "Whoa. Sorry. I can get it."

"Fucking bullshit," I hissed and stormed out of there and headed to my bedroom so that I could get dressed, hearing him grumble something about him probably not getting pancakes, either.

My bedroom looked like a crime scene, so I started trying to put things back where they belonged. I got my boxes of Christmas decorations back in my closet and put the suitcases away.

Because I'd dragged my dressing table over to the door and it was now back, everything from that was all over the place, too. Bottles of perfume, a big vase filled with make-up brushes toppled, several nail polishes, they were all over the rug. A blush palate had broken and made a mess all over my rug. I spied his black Duffle bag from the cabin and the clubhouse on my floor and I glared at it. If I didn't know he's lost almost all his belongings in a fire, I would've thrown that stuff off the roof terrace. I couldn't though. So, I just got angrier.

I began slamming bottles and jars back onto my table and wasn't being very gentle about it when I heard, "Hey."

I whirled around, and Ella was standing there. And she looked alarmed.

"I've gotta get to the salon," I said quickly. "If you have anything to say to me, do it there while I open up. I need a minute to get dressed."

Ella's expression fell, then she took a step back. I closed the door and tried to gather my senses.

I hadn't seen or spoken to Ella in days and days. And I just closed the door in her face.

My God, I was coming undone. I'd ended it with Rider. I was probably losing my salon and my apartment. And I was trashing my relationship with my best friend since kindergarten.

God. I had to get my head together. My luck, my mother would show up here any minute.

After a minute with my forehead pressed to the door, I turned around and got dressed in a pair of black trousers and a black blouse, to match my mood. I put on high heels and quickly put some basic make-up on, ignoring his dopp kit in my bathroom and his toothbrush sitting there beside the sink. I grabbed my phone and my bag, and left, not even making my stupid bed.

I always made my bed.

"HOW'S HER HEART, RIDE?" Ella was calling out to Rider when I got out back. She was standing there with Deacon and she looked pissed.

"I'm working on winning it," Rider said, looking at me, sitting on his motorcycle. The motorcycle he'd taken me for my very first ride on. Why was he still here?

"Don't bet on that," I snapped as I gave him a dirty look.

The way he looked at me turned my bones to water.

"Oh, I *am* betting on it. In fact, I'll bet my Harley." He communicated something with a jerk of his chin and I glanced back and saw he was looking at Scooter, who was behind me. Being my literal shadow. Rider looked at me again and his eyes pierced through me, lanced my gut. I tried to hide what I was feeling.

I'm pretty sure he saw right through it. He put his shades on and left, on his bike.

My chest was aching.

His car was still here, too, so obviously he had plans to come back.

I had eyes on me. Ella's and Deacon's and Ella's were filled with concern. I stormed through the alley to the front door of the building, unlocked it, and went to my alarm panel, hitting buttons and flicking lights on. Ella was in the utility room with me a minute later. I offered her a coffee.

"Yeah," she agreed to coffee. "And girl talk. What time is your first appointment?"

"Not for an hour."

"Good."

Ella shut the door. I burst into tears.

Ella's jaw hit the floor and then she wrapped her arms around me and I buried my face into her blonde curls and kept bawling.

And then I filled her in. On everything. And I cried in her arms. And she cried with me. We used ¾ of a box of Kleenex. And she got mad at Rider *for* me. And she got mad at me, too. She told me I needed to talk to him. To let him in, so we could work it out. She told me that it was going to be worth it.

"To be his. To have that big extended family. To be my sister-in-law. Because I know in my soul that one day I'll be marrying Deacon. And I can tell. Rider? He's got work cut out for him, but if he's anything like he seems like he is, he'll do that work, Jenna, and you'll get your happily ever after."

I told her I loved her, but she needed to give me space on this. And like the good friend she was, she did. She gave my hand a squeeze, promised we'd do a girlie night very soon. She ordered me to be nice to Bronto, said she'd heard I was sending him careening toward a nervous breakdown because I was giving him so much shit. Hardly. I agreed to be gentle with the six foot five three-hundred-pound scary biker. <insert eye roll>.

And then, ten minutes after she left the salon, my effing fricking fracking mother showed up.

Damn it!

18

It was only ten minutes before opening. Ella had gone, and Scooter was sitting in my waiting area, reading a Maxim magazine. I'd already made him remove his boots from my coffee table, but he was still sort of sprawled.

My mother was at the locked door of the shop. Lips pursed. Eyes narrowed. Flanked by Bronto and his grandmother.

Bronto looked like he'd prefer to be anywhere but here. His grandmother was smiling and waving at me through the glass.

I unlocked the door and knew my face was betraying my emotions. My mother scowled at me as she pushed past me, her shoulder knocking mine and physically causing me to stumble. Bronto looked alarmed and glanced at Scooter.

His Gran, written in my book as "Theodore's grandmother. N. C". N: new. C: coupon, was smiling at me, having missed it.

Pippa wasn't in yet. She didn't have her first appointment for an hour and a half. Plus, she'd told me the night before that she was taking her time for at least a week in the mornings, since she'd opened *and* closed every day while I was gone.

I gave my mother, dressed in a bone-colored power suit, tan blouse, and sensible bone-colored heels, a tight smile and said, "Good morning. Can you give me a minute?"

Her eyes narrowed as she looked over her shoulder at Bronto, dressed in status quo Dominion Brotherhood attire, and then her eyes bounced to Scooter, who was sitting in one of my barrel leather waiting-area chairs, dressed almost the same. Jeans. Leather vest. T-shirt. Looking very much like he'd slept in his clothes, which he did.

"Good morning, Theodore's gran. Great to see you." I craned my neck to see around Mom and gave Bronto's gran a smile.

Bronto's gran moved in and put her arms around me. She was a short, stout woman with chubby cheeks and big silver curls. She had on an unbecoming shade of bright red lipstick and blushed cheeks that looked like they'd been made that way with the same lipstick. But, lipstick shade didn't matter. She was awesome.

When she let me go, she reached into the Ikea tote bag hanging from the crook of her arm and produced a circa 1972 olive green metal cookie tin. "More snickerdoodles. This is your tip. You return this tin, I'll refill it."

"Oh wow. Thank you," I hugged the tin to my chest like the cookies were a precious gift, which they were, and put the tin down on the reception desk.

"I have my coupon." She presented it to me with a beaming smile.

"Awesome. You're first today, so let's get you comfortable and then we'll try our hardest to make you even more gorgeous." My heart seized at the G-word that'd just come out of my mouth. Ugh. Time to ban it from the Jenna-cabulary.

"Take my coat, Theodore," she directed Bronto.

"Wash and set, Theodore's gran?" I inquired.

She nodded. "Yes, please."

"Okay, you're a teensy bit early, so how about you sit in that chair or on that sofa there (I had nice matching black leather furniture in my waiting area) and give me two shakes to get you a cup of tea and have a fast chat with my mother, here, and then I'll—-"

"Oh, this is your Momma? Hello!" She reached for my mother's hand. My mother was a banking industry *suit* and she put on her fake smile and shook Bronto's gran's hand.

"Hello. Karen Murdoch, nice to meet you."

"I'm Theodore's grandma. Your girl is just an absolute doll!" It was as if Mom had a clue who *Theodore* was.

"Thank you. We're pretty proud of her," my Mom said with a closed mouth exaggerated smile, and I almost barfed. She was so full of it.

I helped Bronto's grandmother to a chair and she chided Scooter. "Scott. Sit up straight, now." He straightened immediately, despite the fact that he was mid-texting or something like that on his phone.

My mother followed me into the utility room. I shut the door and immediately launched into my defense. "I only got back last night, and I have a full book this morning, Mom. So, if you're here to rip me a new one..."

I'd immediately started busying myself with tea-making and didn't make eye contact. She didn't respond. So, I made eye contact.

Mistake.

Her fake smile mask had already slipped. "Dinner at home tonight. 6:30," she hissed.

I rolled my eyes. "Why don't you just tell me now if you're gonna fuck my life up."

She gasped. "Don't you speak to me that way, young lady!"

"Mom." I was exasperated. "I've had a very, *very* bad few days. Please. Please, don't do this to me right now. I have to get my head together." I put my hands in my hair. My chin quivered. I took a breath.

No crying. NO crying. For someone who hadn't shed tears in years, I was sure making up for it these days.

She watched me with narrowed eyes.

I heard the bells of the shop jingle. I pulled myself together, so I could go out and see who was out there, but the door opened almost hitting my mother and Rider was in the utility room with us, looking tweaked.

I jolted.

He looked at me from head to toe and back to head. This wasn't an ogle. This was an assessment of my well-being. And he didn't look like his usual self. He had a baseball cap on backwards and was wearing mechanics overalls with a pair of dirty sneakers. I was a little bit thrown. He smelled like motor oil.

His eyes searched mine for a split second. My lips parted in question, but before I could ask anything, he turned to my Mom.

"Mrs. Murdoch? Rider Valentine." He extended his hand.

She looked up at him with surprise.

"Nice to meet you," he said.

She gave him a once over and looked at him much the way Rider's mother had looked at me. Judgingly. Finding me lacking. I didn't like the way she looked at Rider. At all. And that wasn't smart, because I couldn't show it to him.

"I see you've got two of your apes watching her. I suppose that's good," she muttered, giving him a limp handshake and then folding her arms across her chest.

"The threat isn't neutralized, like I told your husband this morning, but it's significantly safer than it was a week ago. I have a man following Jenna at all times. We're regularly patrolling this street and I'm with her at night."

"Of course you are." she rolled her eyes.

"Now, she's got a full day, so we should continue this conversation at dinner."

Mom gawked at him.

I gawked at him.

"Dinner?" I asked.

"I spoke to your dad on the phone this morning, gorgeous. He invited us to dinner."

I glared at him, lips tight, but didn't say a word.

Mom was giving *me* the same glare. "Your father didn't tell me of this."

"It's news to me, too," I said, showing my palms in defense.

"See you at six thirty then, don't be late," Mom said and turned on her heel and left.

I was getting a headache.

Where to even begin with this?

Rider's eyes were on me. "You okay?"

I glared at him. "You're not coming to my parents for dinner."

"Yeah, I am. Your father invited me."

"No," I insisted. "You're not going."

"I am."

"Then I won't," I said.

He laughed a little, but not with his usual humor.

I fetched my phone from my pocket and dialed my dad's number.

He barely got his Hello out when I spoke fast. Way fast. Too fast.

I sounded like an auctioneer or something.

"Dad? I'm not coming for dinner tonight. Rider and I broke up and it's over and I'm home and his MC are watching out for me while things are still a bit off, but you don't need to have him for dinner. I'm not coming either. I need a few days to sort my head out and Mom's being... Mom. I can't deal with that today. I really, really can't."

"Uh..." Dad said into the phone.

Rider grabbed my phone out of my hand.

"Hey!" I protested.

"Paul? Let's reschedule dinner. I showed at Jenna's salon because your wife was here, pretending you didn't tell her not to come. She and Jenna were about to get into it, but Jenna needs time. How about I call you tomorrow?"

"Give me that phone." I tried to get it. He didn't give it up. He held a hand out, which landed on my chest, and he kept me back.

"Right. Nope, we're good. She's just in a mood." He held the phone a second and then chuckled. My father said something that made him chuckle? What the eff?

"Yep. Okay. Bye." He ended the call and passed the phone back to me.

"I can't believe you!" I breathed, sort of. I was almost out of breath.

"I told Scoot to let me know if she showed. I rushed over to make sure she didn't hassle you. I already told your father we were back, and he wanted us to come to dinner to talk it all out instead of her causing a scene at the salon. He's gonna be pissed she showed up here after he specifically told her not to."

"He... huh? You... what? What the...?"

He folded his arms across his chest. I gave my head a shake.

"Just go," I said.

He raised his eyebrows.

"Bronto's grandma is waiting for me. Her tea's getting cold." I reached for the cup sitting on the counter beside him.

He grabbed my wrist and pulled me to him before I got to the cup. His mouth was a half an inch from mine.

"I get brownie points for gettin' rid of your ma?"

I shook my head and looked the other way and lied. "No."

"No?" He sounded playful. Like this was just another game. And it wasn't.

"Let go."

"Don't wanna. I wanna kiss. That's your price for me gettin' rid of her."

"Safeword," I whispered.

He let go of me and shook his head with a disgusted look on his face.

"You're a piece of work."

"You're a piece of something," I accused.

His angry expression melted and then he laughed. Laughed! He pinned me against the closed door with his hips.

That wasn't the reaction I was going for.

I pushed against his chest.

He moved in and kissed me. I grunted, while trying to shove.

He tried to part my lips with his tongue. I shoved hard. He went back against the counter and I grabbed for the door knob so that I could escape. I'd get that tea in minute. After he was gone.

There was a knock, just as I was about to open the door.

"Jen? Sorry, I need something outta there." That was Pippa. She was early.

Rider's hand appeared beside my face. He was holding his palm against the door.

"Let go," I demanded.

"You try slammin' any door in my face again, I'll wedge my boot in, Jenna, before you can do it. I'm not letting you go. We both know you really don't want me to. You're just scared."

"Whatever," I said, but my voice broke in the middle.

He let go of the door and I stormed out.

I wasn't going to let myself dwell, all day, on how he just saved my ass from my mother's wrath. I wasn't going to dwell on how fast he got here.

I wasn't going to dwell on how it felt that he was still saying he wasn't giving up on me.

I wasn't!

(But, of course I did. I dwelled on it all day long.)

IT WAS 7:30 BEFORE I got out of the salon. Scooter looked supremely bored. He'd perked up when Deanna came in to say *Hi* and refresh my waiting area supply of brochures for her wax warmers an hour earlier. Her boys climbed all over him like he was some monkey bars while she, Pip, and I had a quick chat. It did not escape my notice (or Dee's) that he seemed to have all the patience in the world for her two little rambunctious monster-tots.

That was a bit of an interesting show, too, because I could've sworn Dee was giving him a shy flirty smile when she left. And he looked interested. Of course he'd look twice. She's a knockout.

But, Deanna had been through the ringer with men. The absolute last thing she needed was another asshole in her life. That was the last thing her boys needed, too, and I didn't know much about Scott, but I knew he'd participated in that gang bang. I'd seen his *thing*, for eff sakes, as he shoved it into that girl's mouth.

I could see why Dee smiled like that. He was kind of cute. Scooter was average height, a bit lanky, blond hair, a bit scruffy, but seemed sweet and had a nice smile. He looked like a combo of biker and all-American guy next door. She could do worse looks-wise, but I had the strong urge to warn her. Because it was about more than the way a guy looked. And she was beautiful, funny, sweet, and caring, and she didn't deserve to get her heart stomped on again.

I think Scott read my mind, because a minute after she left, I must've looked deep in thought with my eyes on him and not liking those thoughts. He was looking at me with a weird resigned expression, his shoulders slumped.

I glared at him and turned my back on him. I hoped that'd be taken as a warning not to fuck around with my friend's heart. If he did, I'd fuck him up.

The day had been busy, and I'd had a few quiet minutes here and there in the utility room with Pip throughout the day where I gave her bits and pieces of the story of the past week in hushed whispers. She was wide-eyed through all the details. I swore her to secrecy. She'd gotten a bit of the story from Rider and from Ella, but I filled in some gaps and when I told her Rider and me were done, but that he was being a stubborn a-hole about it, so I just had to wait for him to get bored of trying, she got alarmed.

"You need to give this a shot, Jen. A real shot. Ride out the storm and see what happens after."

"Nope," I'd said. "Can't."

"You mean won't."

"Fine. Won't."

She'd given me an assessing look and hadn't said anything further. She looked like she was plotting something. I didn't like Pippa's schemes. The only person better at a scheme was me. Usually. Before I got cock-bombed by Rider Valentine.

Yep, that's how it was. If Ella got put in a cock-fog, then I got hit with a cock-bomb. I pitied the poor girl who next landed in a Valentine's sights.

When I closed up, Scooter headed to the parking lot instead of up the back stairs with me and Pippa.

I looked at him quizzically.

"Ride's up there," he informed. "What time you want me here in the morning? 9:30?"

"Whatever," I grumbled and climbed the stairs. Before we got to the back door, I looked over my shoulder at Pippa.

"He's not out here."

"He's inside," she said.

"How'd he get inside?" I asked, checking the door, which was locked.

She winced.

"Pip..." I groaned.

"I gave Scott a key this morning and he gave them to that delicious biker hottie with the dark hair and dark eyes. He made some copies," she said. "What's *his* name?"

"Jesse?"

"Hm," she made a noise.

"Why are you looking at Jesse? You're moving in with Joe soon!"

She looked remorseful and shrugged. I didn't know if she was remorseful about the key or about looking at Jesse like potential man meat.

"Everything okay with you and Joe?"

She made a so-so motion with her hand.

"What's going on?"

She wrinkled her nose up. "Later. Ears in there."

I unlocked the door and decided to end this for once and for all.

SIX HOURS LATER

It was pitch dark, but, as I knew that room like I knew my own, I climbed the stairs and approached the bed.

Immediately, a head popped up and he was reaching toward the nightstand.

"It's me," I said quickly.

That was Deacon's head.

"Jenna?" he asked.

"Yeah," I whispered.

I rounded the bed and climbed into Ella's side.

"Hey?" She lifted her head from the pillow.

I started bawling.

She put her arms around me.

"Oh no... what happened?"

I was too upset to put my filter in place. Or worry about crying in front of a guy. Because this was Ella's guy, not mine.

I didn't have a guy. I had a problem.

"Why do I keep falling on his dick when he's such a fucking dick, Ella? Whyyyyy?" I whined.

"Fuck..." I heard Deacon's masculine voice grumble.

"Oh sweetie! What happened?" Ella asked, stroking my hair.

"I'll give you two a minute," Deacon said, getting up and looked like he was getting into a pair of jeans. It was dark enough that I only saw his outline.

"A minute?" I asked, "Maybe you better go find yourself a sofa, big guy. If you think I'm not sleeping here because you're in her bed now, you gotta learn... we've been besties since we were five and six. If you break her heart, she's climbing in with me. Your asshole brother breaks mine, you're taking the sofa."

It was dark, so I couldn't see his face, but he leaned over, grabbed a pillow, kissed Ella's forehead, and then leaned over a bit more and dropped a kiss on mine, too.

Oh God.

I stared, dumbfounded, as he vacated the premises.

"He's awesome," I told Ella, through tears.

"Yeah," she agreed, sounding all dreamy-eyed.

"WHAT HAPPENED?" SHE asked. And I told her about the day I'd had as well as what'd happened with Rider that night.

"How does that lyric go? If I'm under him I ain't getting over him."

"Wow, Jenna. Sorry, but I bet that was hot."

"Ella..." I groaned.

"Sorry. It sounded smokin'. You really wanna get over him? I think you should go home and get back under him."

"Screw that. Life in Cockfog Land is messed up. I'd rather be in the driver's seat, thank you very much."

"Really? Really?"

"I..."

"Think about it," she challenged.

"No," I whispered, being honest with the only person in the world I felt like I could be 100% honest with. Well, 99% honest. I still couldn't ever tell her I made out with her cousin just after high school grad.

"Okay?"

"But, I'm so...what if he hurts me? I don't like what he's turned me into. I'm pathetic."

Ella shuffled and got more comfortable. "My dad gave me a pep talk not long ago and reminded me of some wisdom. Go out on a limb. That's where the fruit is."

"Hm," I said skeptically. And then she yawned.

"Go to sleep," I told her. "Sorry to barge in on you and your beautiful biker. I have to get used to not being able to do this."

"He doesn't seem like he minded," she said.

"Thank you for being my bestie."

"You're welcome," she said, through another yawn, which also made me yawn.

"I think you got a good one," I told her.

"I know I did," she said with conviction. "And I think you did, too, Jenna. You're just fighting him because you're afraid. I talked to Pippa tonight and we both agree. You—-"

"Ella, don't."

She stopped immediately.

I didn't love that my two closest friends were discussing my love life and what they thought I should do. Then again, me and Ella discussed Pip. Me and Pip discussed Ella. It's just how it went.

But, I *did* love that as soon as I gave her the '*don't*', she stopped.

She fixed the blankets over us.

"Do you want to talk about it?" she asked.

"No," I said.

"Okay."

I loved Ella.

"I'm not laying in any wet spots, am I?" I asked.

She cackled. "Not tonight. We did it in the shower before bed. I put these sheets on this morning."

"Good," I muttered.

"But, fair warning. Show up like this again, not only might you wind up in the wet spot, but Deacon might shoot you. He almost got his gun."

"Yikes. And enough said. No more sleepovers."

"No way. I love our sleepovers," she said.

"I do, too. It's been too long."

"Now that we've got beautiful but badass gun-toting bikers in our beds, we just can't have impromptu sleepovers without putting ourselves in jeopardy of guns and wet spots. Let's do one at your place. In like... a week?"

"Done," I said, and then I wondered what my life would look like in a week.

"'Night."

"Night bestie. Love you like crazy."

"Love you, too," she said.

I REPLAYED THE EVENTS of that night in my head about three times before I finally fell asleep.

I'd gone into my apartment after unlocking the door and found him asleep on my bed. Crashed. On top of my peachy-pink comforter, but on it like he owned it. Like he had every right to be there. He was in jeans, boots on the floor, wearing that grey and blue flannel shirt I'd flung at him the night before, a different white t-shirt underneath, and a pair of grey jeans.

I dropped my bag on the floor and glared at him.

He kept on sleeping.

"Rider," I said.

He didn't move.

"Rider!" I tried again, louder.

He smiled a little. Was that in his sleep or was he playing a game?

I stood there. His breathing was even, as if he was really sleeping.

I said his name again. Twice more. No movement.

So, I went over there and went to nudge his shoulder, and that was when he grabbed me and then I was flipped, put on my back on my own bed, and he was lying directly on top of me, smiling.

"I made the bed for ya," he informed me as his lips came down on mine. "You musta forgot this mornin'."

I turned my head away. "Off me."

He chuckled.

"Get off," I ordered.

"Oh yeah, baby. Let's get off." He grinded against me and he was hard.

I smacked him across the face and he jolted. I'd hit him pretty hard.

"Get out of here," I hollered.

"That's it!" he declared and then flipped me, and I was over his lap and he was yanking my dress pants downwards. They didn't go far, the waistband didn't allow for it, so he got his hand underneath and ripped the fly open and then yanked them. I heard the fabric protest as he yanked.

"Hey!"

I did *not* think so.

He slapped my ass.

Ow. Fucking ow!

And then he hauled my panties down and smacked it again, this time on my bare ass!

"Rider Valentine!" I screeched.

"You gotta learn to stop slappin' me. Next time, I don't just spank this sexy, *sexy* ass. Next time, I tie you down and make you edge until you're pleading for mercy."

I kicked and writhed, fighting as hard as I could, but he had a firm hold of me.

He ran his palm up and down my bare butt and then his finger slipped down in between my ass cheeks and he got a finger part way inside me.

"No!" I hollered, "Don't you dare." I struggled like my life depended on it, and got away from him.

I was on my feet, yanking my pants up.

He leaned back on his elbows and smirked at me.

I shook my head.

My ass was feeling like it was on fire.

"What do you want for dinner?" he asked, casually.

"Huh?"

"Dinner."

I looked at him like he was insane. *Because, he was insane!*

I stood there, rubbing my fanny, and staring at him in disbelief. He wandered out of the room. I kept standing there, dumbstruck.

Pippa poked her head in. "Goin' to Joe's. Spending the night. See you in the morning."

"Don't leave me!" I hissed.

She looked at me with confusion.

"He... don't leave me with him!"

She rolled her eyes. "C'mon. Don't be silly."

"No, Pip. Seriously. He just gave me a spanking. A spanking!"

"She slapped me in the face!" Rider called out, defending himself.

Damn it.

Pippa smirked. "I'm goin'. And for the record, I'm Team Rider."

My mouth dropped. Horrified.

"I talked to him at least four times while you guys were gone. And I listened to your side today, and I'm sorry, but... Team Rider. Let that wall down, Jenna. If you don't, some other girl will. And then how will you feel?"

I gasped. I was speechless.

She snickered and hooked her overnight bag over her shoulder, and then she left.

Turncoat.

"How 'bout pasta and chicken?" Rider called in. "You got that stuff here. Don't think we even need to hit a store."

"I don't cook," I shouted. Pippa cooked. I didn't.

"I do," he informed. "Groceries. Cute animals. The whole shebang. Or did you forget?"

I didn't answer him. I went into my bathroom, locked the door, and took a long soak in bubbles with a sparkly pink bath bomb.

I stayed in there until I was way too pruny, and then when I came out, I locked my bedroom door and got into bed. I was in the most un-sexy pajamas I owned. They were flannel man-style pajamas in pink and grey checkerboard. I had fluffy pink slipper-socks on, and my hair up in a sloppy bun. I got my bag from the floor and grabbed my phone and curled up in bed, scrolling through Instagram.

My stomach was growling. I could smell the food and it smelled good. I smelled what smelled like garlic bread. And I couldn't resist it any longer.

Finally, I stomped out.

If he was going to cook food in my kitchen, I guess I'd eat it. I hadn't eaten all day. Jesse dropped off submarine sandwiches, bringing me an eggplant parm one at Rider's behest, and I never ate it. It was still in the fridge in the utility room of the shop.

"I was just about to come get you," he said. I looked around. It was ready. Even though the kitchen was kind of trashed from the mess he'd made, he'd even set the table with candles and everything.

I folded my arms across my chest.

"Why are you bothering?" I asked.

"Because, I'm taking care of my girl. Scoot said you didn't eat all day. Pippa said you were a wreck. So did Ella. I'd've run you that bubble bath if you hadn't run it yourself. Now, I'm gonna feed you and then..." he looked off into space and then waved the wooden spoon in his hand around in the air, "Give ya three or four orgasms." He shrugged, "Yeah. That should do it."

I could not believe him.

He put the spoon down and grabbed two plates from the counter. They were filled with Fettucine Alfredo, broccoli florets, and topped with bacon and parmesan. There were strips of grilled chicken in there, too. He poured me a glass of red wine and grabbed himself a bottle of beer, and then he sat down. There were bread sticks there in a basket. Where he heck did those come from?

"Are these from Olive Garden?" I asked, lifting a bread stick.

"Yeah. Got Pudge to grab them for us. He dropped them off five minutes ago. I cooked the rest. But these are the shit, so I asked him to grab 'em."

I effing *loved* Olive Garden bread sticks.

"Did Ella tell you how much I love these bread sticks?"

Was Ella scheming with Pippa?

He shook his head innocently, "I got them 'cuz *I* like them, and I knew Pudge was on his way back and would pass it on his way home."

I sat down. I had no idea who Pudge was, but I didn't care. I was famished.

I started to eat and felt like there was a lump in my throat. I had to stop myself from having a repeat of the night he made me eat *Bambi*. I couldn't burst into tears every time he cooked food for me.

Wait. This had to be the last time he cooked food for me. I had to make this stop.

I ate two bread sticks and half the plate of pasta (and it was really, *really* good) and I could not take it anymore. *No* crying. I had to stop myself from crying. So instead, I suddenly got very, *very* angry.

I downed my glass of wine and jumped to my feet.

"This is bullshit!" I snapped.

His fork was half way to his mouth and he was frozen, staring at me, looking thrown off.

"You have to go."

"No," he said and shoved that forkful of food in his mouth.

"No?" I challenged.

He took his time chewing, while I waited for him to answer. Finally, he swallowed and got up. "More wine?" he moved toward my fridge.

I moved toward him and I shoved him from behind.

"You have to go."

He spun around, and his brows went up.

"You want me to get pushy, too?" he challenged.

I shoved him again. "This needs to st-op."

Damn voice breaking in the middle like that.

"Jenna." His voice went sweet.

"No!" I pointed at him.

"Don't you point at me, Jenna Murdoch!" he said, teasingly, mockingly, and exaggeratedly went to slap my finger in a girlie slap way. I hauled off and meant to punch him in the arm, but he caught my fist before it hit the target.

Yeah, yeah... I know it's not cool to be violent. To have a double standard. But, this guy was driving me to violence! He wouldn't leave. He was acting like we were still together. And if he kept his shit up, I'd have to cave, and caving would inevitably lead to heartache. More heartache. My heart already hurt too fucking much.

He twisted me around so that I was facing the wall. My eyes closed out of frustration.

"You mad at me? Good. I want emotion from you. I want it all. Give it to me. Let's fight this out. Let's do what we need to do to get back on track. If I have to force a reaction out of you, so be it, but we're gonna be getting back on track, Jenna." He kissed my collar bone.

I spun around. He let me. We were facing one another.

"Go."

"Go ahead and hit me then. Get your frustrations out. I know this has been frustrating. I know you're pissed at me. But I'm not giving up here. A relationship is supposed to have ups and downs. Both people in it need to work at it sometimes. I'm willing to do the work. You gotta be, too. Let's fight it out. Then we'll make up." He wiggled his eyebrows.

I huffed. "Fighting is not foreplay, Rider Valentine!"

"Think you're wrong there, gorgeous. Works out fuckin' great. Cause one minute, you're yellin' at me. The next minute, my hand is in your panties and your tongue is in my mouth... what's not healthy about that?"

And then... and then I don't know what came over me. The idea of his hand in my panties and my tongue in his mouth? I threw myself at him.

And he caught me, both hands on my ass. I wrapped my legs around his waist and attacked his mouth with mine. He walked us to the bedroom and we went crashing down onto my bed, then he rolled, so he was on his back, me on top.

My mouth was on his, my hands in his hair. I was practically humping him, needing friction through my crazy-unsexy flannel pajamas. He started pulling the pants and my undies down. I began undoing the buttons on his black button-down shirt.

I released the elastic holding my hair in a bun and my hair went spilling down around my shoulders. I pulled the elastic out of his and his went spilling over me as he was turning me over to my back and undoing my pajama top's buttons.

I raked my nails up his back under the t-shirt he had on underneath and he arched his back and hissed.

I did it again. Angrily.

And his eyes lit with something that turned me to a puddle of ... horny. I couldn't think. I couldn't articulate. I could only *feel.*

I grabbed his hair and dragged his mouth to mine.

"Hate fucking," he said. "Great idea, right? Take your frustrations out on my cock, gorgeous girl. I can take it."

That didn't piss me off. If anything, it fueled my lust. Yeah, I was going to unleash all my frustration right there, right then.

I kissed him feverishly. My tongue sought his and twisted up with it. And then my nails went down the back of his jeans and dug into his ass cheeks.

He thrust his pelvis at me and we rolled again, toward the middle of the bed, me on top. I scampered up to my knees, yanked his zipper down, yanked him out, lined him up, and slammed down on him, taking him in to the root in one quick motion.

Ouch. Too fast. I winced, but it didn't stop me. His hands went to my boobs. I slapped them away and then I slapped his face.

His eyes went wide, and he grabbed my wrists and pinned them behind my back, sat up with him still inside me, and attacked my throat with his teeth.

My head rolled back, and I let out a breathy moan, got a hand free, and grabbed his throat and shoved his head back. He landed on his back, catching my wrist as he went down. He bit down on it and growled at me.

I moaned and rocked forward. His fingers went between my legs and started rubbing my clit. I rocked to and fro some more, then I attacked his throat with *my* teeth. He raked his nails up my back. They weren't long, but I still felt the scrape. It felt amazing. That, with everything else going on, the friction inside, his fingers circling my clit. I shivered and started to come. Hard. Loud. Spectacularly. Saying his name.

I collapsed on top of him for about three beats, and then he flipped me and threw my legs up over his shoulders and slammed back inside of me. I yelped and grabbed for his hips to keep him connected with me. My eyes rolled back in my head and the orgasm I thought was over wasn't. It started back up again! I was so over sensitized, I was whimpering like a puppy. Trying to get away and keep him attached to me at the same time. I was writhing. And he wasn't stopping.

He was twisting my nipples, biting my shoulder, nipping at my neck, fucking me so hard, skin slapping against skin, him fucking me at a weird sort of diagonal angle that felt just *so* good that I thought I was going to die. And then he was exploding in me. I felt it as he powered forward and the veins in his neck were straining. His mouth was open and then he let out a primal-sounding grunt that melted into a vibrating exhale. He pulled my legs down and then went to a complete dead weight on top of me.

I was breathing hard. *So* hard, having trouble catching my breath.

My girl-parts were on perma-tingle mode. They felt like they'd never be normal. My nipples were actually buzzing, or so it felt like.

"That's what I'm talkin' about," he said into my ear in a low and husky sexy voice. "See? Hate fucking *can* be like couples' therapy."

I blinked.

He kissed my lips, backed up on his knees, smiling at me, and then he pulled the blanket across to cover us up. He pulled me close and wrapped his arms around me tight. "Any time you get pissed at me, you're welcome to do that to bleed out that rage, okay, beautiful?" He kissed my mouth tenderly. So tenderly. And then he sifted his fingers through my hair and kissed one and then the other eyelid.

I started to panic. I had to go. I had to go!

"Shhh." He pulled me tight to him and shifted so that my head was on his chest. "Listen, Jenna. Just listen."

God, no. I was gonna cry. I couldn't listen. I'd wanna listen until the day I died if I didn't get away from him right effing now.

I pulled away. "I have to pee."

He hesitated.

"Badly," I added.

He let me go.

I headed out the door instead of to the ensuite bathroom.

"Where ya goin?" He sat up.

"The other bathroom. I ... need something in there."

Once I cleared the doorframe of my room, I took three steps and then ran the rest of the way to Pippa's bedroom and rifled through her closet until finding and throwing on Capri yoga pants, a tank top, and a sweatshirt. I slipped on a pair of her ballet flats, then quickly went pee in the other bathroom and then I ran for it, grabbing my keys and nothing else and dashing down the stairs to get to my car, thinking *Oh God, what have I done?*

That was how I ended up in Ella's bed.

19

The next morning, Deacon came in, bringing us both coffee. Ella was already in the shower, so it was just me lying there, trying to wake up, but also trying not to let my brain punish me for last night's actions by re-playing them on a loop some more. They'd done that half the night.

"Ride's waitin' for you. He crashed in Beau's playroom on an air mattress last night." Deacon arched his back, his hand at the small of it. "That room is full of air mattresses and every one of them sucks."

I winced. "Sorry." And then what he'd said registered. "What? Rider or Beau slept there. What?"

"Ride slept in there. Had to tell him you were here, babe," Deacon told me. "He was out of his mind last night, flipped that the Jackals might get to you."

Shit.

"He wanted to come up here last night. I talked him down. Convinced him to let you sleep."

"Thank you," I whispered.

He waved his hand in a 'don't worry' gesture.

"Where's the rest of your family?" I asked. "Everyone's staying here?"

"Spence, me, and Dad were in Beau's playroom. Dad on a pull-out, us on air mattresses. Jojo's in Beau's bedroom. Beau was sleepin' in the play room with Dad and Spence, on his own air mattress with Chakotay, thinkin' it was a bro party, but when Ride got here, Rob pulled him and put him in bed with his ma so Ride could crash on that air mattress. Rob slept on the couch. Kid's a sprawler."

A full house. That was already full, and I'd gone and made more than one person uncomfortable last night.

Shoot. *Me and my effing drama.*

"Ride's in the playroom waitin' to talk to ya," he repeated. "Don't dodge him and make him worry about you again."

"I won't. Sorry to be such a pain in the ass, Deacon," I said.

"Don't worry about it." He smiled at me and went to the bathroom. I could hear the shower running so I was guessing he was climbing in with Ella. I vacated the premises, hesitantly climbing down the attic stairs to the second floor. Rider wasn't there.

I could hear a hair dryer going in the bathroom and all the other doors were opened, rooms empty, so I assumed Jojo was in the bathroom. I went down to the main floor and could see and smell the makings of breakfast preparations in progress, but the kitchen was empty of people. I looked out the window. I saw Rider coming toward the house. From my parent's lawn. Oh God. *What*?

His expression was cool, almost cold.

I backed away from the sink and stood there, in the middle of the kitchen, feeling sick to my stomach. Feeling all sorts of ugliness crash over me wave after wave.

I'd taken off and made him worry. Worry about me with the Wyld Jackals out there threatening. I was a horrible witch. That didn't even dawn on me last night.

Deke came in, through the breezeway that led between the garage and the kitchen. That's where Ella's dad always hung out, in his man cave with his buddies, his music, and his bongs. Deke went straight to the coffee pot, two empty mugs in hand.

"Pink Lady," he greeted with a wink. I heard peals of male laughter from multiple voices on the other side of that breezeway and knew that the gang was hanging out in the garage.

Rider stepped into the kitchen and his eyes landed on me. Cold. Angry.

I winced internally. Shit. I didn't want to cause a scene in front of Deke.

"Jennajennajenna. Jenna! Look!" Beau, Ella's six-year-old brother, skidded into the kitchen and saw me and Rider in a face-off.

"Deacon got me a new shirt!" He was wearing a little Dominion Brotherhood hoodie. He looked adorable.

"Nice!" I said with enthusiasm, ruffling his blond hair.

"You're marryin' Deacon's brother?" he asked.

I froze.

"'Cuz Lella is *for sure* gonna marry Deacon and you're already family so that'll make you like... double family."

I ignored the lump in my throat. "Uh..."

"Didn't your ma tell you to get your backpack, Beau?" Deke asked, spooning lots of sugar into one of those coffee cups. "You're gonna miss that bus. Your pop said he doesn't have time to drive you to school again today."

"Oh, shit. I'm gonna be late!" Beau dashed toward the stairs.

Beau had the mouth of a sailor.

"Gotta bounce, Dad," Rider said. "Call you later." And then Rider turned his eyes to me. "I'll see *you* there at six thirty for dinner with your folks." His thumb jerked toward my parents' house.

"Pardon?" I asked.

Not this again.

"Six thirty." He gave me a hard look. "You be there or we're gonna have a problem, Jenna."

"What?" I repeated, glaring at him.

"Don't make me do this dinner with your folks on my own. I will. But, I won't be happy about it. Come to think of it, meet me here, 6:15, so we can walk over there together."

"Ri—-" I started.

"Jenna! Good morning!" Ella's mother strolled into the kitchen. "Do you want some frittata? I have three big, *big* ones cooking in the oven. I'm also making battered French toast sticks. Just for you, unless you wanna share." She pinched my cheek as she passed me.

"Uh, mornin'. No thanks, Bertie." I loved Ella's mom's French toast sticks. She always made them on my birthday. And when I was sad. Shit. She must've known.

Rider reached for my hand to get my attention. It wasn't sweet. Not at all. There was no emotion on his face.

"Gimme your car keys. I'm leavin' my bike here, takin' your car. Spence'll drop you at your salon. I'll get Scoot to drop you here after the salon."

"Uh..."

Why was he taking my car?

"Her keys are up in my room, on top of my make-up table." Ella materialized.

"I'll get the car key off, leave your house and salon key there," Rider said.

I glared at my best friend.

She gave me a cocky smile.

Evidently, Ella was Team Rider, too.

Rider leaned in and gave me a quick kiss and then he turned on his heel and headed toward the stairs.

"Rider?" I said to the back of him, but he kept going.

Spencer had come in from the breezeway. "Yeah, I'll give you a lift. After frittatas. Whatever the fuck they are."

FML.

The kitchen was a little mayhem-y as people were getting coffee and Bertie was cooking while Rob tried to get Beau to wear matching shoes so that he could get him to his school bus stop on time. He finally gave up on matching shoes and settled for any shoes. I'd seen Rider leave with my car and then I slipped out the kitchen door and marched over to my parents' house, seeing that Dad was in the driveway, but that thankfully Mom had already gone to work.

"Dad," I said, pleadingly, catching him about to get into his car.

"Oh. Hi," he said with a little smile. It sort of looked uncertain. Dad also looked tired.

My father was always well put together. Always clean shaven. Never a hair out of place. And he wasn't disheveled, but he looked tired. Older. I didn't like the way it made my stomach feel.

"Dad, cancel this dinner. Please."

He looked confused.

"I'm trying to... break up with him and he's taking this protection thing seriously, and I just... I need to not do this with you and Mom and him tonight. I..."

"Honey," Dad looked alarmed. "What's going on?"

I started to come unglued. Dad grabbed me and pulled me into a hug, seeing it.

God, it had been years since he'd held me like that. Years. I just fell absolutely apart. He ushered me inside and we sat on the couch.

He got me a bottle of water and a box of Kleenex. I somehow managed to get myself together.

"I can't do this dinner tonight. Mom wants to rip me a new one. Rider wants to protect me from her. Which is kind of sweet, but I'm trying to break up with him and that's not going well and it's just gonna keep getting harder if he keeps doing sweet things like being a buffer between me and her, and if you guys are gonna take my salon, just tell me now, Dad. I don't wanna do this with an audience at the dinner table with linen napkins and Mom's good china, and..."

"Jenna, breathe," Dad said.

I stopped talking and looked at him expectantly.

"No one's taking your salon," Dad said.

"No?"

"No," he said firmly.

"She's been threatening and—-"

"That shit stops."

My eyes bulged. My father rarely cussed, unless it had something to do with golf.

He let out a sigh. I slumped in relief.

"She and I were going to wait to do this, since all the trouble with you and this fella you're dating began, but..." he looked at me and a muscle jumped in his cheek. My dad looked... nervous.

My heart sank.

"We're separating," Dad said.

My eyes were huge.

"Se-separating?"

He nodded. "It's been a long time coming."

"Who? Whose idea..." I started.

"Mine," he said quickly.

I nodded, trying to let it sink in. Wow.

"Jenna, I... I haven't been a perfect husband. And..."

"Are you joking? You're a fucking saint to put up with her."

My father's expression fell. And it was already way, *way* close to the floor. He shook his head, looking guilty.

There was a loud and aggressive knock on the door. Dad rushed to it.

Spencer, Deacon, and Deke were all there, all looking tweaked. They saw me behind Dad and all of them visibly relaxed.

"Don't do that again!" Spencer snapped.

"Excuse me?" My father's back went straight as an arrow.

"Dad, it's okay," I said. "Dad, this is Rider's dad and his brothers."

"You just disappear? One minute you're in the kitchen and the next minute we can't fuckin' find you! With all that's goin' on, what're you thinking?"

I winced. "Sorry. I needed to talk to my dad."

Deacon and Deke were both calmer, but Spencer was supremely ticked at me.

"Next time just say somethin', yeah?"

I nodded a little. "I need another minute with my dad, okay? I'll be right there."

"Deke Valentine. Good to meet ya." Deke extended his hand toward my dad.

"Paul Murdoch. You as well."

"Deacon." Deacon held out his hand. Dad shook it.

"Spence." Spencer held out his. Dad shook his, too.

"We'll watch out the window. Frittatas're ready," Spencer said.

"I don't want any. Go ahead."

"Bertie made a mountain of breakfast food. You should bring your Dad. Come have some," Deacon said. "She said her French toast sticks are your favorite."

"I'll be there in a minute."

"Thanks very much. Another time maybe," my dad said. "I have a meeting to get to."

They all said their goodbyes and Dad shut the door.

He let out a breath. "We have a lot to discuss. But I really do have to go. Sorry to drop a bombshell on you like that, honey, especially since you already seem so stressed out."

"Wow. I mean, it's still kind of sinking in." I shook my head.

"I want it amicable. But, your mother... she..." Dad winced and let that hang.

I could only imagine.

"Listen," he glanced at his watch. "Do you want to go to lunch? We can talk some more? I can pick you up at the salon at around one?"

"I'm fully booked today, and people are already probably a bit miffed about last week. I don't wanna do this dinner tonight, Dad. I'm sorry. The Rider thing is complicated and... can we reschedule?"

"Sure." Dad nodded. "I'll talk to your mother and we'll set another day."

"Okay."

Phew.

"You're not losing your salon, Jenna. You've worked hard. I see that. I won't allow your mother to sell."

I breathed a sigh of relief. Dad pulled me into another hug.

"I've missed these," I said in a small voice.

"Me, too. Lotta things are gonna be changing, honey. I have to talk to you about a lot of things."

I nodded and fought back more tears.

"We've both got a busy day, so I'll call you tomorrow and we'll go from there."

I nodded again.

"I'll watch you walk across. Make sure all is good."

"Okay, Dad."

I walked back over to Ella's house and waved at him before going inside.

And then before I got a chance to get lost in thoughts of last night or thoughts of Mom and Dad splitting up, I got wrapped up in a crazy hectic breakfast with way too much food with Rob, Bertie, Deacon, Deke, Ella, Spencer, and Jojo. And I got to meet Chakotay, too (Spencer's German Shepherd).

Spencer drove me to work in his pickup truck. He was quiet and angry and let me have it a little bit again, saying he'd answer to Rider if anything had happened to me this morning, since Rider left me in his hands. He also told me Rider was not in a good place the night before when I took off on him. I apologized for it again, and he was still miserable. I suspected it wasn't only about me, but I didn't have the head-space to give it too much thought.

So, I didn't. I let him drop me off at the salon and I got there ten minutes late. My appointment was grouchy at first but thawed toward me half way through her roots being done.

And then Paige *Skank* Simpson walked in.

"Hello Jenna. Do you have any Bubble and Bubble shampoo?"

"You mean Bumble and Bumble?" I asked.

She looked at me like I was an idiot. "No. I'm pretty sure it's Bubble and Bubble."

I didn't have time for this bitch's nonsense. I was a shampoo aficionado.

"No, I don't carry Bubble and Bubble." I rolled my eyes.

"Oh. Well, I guess I'll need to go to a higher end salon."

"Yeah, why don't you do that?" I snapped.

I noticed that Scooter was watching her carefully. He wasn't sitting. He was standing. And he was almost in her space.

She glanced at him. "Can I help you?" she was all huffy with him.

"You can move along," he said with zero patience and a lot of assertiveness.

She gave him a sour look. "Tell Rider I say hey," she winked at me.

Fucking bitch.

"I'll do that," I said. "Next time I'm riding his face I'll be sure to think of you."

I heard a gasp of surprise. *Shit.* My customer.

I held my glare while Skank Paige stormed out on her high heels, her split-end-ridden hair flapping in the breeze.

"I'm so sorry, Mrs. Gustafson," I called out.

Her eyes were huge. She looked back down to her magazine.

"You were aggressive," I said to Scooter.

"She's a mole," he said through gritted teeth.

"Mole?"

"Shh. Yeah. She's been reporting to the Jackals. Takin' pictures. Causing all kinds a shit. Didn't know what she was doin' in here. Probably scoping the joint to see if you had protection." He was dialing on his phone. "She keeps tryin' to catch the eye of members, now prospects too, so she can report back to Gordino, Ipswich Jackals Prez." He started talking into his phone. "Jess. Need a ride-by and an hour or two of sentry. Four or six AS-

AP. Jenna's House of Allure. Yep." He hung up and dialed again. "Ride. Jackal mole Paige at Jenna's tryin' to stir shit.... Yep already did. Jess's sortin' it. She's fine. Tore a strip off that gash. Shoulda heard what she said."

I got right in Scooter's face and slashed my index finger across my throat in warning.

"Tell ya later. Mixed company. Right. Bye." He snickered and was about to hang up.

"Wait. Tell him dinner is canceled at my parents."

"You wanna talk to him?" Scooter asked.

"No! Just... just tell him."

"Ride? Jenna said-—Oh. Right. One sec." He looked to me. "He heard you. He already knows. He wants to know what cute animals you want him to pick up for dinner?"

I ignored him and went back to Mrs. Gustafson.

She was terse with me the rest of the appointment. I gave her the wash and set on the house and gave her an extra wash and set coupon for next time. She perked up a little with that.

My elderly lady clientele list wasn't real big. It just figured with my luck that it'd be one of them in my chair when that happened.

IN THE MIDDLE OF THE afternoon, I got my period.

Well, at least I wouldn't be falling on his dick for four or five days. Maybe he'd get tired of this game by then.

My phone made a text noise.

It was Rider.

"Pork chops or ribs?"

I wrote back.

"Don't worry about me for dinner."

I texted again.

"Don't worry about me at all."

He wrote back.

> **"I'm off before you today. I have time to cook. What do you want me to make?"**

How did he even know what time I finished today? Were his prospects looking at my appointment book? I rolled my eyes and put my phone in my reception desk drawer.

He showed up a few minutes later.

And with lots of fanfare. I heard the pipes over the loud hairdryer in my hand. Four motorcycles pulled up out in front of my salon and parked. Rider on his motorcycle, looking hotter than should be legal (damn it), plus Deacon, Jesse, and a very tall slim redheaded guy with a ZZ Top length beard (I'd never seen him before) all stood outside while Rider came in, leather vest, blue jeans, black boots, black thermal. Low man bun. Scruff on his face. Anger on his face. Delicious-looking.

Grr.

I was in the middle of blow-drying a teenage girl's hair, but he got to me, took the dryer out of my hand, and flipped it off, saying, "One sec." to the girl. He walked me into the utility room. He shut the door.

"You didn't answer me about dinner," he said.

"I have clients. I'm busy."

"Fine. Sometimes I got my hands in a hood and can't answer a text right away, too, but Scoot told me you sat for ten minutes eating cannolis with Pippa before that girl came in, so you had ten minutes where you coulda took ten seconds to write back to me and tell me pork chops or ribs."

"I don't have to text you back. And I don't want either. Is he my protector or is he just your spy?"

"You don't like 'em?"

"What?"

"Ribs or chops."

I sighed. "No. I don't."

"Then I'll make you something else."

"Don't bother. Let me out. I have another person in the waiting area."

He shook his head.

I doubled over with a wince.

"What's wrong?" He was on alert.

I let out a breath and straightened. "Nothing. Just go, okay? I don't care what you make for dinner. Okay? I don't like meat with bones in it."

"Meat with bones in it?"

"No."

He laughed and scratched his jaw. "I got so many comebacks right now..."

I winced again. I had to get to my bag and take some ibuprofen.

"Are you sick?"

I rolled my eyes. And then I decided, fuck it.

"I got my period."

He pursed his lips.

"Yeah. So no hate fucking tonight."

He smiled. "I got no problems running red lights, gorgeous."

I looked at him a second and then the meaning behind his words permeated.

"Ew. Gross. Get out. Let me get back to work."

"How 'bout cheeseburgers?"

"Whatever." I waved my hand at him as I headed back to my client.

He spoke to Scooter in the waiting area and then they stepped outside (the three other bikers were still out there, all with their backs to my window, looking like bouncers) and they were talking for a minute. I was blow drying, but half watching them. I saw Rider's head go back in raucous laughter. And then he looked at me and gave me a *thumbs up* and blew me a kiss.

Blew me a kiss. What was it with him?

Scooter looked at me and laughed.

Scooter had obviously told him what I'd said to Paige.

I'd have thought Rider would still be miffed about my taking off last night. He'd gone from waiting to talk to me in Beau's playroom to deciding to go to my parents' house, to laughing and blowing me kisses while talking about what he was gonna make me for dinner.

Whatever. Games. Him and his games.

Scooter, Jesse, and the ZZ Top biker stayed outside for the next hour. (Deacon and Rider rode off). Rider came in at 5:45, sending Scooter home, and sat in my waiting area until I closed at 6:00. Pippa had already left at 5:00, planning to go out on a dinner date with Joe.

Two minutes after she left, she sent me a text.

#TeamRider

I rolled my eyes.

I ignored Rider while I closed up. He followed me out front and up the front stairs.

I went immediately into my room and locked the door. Two hours later, I walked out to get a drink and he was cooking burgers on Pippa's George Foreman grill. They smelled really good.

On the middle of the kitchen table was a package of six chocolate frosted cupcakes with pink sprinkles on them. I stared at them.

"Figured you might need those today with that Aunt Flo business." He waved the spatula he was holding in the air and then went back to his cooking.

I went back to my room.

"Food's ready" he called in not long later.

"Not hungry," I called back, lying.

He said nothing in response.

I watched television in bed.

He came in at around 11 o'clock. I guess he'd been watching TV in my living room. I guess I'd also forgotten to lock the door. Just as well. I didn't need my doorknob broken.

He shed his clothes and got into my bed. Naked. I tried to keep my eyes on the TV.

He spooned me, but there was a layer of blanket between our bodies. I just stayed there, not reacting.

He didn't do anything about it.

He fell asleep.

I stewed in my warring feelings for the next hour, then I slipped out and sat at my kitchen table and ate two chocolate cupcakes, washing them down with two huge glasses of milk.

I heard a key go into the lock and then the door opened. Pippa walked in while I had a too-full mouth.

I swallowed it down and said, 'Hi." I took a big sip of milk.

"Hi," she said, and she looked upset.

"I thought you had a date with Joe."

"I did."

"He didn't come back with you? That's rare."

"Yeah. He's a fucking goof."

"Oh?" I nudged the package of cupcakes in her direction.

"I don't wanna talk about it tonight," she waved her hand. "I'm goin' to bed."

"'Night," I said. I rinsed my glass and put it in the dishwasher. The kitchen was trashed again. Rider could cook, but could he not clean?

I loaded the dishwasher, hand-washed the Foreman grill, and then I went to my bathroom, brushed my teeth, and got into bed.

He immediately pulled me to him and pulled my head to his chest.

"What were you doin'?"

"Cleaning your mess. Can you not clean up after yourself?"

"I cook. You clean."

"I didn't eat, Rider."

"Bet you ate cupcakes." I heard the smile in his voice.

I tried to ignore the sound of his heart beating. I had to pull away. I turned my back to him.

He spooned me. I was too worn out to wrestle. And my belly hurt. I winced at a cramp and my hand went to my stomach. His hand sweetly moved under my hand and he rubbed my stomach and kissed the back of my neck.

I fell asleep, a lump in my throat, wrapped up in his arms.

20

Several Days Later

It wasn't easy, but I kept trying to keep my distance. He kept doing what I was ascertaining was his *thing* for the next two days.

But, then, things changed.

The first two days he was texting to ask about dinner, walking me upstairs after I closed up. I noticed he'd kept my car key after the night at Ella's, likely so I couldn't take off again.

He organized protection for me during the next wedding on my roster, where me, Pippa, and Ella took care of hair and make-up for the bride, my client Mindy, and her handsome groom. I hadn't told him about it, so figured Pippa must have.

Turncoat.

The first two nights Rider cooked me dinner I didn't eat, and messed up my kitchen, and then he slept in my bed with me, being cuddly after I'd fallen asleep.

The night after burgers, he made a stir fry that I didn't eat. I ate a peanut butter sandwich over the sink at midnight after he fell asleep. He spooned me again when I climbed back in. For some reason, I didn't pull away.

The night after that, he cooked pre-breaded pork schnitzel (no bones) and scalloped potatoes (from a box, but they still smelled good), and boiled some corn on the cob. I made a tuna wrap and ignored the food and cleaned the kitchen up after his massive mess. Again.

The next night was the wedding. I ate there. The bride sat me and Ella and Pippa at the singles' table. I didn't even party. I was a stick in the mud, so deep in my misery. We left early.

The next night, he didn't come home, left me with Jesse. Jesse had shadowed me that day while Scooter did something with Deacon and then watched Ella. Scooter turned up later that evening though, as Jesse had to do something for the club and I overheard them say that Bronto would take care of Ella the next few days, Scooter of me.

I was tempted to make Jesse's job hard the day he watched me, feeling no love for him after the way he'd kidnapped me from Ella's room, but I didn't have the energy for it, so mostly ignored him and that seemed fine by him. He was quiet and very watchful, looking over anyone who came in skeptically and double-checking the doors in and out of my apartment and salon. He did a walk-through of the apartment before he even let me step more than two feet into my kitchen. Way more thorough than Scooter and Bronto.

Rider came in at four o'clock in the morning and he had a black eye. I saw this when I woke up that morning, noting he hadn't spooned me when he came to bed, seeing him fast asleep in bed with his eye all purple and swollen.

I slipped out and didn't see him until the next morning. He'd gotten in late the night before (again) and we hadn't seen one another. He tried to cuddle me, and I elbowed him in the ribs for it. He stayed on his side of the bed after that.

Listen to me. His side. As if he had a side of ***my*** *bed.*

I saw him that morning and he looked tired, roughed up, and grouchy.

And I was grouchy, too. I'd been grouchy all week in front of him and sullen when he wasn't around.

Scooter wasn't there, and neither was Pippa. She had something going on, too, and she was keeping mum about it. She was gone the past two nights and had cancelled all of her appointments during the day both days. I asked what was wrong via text and she replied that she'd 'tell me later'. I was busy. A few walk-ins came in for brow waxing the day before and I'd done them and put the money in Pippa's lock box for her, so her days off wouldn't be too bad of a hit.

Rider went in to the bathroom as I came out after my shower and didn't even say good morning.

Maybe he was getting sick of this game.

Good.

(So, why was my heart hurting?)

I went down to the salon, and ten minutes later was getting scolded by Scooter, who, it turned out was in the shower in my other bathroom while I'd left, thinking he wasn't there.

I rolled my eyes. "I didn't know you were there."

"Jenna, come on! What's it gonna take with you?"

"I don't know who the fuck you think you're talking to!" I fired back. "But—-"

Rider came in. "Hey!" He got between us, blocking me and getting in Scooter's face.

"She walked down here without saying anything. She usually doesn't come down till 9:30, 9:45. It's 9:10. I thought I had time to get a shower. Anything could've happened to her and it'd be my fuckin' fault."

"Cool it," Rider ordered.

Scooter stormed out front and lit a cigarette.

Rider turned to me, his eyes narrowed.

"Gotta make everyone's life miserable?" he asked, giving me a disapproving once-over. "If we get through this thing without you gettin' hurt it'll be a fuckin' miracle and no thanks to you, Jenna."

My heart stuttered.

He rolled his eyes. "I need my fuckin' head examined."

And then he stormed outside and said something to Scooter, his hand reassuringly on Scooter's shoulder.

I turned around and stormed into the utility room and slammed the door.

I paced in there, in the tiny space that had a counter, a sink, a small stacked washer and dryer, and a long shelf filled with supplies. I couldn't pace far, obviously, but I did it angrily and I was angry at myself.

I heard the door chimes and figured it was Scooter, so I busied myself. And then I made a coffee for me and one for him and I brought it out to him.

He was sitting there in my waiting area, talking to Deanna.

"Uh, hey," I said to her, passing him a mug.

"Thanks," he said warily.

"Sorry about this morning," I said, looking him in the eye.

He nodded. "Just don't want anything to happen to ya is all. Things have been stressful. I dealt with these guys first hand, you know that Jenna. I'm watching, my hand ready to grab my phone or my gun at all times, and..." he took a breath. "I just don't wanna see you get hurt."

"Thank you. I'll be better."

He nodded, flexing his jaw.

I tried to play it cool, imagining he wouldn't want anything revealed about what'd happened to him on the side of the road. It couldn't be easy for him to know I knew about it, even.

Deanna's eyes were bouncing between us.

"Where are the boys?" I asked her.

"Oh, I got them into daycare. First day. I have a meeting at the cab office with Ella's dad, Rob. He wants to talk about some stuff. Hours. Responsibilities. I thought I'd pop by and ask if I can borrow a flat iron for like, ten minutes, so I can look my best. Mine bit the biscuit."

"Of course," I gestured toward a salon chair and she rushed over and turned a hair iron on. "But don't worry about Rob. You could show up in a burlap sack with your hair a tangled mess and he'd take one look at you and know you're good people."

She smiled at me.

"I can sell you a new Chi at cost," I added.

"Maybe," she smiled, but it didn't reach her eyes. She was always tight for money.

"Isn't your birthday coming up?" I asked.

She shook her head. "Stop it."

She totally knew I'd be giving her a new flat iron for her birthday.

"Stop what? Never mind my question." I winked and turned back to Scooter.

Scooter was looking at her smiling like she was a movie star and he was star struck.

I was excited for Deanna to get more opportunities at the cab company. Ella had told me that her father was taking over the taxi company, that he'd bought it with help from Deke from the previous owner. Ella was moving to work at the bike dealership with the Valentines, so she'd recommended Deanna for more hours and responsibility. It'd be a good thing for Dee, who could use the money as well as the confidence boost.

"Coffee, Dee?" I offered.

"Yes, please! My hero!" She clapped her hands.

The bells jingled, and it was the mailman, who needed me to sign for something. Probably the new cosmetics line I'd be selling.

"I'll get her coffee," Scooter offered.

I gave him a warning look.

He'd better be careful with her.

He looked me right in the eye, meaningfully and my warning melted away.

What I saw there in his eyes? I suddenly had no qualms at all about him pursuing Deanna. But as soon as she left, he was going to get a talking-to anyway.

Behind the mailman was an early customer, and then Ella with Bronto were also coming in. Ella had said she was stopping in for her own flat iron today. I also had a wad of cash for her from the wedding we'd done on the weekend.

Lulu had come in and covered a couple appointments on the Saturday while we did the wedding and in the few minutes we chatted, I knew she'd fit in here very well. If I hadn't been sinking into the depths of depression, I would've thought of all sorts of trouble to get into with her.

She was 21, barely five feet tall, liberally tattooed, had purple hair, about a half a dozen piercings between her lip, her ears, her belly, etc. And she was a wiz with hair.

I'd told her that I wanted her to come work here. She was doing a temp job for two weeks and then she was going to take over Deb's chair on the days Deb didn't work, for starters.

Speaking of Deb, I hadn't seen Deb since before the kidnapping fiasco, but had texted her to thank her for helping out so much. She'd texted to say she was looking forward to hearing about my new man. I ignored that comment and asked about her girls' getaway and she replied to say she'd enjoyed her Vegas getaway a lot but that she had a personal issue and would be taking a few extra days off.

Bronto and Ella weren't there for long and I made it a point to be extra-nice to Bronto.

"You been watching *Breaking Bad*?" he asked.

"Nope. Waiting for you," I told him.

He smiled. "I've seen the whole series twice before I started watching with you and Pippa."

"It doesn't matter. We made a deal," I said.

He smiled big at me. "I'll try and switch with Scoot for the next couple days. Let him shadow Ella."

"Sounds good," I'd said. "I'll stock up on Cheese puffs and Reese Puffs."

He smiled even bigger. "I'll bring Snickerdoodles."

"Perfect."

"How's everything?" Ella asked me when Bronto wandered outside, saying he was heading to the bakery next door for a snack.

I gave her a shrug.

She pulled me into a hug. I hugged her back, feeling so down in the dumps I wanted to just slink into a dark room and stay there forever.

"Hang in there," she told me, and I'd nodded. Deanna slid up close to us and whispered, "Soooo...what's Scott's story?"

Ho boy.

She and Bronto left.

Thirty minutes later, Deanna had already gone, after I'd told her we didn't know if he had a girlfriend or not and that he seemed like a good guy. She wanted to know why he was my bodyguard and why he had one hand ready to grab his gun at all times and I told her it was complicated. She told us she wanted in on our next girls' night out, so she could get the 'scoop'. And the glint in her eyes told me that Deanna definitely had a thing for bad boys with guns.

Yikes.

I had a lull between appointments, so I was sitting at my reception desk, playing on my phone, my mood in the dumps, and then my heart sank even deeper when Scooter jumped up out of his seat in the waiting area and looked at me with wide-eyes.

He started hitting buttons on his phone.

"I just got a text. Bronto got shot. Two bullets. And Ella got taken by Jackals."

My phone fell out of my hands and crashed to the floor as my hands came up to my mouth.

Half an hour later, during which time Scooter was on the phone a lot and I closed my salon and cancelled the appointments for the rest of the day and shut the blinds and set the alarm, at Scooter's demand, my phone rang. It was my mother. I rejected the call.

A text came through from her.

"Why is the salon closed in the middle of the afternoon?"

Oh Fuck off, Mom, I said aloud to my screen, not to Mom (unfortunately) and put my phone down. Her spy had to be close for her to get word *that* fast.

My phone started to ring again, and I'd wished it'd smashed to bits when I dropped it, but the screen read "Rider" instead.

I answered it.

"Hello?"

"We know where she's at. We're gonna get her back and her cousin's involved. Fork's with her now and he's gonna make sure nothin' happens. She's gonna be okay. But, you stay there. Let no one in, and keep the blinds closed. Alarm on."

I made a sobbing sound.

"Okay?" he asked.

"Okay," I whispered.

He hung up.

I paced some more.

Scooter got word that Bronto was in the hospital, the gunshot wounds not lethal. One was in his arm and the other in his butt.

He was going to be okay.

AN HOUR OR TWO LATER, I had a text from Rider.

"We got her. She's in Deacon's arms. And she is 100% fine."

Thank God. I burst out crying.

"Ok. Thank God."

Scooter's phone made a text sound and he let out a breath of relief, too.

"Let's go up to my place." I reached for my purse and my keys. "I need a drink. Let's hit the store for some booze first," I said.

"Lemme get the okay first," he said and dialed on his phone.

He got the okay and we headed out.

At the store, I filled my cart with booze, including what I'd seen Rider drink the last few times he'd had a beer in his hand. Plus three bottles of assorted booze, two bottles of wine, and I told Scooter to toss a dozen of his favorite in the cart.

We got up to my place and I ordered pizza.

I called Pippa. She sounded funny and she tried to blow me off.

"Wait. I'm calling to tell you Ella got kidnapped."

"What?" she yelled.

"She's okay now. It was over within a few hours. I don't know the whole story, but Bronto got shot twice. He's gonna be okay. I don't know if all this crap is over, but...yeah. That's the day we had. What's up with you?"

"Uh... just dealing with some stuff."

"Some...stuff?" I inquired.

She didn't answer me.

"Philippa Christine Griffin!"

"Ouch," she replied. "Don't you whole name me, Jennifer Whatever Murdoch."

She didn't know my whole name. Two people did. Besides the people that gave me that name. Ella and Rider.

"It's Genevieve."

She held the phone.

"Genevieve Maybelle Murdoch." I said, with disdain.

She still held the phone.

"That's how much I love you. Other than the people that named me that, there are only two other people who know that. Unless you count doctor's offices and schools, as well as my bank."

"Shit," she muttered.

"And the government..." I added.

"I get it," she whispered.

"And now probably Scooter," I muttered, knowing he was in the next room.

"That's how much I love you," I repeated.

She sniffled.

"What's going on with you, Pippa?"

"Joe," she whispered.

I waited.

"He's been drinking."

"No." I closed my eyes.

"And doing heavy drugs."

"Fuck. Where are you?"

"His place. I'm trying to help him detox right now. I think he's on the other side of it. We'll... we'll see."

"What can I do?" I asked.

"Nothing. Just stay safe until all this biker drama is over and then girls' night. You, me, Ella, Andie. Dee. Lulu maybe."

"Okay," I whispered. "If he keeps drinking, you have to pick you, Pip. It could get worse, like it did before. You pick you, okay?"

"I know," she whispered.

"Girls night. I'll make it happen."

"Good. Love you, too." She said and then she added, "Gotta go. Bye."

"Bye."

"You're a good friend," Scooter said.

I looked over my shoulder. I was in my kitchen. I thought he'd been in the living room.

"Don't know what all that was about but just thought it was worth sayin'. It's been noticed."

I smiled. "I'm a good friend to Deanna, too."

His eyebrows quirked up.

"And she doesn't just have big boobs, Scott. She's got a big heart in there, too. She's been fucked over bad by guys. Real bad. Cheated on. Abandoned when she was giving birth. Fucked over. More than once."

His face went to stone. He knew where I was going with this.

"Her two sons have been fucked over by the guys who've exploited Dee Dee's big heart, too. So, just sayin'... don't go there unless you're not going to be screwing any of the three of them over."

He sucked on his teeth behind his lips and looked pissy.

"But, just sayin..." I added, "If you *do* go there and it does work out, she'll be a lucky girl. So, you've been warned, but... she asked what your story was. Wanted to know if you had a girlfriend. Want me to text you her number? I'll even babysit for the first and second dates. But no overnights until the fifth date. I'll babysit then, too."

His eyebrows shot back up.

On that parting shot, I retreated to my bedroom to get into some comfy clothes. I texted Ella.

"They say you're okay. You really okay?"

She replied not long later.

> **"I really am. It was really icky, but nothing happened. I just need to bleach my memory. Come over tomorrow night. My parents are having a party. With BBQ. And Rummoli. It's a 'yay! Elizabelle didn't get raped by her uncle and his cohorts' party. You simply MUST come. Cue dueling banjo song from Deliverance."**

Um...yikes.

She'd inserted a bunch of emojis of boingy eyes and green puke-faces after her words.

"I'm there. I'll bring some hooch."

"XO"

"XO"

Rider showed up about ten minutes into us eating pizza.

Scooter and I were both on the couch, watching old episodes of South Park. I hated this show, but he'd put it on while I was in the other room and I didn't want to be a kill joy, feeling blessed about Ella and all, so I sucked it up.

Rider walked in, waved at us without looking at us, nabbed a pizza slice from the coffee table, and went toward my bedroom, pulling his shirt over his head, then taking a bite on his way there.

I sat there, slumped. He didn't even look at me.

Five minutes later, I went into my bedroom and heard the shower running. The bedroom floor was littered with his clothing and the past few days I hadn't cared enough to complain about it.

I glared at my rug angrily and then scooped up all of his clothes off the floor and tossed them into my half-full basket. I wandered to the kitchen with that basket and turned on a load of laundry (I had a stackable set the same as what was in my salon behind bifold doors in the kitchen).

I turned around and there he was, getting a beer out of the fridge. He went back into the living room.

Scooter was in the kitchen with me, his car keys in his hand. "You wanna go see Ella? I can take you."

I nodded profusely and grabbed my purse and slipped on a pair of shoes and just before heading out the kitchen door, I stopped.

"Does Rider know we're going?" I asked.

"His idea," Scooter replied and headed for the door.

My heart was in my throat. Okay, how to decode this?

Was he being sweet by letting me go see Ella after what she'd been through, or was he getting rid of me because he was back now and didn't want to be in my presence?

If he didn't want to be in my presence, he didn't have to be. He could leave me under the care of his prospects. He wasn't taking me to see Ella, so clearly, he didn't want to go there with me.

But, he was using my place as a crash pad so maybe he didn't want to be around me and was planning to go to sleep before I came back so he wouldn't have to deal with me.

My heart hurt. My brain hurt. I was being *so* stupid.

WE GOT TO ELLA'S AND the whole family was in the kitchen, Ella's family and all of Rider's, (except Rider and Jojo. And his mother, of course)

finishing up dinner. Jojo had been in to the salon a few days before to get a trim, her very first Brazilian (which was a laugh. Pippa takes great joy in the pain of a girl's first Brazilian. I was there holding Jojo's hand) and an eyebrow wax and she'd already headed to her friend's place in New York. When we walked in, I caught sight of Deacon holding Ella in his arms, her head back and her eyes aimed up at her tall beautiful biker man. Stars in her eyes. Love in his eyes. I felt a stab of jealousy.

I wedged myself into their clinch.

"Cutting in!" I announced.

Deacon backed off with a smile and I wrapped my arms around her.

"Thank God you're okay!"

We hugged and rocked back and forth for a good few minutes. Beau ran over and got in between us and we hugged him, too.

Ella's Mom put on a pot of coffee. Me and Scooter sat down.

Spencer was eyeing me. "Where's Ride?"

I shrugged.

He clenched his teeth and looked at Scooter and they must've done some sort of badass biker non-verbal communicating thing, because Spencer gave him a nod and then got up from the table and went outside. Scooter followed, telling me he'd be out there and reminding me not to leave the house. I answered him by rolling my eyes and saying, "Duh."

He flexed his jaw at me and then went out to the garage.

"How are ya, Jenna?" Deke sat down in Spencer's empty chair (after flipping it around backwards).

"I'm....okay." I said. "Super relieved you guys got Ella back fast."

He nodded. "Things're good then?" He asked.

"Uh huh," I muttered.

"With everything?"

"What are you asking me, Deke?"

"You and my son? Things good there?"

I gulped.

He smiled. Big. Wow. That was forward of him. Rider's dad was a looker. He was around fifty, maybe, and he had a deep Trace Adkins voice. Deacon looked a lot like him, but Rider definitely had his smile.

I pulled my lips in and felt my shoulders rise as I sort of tried to shrink within myself.

"Just between you and I, he's not a pro at this relationship stuff, so cut him a bit of slack, okay? For the record, I think he wants to be."

I guess word had traveled that things weren't going so well with me and Rider.

"It's not him," I whispered. "It's me. I think he's way better at it than I am. And I have no excuse as I've been in relationships before."

Where was my filter? *I* broke up with Rider, Rider was ignoring my breaking up with him, and here I was, acting sorry for my fighting to stay broken up.

Deke looked as surprised as I was.

"Then why are you here, not with him wherever he 's at, makin' it up to him?"

I blinked a couple times.

He gave me a warm smile and then booped my nose and walked out toward the garage calling out, "Wanna go for a smoke, Deke? Why, don't mind if I do."

"Rob'll join ya," Ella's dad Rob comically chimed in and followed Deke out.

Ella and Deacon were all cozy and googly-eyed by the kitchen counter, so I looked to Scott, who was coming back and eyeing the cheesecake on the table.

"Can we go?" I asked quietly.

"I'll get you a slice to go, Scoot," Ella said.

I got up and headed for the door. "I'm so glad you're safe."

"Thanks for comin' over. See you tomorrow night for barbeque and Rummoli. Right?"

"Right. I wouldn't miss your 'Not raped by your uncle' celebration."

Deacon's back went straight, and he did a double-take.

"Ella named it, big guy, not me." I waved my hands defensively.

He looked down at her. "Not fuckin' funny, Kitten."

Ella blushed but rolled her eyes.

I hugged her. Deacon hugged me, and I waved at the garage as we stepped out into the driveway. Rob, Bertie, Deke, Spence, and Spence's dog were out there. I got waves and a wagging tail.

Scooter got into his car, I got into the passenger side, and we pulled out, just as my mother was pulling in.

Eeks.

I hoped she didn't see me. It was dark, and I wasn't in my car, it was Scooter's Hyundai Accent.

He drove us back to my place. In silence, because my mind was on my troubles, which were not few. Beyond all the Rider stuff, I'd eventually have to face Karen Murdoch. Ugh.

WHEN I GOT HOME, THERE was no sign of Rider's motorcycle or his car. It had been his Harley here when we'd left. I into the apartment, all the lights were out. No note. Nothing.

I flipped the laundry over from the washer to the dryer, put on another load, then put the pizza away. I said goodnight to Scooter, who was lounging, eating cheesecake. I went to bed, thinking about getting myself my planned two cats. Someone to love and cuddle with.

I closed my eyes and it took ages for sleep to find me.

Rider didn't come back that night. At all.

21

O*kay, so where should I put his clean laundry?*

After way too long debating it, I settled for a neat pile on top of my dresser.

It was time to head out to the Forker family game night slash '*thank goodness Ella was not-raped-by-her-uncle*' celebration.

I'd already closed the salon and was with Pudge, the tall ginger biker with the long beard that was standing sentry after the Paige scene.

Pudge wasn't pudgy. He was super slim, so I guessed the nickname was sarcasm. Pudge was also a definite felon who had no qualms about using a gun. When we got into the apartment after he walked me up from the salon, he'd put a big-ass knife and two guns on my coffee table before putting his boots on the table and sitting back with my remote.

I didn't bother telling him to get his boots off my table, like I'd have told Scooter, Bronto, or even Bad Ass Jesse. Pudge could keep his boots on my table if he wanted to.

He was a man of few words, but he'd told me he'd moved here from Bismarck a week and a half before to help take down those "Lowlife ass wipe jack wagons".

He said he'd been in the Doms for eight years, since he got out of 'state' and I knew 'state' didn't refer to state college; it referred to the state prison. He was a definite badass, had all sorts of mean tattoos, but he was good protector material. I felt safe. I wished he'd been there when Bronto got shot in the ass. I doubted Ella would've gotten taken from Pudge.

Then again, maybe they would've shot to kill instead of to maim if it hadn't been a prospect there that day.

He'd only brought his motorcycle, though, and I was apparently not allowed to ride on the back of a bike that wasn't my 'old man's', so he drove my car and we went to Ella's.

I didn't want to take my car. I didn't want my mother to see it parked at Ella's. And I couldn't talk Pudge into parking down the street, so she wouldn't see it. I tried to explain that I was hiding from my mother and he looked at me like I was loony tunes.

I gave up the argument and went inside, seeing a houseful in the Forker kitchen. All the extension leaves were in the table, taking it from being big enough to seat a dozen to making room for another half a dozen. There were at least fifteen chairs around it. Several were lawn chairs brought in from the garage. The Rummoli board was in the middle.

I had a tote bag with my Rummoli jar of pennies, nickels, dimes, and quarters, and saw three other jars on the table. The kitchen counter was set up with a cheese and cracker tray, a bowl of chips, Ella's nacho dip, Rob's crab dip, a big crock pot that looked to be filled with pulled pork, two big bags of buns, and two foil-covered cookie sheets lined up with toasted submarine sandwiches cut into thirds, that looked and smelled like Ella's meatball subs (which rocked).

Pudge immediately went to the food. I sat down between Ella's Dad's friend Jase and Spencer. People wandered in from the garage and elsewhere in the house and Ella came over and hugged me and then sat on the other side of Spencer, her big jar of change in front of her. And then the rest of the group filed in from the garage, last of which was Rider. He sat across the table from me and his eyes landed on me.

My heart hurt at the stone-cold look on his face. I wanted to flee.

But, I couldn't. People bought change from my jar to gamble with, including Rider, as Ella's and her mom's jars were much lighter than usual, and then Ella explained the rules of the game to the Valentines and ended with,

"Let the betting begin!"

The mood was jovial, other than Rider and me. Most of us played, but Rob's friends watched, coming in and out of the garage, bouncing between watching us, and congregating around the food-filled counter. We played a few hands, and then I won a big hand and my mood shifted and I did a little happy chair-dance over my healthy-looking pile of pennies and nickels, which was probably less than $2, but it was the win itself, not the size of the win. I'd been playing this game almost monthly since I was a kid, so I took Rummoli seriously.

The next hand, after my $2ish win, I had a full house: two fives and three threes, so I started betting.

Everyone playing (there were eight of us) passed, except for Deke, who raised me. Rider raised him. I raised it. Deke opted out. Rider raised it again. I raised it again, with a death-challenge in my eyes.

Finally, he threw a set of keys on the center of the board.

I stared at them, confused.

"My Harley."

"Your Harley? Over a card game?" I was astounded.

This wasn't about the card game. But it was a stupid bet. And the room knew. They were all watching The Jenna and Rider Show with avid fascination.

"Yeah," he bit off.

"I don't have a Harley to bet with," I snapped, my voice filled with venom.

Why was he being so ridiculous?

"I got an idea." He pulled his phone out of his jeans pocked and typed something. My ass binged. I reached for my phone and pulled it out.

> **"You win, you get my Harley. I win, you give me control tonight. One night. My rules."**

I put my phone face down on the table and glared at him.

He was waiting. His eyes were ablaze with anger. The room was waiting.

"No fair," Ella pouted. "Secret bets are not fair."

"I can imagine what it says," Spencer shrugged.

"Jenna will tell me later." Ella said, resigned.

I shook my head. "Fold." My shoulders slumped.

"Chicken shit," Rider said, his eyes still angry.

My anger returned, and I glared.

"There she goes again, writing checks she has no intention of cashin'..." Rider mused, being an absolute prick about it.

"No. Cancel my fold. Call," I said, angrily and dropped my cards on the table, face up.

He gave me an evil smile and then dropped his cards.

Shit. Shit. Damn. Straight flush.

Damn. No.

Spencer hissed. "Ooooh. What'd he win?"

Spencer tried to grab my phone. I grabbed it first, and shoved it in my pocket, my face going red.

"Let's break for food," Deacon suggested. "One of those meatball sandwiches is callin' my name." He moved to the counter.

Rider scooped up his big pile of winnings and kept it in front of him and gave me a look of promise.

"Need a drink, Rider?" Ella asked.

"I'll get one, thanks, Ella," he said to her, but his eyes were still on me and flirty and ... holy shit, I had to cross my legs. My body reacted in a way that... I was tempted to drag him out of here.

But, then his expression changed, and it was cold and angry, and a bucket of ice water was thrown on my libido.

Was I going to be treated to an actual hate fuck?

A real one? How bad would it be?

I felt sick.

"Gettin' some food, Jennabean?" Rob asked.

"Yeah, of course."

"Made my famous chili and my pulled pork." He gestured toward the kitchen counter and I noticed Pudge ladling out a big bowl of chili from another crockpot I hadn't clocked yet.

Pudge hadn't been playing cards. He hadn't even gone out to the smoking area with the others when they'd gone. He'd been grazing at the counter the whole time. I was getting a good idea of why he was nicknamed Pudge. Maybe he should've been nicknamed Tapeworm. I didn't verbalize that thought. I moved to the food and made up a plate with a tiny bit of everything so that no feelings would be hurt.

Rider was beside me.

"Got you a drink. Come sit," Ella said to me, walking by with two cans of Pepsi and one can of Coke in her arms.

"Fuel up, Starlet," he whispered in my ear, leaning over me to grab a napkin. "You're gonna be burnin' a lotta calories tonight."

My blood went hot. My face went red.

I moved away from him and went to the living room and sat on the couch beside Ella, who had Deacon on the other side.

Ella gave me a big-eyed look. "I think you're in trouble, sister..."

I gave her big eyes back and then rolled my eyes as if it was no biggie.

But, shit. I had no appetite. None.

AFTER THE GAME FINALLY ended, Ella's mom Bertie the winner, I couldn't find Pudge. I was in the garage, peering at the driveway. My car was gone.

I felt a bit panicky.

"Let's go," Rider said to me under his breath, on his way past me as he headed outside.

My panic levels escalated. I stood there, feeling like I was under a cloud of impending doom.

"G'night Pinkie," Deke gave me a quick hug.

I must've had horror all over my face.

Spencer was in my space, giving me a hug and whispering, "Have a good night, payin' your debts."

I laughed nervously and tried to play it off like it was no big deal, but I felt like my knees were knocking together when I headed down the driveway after saying *bye* to everyone.

He was sitting on his motorcycle, waiting for me, a helmet in his hand. An unreadable expression on his face.

Shit. I was afraid of this.

His motorcycle. My chariot. My chariot awaited me, to take me to... where? The pits of Hell?

He got off the bike and put my helmet on me, buckling it up, looking into my eyes with a smug smirk that was evident even though it was dark out.

Rob, Uncle Lou, and Jase stumbled off into the night, saying their goodnights as they headed somewhere on foot. Rob's buds both lived in the neighborhood, so I guessed they were going to one of their houses.

I glanced at my parents' house and all the lights were off, only Mom's car in the driveway. It was after midnight. Had Dad already moved out? Wait. Was he giving up the house? This was his childhood home. He couldn't move out! I felt even more panicked. She'd sell it in a heartbeat. I had visions of catching my kids at the bottom of that big wide polished painted white wood banister, letting them slide down it as much as they wanted. Once they were old enough to do it safely, of course.

"Get on," Rider said, no growled.

I hadn't told him about my folks, so maybe he thought my increased registering horror was only about him.

I climbed on and he started up the bike and then he rocketed away, making me grab him and hold on for dear life.

He drove back to my place too dangerously for my tastes, and I didn't enjoy that ride. At all. In fact, it was scary!

When he parked, and I got off, I started shouting.

"You trying to get us killed?"

He had a scowl on his face as he got off the bike.

"You're an asshole, Rider Valentine!" I stormed up the stairs to my apartment.

"Yeah, well, you're bein' a bitch, Genevieve Maybelle Murdoch."

"God, you're such a jerk," I hissed and slammed my bedroom door in his face.

He opened it and was in there with me. "Don't forget, Genevieve, you have a debt to pay. Get undressed."

I stopped in my tracks. "You're gonna make me do this?"

"A bet's a bet."

I glared at him. "You can't be serious. Making a girl who can barely stand you, fuck you?"

"A bet's a bet. My rules. And serious as a heart attack." He undid his pants and pulled his belt out of the loops. He held the halved belt in his hand. I stared at it in horror.

"Get undressed."

Oh my God. What was he gonna do with that belt?

This was *it*. I'd pay my debt tonight. Fine. All right then.

And, that would work Rider Valentine straight out of my system. Like the flush of a toilet. Whoosh. Gone.

Asshole!

I was wearing a cute cornflower blue babydoll tee, faded boyfriend jeans, and my baby blue Converse slip-ons, no socks. I kicked my shoes off and then undid and dropped my jeans. I threw my shirt off angrily, momentarily getting stuck in it. I was wearing a baby blue thong and a white lacy bra. I stared at him and blew my hair out of my eyes.

He took in my body hungrily with his gaze and then he threw his brown Henley over his head and dropped it, then dropped his dark blue button fly jeans. I noticed that the pile of clean clothes on my dresser had shrunk and realized the brown Henley was one I'd folded after laundering it the day before.

He took a step toward me and grabbed for my ass cheeks, pulling me to him.

I looked up at him, holding my elbows with opposite hands, not looking down at his nakedness.

"You wanna go do anything to get ready for bed, do it now." His voice was husky. He gave my ass a squeeze and let go.

I backed away from him and went into my bathroom and shakily washed my makeup off and brushed my teeth.

I was so shaky. What was I in for tonight? What would I endure before flushing the rest of him out of my mind forever? I heard Luke "Lick" Hanson's voice in my head.

> *"Yeah, you fuckin' whore, we're gonna fuck all your holes until they bleed."*

I finally went back into my room, not able to procrastinate further. The lights were out, and he was in my bed. I left the bathroom light on and closed the door half way. It was probably too bright, but I needed to see. I needed to make sure that I got the full affect of his anger so that I would be able to flush these feelings away.

He threw the blanket over and patted my side.

I climbed in, still in my bra and panties, not knowing for how long.

He tossed the corner so that the blanket floated down on top of me, then he pulled me to him and kissed me. I braced, but it was slow, sweet, gentle. I was stiff at first, but eventually melted into it.

And then I pulled back to catch my breath.

"First rule," he whispered, "No pulling back."

"What other rules do I have?" I asked, haughtily.

"No other rules," he whispered, and his mouth was on mine again.

He kissed me briefly this time and then pulled me close. My head was on his shoulder, his arm wrapped around my waist.

And... nothing.

He was just lying there.

My eyebrows furrowed in confusion. I stayed put. He pulled me closer. Okay, I was braced for whatever was about to happen.

He sifted his hand through my hair and kissed the top of my head and pulled me over more so that my head was on his heart.

And there was that sound again. The sound of his heart beating.

A minute went by.

Two.

Three.

"Rider?" I asked.

"Hm?"

"What... what is this?"

"Go to sleep, gorgeous."

I blinked.

"What kind of game is this?" My voice was barely a croak.

"No game," he said.

"Bullshit," I snapped.

"No bullshit, Jenna."

My chest was burning. There was this searing pain in my shoulders, this... aching. It ached so much.

Don't cry, Jenna. No tears!

His hand sifted sweetly through my hair again.

I lifted up on an elbow and looked down at his face, which I could see well due to that bathroom light.

"Are you serious?"

"A hundred per cent."

I blinked.

But...

How could I get him out of my head if he wasn't going to *hate fuck* these feelings right away... if he wasn't going to make me actually hate him?

"You won the bet," I whispered.

"Yeah," he agreed.

"And you're not gonna make me actually..." I let that hang.

"I get what I want tonight from you. This is what I want."

I didn't know how to decode this.

What the fudge was he playing at?

I scratched my head and gave my head a shake.

"You wouldn't have really taken my Harley if you'd won, would ya?"

"Fuck yeah!" I said without hesitation.

Laughter burst out of him. Hard, unabashed, and fucking beautiful. He rolled me and pinned me. He was he was kissing me breathless.

I started kissing him back. And then I couldn't take it anymore. I rolled him and climbed onto him and thrust my hands into his hair.

"We don't have to do this tonight," he said.

"I want to," I said and undid the clasp at the front of my bra and threw it off. His eyes went right to my boobs.

I climbed off, peeled my panties off, and then climbed back on, lined him up and slowly lowered myself until he was all the way inside.

He threw his hands over his head and watched, eyes heated.

I ran my hands up and down his chest, played with his nipple piercing, and then I started to pick up the pace. And then I slowed, going slow, deep, circling.

"You gonna take yourself there?" he asked, his voice almost guttural.

I nodded enthusiastically and put my hand at our connection and began to rub both of us. My other hand went to his nipple and toyed with it. I started going faster, circling with my hips, throwing my head back as I absorbed the sensations, how good he felt. I took myself, with my fingers, to the edge. I looked down at him and he was watching, looking possessed with lust, his knuckles braced against my mauve headboard, his biceps straining, like he was fighting against taking over, the way he wanted to do.

I grabbed his hands and weaved his fingers with mine, and started rocking harder, faster, bigger circles, tightening my inner walls, and he let out an almost roar as we rocked so hard my headboard started thudding against the wall.

We came together.

I finished with my face buried in his throat.

My eyes were shut tight, my heart hammering with a threat to fly right out of my chest, and his hands sweetly ran up and down my back.

He kissed my throat and gently moved my hair, which was all over his face, out of the way, getting it into a ponytail in his fist and tugging so that I had to look at his face.

Rider likes it rough. But, he can also be incredibly sweet. You could say that he pulls my hair. And my heart strings, too.

I was smiling, I think. Blissed out.

"Had a feeling this was how it'd go down."

"Hm?" I asked, still recovering from a definite top 3 orgasm *ever*.

"You. This. You wanted it. You played your little game pretending you didn't. But you wanted me. As soon as I backed off, I knew this'd happen."

My heart dropped.

Another game.

My expression must've dropped, too.

"It's okay, however we got here, gorgeous. It's all okay by me."

Well, it wasn't okay by me.

"Everything is a game to you," I choked out.

He shook his head. "No." He let go of my hair.

"It is. It's all a fucking joke." I started to pull away.

"Get back here..." he sounded angry.

"Fuck you."

"Listen to me..."

"No. Screw off."

"Jenna! Fuckin' listen to me!"

I stopped and waited to see what he was going to say.

This game we were playing? I didn't know how would end. He was systematically breaking down my walls. On one hand I wanted him to stop. Go away. Dirty rotten scoundrel. On the other, everyone gives up on me, eventually, and part of me doesn't want him to give up on me, ever. His 'no matter how hard you fight, I don't give up until you submit" was kind of endearing.

But this? Did this guy take anything seriously? Jojo said he used humor to deflect. But, come on. This was ridiculous.

He was just staring. Smiling.

I shook my head in disgust.

"Go find your next conquest. I'm not playing games anymore, Rider."

"Me neither, Jenna. Stopped bein' fun. No more games that aren't fun. Let's shake on that."

"What?"

"You've been playing your games, too. Pushing me away, I let you think it's workin' and then you panic and try to reel me in again. Keep me hooked, right?"

"I'm not playing games."

"Maybe you don't think you are, baby, but you are. And you're getting really predictable."

"Monogamy, monotony?" I challenged, pulling the blanket up to cover my nakedness.

"Nothing even remotely monotonous about you, beautiful. Even when I can predict your next move."

I sighed.

"No more games. How 'bout we both agree to that. You give this an actual honest chance."

"I gave it a chance, but..."

"You gave up at the first sign of trouble, babe. You were lookin' for a reason to give up from the start and I wasn't even close to lookin' for an out. Not once. I was getting deeper by the minute. Any idea how much that hurt?"

I blinked. I was hurting him? No. I was protecting myself, so he wouldn't hurt *me.* There was a lump in my throat. God, I didn't want to hurt him.

I shook my head, dumbfounded. "So, okay, how does this go, then? I stop letting you chase me, I let you catch me, and then you get bored?"

He froze.

"This still a game to you?" he clipped. "Even right now?"

"Seems like you want games, Rider Valentine. If I wanna keep you, I have to play, keep things interesting, right?"

He growled in my face, "This isn't a fucking game. Not anymore. Fight, don't fight. Either way, I'm not letting up on you, I'm not letting you slip through my fingers. Ever."

"Stalker," I scoffed and jumped out of bed and headed toward the door, figuring I could grab my robe from the hook on the back of it. Go sleep on the couch or in Pippa's bed if she wasn't home again.

"Not joking, Jenna." He caught my arm and wouldn't let me pull away.

"Why are you doing this?"

"You know why."

"I do?" I looked at him bewildered.

"You know you do."

"I don't, Rider. I really, *really* fucking don't."

He moved into my space, pinning me with his body against the door and he went from looking on the verge of rage to sweet.

"Because I love you, gorgeous. The wild parts, the sweet parts. The bitchy parts. All your parts." He grabbed my ass into both hands.

He loves me? *Loves* me?

I couldn't even blink for the longest time. Until I finally did. And that was the third time that I, Genevieve "Jenna" Maybelle Murdoch, cried in front of a boy.

"Why would you love me? I'm a materialistic biker-bigot dead lay." Tears streamed down my cheeks.

"No." He shook his head and put his thumbs to my cheeks to catch the tears. "You're high maintenance, but I've decided that it's worth it. You're generous. You give so much. And you're getting better in bed every time I fuck you. I'm clearly an excellent fuckin' teacher, because you're getting seriously good at it. Though, you're not through training yet. Got at least 1000 more lessons for ya. Then we'll see where you're at."

I closed my eyes tight and planted my face in his chest. He walked me back to the bed and we tumbled down onto it and he wrapped me up in the blanket and kept his arms around me.

"You don't love me," I whispered.

"I just said I did."

I shook my head. "You're so m-mean."

"Mean?" He sounded amused as I was crying into his chest.

"How am I mean?"

"You do all these things, all these crazy sweet things after breaking my heart telling me I sucked in bed."

"But, you did, babe."

I laughed. And he laughed too, and wiped my tears.

"But you don't suck now, Jenna." He kissed my mouth. "If I didn't say anything you'd just keep taking what I give you and just fuckin' lie there. At least when you were fighting me off, you were doing something. And you're really fuckin' good at it when you hate fuck me."

"You hate fucked me first and that wasn't nice, either."

"That wasn't even a hate fuck. I made a joke. One of these days, you're probably gonna piss me off enough for us to have some serious angry sex, but what I'm startin' to see from you, I could see you intentionally pissin' me off just to get that. You'll get off on it that much."

I gave him a twisted-up expression. "Uh. I doubt it."

"We'll see."

"Maybe I should make *you edge and* beg for it."

"Maybe you should." He squeezed me tighter. "Maybe you should think up all sorts of fun sex games for us. I'm already making my list."

I started to laugh.

What a crazy night. Crazy few days. No weeks.

My laugh melted away and I was feeling all sorts of feels all through me.

He loves me?

He'd never been in a serious relationship before and a few weeks into this, he decides he loves me?

Could I trust this?

"Jenna," he said, sounding serious.

I looked up at his face and then wiped the tears, which were blurring my vision, away.

"I'm not joking. Every day I see something I seriously fuckin' dig with you. Something new every day. Scoot's been giving me reports, you know. All the guys. They've all got good things to say."

"Except Jesse," I said.

"Even Jesse. You're a good person. A great fuckin' person. Stuff you do for your friends. Your customers. Me."

"I've been a pain in your ass," I muttered.

"Yeah. But watching you push me away was entertaining. You make me laugh. You keep me warm at night. So fuckin' sweet the way you snuggle up to me. You did my laundry even when you were pissed. I seriously dig your towels and your sheets. You clean up my messes. You defended me to your Ma, even when you were furious with me. Looked like you wanted to take my own mother on a few times to defend me. You took my sister under your wing like she was as close to you as Ella and you'd just met her. You even defended Gia just because Joelle said she was good people. The way you were there for me during the funeral? Shit. Yeah, and you're very, *very* easy on the eyes."

I rolled my eyes, but I had a smile on my face.

"I love you, Genevieve Maybelle Murdoch."

I choked on a sob.

He smiled at me.

"Please don't break my heart."

His smile slipped.

"Please don't." I was sobbing, then began rambling auctioneer-fast again. "I don't even cry in front of guys, because I got hurt when I was seventeen and I gave him my V-card and he was screwing a bunch of other girls when we were supposed to go off together in his VW bus after high school and he made fun of my crying in front of the whole school, so I've been so careful since then. Every guy I date gives up because I'm high maintenance. And because I keep them at arms' length and I try to be the good time girl. The fun girl. But, inside I'm just... my mother doesn't love me. She's always been disappointed in me and hated my grandmother Genevieve, and when she calls me that name it's just to remind me she finds me such a disappointment, so please don't call me that. And my father doesn't love her. He told me the other day they're separating and I'm afraid she's gonna go postal and eviscerate him and me. And I just—-I love you, too. Like I've never loved anyone."

He looked surprised.

I ran my thumb across that pillowy lower lip of his. "You take care of me. And no one ever has. And you're sweet and charismatic and make me laugh, and you are so fucking handsome you take my breath away. I love that you're tall and your eyes just do me in. The best sex I've ever had, Rider, even if some of it is way freaky-deaky."

He chuckled.

I kept talking. "You make me let go in a way that no one ever has before. I want that rainbow, that joyride with you... *so* much. I try to be a good time girl but inside I'm such a fuck-up because of how my house was growing up. And I want lots of kids and a big family and to spoil them all with love, not stuff. And I want them to ride the banisters and laugh as loud as they want, and do backwards somersaults if they want to."

"Then that's exactly what you're gonna have," he vowed. "Gymnastics classes for all of them."

Wow, that was a whole lot of verbal diarrhea.

"I can't believe I just said all that," I announced with a wince.

He shook his head. "Don't you ever be afraid to say anything to me."

I gulped.

"Why didn't you tell me your parents were splitting? Has that been fuckin' with you on top of everything else?"

I nodded.

"I'm also worried about Pip. Joe's off the wagon and she's not in a good place. She's trying to help him detox. And last year, he beat her up when he was drunk. She forgave him after six months clean and gave him another shot. But, I don't know if it's good that she's still with him. If he did that last time?"

Rider went stiff.

I sighed. I was suddenly exhausted. And yet exhilarated. I felt like I'd been through a war. Had I made it to the other side?

I looked at him.

He caressed my face and then he started talking, looking impossibly deep into my eyes.

"My head's been fucked for a while. Shit was rough with my parents splitting. Joelle's paternity. My mother's cheating with the enemy and all that shit. She's a fuck up."

I was all ears. He was opening up. Jojo said he didn't open up. But he did with me after Lick's funeral, and he was doing it now, too.

"I have a lotta guilt about Lick. Had it before he died. Those years he lost when I shoulda lost the same years and didn't. Tried to make it up to him when he got out. We got in so much shit together, makin' up for that lost time. And now he's gone."

I caressed his face.

"Never knew how it'd be having someone. All I saw with my folks was him giving, her taking. Her fucking him over. Deacon got repeatedly fucked over by women, too. Spencer wanting love and getting rejected whenever he put himself out there."

I nodded.

"And then when D was ready to go all in with Ella? Seeing what they were building? I wanted something like that. Thought maybe we'd have it. Me and you. I didn't know if it was a pipe dream."

"Relationships can be hard."

He smiled. "I see that."

"Especially when you try to build one with a drama queen high maintenance pain in your ass."

He hooked a hand around my neck and brought his lips to mine and then he kissed my forehead, too.

"You're worth it. The moments we've had when things haven't been caught up in drama. Even some of those. I see what I'll have with you. If you let me."

"I want to."

I snuggled in and we were quiet a minute.

He loved me. He was opening up. I was, too. This was amazing.

"Can we go for a ride?" I asked.

He smiled. "Absolutely. This is another reason I'm in love with you."

God. He was so sweet sometimes.

We got dressed and gassed up at the local Circle J. And then he drove until dawn, me wrapped around him, him taking us down all sorts of winding roads, on the highway, through the country.

When the sun was up, we went to a nearby diner for pancakes.

Deacon and Ella were there. But, they looked like they'd rolled out of bed and come.

"You two are up and about early for a Sunday!" she exclaimed as we approached their table, holding hands. She looked at our hands and gave me a huge smile.

Sunday was typically my only sleep-in day.

"We haven't been to bed yet," I informed her and reached down and scooped a strawberry off her waffle and popped it in my mouth.

She smirked.

We sat down and ate with them, mine and Ella's very first biker double date. And then Rider and I went back home and made slow sweet kissing-one-another-everywhere love before falling asleep. And since it was Sunday and I didn't have to open the salon that day, we slept almost all day.

22

Sunday Night

We were back in bed, cuddling and talking, hours after going to the Olive Garden for dinner on his motorcycle. In fact, we were having Olive Garden post-sex leftovers when my phone rang.

I reached for it and then backed away like it was a poisonous snake. The screen read:

Mom Calling

"Should change her ring tone back to the death march," I grumbled and curled back into him.

He laughed.

"She caught me: pocket dialed me once when we were together and heard the ring tone and got really angry."

"I bet," Rider said, putting the end of a bread stick in his mouth. We got extras 'to-go' with our doggie bags.

"Answer it. Be brave," he encouraged. "I'm right here to take over if she goes cunt-a-saurus on you."

I winced and put the phone to my ear.

"Hello?"

"Hello?" she sounded surprised that I answered.

"Hi Mom."

"Jenna."

There was awkward silence.

"How are you?" I tried.

"Very funny," she replied snidely.

My stomach dropped. I hadn't been trying to be sarcastic with her. Not remotely.

"I wasn't trying to be funny," I said softly. "Sorry I missed a few calls. Things have been—-"

"Yes, I know. Anyway, dinner at the house tomorrow night. Will that fit into your schedule?"

"Dinner at the house tomorrow?" I parroted.

Rider gave a single nod of his head, as if to encourage me and show he was fine to come. And suddenly, him at my side, I sort of felt no fear about it.

"Sure. Can we bring anything?"

"Don't be ridiculous. Six thirty. Don't be late."

"We'll be there, or we'll be square," I said, feeling like *eff this*, I wasn't going to act all contrite. I hadn't done anything wrong.

"We?" she repeated.

"Mm hm," I said. "Rider and me."

I wasn't surprised she was going to try to have it be me without Rider. After all, he had tried to shield me from her more than once already. I felt a burst of affection for him. He needed a blowjob.

"I didn't invite Rider."

"Well, it's a package deal this time, Mom," I insisted.

She let out a sigh. "Fine. Just remember, you did this. Six thirty." She hung up.

I rolled my eyes at her warning and put the phone down and then I climbed onto him, straddling him.

He had his hands behind his head, fingers woven together, head resting against my mauve headboard. Chest bare. A pair of slightly baggy Adidas running pants on.

I walked my fingers up his abs and then found my hands on his shoulders.

"Good to get this done with, gorgeous."

I nodded. "It's gonna be ugly. She just kinda warned she'd make it *extra* ugly to punish me for insisting you come."

He shrugged. "What I've seen and heard every time you've talked to her, it's only her that's ugly. Just keep doin' you."

God, he was amazing. I threaded my fingers into his hair and kissed him.

"Good thing we both ate about a hundred of those garlic bread sticks. Otherwise this might be a gross kiss."

"You ate a hundred. I ate three," he informed me.

I started laughing. He was probably right.

He rolled me and snagged the side of my panties with his thumb.

"Again? Already?" I rolled my eyes. "God, you're insatiable. I put all sorts of effort in last time, so if you're prepared to do all the work."

He smirked and then he went down on me. And I did not make him do all the work.

He got to finish in my mouth.

LATER THAT NIGHT, I asked him for an update with the Wyld Jackals war.

Holding one another in bed, in the dark, he told me that Mantis, the president of the Jackals back in Sioux Falls had been shot in the leg by Christian Forker, Ella's cousin. He'd gotten away, though, and was likely in hiding. Rider said that Edge was hunting him, and Rider said it with a coldness that made my blood chill.

Yikes.

Christian Forker had gone underground for a bit, waiting for some things to "play out", whatever that meant. I guess he was a wanted man with his club, for saving Ella, for shooting a club president.

Key, the Ipswich VP had been killed. Gordino, the Ipswich President, was laying low right now. Half his guys were either dead or in jail. Ella's Uncle Willie was still in the hospital with complications due to head injuries after being thrown from a moving vehicle during Ella's drama.

Rider also said that the Jackals had lost respect of the last remaining clubs who were still willing to do business with them, so they were running out of options and a few more key moves would mean it'd be easy to patch over that club.

Chances were that Wild Will Forker, Ella's sicko uncle, would be released into police custody from the hospital due to what had happened with Ella being abducted.

Rider didn't elaborate, but said they were still talking about how to finesse things with the police. He assured me they were working *with* the police, but said a lot of things were being played fast and loose.

The cops wanted the Wyld Jackals taken down and were willing to overlook some things to get that result, but the Dominion Brotherhood still had to be careful with how they played things. Rider said there were other clubs involved, and it wouldn't be long before the Wyld Jackals were just a bad memory.

"What's happening with your mother?" I asked.

I felt his body stiffen in the dark.

"We tried to talk sense before she got beat up. Fell on deaf ears, obviously. Still don't know who beat her up. She felt cornered, but wasn't willing to be reasonable. My guess is she either got beat up for another reason and blamed it on Mantis to use it to her advantage or, more likely, she got someone to beat her up, so she could fabricate that story and buy some sympathy. Dad told her she has until the end of September to get herself a place to live. He's selling the house, won't have her there throwing parties and causing shit so that it won't sell. He's done covering all her bills. She started selling shit that wasn't even hers to sell, so she's done. With Joelle gone to New York, he wants to just shut the place down for the real estate agent. Me and the boys'll go make sure it's ready before the sign goes in the lawn."

"I can help," I told him.

He smiled and tucked my hair behind my ears. "Thanks, baby."

"Why didn't your dad ride a motorcycle at Luke's funeral?" I asked.

"He lost his license for a bit for a DUI."

I was sort of surprised.

"Mom fucked with his head. She told him Joelle wasn't his. He had to wait on a paternity test. Then he got rip-roarin' drunk and drove his car into a tree. Good thing it was a car, not his bike, or he wouldn't have survived. It was touch 'n go there for a bit."

I bit into my lip.

"He gets his license back soon. It wasn't a good thing, but it's what finally got him to wipe his hands of her for good. So, it was sort of a good thing."

"Yuck."

"Man's put up with a lot of shit from her the last twenty-eight years. We're all done, though."

"I hope you guys can somehow fix it."

"Ain't likely. Hope you and your ma can patch things up or our kids won't have a grandmother."

My heart felt like it was going to split open wide and that butterflies and flowers would burst out of my chest. He was talking about kids with me.

"Ella's mother is awesome. So's your Aunt Delia. They'll be okay in the grandma department," I said.

He pulled me closer.

Yep, just a few weeks of knowing each other and discussing our future kids? These Valentine boys didn't waste *any* time.

MONDAY MORNING

I was sweeping up hair at the salon and chit chatting with Andie, who'd come over from the bakery next door to bring us a box of biscotti and do some gossiping.

I didn't say much about my biker drama. A) I had Jesse sitting there in the waiting area. B) Andie was a friend, but I didn't want to flip her out. She'd missed most of the drama the past two weeks.

She knew I was dating a Dom member and that Ella was dating his brother. She didn't really need to know about rape, murder, videotaped gang bangs, kidnappings, and all the drama we'd endured.

Andie was our age, really pretty, but no way was she the type to date a biker. She had pretty eyes, pretty hair, was really petite height-wise, voluptuously curvy otherwise, and shy. She liked to come out dancing with us, occasionally got a little bit rowdy, but the moment a guy showed her attention, she went super-introverted.

She was currently eyeballing Jesse, though. Probably difficult *not* to. He was pretty damn hot, sitting there casually sprawled, eating a biscotti, in just a black muscle shirt and dark jeans and motorcycle boots. Tattoos and muscles on display. His Dom prospect vest laying on the chair beside him. He was scrolling something on his phone, yet he still seemed totally alert with our surroundings.

I had a customer in the chair whose color was processing, another customer under the dryer. Pippa was between appointments.

And that was when Daniel Sotheby walked in.

In a suit. Looking handsome. Looking at Jesse with concern as his eyes bounced back and forth between Jesse and me.

Biker Bigot was my first thought.

"Oh... morning..." I said and stuck the broom in the utility room and went to the reception desk. He eyed me from head to toe and back to head again, then smiled.

I was wearing a tan suede pencil skirt with a sexy front slit, a pale pink low-cut blouse, and pale pink stiletto sandals. My hair was in a sleek ponytail this morning. I had my last appointment at 5:30 today and figured I'd save time getting ready for dinner at my parents by dolling myself up a little bit this morning.

Rider hadn't seen me as he'd left for the garage while I was still in the shower, so I was looking forward to his opinion of my outfit.

Badass Jesse had even done a bit of a stumble when I'd walked into the kitchen to meet him, so we could head down the stairs. He did a slow perusal of me. He hadn't said a thing and went 100% business (in his bikerly way) with me after that, but a girl can tell.

Now, I was seeing an appreciative gaze coming from Dan.

"Hi. You look absolutely gorgeous today, Jenna." He smiled.

"Thank you," I said, but I kept myself stiff, formal, and not feeling anything at his use of the g-word, the way I felt it with Rider.

"You got time for a cup of coffee?" He jerked his thumb toward the direction of the coffee shop.

"I don't; sorry," I said.

I glanced at Jesse, whose eyes were on him and his jaw was ticking. Sheesh, that look on his face? I'd hate to see how he'd look at a guy looking at *his* girl instead of his buddy's girl.

"Oh. Shoulda called," he said.

I gave him a tight smile. "Actually, I've started dating someone, and..."

His eyes went cold. "The guy who replied to the last text I sent?"

I smiled. "Yeah. I saw that. Sorry about that."

He looked over his shoulder at Jesse, annoyed.

"That's not him, but that's his friend, and, yeah. We're early on, but, I just wanted to be straight with you."

"It's early on? Don't lose my number," he told me.

"It's early but I'm fairly certain he's *the one*."

He looked disappointed.

"I have to check on my customers. Have a good one."

His eyes did a sweep of me. "You, too, Jenna." And then he gave me a warm smile.

This guy was definitely a potential catch. But, I was taken. Happily taken.

Andie was looking at Dan with unconcealed lust as he left.

Maybe I should set them up.

Jesse was texting on his phone.

"Are you ratting me out?" I asked after Dan left.

"Absolutely," Jesse said. "But, you get good marks for how you handled it."

I snickered and went back to check on my customers.

6:15 PM

Rider texted to say he was outside the back of the salon. Jesse and I walked back together and as I approached his orange Charger, he got out and walked around to the passenger side.

He waved at Jesse who got on his bike and pulled out.

And my beautiful biker looked good. No. He looked *good*.

His hair was loose, he was clean shaven. He was wearing dark jeans and a royal blue and jade green striped button-down shirt. He had on motorcycle boots, but they looked like they'd been polished. His eyes were piercing.

I got to him and he dipped me, Hollywood style, and it took me back to the night we met.

My face split into a smile.

"Where have you been all my life?" he asked, his voice husky. He approved of my outfit.

"Waiting," I told him.

Yeah, that sounded rom-com cheesy, and it might've even been the exact line used in a 1980's John Hughes Molly Ringwald movie, but it felt absolutely amazing to have him look at me like that and hold me like that again, the look in his eyes somewhere between adoration and possession.

"I'm so fuckin' in love with you," he told me.

There was a lump in my throat. "Me, too."

He pulled me back up to vertical.

"And I got your back in there with her tonight, okay, Jenna? No matter what she throws at us, we're gonna be okay. Okay?"

I nodded.

God, it felt even better to have someone have my back than I could've imagined. He opened the door for me and I got inside and blew out a breath of relief, steeling myself for the night to come.

I KNOCKED ON THE FRONT door.

"You're knockin' on the door of your childhood home?" he asked, standing behind me.

"Yeah. I don't live here anymore."

He shook his head, perplexed.

I got it. Ella would never have to knock on the door of her parents' house. Ever. I didn't have to knock at her house and I wasn't related by blood. But this house? Yeah, it would be frowned upon if I didn't knock.

One day though, if Ella and Deacon had kids and we had kids, our kids would be first cousins. I'd be related to Ella's family by blood.

God, that felt good.

I smiled at him.

He smiled back. He had no idea why I was smiling, but his smiling back at me gave me strength.

Mom opened the door and gave us a cursory eye sweep and waved us in.

Rider had a bottle of wine. I had a box from Andie's bakery that was filled with macarons. Mom's favorite.

"Nice to see you again, Mrs. Murdoch." Rider held his hand out.

Mom took it and shook his hand.

"Dinner's nearly ready. Please come to the dining room."

Dad was already sitting at the head of the table.

"Hey Dad," I went to him and kissed his cheek.

"You look lovely, Jenna," he said.

"Thanks. Dad, this is Rider."

Dad stood, and he and Rider shook hands.

"We met, Jenna. When he came over that morning."

"Oh yeah," I said.

"How's things, Paul?" Rider asked.

"We'll see," Dad muttered and gestured for Rider to sit down.

It was a table for six, but only four places were set. Rider and I were closer to Mom than Dad. Mom returned from the kitchen where she'd gone to get rid of the things we'd brought.

Dad's smile melted away at Mom returning to the dining room.

"What's for dinner?" I asked. "It smells great."

"Prime rib. I took a half day off to cook." She put the butter dish and a dish of horseradish on the table.

"Mm, sounds good," Rider said.

"Be right back," Mom said and went back to the kitchen.

I looked at Dad. He looked better than I'd last seen him.

"Jenna, we have to talk after this. I don't know if she's going to say some of the things I wanted to say to you privately, but—-"

"You mean, in case I tell her about your whore, you want to make excuses for all you've done?" Mom was back.

Holy shit.

My eyes widened. I tried to swallow down a lump in my throat. It remained where it was.

Rider's eyes were on me. I felt steady just looking at him.

He gave me a meaningful look.

Dad's eyes closed, and he let out a breath.

"Wine?" Mom asked and had a bottle, not the one we'd brought, in her hand.

"Yeah. Make it a double," I muttered.

"Rider, I'm sorry, we meant for this to be just a family dinner. Jenna insisted you were coming so unfortunately you're not seeing us at our best." Mom was completely composed, but also seemed a little bit higher strung than usual.

And that was saying something.

"You see, my husband of twenty-six years is ending our marriage and he's been having an extramarital affair for three and a half years."

My heart dropped. She finished pouring my glass and moved to him.

Dad's eyes were still closed.

"That means that when we spent our silver wedding anniversary renewing our vows, he was fucking someone else on the side. Now, Genevieve, since his whore is the whore he purchased your salon from, you'll probably understand when I tell you that as his wife who's entitled to half of his money, I want to sell immediately and liquidate all our assets so that they can be split down the middle."

Rider's glass was now full.

What? *What? Debbie?*

What? I don't think I'd ever heard Mom use an F-bomb.

"Oh, you heard me," she answered my unspoken *whats.*

"Dad?" I was in shock.

Dad's eyes opened and were on me and they were filled with remorse.

"I didn't want you to find out this way. I wanted to talk to you."

Mom laughed with venom in her voice.

"I should have known. He has the perfect business for you, the perfect arrangement for the former owner to show you the ropes and stay on until you're all set. Then he divorces me and moves on with her. She's already a friend to you and swoops in to take my place and you're instantly on their side."

I heard the 'ding' of a kitchen timer and it sent Mom back to the kitchen. She strolled in there, casually, like she hadn't just dropped a bomb on me.

"Dad?" I asked.

"I'm sorry you had to find out like this."

I gave my head a shake.

Debbie was awesome. She was not far off Mom's age, just a few years younger, but she was youthful, fun, interesting, sweet. She'd been amazing to me. She said she wanted to retire, work less but still cut hair for a while, so I'd taken over the business and she was staying on, renting a chair, for 2.5 to 3 years to help with the transition. I'd taken over her apartment over the shop and she'd moved into a really nice little Victorian house not far away.

She talked about sex, but she never talked about dating and she was a stunner. Now, I kind of understood. She had a love life. With my Dad.

She and her friends had just gone on a girls' trip to Vegas.

Shit. My Dad had said while I was in lockdown in Sioux Falls that *he* was going on a business trip to Nevada.

Did Mom catch him?

Mom came back out with the pan with the roast. Surrounding it were roasted Parisienne potatoes and roasted baby carrots. She put it down and went back to the kitchen, calling "I could use a hand carrying out the rest, Jenna."

I got up and followed her.

"Mom." I felt so sad for her. She wasn't nice. She was mean to me and barely nice to my father. As for their twenty-fifth renewal, she'd organized that in the garden with their friends and it'd felt fake even back then. I doubted Dad had a choice.

But he'd been cheating on her for all this time? With Deb. Deb! I considered Deb a friend. Deb knew so much about my life. I'd sat and moaned to Deb about my mother a hundred times, for heaven's sake. I was feeling betrayed right now, too.

"I guess you think I deserve this," she said, pouring gravy from a pan on the stove into her fine bone china gravy boat.

"No. Not even a little bit." I said, my arms cradling myself.

"You'll be on his side after he pulls you aside. He's always spoiled you."

"What? My father didn't spoil me. Neither of you did."

"Bring the rolls." She walked out with the gravy boat and I followed with a basket of rolls.

She put the gravy on the table.

Rider was sitting there looking at me. My father was sitting there with a face like stone.

Mom smiled and said, "So, in light of the circumstances, we'll need to liquidate all the assets and split them. Including the salon and the building the salon and apartment are in." Mom started to slice the roast like she wasn't talking about slicing my life into pieces.

Dad's face went hard.

"Except this place." She looked around with disdain. "Your father had his mother make this part of your trust fund. I'll move out and then he'll either take it until you want it, or he'll give it to you, I guess."

"Mom..." I started.

"Karen. I'm sure we can deal with this without dragging Jenna's business into it."

"No." She pointed the knife at my father.

Yikes.

She went back to slicing.

"Mom, I know there's a whole lot happening here, but maybe we should all just..."

"No." She started serving the meat. She served Rider first, then Dad, then me, then herself.

She started ladling vegetables onto Rider's plate.

"Your father has spoiled you rotten. You have not shown the level of responsibility required to run a business, Genevieve. It's better we just end it now."

"I'll buy you out, then," Dad said. "This thing is between you and I and it shouldn't touch Jenna."

"There you go again. Indulging her bad behavior. Look at what she's doing!" Mom gestured at Rider.

Rider's eyebrows shot up.

"And she takes off for days leaving her business in the hands of your whore and her nail technician. She couldn't care less about responsibility."

"I love my salon. I'm doing well with it. I—-"

"You're a frivolous young woman who needs a reality check!" Mom hissed.

I shot to my feet. "Are you kidding me? Reality? I lived in a house with two people in a loveless marriage who tolerated me, at best, because of how much of a disappointment I was. Despite that, I put myself through beauty school. My business might only be my business because of Dad's arrangement, but I never asked for that. I don't ask either of you for anything. Affection. Support. Love. Not a thing." I threw my napkin on the table. "I was in hiding because someone wanted to rape and kill me, not that you'd give a shit. If you want to take my salon, have at it. I no longer give a fuck."

I stormed out. Rider was right behind me.

My first instinct was to climb Ella's staircase to her attic. That's where I always headed when I was furious with my mother. Because that was all I had. That wasn't the case any longer. I had a man who loved me. I spun around and faced Rider in the driveway. "Please take us for a ride? Please?"

"You got it, gorgeous." He kissed my forehead and opened the passenger door of the Charger for me.

We got to his garage, I hadn't said a word on the way, and parked close to the burnt-out Deke's Roadhouse. He unlocked the garage and took me in through the side door. His regular Harley and his vintage bike were both there. There was also a half-built bike in a similar style, but with pink in it. I touched the body of it.

"You making this for a girl?" I asked.

"Yep," he said. "You want one, too? Teach you to ride?"

"No." I shook my head. "I like that I can just hang onto you and enjoy the view." I stared off into space.

"Jenna..." He approached me.

I looked at him.

"I'm not gonna cry over that," I informed him.

"Okay, baby." He put his hands to my jaw and caressed the apples of my cheeks with his thumbs. "But if you need to, lean on me, gorgeous."

I put my arms around him.

My phone was ringing from my pocket.

I glanced at the screen.

Mom Calling

I answered.

"Hello?"

"End things with him and show you're ready to be a responsible adult and I won't drag your salon into the divorce."

I held the phone.

"Your choice. Let me know by tomorrow."

"I don't have to think about it, Mom. I'll give you my answer right now."

She held the phone.

"Take it. Take it and sell it. I don't care. I'll work at another salon until I get my trust fund and I'll buy another one. I don't give a shit. He means way more to me already than that. You're doing me a favor here, because this cuts the strings. We're done. Enjoy yourself, Mom. Have fun basking in your bitterness knowing you've won."

I ended the call, shoved my phone in my pocket, and put my ear to his chest.

Thumping steady and sure. This was all I needed right now. This, and the open road.

"We goin' for a ride?" I asked, looking up at him.

He looked furious. "I heard what she said, Jenna."

"It doesn't matter."

"She offered to let you keep it if you gave me up."

"Yeah." I said, a sourness working its way through my mouth, my stomach.

"She'll probably change her mind after she gets a chance to cool down. She's just striking out at whoever she can because she's so angry."

"She won't change her mind, Rider. And it's okay. I'm *so* ready for her to have zero leverage over me, it's actually a bit of a relief."

I felt that, yeah, but I loved my salon. I hated that I'd also be taking away from Pippa, who would have to find another salon to work at.

And Pippa was supposed to be moving in with Joe, but the way things were with them right now? She wasn't talking, but I could tell things weren't good. I didn't like the idea of her having to move out of our apartment and in with him if she had any doubts.

"I love you," he told me.

I smiled. "I love you, too. Take me for a ride, please?"

"Let's go. Tap my left elbow if you want me to pull off. My right one, when you're ready to head back home."

We took his Harley and drove for a good hour or hour and a half, before I tapped his right elbow and he took us home.

I WAS SITTING ON THE edge of the bed, deep in thought, while he was in the bathroom a long time, the water running.

Finally, he poked his head out and crooked his finger at me.

I got up and walked into the bathroom. He'd run me a bubble bath. My scented warmer light was on, the lights off, and he put two plush lilac towels with satin edging on the vanity for me.

"Thanks, handsome."

He kissed my forehead and left me to it.

I came out of the bathroom a half an hour later, relaxed and sleepy. He was in bed, watching television.

"You didn't like the purple towels?" he asked.

"Those are my good towels. I don't use those," I said, tightening the beige bath towel wrapped around me.

He chuckled. "Why have 'em if you can't use 'em?"

I smiled. "Because they're pretty."

"Yeah, well so are you, and I certainly plan to use you," he teased.

I crawled up onto the bed in just the towel.

"If I use them constantly, they might not be pretty. If you use me constantly, I don't know if that'll be pretty, but it sure will feel good... so I won't care."

He snickered and undid my towel and tossed it. I crawled under the blankets with him and snuggled in.

"We didn't get dinner. You hungry?" I asked.

"Not really," he said.

"Me either."

He didn't make any moves, despite my nakedness, his nakedness.

I was glad. I wasn't feeling sexy right now. I was feeling very, very tired. And sad.

He rubbed my back until I fell asleep with my head on his chest.

MY DAD WAS WAITING for me at the salon when I got down the stairs in the morning. He was standing there chatting with Scooter, who was today's shadow. Rider had already gotten up and showered to leave for work before I was out of bed, kissing me sweetly, telling me to have a good day and to call him if my mother tried to hassle me.

"Hi Dad," I said.

"Hello, honey. Got time to talk before you open?"

I nodded, and we went into the utility room, leaving Scooter in the waiting area.

"I'm sorry you had to find out that way," he said as I started up the coffeemaker.

"Me, too," I said.

"In Deborah's defense, she didn't like the lies. She gave me an ultimatum about it. Made me put a timeline on it. I pushed it off a few times, not wanting to hurt anyone. I'm lucky I didn't lose her."

I passed him a cup of coffee and started a new one for me.

"Your mother and I haven't been happy for a really long time. If we ever really were."

"Yeah, but lying doesn't make it better. It's cowardly, Dad."

He looked down. "I know. I've been trying to get caught for six months. I think your mother knew for about two years. I think she suspected it when we had to have that meeting with Deborah to sign all the papers for the salon. She started punishing me even more but never confronted me. I think it was more fun for her this way."

"How did it all come to a head?"

"The night we saw the news about that woman that got murdered and we couldn't reach you. We were arguing. I was leaving for Vegas that morning and I was telling her that I wasn't concerned about Rider. See, Deborah's closest friend Laura used to date Rider's father, so she filled us in on the kind of people you were with. And honey, that added to talking to Rider on the phone? That put my mind at ease. I was trying to settle your mother down, and finally I blurted how I knew that the Valentines were good people. It just spiraled out of control from there."

I blew out a breath.

"It's on me. I accept responsibility. And now she's gonna make everyone's life miserable. I'm seeing my lawyer. I want to find a way to keep the salon out of it. Our original arrangement should stand. It might make things take longer, but I'm not willing for you to take the brunt of this."

"No, Dad." I shook my head. "That puts me in the middle of this thing with you and her and I don't wanna be."

"She's gonna tie up all our assets, or I would've—-"

"I know."

"The house is in your name in trust. I did that when my mother passed, so she couldn't sell it out from under you if things came to this. Even then I think I knew we wouldn't last forever. I could ask my lawyer about it. If you sell it, it would be more than enough to—-"

I shook my head. "No. I'm gonna raise my children in that house."

Dad's expression went soft.

"They're gonna slide down that banister right into their daddy's arms."

Dad's eyes filled up.

When I was about four, I slid down the banister and Dad caught me at the bottom. And I thought I'd be in trouble, but Dad's eyes were sparkly, and he was laughing at me and my inability to hide how much I'd loved doing it. And Mom caught him and screamed at him for it. And screamed at me for it.

I knew he remembered it as vividly as I did by the look on his face.

"I'll buy a new salon when I turn thirty."

"I'll try to find a way..." he said.

"No, Dad. Thank you for being willing to try. Thank you for all the faith you showed me when you decided to do this. I'm not happy about the lies and I wish you'd gone about ending your marriage a different way. Adultery is not okay. But, I appreciate—-"

"Jenna, your mother and I haven't had a real marriage in more than ten years. I was celibate for years before I met Deborah."

I winced. Still. Adultery was adultery.

"You should've ended it with Mom before you went there with Deb."

He nodded. "I know."

"And Deb should not have pretended to be my friend all this time."

"She is your friend. She loves you, honey. I'm gonna marry her."

I blew out a breath. I loved Deb, too. But, this was really, *really* ugly.

"I'm gonna need time," I said.

"I know."

"But I do love you, Dad."

"I love you, too, Jenna. And I'm so very sorry for not shielding you from her better. She made me so angry and you were always just so resilient. I hated how she treated you we would have terrible arguments when you weren't there. But you always just bounced back from her nonsense. I've always been in awe of that."

"I didn't bounce back, Dad. I just hid it really well. You should've shielded me better. I didn't think you cared."

My father looked like he'd been hit in the gut. He swallowed.

"I've gotta open," I whispered.

He took a sip of his coffee and put the cup down.

"I'm meeting with my lawyer this afternoon. I'll let you know what he says about all of this."

"Don't bother, Dad. I think a fresh start might be better."

Then I wouldn't have to deal with Mom. I wouldn't have to work side-by-side with Deb, his mistress. I could make a clean break.

Even though it hurt like hell.

He kissed my cheek and left.

I stood there a minute, looking around. And then I heard Pippa's voice. She was saying hi to my dad.

I closed my eyes, stress filling my belly. I hated that I was going to have to break this to Pippa.

And Lulu. I'd have to tell her she didn't have a new job to start next week after all.

Fuck my life.

At least I had Rider.

As if he'd read my mind, he was phoning me.

"Hi."

"Scoot said your dad just left?"

"Yeah."

"You okay, gorgeous?"

"No."

"What can I do?"

"You got a cool mill lying around I can borrow so I can buy this place?" I didn't even know how much it would be listed for.

"Not exactly, baby."

"Yeah, that's all right. Lana's Hair Salon might have a chair for rent. Or maybe Fran from another salon will hire me. She's three blocks from here."

"Yeah?"

"I'm gonna need to find an apartment," I mumbled. I loved my apartment.

"We'll get one together," he said.

"Already?" I asked.

"Some reason we should wait?" he asked.

"Nnnnno."

"Then check the want-ads. I got money put away, so we'll be fine."

"Huh?"

"I don't know your cashflow situation, gorgeous, but I got money in the bank. Don't stress about cash. I can cover us."

I blinked.

How amazing was he?

"I'm not destitute yet, don't worry," I said softly.

He didn't answer.

"But thank you, Rider."

"Love you, beautiful. Gotta go. Customer here. You okay?"

"I will be," I said. "Bye, handsome. Love you, too."

"See you tonight. But, what non-cute grocery item do you want for dinner?"

"How about I make *you* dinner?" I suggested.

"You said you can't cook."

"I can't. But I'll try."

"Naw. I'll cook, you do the dishes. We got that down pat."

"Yeah, but you're really messy."

"But you like my food."

"Yeah, you're a damn good cook," I said.

"Gotta go, babe. I'll thinka somethin' to wow you with."

"Okay. You could make any of the food I didn't eat last week when I had my head up my ass. Okay?"

"Okay," he chuckled.

"Love you so, *so* much, Rider."

"Love you more. Bye, gorgeous." He hung up.

Ella was in the front, with Pippa and Scooter and Pudge, when I got out. Pudge was Ella's bodyguard today. He went out for an egg McMuffin and hash brown run while I filled in Ella and Pippa on all the news.

Ella and Pippa felt awful for me, and Ella immediately declared it a girls' night out. We needed to go get drunk, she said. So, she and Pippa rounded up Andie, Lulu, Dr. Lola, and Deanna, and we all went to a bar after work, two biker bodyguards with us.

I had good friends. I had a great boyfriend.

I'd be okay.

RIDER KNEW I WAS HAVING a girls' night out. He left me to it.

When I got home at about 1:30 in the morning, more than a little bit sloshed, he was sitting on my couch, a beer bottle balanced on his knee, held by the neck with his hand.

"Hey-yah," I leaned on the doorframe. Pippa staggered toward her bedroom. She was smashed drunk, too.

Scott was behind me. "You good?" He was addressing my man. My beautiful biker man.

God, my biker was beautiful.

Rider waved. "Yeah man. Hit the road. See ya here at 9:30."

"Night Jenna," Scooter said.

"Thanks for beaming me home, Scotty." I giggled and then informed Rider, "Scooter and Deanna made goo-goo eyes at one another all night long. It was adorable!"

Scooter rolled his eyes. "Lock up."

"Roger, dodger." I saluted him, following and turning the lock on the kitchen door and putting the chain on.

"He must be so bored hanging out with me most days," I said, coming back to the doorway of the living room. "How does he survive doing that all day?"

"You're fun to watch, I'm guessin'." Rider flicked the TV off and put his beer bottle on the table.

"You think so, but you like me. No. I mean financially."

"He gets paid. I pay him."

"You pay him?"

"Yeah. Prospects are at our beck and call, get a small cut of the club's earnings, but a situation like this, full time bodyguard, I'm paying him, so he can pay his bills. It's a job."

"Oh. All this time?"

"Yeah. Him, Jess, Bronto, whoever's watching you."

"Must be quite an expense."

"It is. You're high-maintenance, baby. I have to pay him a premium. High maintenance is even higher than the usual danger pay."

I laughed.

He was stalking toward me.

"You drunk?" he asked.

"Little bit," I held my hand aloft, my index finger and thumb a few inches apart. And then I threw my arms wide to make it look like a lot.

He stepped up to me and put his arms around me.

"You have a good night?"

"It felt really good to let my hair down and dance. Me, Ella, Pippa, all of us. We danced our asses off."

"Shit," He grumbled.

"What?" I asked.

He walked me toward the bedroom.

"I missed watchin' you dance."

I laughed. "I wanna dance some more. But I wanna do the no-pants dance. Like Men-Without-Hats, but Jenna and Rider-with-no-pants. Ha-ha."

"Sounds good to me," he said and undid my jeans button.

I put my head on his shoulder.

"I'm sad," I mumbled.

"Baby?" he took my face in his hands.

"I don't wanna move." I pouted.

"I'm sorry, babe."

"I wanna live here for the next few years, enjoy the roof parties, the closeness to the bakery and my salon and that coffee place down the street with the really good BLT wraps, then I wanna move into my parents' house and raise our babies there."

"Sounds like a good plan."

"But I have to move and someone else is gonna have the salon and probably rent the apartment out and it'll ruin the roof people group, too, because what if whoever moves here doesn't like roof parties?"

"That'd suck for the neighbors."

"I love my neighbors. They're gonna be so sad, too."

We were now lying on the bed together.

"Pippa's moving in with Joe. She and I are gonna talk to Lana about working there. We don't wanna work at Fran's. Her husband hangs out and he's creepy. And we wanna work at the same place." I sighed.

He was playing with my hair.

"I'm sad." I repeated, my eyes drooping.

"I'm sorry, Jenna," he whispered.

"If I turn into my mother, just divorce me, okay? Don't cheat on me behind my back."

"You won't turn into your mother."

"I hope not."

"And I won't cheat. Not ever. Promise."

"I love you."

"Love you, too, Jenna."

"I won't be sad for long as long as you don't leave me."

"I won't leave you, baby. Promise."

"Okay."

And then I fell asleep.

23

The Following Saturday

My salon had just closed for the day. I'd gotten changed into workout clothes and went down to see Rider, who was in my parking lot with Jesse.

Business was still ticking on, though I knew the listing had gone up quietly. I hadn't been broadcasting it, but a few people had seen the listing and started asking questions, which wasn't fun.

I'd been non-committal with my answers, saying, "It's not easy to run a business. Just lookin' at my options." But inside, I was so effing sad.

I hadn't seen my mother. At all. Not a word, not a text.

I hadn't seen Deb, either. She sent me a long text telling me that she was sorry about how things had come to light, that she cared about me and was going to give me space, that she wasn't coming in to work until I invited her to come.

If I didn't want her back before the salon changed hands, that was okay, too. She told me she knew two upscale salon owners in Aberdeen who she would be happy to introduce me to if I wanted to work at either of their salons. My response was a 'thumbs up' emoticon to Deb. I didn't have any words for her yet.

The business was in my parents' names, but all the bank accounts were in my name; Dad hadn't allowed Mom to put her name on them when our arrangement was made, so I just kept on like normal, with the exception of the day the real estate agent, not from my Dad's firm, came in and had pictures taken and asked questions about the building specs so that he could set up the listing.

I wasn't surprised my mother went to another realtor. I also wasn't surprised it was sprung on me, rather than an appointment being made. It was Karen Murdoch's style to inconvenience me while also shredding me.

I wasn't a bitch, though suspected this surprised him. He likely got a warning from my mother. But, I was cooperative. He told me that if I was helpful with the transition to the new owners and they did plan to keep it as a salon, I could wind up with a job, if I wanted one. I might even be able to rent the apartment, if they were willing to keep it as a rental unit. It was all a 'wait and see'.

Working here without it being mine? I didn't want that. I didn't say it to him, though. I was polite and professional. Living here while someone else ran the salon? No way.

Things with Rider and I were good. No, great. There was the cloud of all this salon stuff over us, but I tried not to let it consume all of my thoughts. At night, he made dinner and I cleaned up his ridiculously big messes.

We made love, we cuddled, he told me about his day. We went for a few long motorcycle rides.

One night, we made dinner and his Dad and brothers came over and hung out and watched a hockey game while me, Pippa, and Ella hung out in my room, watching a girlie movie.

I finally had a guy that I could lean on and I was worried my cloudy mood was going to make him get sick of me. But, he rolled with the punches. He was patient and loving and so sweet and nurturing. It was the only thing saving me from being in a full-fledged depression.

Things were quiet, for the moment, with the Wyld Jackals. Until that day. That day, the Jackals answered my earlier question about whether or not Rider and I would get out of this unscathed.

RIDER WAS WORKING IN the parking lot behind my salon on a new bike. He'd decided to tinker with one of his builds and was doing it here instead of at the garage since the garage was jam-packed due to a surge in business. Spencer had come by, bringing all the bike pieces in his pickup truck, parking here, and taking the Charger with him, planning to do a swap later.

I'd peeked out a few times, thinking that if I were keeping the salon, I'd have wanted to find out how much it'd cost to build a garage back there, just for his personal stuff. That way he could do his tinkering while I worked on Saturdays, which was when he usually worked on his custom bikes. The terrace overhang would be the perfect place to snug a garage into.

Since the salon was being sold, it was a non-issue.

"I have to go out," I informed him.

Right then, we heard the roar of pipes. He stepped away from the bike he was working on and glanced down the alley and saw that on the main strip, a parade of motorcycles was going by. At least four or five of them. Wyld Jackals. Again.

Shit.

"Yikes," I said.

Rider made a face. "That's the third time they've done that today. Don't like this." He glanced at Jesse. "They're driving by the Valentine block and the Forker's house, too."

"Rider? I have to go out."

"Now?" he asked.

I glanced at my watch. "Yeah."

"You can't wait twenty minutes?"

"If I do, I'll be late."

"I can't take you. Gotta finish this and get all this shit put away."

"I'm gonna be late if I don't leave in two minutes," I said.

"Jesse? Shadow Jenna?"

Jesse was watching him, smoking a cigarette. He gave a nod.

"I don't think you want that, Rider," I advised.

Rider looked at me like he was losing patience with me.

I stared at him a beat. He stared back. And then he looked sorely pissed. "Are you fuckin' serious right now? All this shit goin' on and you're gonna gimme a hard time about keepin' you safe? Jackals driving up and down this strip like they're ready to prove something and you're being like this?"

"Nnnno...."

He gave his head a shake like he couldn't make sense of me.

He was in a shitty mood today, for some reason.

"You want me to cancel my plans? If it's not safe..."

"No. We need to live." He looked to Jesse. "Keep alert."

"Of course," Jesse muttered and looked at me.

"You probably don't want Jesse to come with me."

I folded my arms across my chest and stared at him. A little smirk on my face.

Jesse shifted from one foot to another, also beginning to look like he was losing patience with me.

Rider leaned forward, just a little. "Jenna. Jesse comes with you. He doesn't take his eyes off you unless you're in the can and only after he's looked first to make sure there's no fuckin Jackals in there, looking to get their hands on you."

"Really? You want him watching me the whole time?"

He looked to the sky, likely for deliverance, and Jesse looked at Rider like he wanted to knock some sense into him for having anything to do with me.

"Fine," I shrugged and adjusted the strap of my Duffle bag that was over my shoulder. "Want me to drive or you, Jesse?"

"Gimme your keys." Jesse held his hand out to me.

"Want a kiss goodbye, Rider?" I asked, placing my car keys in Jesse's palm.

Rider looked at me like he wanted to strangle me, rather than kiss me. I had a feeling I might finally get myself some of that *actual* angry sex today. He hadn't asked where I was going, but I was in workout clothes, so he must've figured I was heading to the gym or to Pippa's yoga studio.

"Whatever." I went to move away, seeing he was too pissed to kiss me. "See you after my pole dancing class." I kept moving.

I was halted, Rider catching me by the back hem of my coat.

"Keys!" He snapped and held his hand out.

Jesse smacked the keys into Rider's hand.

Looked like Rider had time to shadow me after all.

"Fuck," Jesse grunted. Jesse looked like a dog who'd had his bone taken away. "Fuck. Couldn't've kept that last line to yourself, could ya, Jen?"

I laughed.

Rider glared at Jesse. "Can you put all that into Spence's truck and wait till he gets here to pick it up?"

Jesse gave him the finger.

I laughed louder.

Jesse started lifting bike parts as Rider grabbed my hand and marched me to my Jetta.

"You're gonna pay for that," Rider growled into my ear as he opened the passenger door for me.

"Naw. You are. 'Cuz you're gonna have to watch fifteen girls swing around poles for ninety minutes and prove to me that I'm the only one of those girls making you hard."

He bit into his bottom lip as he shut my door.

As he rounded the vehicle, he adjusted his jeans at the crotch on the way.

WE WERE LEAVING THE studio and he was quiet until we got into the car. When we got into the car, me tossing my Duffle into the back seat, he turned the ignition and put a hand to two and a hand to ten on the wheel. Rider blew out a slow breath and then said,

"You're in so much trouble, Missy."

I snickered.

I hadn't exactly been honest with him. I had one-on-one classes with my instructor, a fifty-year-old dancer who had retired from exotic dancing, but she had a waiting list for her classes, because she was damn good.

And she told me that I was good enough on that pole to go pro. It helped that I had danced until I was 14 in jazz, tap, ballet, and contemporary, so I had rhythm. I'd been taking her pole-dancing classes for almost two years and I knew I was good.

I called her a few days ago to renew my once-per-week membership, which was an expensive membership being one-on-one coaching. I knew my future was uncertain, but before all this drama, I loved it and I loved what it did for my body, so decided I'd give something else up to be able to take these classes.

I ate junk food a few times a week (or 100 garlic bread sticks) and somehow managed to keep svelte thanks to these once a week classes and twice a week classes with Pippa the Yoga and Pilates Sergeant. Pippa wasn't all sweet and namaste with me. She yelled at me when I wasn't perfect in pose.

I'd never had a guy see me do my pole dancing class before, and I knew I'd impressed him.

"I'd be in more trouble, I'm sure, if I'd let Jesse bring me."

"Fuck." He closed his eyes and shook his head. "That's for damn sure."

And then he put an arm around my seat and looked over his shoulder as he backed out of there.

Two minutes later, we were on a backroad by the town dump, a deserted service road that no one really used.

"What are we doing back here?" I asked.

"Get over here." He turned the car off, unbuckled my seatbelt, and then hit the button to recline his seat.

I climbed over, still wearing my workout tights.

"You got something else to put on in your bag?"

"Yeah. Why?"

"Bottoms?"

"Yes...."

He looked down and grabbed the crotch of them with both hands and shredded them between my legs, exposing my panties.

I gasped.

"Rider Valentine!"

"Give me that mouth," he demanded and then grabbed the back of my neck and pulled me to his waiting lips.

"Work my fly undone," he ordered. "And take your spanking and fucking like a good girl."

Holy shit.

I did it and rubbed all over his piercing.

"Get me in you."

"Mm. You want in me?" I teased, rubbing my thumb over his piercing."

He growled in my ear, "Right now, baby." He slapped my butt.

I obliged.

It was fast, and it was furious. And my ass was definitely pink, because he slapped it about five times.

I whispered in his ear, coming down from my orgasm, "I want you to fuck me on your bike."

He raised his eyebrows and yanked on the length of my hair and attacked my throat with his teeth.

"I wanna ride you, while we ride..." I walked my fingers up his chest to his mouth and ran my index finger along that sexy, pillowy bottom lip.

His eyes lit with fiery lust. "That'd be dangerous. Operating a dangerous machine ... dangerously." He laughed as he said *dangerously* and I giggled.

"I operate dangerous machinery every time I climb onto you," I told him.

"Mm. Best get off the dangerous machine, so I can drive us home. Next time we fuck in a car, let it be mine. Not enough room in here." I laughed and then I climbed between the front seats into the back and got into my Duffle bag to get my yoga pants out.. I switcheroo'd, and was still in the back seat, stuffing the ruined tights into my bag when I heard, "Fuck! Buckle up!"

"Wh...what?" I heard the sound of motorcycle pipes. He turned the ignition and we rocketed forward.

I looked over my shoulder and saw four motorcycles behind us, gaining on us.

Did they follow us?

"Fuckin' cunts! Why can't we be in the goddamn Charger?"

We were driving fast. I still wasn't buckled up. I struggled to get the seatbelt fastened, because the motorcycles were trying to catch up to us.

Rider took a sharp right at the last second on a back road and the tires squealed as he did it, gravel flying everywhere.

I had one hand pressed against the door and the other clawing the back of the seat in front of me.

Oh God!

I was thrown around in the backseat a little, bouncing from one side to the other. We were spinning out and somehow, I miraculously got the middle lap belt done up. Then, there was the sound of screeching, the smell of burning, and glass breaking, metal crunching, as we smashed into a van. My front airbag was out, and Rider was wedged between his seat and the air bag.

I heard a loud ping noise and then a whole bunch more of them. I ducked and covered my head, staying low.

I heard a couple more ping noises. We were being shot at! I got the seat-belt off and turtled in the space between the passenger seat and the back seat.

My God! Rider!

And then I heard sirens off in the distance. I heard and felt the vibrating roar as motorcycles pulled away. The van that we'd t-boned into backed away and pulled away, too.

Seconds passed while I was just, I don't know, blinking? And the sirens were louder. I got up from my crouch and looked into the front seat and there was blood on the air bag. Rider was slumped into it. Unconscious.

"Rider?" I climbed between the seats.

He was definitely unconscious. His face was bloody, a cut over his eye.

"Baby?" I croaked.

I checked myself. No holes, no blood. The windows were all broken and there was blood on the windshield, blood on the dash, the air bag.

I choked on emotion.

I saw the flashing twirling lights through the spider web of my wind-shield. The cops.

The fire department and ambulance followed a minute or two later.

I heard them say he'd been shot. At least twice.

The front end of my Jetta was smashed in, but they got to him, got him out of there and onto a stretcher.

Someone talked to me. Someone got me to the back of the ambulance and checked my vitals. But I was just crying and begging Rider not to be dead as they were working on him.

I was banged up from bouncing around inside the car, a cut over my eye, a bump on the back of my head, but I was otherwise unharmed. Except on the inside. My heart was breaking. They had an oxygen mask on his face. They were leaving with him and me in the ambulance.

He was bleeding from his arm and from the right side of his chest and he wasn't waking up amid all they were doing.

ELLA AND DEACON, SPENCER, Deke, and my father and Deb were all in the waiting room with me. I didn't know how they knew to come. Spencer got there first. I hadn't stopped crying when I was asked questions, so I don't know how anyone understood me when I told them our names.

They took him and now I was pacing. I couldn't sit. I had a bit of tape over my eye in lieu of stitches. An ice pack for the back of my head.

I was pacing because Rider was in surgery.

I was pacing, because my heart was not inside my body right now. It was in Rider's hands. If he didn't make it, I would not survive. I would not.

I'd never ever felt like this. I'd never been through anything this frightening, this gut-wrenching. He was just lying there. My strong, vibrant, sparkling-eyed biker was just lying there, bleeding.

When Spencer got to me first, hugging me while the police fired questions at me, I wasn't doing well, I wasn't helping the police because I was falling apart. Spencer made me look into his eyes and told me to take deep breaths and calm down. And then he told me that I needed to talk to the police to help them catch the fuckers that did it, so that was when I was able to get coherent sentences out.

I'd talked to the police and told them about the four or five motorcycles that had been going up and down the street all day long. If someone identified who those four bikers were, and someone had to have seen them from all the busy shops along the street, that's who the cops could arrest. That's who either tried to kill us or who helped. That's who might have succeeded in killing my beautiful biker.

I wasn't sure if bullets came from the van, too, but I think they did.

Please no.

I spewed out as much detail out as I could, crying in Spencer's arms the whole time.

"He flatlined on the way here, in the ambulance, Spencer. His heart stopped beating for a few beats, but they got it going again. If he doesn't make it, I can't, I can't..."

It absolutely undid me to see them pumping his chest.

Spencer kept hugging me and rocking me until Deacon, Ella, and Deke arrived next. Ella took over the hugging and rocking then, until I couldn't handle being hugged anymore.

By this time, Scooter, Jesse, and Bronto were with us. It was the first time I'd seen Bronto since he'd been shot. Andie and Pippa were there for a bit, but it was really crowded, so they left.

They all hugged me, but I was numb through the countless hugs and finally pleaded for people to stop hugging me.

More bikers showed up and Spencer and Deacon stopped them from crowding me. People brought coffee and donuts and pizza and more coffee and I was sick of getting asked if I wanted something so I just kept pacing, not wanting to be hugged or touched anymore.

After hours and hours of pacing, the doctor came out and asked for Deke, knowing he was Rider's father.

Deke stood and put his hand on my shoulder. Ella got to the other side of me, there, in case, in case...

Deacon and Spencer were behind us. Ella's Dad behind them.

"Please, please, please, God, please," I chanted.

Ella was crying softly, holding tight to me.

I heard Deb's voice hitch. She, too, was crying. She'd come in with Dad and they'd both hugged me before I cut off all the hugging, but I don't think I was really *all there* at that point. I just kept pacing for hours and hours, refusing offers of coffee and food and whatever the eff.

The doctor started to speak, and the place was so quiet you'd hear a pin drop.

"Mr. Valentine, your son made it through surgery. The two bullets are out. We almost lost him twice during surgery. His heart stopped beating, but we got him back."

My knees were Jell-O and they wobbled. Deke supported me by putting his arm around me. Deacon moved in behind Ella and put an arm around each of our waists.

"Tonight is critical. We have to just wait it out. It'll probably be a long night. You're welcome to visit with him for just a minute, but only one at a time. If he makes it through tonight, we can be cautiously optimistic."

I pulled away from the teary-eyed Ella and then I was following the doctor, Deke behind me. I glanced back and saw Deacon holding Ella, looking so angry. Ella's hand was on his jaw. She was trying to comfort him.

Spencer had his forehead and his palms against the wall.

Deke and me went in together, completely disregarding what the doctor had said.

Rider was connected to all sorts of machines, a breathing thing in his mouth. His chest and shoulder were bandaged.

I leaned over and kissed his forehead.

Deke leaned over and did the same.

"Don't you leave me," I demanded.

Rider didn't answer me.

"Don't you dare, *dare* leave me, Rider Valentine. You're in. You finally got inside my Kevlar and I need you to stay there."

I could hear his machines. I could see all these numbers and graphs on the screens that told me he was still alive. I felt like I was falling apart, though. If he didn't make it?

I started to lose it.

"He fought his way back three times, Jenna. Three times they've got his heart going again. He's not givin' up. Don't you give up, Ride," Deke ordered. "Don't fuckin' stop fightin'. You got a girl here waitin' for ya. We don't let those fuckers win, son. They do *not* get to win."

I sobbed some more and sat in a chair beside his bed and put my hand on his. I kissed his knuckles and then I carefully put my head to the left side of his chest, cautious not to disturb any wires. I could feel it, sort of.

"I don't wanna hear these machines. I wanna hear his heart," I told Deke.

"Jenna, darlin'... these machines here *tell* you his heart is beating." His voice was gruff.

"But I wanna hear his heart properly. I know it sounds stupid, but... when I'm upset or freaking out, he always calms me down by getting me to listen to his heart," I told Deke. "These machines are too loud."

He gave me a nod and left the room.

"Please don't leave me, Rider. I love you so much. I'm just getting my taste of that rainbow. We're supposed to joyride through life. Winding roads. Babies. Sex games. Angry sex. Riding the banister. I want all of that with you. Even the bad days. I'll take a thousand bad days to have just a few good ones with you. You come back to me, okay? I'll stop pushing you away. I promise."

Deke was back with a stethoscope. I didn't know where he got it, but I gave him an appreciative smile and put it on and put it to Rider's chest and closed my eyes to listen. I moved the circle thing around until I found it loudest. I listened to the steady beat of his heart and tears just kept rolling down my cheeks, but I *knew*, I knew he'd come back to me.

They wanted me to go, but I wouldn't. I stayed in my little chair beside his bed and stayed out of their way. Deacon came in. Ella came in. Spencer came in. That was it. They took turns trying to get me to eat or drink, but I couldn't. I wouldn't. I heard them in the hallway talking and saying they'd called Jojo and told her. And then they kept talking about shit with the cops, about something about Gordino. I asked them to *please* go talk somewhere else and let me listen to his heart with my stethoscope in peace. My eyes closed, holding his hand. They left.

I guess I finally fell asleep, but woke up feeling my hand getting squeezed.

He was squeezing my hand. I straightened.

"Rider?"

He opened his eyes just a little and squeezed my hand again.

I pushed the button for the nurses, who were probably already on their way as they were watching his machines from some other desk, too. They started taking his vitals and asked me to step out in the hall.

I did, but stayed in the doorway so I wasn't out of his sight.

His breathing tube got pulled out and I was invited to come back. I gave him some ice chips, and then he squeezed my hand and pointed to the stethoscope around my neck with a confused look on his face.

"Oh, I wanted to play hot dirty doctor with you. I've been waiting for you to wake up." I whispered this.

The nurse who was there smirked.

"Could you go tell his dad he's awake? I don't wanna leave him."

She smiled and left us, saying, "Yes. The doctor's gonna come, too, so pause the doctor game."

She winked. I smiled at her and looked to Rider. "I was listening to your heart. It was settling me down. I was so scared."

"C'mere," he whispered, his voice all scratchy.

He reached for the stethoscope and I leaned forward. He put the circle on my chest kind of fumbly, he was definitely doped up, but I caught his drift. I lifted it up off my neck and put the circle to my chest and then put the ear pieces in his ears. I moved in and he drowsily reached forward and adjusted it until he found the right spot and then he listened to my heart, closing his eyes and smiling.

God, I loved him so much.

I closed my eyes and said a prayer of thanks.

A WEEK AND A HALF LATER

Debbie took care of the salon until a few days after Rider was home from the hospital. She and I didn't talk, but Dad had asked if I wanted her to take care of it and I'd gratefully nodded.

When she had been at the hospital and hugged me, then backed away and stood there with my father, I hadn't even registered at the time how right they looked together. I was too busy falling apart and praying that the man I loved wouldn't die.

Deb was dark-haired, like me, like Mom. She was shorter, petite, pretty, and bubbly. And she fit on my father's arm like she belonged there. He looked worried, for me, but he looked happy with her.

My dad told me, at the hospital, that he'd told my mother what'd happened, that we were in a car accident, that we'd been shot at. That I hadn't been hit, but that Rider had been shot twice and nearly died.

Mom didn't text or call, and she certainly didn't come.

I didn't care. I didn't need her. I had a family. A big, huge, beautiful noisy obnoxious loving family who were driving me crazy trying to take care of me, do things for me. People who accepted me as I am.

The crowd of bikers at the hospital had been seen in more than one pow wow. I knew they were planning their retribution. And I wanted to get in line with them, learn to shoot. Annihilate those bastards who had raped and killed Jet, who'd killed Lick, who'd sodomized Scooter, who'd tried to hurt Ella, and who'd almost taken Rider from me.

Rider was in the hospital for several days. Me at his side other than to sleep and shower (though I slept at the hospital that first night) and then we were home for a few days when I got the call from the real estate agent.

My business had sold.

Already.

IT HAD GONE INTO A minor bidding war between two buyers who must've seen it while Rider was in the hospital. No one had called me to say they were looking at it.

The winning bidder wanted to take possession within two weeks. The bidder wanted to meet with the current manager in two days. And that would be me.

I wasn't happy. To put it mildly. I knew this was coming, but couldn't believe my mother hadn't put it on hold with me almost losing Rider.

I was freaking out about having to move, having to pack and get us a place when Rider was still recovering from two effing gunshot wounds.

He was recovering well, and he was definitely enjoying how much I was pampering him. I couldn't cook well, but I warmed up soup and made him deli sandwiches and bagels with smoked salmon cream cheese. I ordered in food. Pudge did several food runs for us and stayed and ate with us more than once. He wasn't Mr. Personality, but he seemed to like hanging out at my place.

Rider and I hung out in my bed and watched movies and played video games a lot.

I brushed his hair and gave him backrubs. He told me when he was well enough, he wanted me to shave him. He told me he wanted me to shave him in one of my salon chairs and said he'd been having a fantasy about us having sex in one of those chairs with shaving cream all over his face.

I told him I'd try to make that happen before the salon changed hands. And then I gave him a blow job but didn't let him take care of me.

I could wait a few days. He didn't want to.

He also asked me about installing a stripper pole in my bedroom, so I wouldn't have to leave the house to go to stripper-cize classes anymore.

I'd winced at that comment, but he teased me for it.

"Hey. I took us to a backroad without protection when we were under threat. Not you, gorgeous. Do not take that on."

He acted angry that I was taking any blame, so I relaxed, not wanting him stressed.

I shrugged and told him maybe we'd set up a pole in our new place. He rubbed my back when I went all sad again, thinking about moving.

We had outdoor patrol set up. There were constant drive-bys and the Dominion Brotherhood presence on my street was strong.

The police could not find any sign of a blue cargo van with signs of T-Bone damage. They did, however, have an idea who had been driving the motorcycles due to the footage from some security cameras around the businesses on my street.

We were waiting to see how that panned out, but Rider told me not to be surprised if it didn't go far. The shootout happened in a more secluded part of town without cameras on every corner. Unfortunately.

But, Rider did tell me that revenge was on the horizon, not just because he'd almost been shot dead, but also because they'd tried to shoot us both. It was mentioned more than once that my car was riddled with bullet holes and it was a miracle we'd both survived and an even bigger miracle that I hadn't gotten shot even once.

For a change, luck seemed to be on my side. I'd take it.

I DRAGGED MYSELF INTO the bedroom after the phone call from the realtor, which I'd taken in the kitchen while folding some clean laundry.

"What's up?" he asked, shifting upright in bed.

"The salon sold," I said softly.

My chin trembled.

"C'mere," he patted the bed.

I climbed up and sat.

He put his arm around me.

"What's the story?"

"I don't know, really. There was a bidding war. Someone won. It's closing in two weeks. We need to find a place to live. I need to find a job."

"Don't worry."

"I have to pack and figure out where to put my stuff, and...maybe they'll take the salon in two weeks and I can get them to give us an extra two weeks before we have to leave the apartment."

"Don't worry about it. We can take a little holiday at the cabin for a few weeks, maybe. Put all your stuff in storage. Then go from there."

"Yeah?" I asked.

He nodded. "Or how about we go to the Caribbean for two weeks? Come back and see what's what."

"I don't wanna be that far yet, Rider. Not with the Wyld Jackals threat still kind of active."

"It's not gonna be active much longer, believe me." His eyes were cold.

"What's going on?"

"Don't ask questions you don't want the answers to." He booped my nose.

I scrunched it up and pretended to bite his finger.

He pulled me close.

"You okay?"

"No. But I will be."

"What would you rather?" he asked, using words I'd said to him after we first got together.

"Hm," I mused. "I win the lottery and buy the salon off whoever bought it and we live here two more years and then we move into my parents' house and start planning a wedding and babies."

"Two years?"

"We need two years for just us at least. Maybe get engaged after a year and then I have a year to plan our wedding. We get married and I get pregnant a year after that and then we have three or four babies, bam, bam, bam. And then I hire a personal trainer and get my body back after all that baby-making and we live happily ever after."

"Hm." He smiled.

"Sound good? Or am I scaring you off?"

"You run the salon, I build bikes, fix cars and bikes."

"And we ride. And much as possible. Sidecars for the babies."

He laughed. I laughed.

"What do you want?" I asked.

"Easy. Wanna make all your dreams come true, gorgeous."

I smiled. "There's gotta be something you want," I said.

"There is."

"What?" I ran my fingers through his hair.

"You to let me take this ass." He grabbed my butt cheeks.

"You know the deal..." I told him.

"Four carats?" he asked.

"Yup."

"Close your eyes, Jenna."

I laughed. And then my heart skipped a beat. What? No.

"Close 'em."

There was no way. No way. He couldn't have bought a ring this soon. Not only not this soon, but he'd gone from the hospital to my apartment and hadn't been alone to go out and do any shopping. His brothers and the prospects and members had been in and out but surely, he hadn't tasked someone with a job *that* important? Please, *God,* tell me Pudge didn't pick out an engagement ring for me.

I heard a drawer open and then I heard some crinkling.

Crinkling?

I felt something weird slide onto my finger.

What? A weird heavy weight was on my finger. Way heavy.

"Open 'em"

I opened my eyes and I busted up laughing. On my ring finger was a very large, very blue Ring Pop candy ring.

"That's gotta be at least twenty, thirty carats, right?"

I threw my arms around him and busted up laughing.

That he could make me laugh like this five minutes after I found out my mother had my dream sold out from under me was amazing. And that was because I had a new dream. And it was to be with him wherever that road took us. Whether I had my own salon or worked for someone else? It didn't matter. Life would be what we made of it.

I didn't let him take my ass that night, though. Despite the gesture. He tried to sweet talk me into it, but I said no.

"Exit only."

"C'mon, baby. I'll make it good. Promise, I'll convert you."

Maybe I'd give it to him eventually.

He made love to me, carefully, sweetly, since he was still recovering. And of course he got his finger in there again just before I came. He was definitely working on working me up to it.

THREE DAYS LATER

I had to meet with some jerk who bought my salon at eleven o'clock. The realtor had left very vague details on my voicemail.

Rider informed me at eight thirty that morning that he had a doctor's appointment and I was upset that I couldn't go with him. He told me not to worry, that his brother would take him. Spencer turned up and they left at 8:45.

I had Jesse shadowing me. I lackadaisically strolled in at 10:59. The salon was open. My mother was sitting there in the waiting area. So was my father.

They were arguing. Of course. Debbie was there, too.

"You guys need to go. I'm meeting with the new owner in, like, one minute."

Mom eyed me up and down.

I barely looked at her. I didn't have time for her nonsense. She knew that Rider had almost died. She knew I'd been shot at. And this was the first time I'd seen her.

"It was requested we were all here," Dad said.

Pippa wasn't here yet. She was busy getting Joe's apartment painted and looking for a new spot to do nails from. She was thinking of setting up a mobile nail bar and waxing business.

I was planning to see what was what with this meeting and then ask Jesse to talk to the other prospects about rounding up some moving boxes for me and helping me pack up the apartment. Rider had distracted me (with his penis or his mouth) every time I'd tried in the past three days to get started on packing.

I'd heard that Deke and Spencer were still staying at the Forker's house, but that they were thinking about breaking ground on a new compound in the spring, behind the existing property. Deke was in negotiations for the land back there.

Maybe we'd go see some houses, too. Maybe we'd get a little for-now apartment, or grab a place with Deke and Spencer temporarily and I'd see what was what with my parents' divorce so that I could consider moving into their house when that was done with.

I saw Spencer's silver pickup truck pull up in front of my salon and I did a double take. What was he doing here?

He and Deke got out of his truck and then I saw Rider.

Wait.

Rider?

He was approaching the salon, wearing a suit, holding a file folder. He'd had a haircut.

A haircut!

His hair hadn't been cut super short, but barely grazed his collar bone, and he was in a suit!

He opened the door and came in. His dad and Spencer behind him.

"Why did you do that and who the *fuck* touched your hair?"

He stopped, looking startled. His lips twitched.

I folded my arms across my chest.

"You don't like it?" he asked.

I shook my head. "I have a meeting like... five minutes ago. All of you have to go. I..." I shook my head. "Why did you go get a haircut?"

"I'm your eleven o'clock," he said.

I gave him a gawking stare.

My mother got to her feet. "What's the meaning of this?"

I glared at her annoying attitude and my eyes moved back to Rider.

"I bought the salon for you, Jenna. The building. All of it." Rider handed me the file folder filled with papers. "Well, Dad helped." He smirked at his father.

Deke gave me a big smile. "After we got into a bidding war with your father."

My mother snickered. "Right." She was filled with disbelief.

My dad was standing there smiling, not looking in the least bit surprised. Deb was smiling, too.

Mom realized that this was really what was happening.

She made the most ridiculous huffing noise I'd ever heard come from her. Her face was beet-red and then she stormed out. Storming out, she stumbled on the runner by my shop's front door and nearly wiped out. I reached to help steady her, but she didn't allow it. She was gone.

If I hadn't been in such shock, I'd have laughed out loud. Karen Murdoch never let people see her sweat, let alone stumble.

Was this really happening?

I grabbed Rider's hand and pulled him into the utility room.

"Are you serious?" I asked, shutting the door.

"A hundred per cent. It's yours, gorgeous. All yours."

"How? You had that much money?" I asked.

"I got a mortgage. My dad co-signed."

"No way would the bank my mother works for okay that. She'd find out, somehow, and nix it."

"Wasn't her bank. In fact, I'm thinkin' she's got a rivalry goin' on with that other bank down the street. And I may've name-dropped a little over there," he shrugged.

"Your Dad really co-signed?"

"I got a nice down payment down. I had money in the bank. It cleaned me out, but he already has an offer on the house back in Sioux Falls and he's splitting the money between me, Deacon, Joelle, and Spence. Isn't even listed yet. Good offer. I'll have my nest egg back in a coupla months. The neighbor wants to buy it for his son for a wedding gift. Money's comin' through for insurance for the Roadhouse to get re-built. Business is pickin' up at the garage and the dealership is selling bikes like hotcakes. We hired Jesse to help out at the garage while I've been laid up, but it's busy enough, we'll be able to keep him on. We're in good shape."

"But to co-sign?" I winced.

"Books looked good to the bank. Your dad submitted copies. Your dad headhunted that realtor, too, that's how we kept things on the DL with your mother. I told Dad you've got money coming to you when you turn thirty, so we'll re-do the mortgage then if you need one at that point. But, he woulda co-signed anyway. I just told him I believe in you."

My God. That felt really good.

"Besides, when we figured out we were bidding against your dad, he said as soon as we moved the paper to our names, your ma would lay off and he could even switch things, get you access to money to buy it off me soon as their divorce is final. If you weren't okay with it being in my name... it'd only have to be for maybe six months or so, dependin' on how long your ma tortures him with the divorce. Then your Dad could buy it from me and give it to you. I got a mortgage with no penalty if I pay early."

"How was Dad gonna do this without Mom knowing?"

"He said he was putting it through his company. He was shuffling things around to keep it for you, so your mother wouldn't know. When we found out we were both trying to bid on it, we talked about a way it'd work out for everyone."

"Why didn't you tell me?"

He laughed. "I wanted to surprise you."

"I've been so stressed," I said.

"I didn't know for sure how it'd all play out. Only got the approvals four days ago. Started the ball rolling as soon as I was able after getting shot."

"But you let me stew for how many days?"

"You gonna forgive me?"

"Of course I am," I said. I was in absolute shock. "I can't believe you did this for me."

He smiled. "It's for us. Your salon but our future. I'll live here, too. You okay if it's in my name for a while?"

"It can stay in your name forever. I don't care. I'm gonna build you a garage out back," I told him. "So you can work on your custom bikes."

"Great idea," he said.

I stared off into space for a moment, letting it all absorb.

"No tears?" Rider asked.

I blinked at him.

He chuckled and folded his arms. "I make you dinner and you cry. I save your business, Pippa's business, and your home, and hand it to you and....nothin'. I do not understand women."

"Who cut your hair?"

He laughed. "Ah, that's it."

I backed him against the door. "Did you let some strange woman touch this hair?"

He looked at me with a heated expression.

"If I did, would you get in a cat fight with her?"

"Damn straight."

"You don't like the haircut?"

"I love it. You look amazing. You looked amazing before. But, yeah. You're like... a girl's wet dream. I have a major lady-boner."

"Yeah?"

"Oh yeah." I ran my fingers through it. It was to his collar. He had a long sideswept bang half in his eyes. It was super sexy. And the dark suit he was wearing? It fit him like it was tailor-made.

"A gay man at that place a few blocks from the garage cut my hair. No female but you is allowed to touch it."

"Good," I smiled. "Why'd you cut it?"

"I'm a respectable business owner. Wanted to look the part."

"Grow it back," I ordered.

He shrugged. "Okay."

"But you need more suits." I ran my hand down his lapel.

"Better buy me some."

"I will."

"Let's go upstairs and you can start paying off your rent."

"My rent?" I asked.

"Yeah. Since I'm not only your boss now, but also your landlord."

I laughed and threw my arms around him. "I fucking love you."

And then I started bawling in his arms.

Epilogue

Three days after Rider gave me the papers saying he'd bought my salon and the building it was in, we were invited over for a Forker Family game night.

I won his Harley off him. He had three jacks and two kings. But I had an eight through queen royal flush.

I let him ride the Harley sometimes. Okay, all the time. But it's known as Jenna's Harley.

This was the beginning of outlandish bets at the Rummoli nights. Sometimes, we made secret bets for sexy time ahead of time. That was fun. We regularly thought up new sex games. We sometimes got weird.

I still think Ella's a bigger perv, though.

A WEEK AFTER HE WAS back to work and feeling 100%, I took him down to my salon after I closed, and we acted out his sexy hairdresser shave fantasy. It would be the first of many After Hours Hair Salon Sexcapades.

It started with me giving him a shave, dressed in lingerie, with those thigh-high socks that I teased about at the Valentine cabin. Rider *seriously* liked those. It finished with me riding him until we both came, while straddling him in one of my salon chairs, never breaking eye-contact. My beautiful biker was *so* hot it wasn't funny.

Many months later, after we got the garage built out back behind the salon, we had sex on his slash *my* Harley in there.

A FEW WEEKS AFTER RIDER bought the salon, Pippa moved out. I was sad. To cheer me up, Rider took me to the shelter Ella volunteers at and we got a shelter cat who had one of her kittens with her. The others from her litter had been adopted. We took them both home.

FOR A WHILE AFTER ALL our drama, things had been quiet with my mother. Life without her was good. But, I felt guilty. She was my mother.

So... I invited her over for Christmas dinner. She said she had plans. She agreed to come over for dinner December 23rd. She acted like it was a pain in her ass. But, she came.

My kitten kept jumping up on her lap and purring. It was hilarious. I had trouble hiding how funny I thought it was.

Rider cooked steak. She complimented him on his cooking.

She insulted my outfit, was 'meh' about her Christmas gift (didn't buy me one) and was snooty about the way I set the dinner table. But, she did awkwardly hug both of us goodbye. She said she was leaving Christmas Eve and spending Christmas with her sister in Miami.

Christmas Day, we had dinner with the Forkers and Valentines at the Forker homestead. My Dad and Deb came, too. So did Deb's friend Laura. Laura had dated Deke years back, when she lived in Sioux Falls, and they were making goo-goo eyes at one another all through dinner. And after dinner, we all went tobogganing. My idea. It became a new tradition (whenever there was a white Christmas). My first Christmas with Rider was the happiest day of my life. (Until the day we got married).

AFTER WINTER WAS OVER, Rider and I had the Valentine family cabin for a weekend, and I decided to play his game again, where he would chase and I would fight him off.

This was my idea. I had my "safeword" and had done a lot of thinking and concluded that our games and his darker fantasies were absolutely unconnected to anything bad that had happened to Jet or anyone else.

I craved his sexual approval and thrived on it. It now drove me crazy to think about surprising him with a new sexual encounter. We regularly took turns amping up our sex life. We had missionary sex in bed, too, but we both worked to keep things spicy. Positions. Locations. Role-playing. I hoped that this wouldn't ever change. I started having some darker fantasies of my own, and he never hesitated to indulge them.

I didn't want him to feel bad about his darker urges. I wanted to be everything he needed. And he was everything I needed, and I trusted him 100%.

We'd put away the axe-throwing stuff. It had gotten dark. We'd had plans to watch a movie and cook some hot dogs over a campfire.

"Rider," I whispered in his ear.

"Hm?" he'd asked, closing the garage and locking up. He was shining the flashlight toward the cabin, so my path would be clear.

I faced him instead. "I want you to chase me. I want to fight you off."

He stopped, and his eyes went wide.

"Serious?" he asked.

I backed away. "Get away. Don't try to make me have sex with you!" And then I started running in the dark.

The light and Rider chased me down and in no time, he had me, up in the air, over his shoulder. I kicked and pounded on his butt, and wiggled so hard that we tumbled to the ground. I tried to get away. The flashlight's beam was gone.

The adrenalin was surging. Especially, being in the dark like this.

He grabbed for my ankle and dragged me back, flipping me to my belly and then he climbed on me.

"No, please no..." I whimpered, pinned under him. We would both have some serious sex bruises after this.

He started yanking his zipper down, while pinning me. I shoved and wriggled, and got to my back. My knee came up, and he grunted and twisted to deflect, then tightened his grip on my wrists and pinned them above my head.

"Don't render *The Beast* useless, gorgeous. Then I won't be able to fuck you and make you come all over him. You want him in your pussy or your mouth? Or your sexy ass?"

"Please, don't. Please don't fuck me doggy style in the dirt. No!" I whined and wriggled and got a hand loose and slapped at him. My palm connected with his cheek and then he flipped me and whacked my butt and then dragged down my track pants.

"Want me to tie you to that tree so I can fuck you?"

"No. Please no..."

He yanked my track pants down straight to my ankles, pinning my wrists in the dirt. My face was in the dirt, too, and crazily, it felt so naughty that it made me wet.

"Spread these legs right now." He rammed inside me. "You like that?"

"Please stop."

He slammed his hips forward and I cried out. He put his thumb to my butt and slipped it inside.

"You like that," he told me. "Don't you, my filthy-dirty beautiful girl?"

I whimpered.

I liked it.

And the next time we played it, I left rope by the tree ahead of time, so that he could use it to tie me up.

MOM AND DAD EVENTUALLY got divorced. Not amicably. She moved to Miami to live near her sister.

I speak to her once or twice a month, let her try to get her little digs in, to insult me, and then I go on about my business, letting it roll off like water over a duck's back. We get together once a year, maybe.

RIDER'S MOTHER CONTINUED to be a cunt-a-saurus, a major thorn in everyone's sides for a while. But, that was another story.

RIDER GREW HIS HAIR back. I'm the one who trims it now.

I gained ten pounds in that first year, because my beautiful biker can *cook*. He loves my ass even more now that there's more to grab onto.

ONE YEAR AFTER WE MET

Dad and Deb's wedding was in Vegas. Tasteful and small, and I was Deb's maid of honor. Dad asked Rider to stand up with him. They'd gotten close. Dad and Deke go golfing on occasion, too. Dad is so different nowadays. I know he has regrets. I also know I'm not about to spend the rest of my life punishing him for them.

I have the same thoughts about my mom. She's the one who has to live with her bitterness. I can choose to let it go. It's not always easy and sometimes anger tries to seep through, but I look at the life I have and all the joy I've been blessed with and that always wins out over the bitterness. The journey with Rider, ending in almost losing him, when I almost pushed him away? It changed me.

While in Vegas, my beautiful biker asked me to marry him! The day after my dad's wedding.

Rider presented me with the most beautiful engagement ring. Well, first it was a Ring Pop, but it was a special-order Ring Pop that said Jenna: *Will You Marry Me?* inside it.

We were out for a romantic Las Vegas dinner in a Michelin star restaurant, to celebrate the one-year anniversary of him dipping me Hollywood style and telling me he was gonna need my number. He had the Ring Pop put in my fancy swan-shaped linen napkin.

He had the real ring in his pocket. It was a four-carat diamond ring.

I said *yes*. And, true to my word and committed to allowing him to cash the check I'd written, I gave him my ass that night. In a hotel room on the Las Vegas strip. It was my idea. He did *not* turn it down.

He was gentle and careful, and it was actually pretty damn good.

Life wasn't always a joyride. We fought. Sometimes over stupid things. Sometimes, (ahem, often) I was a drama queen and occasionally climbed in bed with Ella. Sometimes, he was an alpha-hole. We had angry sex sometimes. We had our share of ups and downs. We saw a lot of ups and downs with our friends and family. *Lots*. But, we were most often Good-time Rider and Good-time Jenna living life full-throttle.

We faced more drama with the Wyld Jackals before they finally got patched over. But, that's another story.

And right after getting engaged, we moved into my parents' house. Ella and Deacon lived in the country, first in Deacon's rock star trailer, and then in their custom-built home that Deacon and his brothers (blood and Dom brothers) did most of the building for, but we all spent lots of time either at our house or in the Forker family kitchen, playing cards, laughing our asses off, and loving life.

After a short time in New York, Jojo moved to town and she stirred up all sorts of drama! But, yep... another story.

We were going to raise our kids in my childhood home, but making sure it was a place with love and laughter, and Rider would catch them as they rode down that banister. But, I'd put bumper pads everywhere first. And make our kids wear helmets. Because, I didn't want them to get hurt.

Eventually, we had kids. Three. Two girls and then a boy. We named our little boy Lucas, after Luke "Lick" Hanson.

PIPPA AND JOE DIDN'T make it. Things went from bad to worse, sadly. There was a whole lot of drama there.

She moved back into the apartment above the salon when we moved out. She moved in with Spencer.

Jojo said Spencer needed a strong woman to whip him into shape, since he was such a handful. Pippa just so happened to be strong enough. But, that's another story.

A pretty damn good one, too.

Playlist:

STAY – THIRTY SECONDS to Mars

Lifehouse – Hanging by a Moment

Ride – Twenty One Pilots
Journey – Open Arms

Scenic Route

BEAUTIFUL BIKER 3. Sneak Peak:

Spencer and Pippa's Story

1

The first time I saw him, he was trying to flirt with my friend, Ella (who was dating his brother). Later that night, he tried to get my boyfriend to score cocaine for him. In the coming weeks, he was typically drunk and jerk-like each time I saw him and sporting much-deserved shiners from first his oldest brother Deacon, and then from his other brother, Rider.

A week ago, I'd actually seen him dodge a punch from his little sister, Jojo. Again, deserved.

So, why, then, did I just wake up beside him in a bed in his room in the Dominion Brotherhood MC clubhouse?

Maybe I'd better rewind. Once you find out how I got here, maybe you'll be able to help me figure out whether or not it was a colossal mistake to sleep with Spencer Valentine.

Dear Reader,

Want more?

Join DD's mailing list at ddprince.com and follow her on Facebook for news about upcoming books.

Scenic Route, Beautiful Biker 3; Spencer and Pippa's love story is now available!

Check DD Prince's website in case more books are available. There is a lot more Beautiful Biker deliciousness to come!

Beautiful Biker Series page:

http://ddprince.com/dd-princes-books/series-the-beautiful-biker-series/

Author's Notes

TEN BOOKS IN THREE years. WOW.

I can't even tell you how much I love this gig.

Big thanks to the following people:

Kass of Full-Proof and Ana of Insta-Grammar. I may not have followed every single suggestion you sent, but you both helped make this book better. Thank you, immensely!

Heather N, for loving Detour so much that you liked almost every single teaser or mention of Joyride over the 1+ year between books. Thank you for beta reading.

To my beta readers, some of who have been beta reading for me since my third book, Truth or Dare. HUGE thanks to all of you: Tai, Marquitta, Shannon, Rebecca, Vanessa, Joni, Kelly, Andrea, Lindsey, Shannon, Maria, Peggy, Sansa, Mariah, Pauline, Ann, Tyi, Robin, Shelli, Heather C, Maureen. Thanks a million for your help & willingness to drop everything when I finally get to that point that I want feedback as fast as humanly possible. LOL. I appreciate your willingness to read that ARC *so* much.

Thanks to all who post about my books in other Facebook groups or recommendations threads online, who tag me in nominations for author awards or spotlight opportunities, and who tell their friends to read my books.

Thanks to my writer friends, too, for your advice, your support, and the laughs.

I LOVE the book community with all of my heart.

XO

PS: Thanks to you, dear reader, for spending time with my books, for spending your hard-earned dollars to buy them.

Join DD's mailing list and follow on Facebook for news about upcoming books, including:

Scenic Route, Beautiful Biker 3, Spencer & Pippa's story.

I am planning to work on and hopefully finish Kill Game in 2018, too, and will also work on bringing my paranormal lovers a Tristan novella asap. Stay tuned!

The Scoop: http://bit.ly/ddprincescoop
http://facebook.com/ddprincebooks
Follow DD on Amazon:
http://bit.ly/ddprinceonamazon
Visit her website at ddprince.com[1]

1. http://ddprince.com

Dear Reader,

Want more?

Join DD's mailing list and follow her on Facebook for news about upcoming books. Hit the Follow button at amazon.com/author/ddprince. And you can find me on most social media sites as @ddprincebooks.

Scenic Route, Beautiful Biker 3; Spencer and Pippa's love story is now available!

Check DD Prince's website in case more books are available. There is a lot more Beautiful Biker deliciousness to come!

Beautiful Biker Series page:

http://ddprince.com/dd-princes-books/series-the-beautiful-biker-series/

*Aiden Carmichael:
hot, bad boy. My boss.
Oh, and a messy, selfish roommate.
Worst roommate ever. In fact, I
hate his alphahole guts.
And I'm not usually a hater!*

**Carly Adler.
Great rack. Cute AF sass.
I get what I want.
And I wanna tap that.**

Alphahole, a contemporary, enemies-to-lovers, roommate, office romance.

Aiden Carmichael is absolutely infuriating. You're going to effing love him!

Learn more: http://ddprince.com/alphahole-now-live/

More from DD:

The Dominator Series

Saved

The Nectar Trilogy

Hot Alpha Alien Husbands

Made in United States
Orlando, FL
07 July 2023

34837045R00261